Dolores Stewart Riccio

The Divine Circle of LADIES TIPPING THE SCALES

The 7th Cass Shipton Adventure

ISBN: 1452852448
ISBN-13: 9781452852447

Printed by CreateSpace, An Amazon.com Company,
Charleston, SC.

Also by *Dolores Stewart Riccio*

SPIRIT

CIRCLE OF FIVE

CHARMED CIRCLE

THE DIVINE CIRCLE OF LADIES MAKING MISCHIEF

THE DIVINE CIRCLE OF LADIES COURTING TROUBLE

THE DIVINE CIRCLE OF LADIES PLAYING WITH FIRE

THE DIVINE CIRCLE OF LADIES ROCKING THE BOAT

For my amazing daughter Lucy-Marie
and her amazing step-daughters
Alison, Kate, Rachell, and Kim

Acknowledging with love the inestimable editing and proofreading skills
of my husband Rick and my sister-in-law Anna G. Morin—
a thousand thanks!

A Note to the Reader

This is a work of fiction. The characters, dialogue, events, businesses, love affairs, criminal activities, herbal remedies, love potions, and magic spells have been created from my imagination. Recipes for dishes prepared by the Circle, however, may have been taken from actual kitchens, probably my own. Plymouth, Massachusetts, is real place, but some of the streets and locales in the *Circle* books are my inventions. Greenpeace, too, is a true crusading organization, but any misadventures here described are fictional.

In a series, families keep growing, changing, and becoming more complicated with time, so that even the author has to keep copious notes. For my seventh *Circle* book, therefore, I'm including a cast of primary characters and their families—to be consulted when confusion reigns. It will be found at the back of this book, along with a few recipes from the Circle.

DSR

LAMMAS, AUGUST 1, FESTIVAL OF BREAD,
FIRST HARVEST OF THE YEAR

CHAPTER ONE

Love does not sit there, like a stone; it has to be made, like bread, remade all the time, made new.

– Ursula K. Le Guin

"The trouble with Lammas is, it reminds you that summer is not forever," I complained. "And to think I may have to spend the last of these lovely days in a jury room crowded with my sweating peers gorging on Dunkin' Donuts. It's just too much of a civic sacrifice." I reached into my new handbag, soft Italian leather, a gift from my traveling husband Joe Ulysses. Taking out the folded blue sheets of my summons, I opened them on the table. "Look here—there just doesn't seem to be many ways to dodge this bullet, so to speak."

"Think of it as a mitzvah." Phillipa hardly gave the pages a glance before turning to peer through the glass door of her wall oven. As she leaned forward, intent upon her delectable creation, the dark fall of her hair shone like crow's wings that matched her shirt and slacks, black being her signature color.

"Mitzvah?"

"A virtuous act, a kind, considerate, ethical deed, a good work performed with joy," she explained. "Jury duty could be considered a mitzvah, and it's good to have a few mitzvoth inscribed under your name when the time of judgment arrives." My friend Phillipa Stern may be a loyal member of our Wiccan circle of five, but she still maintains her Jewish roots.

"Oh, yeah? I don't remember that you ever served."

"No. But I did get called once."

"Yes? And then what?" I asked suspiciously.

"Well, it happened to be right in the middle of taping several back-to-back shows for *Kitchen Magic.* Thank the Goddess I'm no longer a TV chef, but wasn't it a kick while it lasted!" Phillipa sighed. A sudden smile lit up her sharp features brilliantly. "Anyway, I managed to get a postponement due to time constraints. Then there was some sort of screw-up, and I never got called back to jury duty. Guess it was luck. Or a bit of magic. Fiona did this little *thing,* I don't know what you would call it."

Fiona, the oldest member of our circle, seemed to have the most psychic clout of us all. Maybe I should ask Fiona to do the same "little thing" for me. But perhaps not. I am, after all, a Libran. And dispensing justice is definitely a Libran specialty. So possibly it *was* my civic duty to serve. I felt just a small frisson of excitement at the thought of facing down another criminal, as I had so often done in my checkered past. *Oops.* I meant *alleged criminal*, of course.

"I guess I'll just go ahead and get it over with," I said. "I wonder what kind of a trial I'll draw."

"Good girl. Probably some boring gang-that-couldn't-shoot-straight stuff. Breaking and entering a garage in North Plymouth. Bring a box of NoDoz. Are you called to the Plymouth or Brockton Superior Court."

"Brockton."

"Hmmmm."

"*Hmmmm?* What does that mean?"

"Brockton's where the more serious criminal cases are tried."

"Suits me. Who wants to judge some petty shoplifting incident? I just hope the courtroom is air-conditioned." I was still weighing the pros and cons. Wavering on decisions is another Libran trait. "Lammas can be hot and steamy."

"Yes, nothing says Lammas like something from the oven." With an oven mitt shaped like Zelda, her sleek black cat, Phillipa removed several pans of cinnamon rolls and set them on wire racks beside her restaurant-size Viking range. Their fragrance was delectable, and I devoutly hoped I would be offered a sample when that fancy-dancy built-in Meile "coffee system" finally finished spitting out our cappuccinos, another divine aroma.

"I'll get you one of those fans everyone was waving at the Scopes Monkey Trial," Phillipa offered, setting down two frothy, steaming cups. She inverted a pan of cinnamon rolls onto a round plate; they oozed with melted brown sugar. "Hot bread. It's supposed to kill you, but who can resist?" She rattled on about something Oscar Wilde had said on resisting temptation, but to me her voice was fading away into the distance.

I'd been staring at the afternoon sun glinting off a copper pot of mums that decorated the long marble table. Moments later, I realized that I'd fixed my eyes on that reflected light too long. I was sliding out of myself, getting dizzy, in that way I do just before I have a vision. Because visioning is *my* "little thing." I'm a clairvoyant, worse luck—a psychic skill I wouldn't wish on my worst enemy.

Now that the spell was on me, in my mind's eye I envisioned a courtroom. I saw myself in the jury box. I saw the haunted looks of bereaved people among the spectators, the shadow of fatigue on the attorneys' faces, the slouch and swagger of the two defendants whose bravado hadn't made it to their eyes. And I heard myself saying, *No one knows the whole story. This is wrong, all wrong.*

"Hey, Cass...where are you going, hon?" Phillipa leaned over me with a concerned expression.

Somehow I managed to give my sixth chakra a good shake and come back to where I was—Phillipa's state-of-the-art kitchen—in a shower of indigo vibes.

"Not a Monkey Trial," I whispered. "More like a murder trial."

~

I didn't get much sympathy at home either. Years of working for Greenpeace had brainwashed Joe with an altruistic mind-set. Not that he was one of those young Banana Republic volunteers who joyously risk their necks in flimsy inflatable crafts going up against rusted-iron whalers. No, he was a sober, sensible (but sexy!) engineer and all-round repairman of mature years who kept the mother ship running through any quixotic adventure to which he was assigned. My call to jury duty paled into insignificance beside the vicissitudes of trying to save the planet from greedy spoilers.

"Hey, sweetheart...it will be fun. You'll see," he assured me with an amused glint in his Aegean blue eyes. "After all, you've always taken an interest in crime, the more dangerous the better. Of course, this time you won't be chasing psychopaths around Plymouth—you'll be safe in a jury box, dispensing justice like Athena, and I can rest easy for a change." Joe pulled me against his compact muscular body in a consolation hug. We were almost the same height; our bodies fitted together with the ease of familiarity, like practiced dancing partners. I felt the impress of the small gold cross he always wore around his neck against the same place where I wore a silver pentagram under my shirt. "If you like, I'll try to fill orders while you're tied up at court," he offered.

Banish that thought! My internet shop, *Cassandra Shipton, Earthlore Herbal Preparations and Cruelty-Free Cosmetics,* is not the kind of business that can be left to well-meaning amateurs. Imagine the customer dissatisfaction if a love potion designed to create passion got switched with a calming tea blend guaranteed to bring soothing sleep. "Oh, don't worry about that, hon." I leaned my cheek against Joe's shoulder. His neat gray beard tickled my ear. Come to think of it, the scent of summer herbs that always surrounded him was a love potion all on its own. "This is actually my slowest season, and I'll probably be able to catch up with orders on nights and weekends. I'd be glad for you to take care of the post office runs, though."

"Anything you say, my pretty one," he leered. "You'll pay, of course?"

Hey, Toots, could you get cracking on a little dinner here? Scruffy whined. Not aloud perhaps, but I always seem to hear his canine thoughts as if they were spoken. From the L.L. Bean faux sheepskin bed where he reclined, he looked up at me through tangled, bushy eyebrows with the tragic expression that he'd perfected. The heartrending effect was somewhat diminished by his offspring Raffles who was dashing around the kitchen in joyous greeting mode.

Simmer down, you dim-witted kid. We're talking food here.

"Hold your horses. I haven't even taken off my coat yet," I said.

Joe let me go so fast I rocked backward on my heels and stepped on Raffles, who yipped painfully and leaped to safety behind his sire.

"Oh, not you, honey," I hastened to explain." Scruffy is whimpering for his dinner."

"Should have known. That was one of the first things you ever said to me, do you remember?" Joe took the wine opener out of the drawer and applied it to the bottle of Merlot on the counter. "You said, 'he talks to me.'"

"And you said, 'he looks smart enough.'" I remembered every word, and all the other crazy, exciting stuff that happened that night, too. "But really, it's a wonder you didn't decide I was totally balmy and run for the ship." *Greenpeace,* a 218-foot ship put into operation after the *Rainbow Warrior* was blown up by French secret agents, had happened to be docked in Plymouth Harbor at the time.

"Alas, sweetheart. It was already too late, you'd enchanted me with your green gaze. Later, when I found out you were a witch...with actual love oils scenting the backs of your cute knees...well, what could I do?" He sighed heavily and poured the wine into two pressed glass tumblers. We smiled, silently toasted each other, and drank. Then we kissed for a while.

Scruffy flopped over on his bed with a loud moan. Raffles rushed over to nose his sire anxiously and was rewarded with a *sotto voce* snarl.

Later...much later...there was moussaka by candlelight in the dining room (something we don't do every day—Joe's idea, and that alone should have alerted me) and two belly-satisfied, burping canines sleeping under the table.

"I figure I'll probably have gone and be back again by the time you have to report for jury duty," Joe said with feigned innocence as we were sipping hot black coffee and nibbling baklava. "Might be weeks before they actually call you."

"Good Goddess, you've got another assignment and you never even mentioned it! So much for all your talk of helping me with orders. You really have no idea when you're going or when you'll get back, right?" My tone was suitably wounded. "Where in Hades are they sending you this time?"

"They're keeping the target under wraps this time, some political issue. I've not even been notified of the date. Just an alert to be ready to ship out *whenever.*"

"*Top secret?* Uh oh. I guess I don't have to be a clairvoyant to figure this out. It's some kind of protest mission against the government, right? For Goddess's sake, just tell me that you're not going to steam into another missile testing site!"

Joe had the grace to look embarrassed. "Just that one incident, sweetheart. And it only involved a little bruising from those hoses they turned on us. Based on a couple of rumors I've heard, it's my guess that we're going up against a foreign government this time, not our own. So, relax, sweetheart. Nothing to worry about."

So he said. The boyish eagerness in his eyes was not reassuring. *One foot in sea and one on shore*, the Shakespearean ditty came back to me. *Men were deceivers ever.*

Instantly, I was afflicted by one of those instant images that flash on and off like a camera shutter. I actually saw myself as Isis searching for the parts of Osiris. The picture faded away as quickly as a dream, and if I hadn't learned to think of it in *words,* I'd have lost the thought entirely. The body-parts scene I'd envisioned was only *symbolic*, of course. Or so I told myself. Nothing could possibly happen to Joe with all the protective blue-white light I was always wrapping around him, and the good luck amulets I hid from time to time in his duffle bag.

"Listen, Joe. Can't you possibly skip this one? Oh not because of the jury duty thing. I'm afraid for you. There's something going to happen. I know it."

"This is what I get for marrying a Cassandra!" Joe grinned at me. Easy enough to see that he relished the prospect of danger. Fat chance I'd have of talking him out of this adventure when his eyes shone with that gleam of anticipation.

"Yeah, well I just hope I can put you back together again," I said. "I do love all of your parts."

Deidre's cap of gold curls shone in the firelight, but clearly, she'd lost the elfin sparkle in her light blue eyes. In fact, she looked positively stressed out, like a gal with permanent PMS. Small wonder, with all those kids to raise alone. She had my profound sympathy. I'd served my time as a single mom, and I knew just how tough it could be.

"What the blazes, I guess I'll take another chance on the Cosmos," Heather muttered, as she crouched over her parchment, earnestly scribbling.

Good. She was keeping her psychic fingers off Deidre and calling for a miraculous housekeeper to manifest at her own front door. I had no doubt the helping hands would appear, but I did wonder what sort of maverick would be sprung on the Devlin household this time.

Personally, my secret wish (which was not much of a secret, either) was that Joe would stay safe through this next expedition—and every one after that. Those Greenpeace crazies were known for pulling off some really dangerous stunts. In the past, environmental crusaders had been run over in their inflatable boats, sprayed with high-speed water hoses by irate government people at test sites, thrown into Third World prisons, and even blown up by foreign covert ops. The less I knew about the plans for this protest, the more I worried. In fact, I worried so much, my upcoming jury duty dilemma almost slipped my mind. I guessed that might be a "Freudian slip," revealing that the inner Cassandra actually didn't want to invent some specious protest. Deep down, I really wanted to report as ordered, if only to see what trouble would turn up to liven the dog days of summer. Could it be that Joe felt the same way?

Fiona drew down the moon into the arms of her spirit. We hummed, chanted, and danced faster, faster, *faster* to raise our cone of power, then threw our arms upward to release our wishes to the Spirit of the Universe.

A little more chanting and dancing, then we ceremoniously gave our parchments to the fire and more or less fell onto the grass. We were inspired, uplifted, and fairly well exhausted. Fiona opened the circle, and we all trooped down to Heather's patio for what is traditionally called "cakes and ale," or as Phillipa had it, "grog and gossip." Tall garden torches created suitably spooky shadows across our witches' party.

Fiona plumped down beside me. Glamour gone, she was her pixilated old self again. She dropped her ancient green reticule between us. Straining my ears, I fancied that I heard a metallic ring as the bag hit the flagstones. Fiona had been known to carry more than butterscotch candies and arcane pamphlets in that miraculous tote, but the pistol given to her by her late husband had been *lost at sea* in our Bermuda adventure. And as far as I knew, it had not been replaced. Her gray eyes took me in shrewdly. "Never go walking out without your hat pin, that's what I say." She winked soberly and patted the venerable bag.

"In that case, I do hope you've asked Detective Stern to get you a licensed hat pin," I said. Phillipa's husband usually could be counted on to keep us legal, too often after the fact.

"What are you saying about Stone?" Phillipa looked up from cutting slices from the braided loaf of barley bread she had baked in honor of Lammas.

"My, that bread does look lovely, dear. Reminds me of an oaten braid my wee auntie Gracie used to make. Called it 'faery bread,' and she should know. Pure Pict from the look of her. *Fir Alban*, as they are sometimes called." Fiona, a mistress of misdirection, soon led the conversation away to the faeries but Phillipa's cool ebony eyes were not fooled.

"Faeries have certainly turned out to be my bread and butter." Deidre passed around a platter of sausage, cheese, and apple wedges. "For a while there, it looked as if I'd never be able to keep up with orders for my gossamer Victorian flower faeries. I swiped the idea from the young minxes who conned Sir Arthur Conan Doyle. They photographed cut-out faeries pasted to sticks, and he believed he was looking at the real thing. I guess the poor old man was besotted."

"Aren't you tempted to start a faery factory and grow rich?" Phillipa held out her glass for the lively Cabernet Sauvignon that Heather was pouring all around.

"*Banish that thought*. I love making dollies and poppets. I actually feel as if each of them carries a handmade blessing into the life of the new owner. But I know I wouldn't love running a factory. Anyway, the rush is over now, and the flower faeries have become just one more reliable item at Deidre's Faeryland." Deidre, whose hands were never still for long, took an embroidery out of her workbag and bent over it closely.

Looking in through the open French doors to Heather's Victorian red parlor, I could see the portrait of a Morgan sea captain—*great, great-grand* somebody—enshrined over the mantle. I fancied that he was observing this domestic scene with approval—Deidre with the soft light of the torches gleaming on her yellow hair, needlework in hand. *How womanly and how deceptive!* Besides being a prolific mother, Deidre had a fey sense of mischief and a magical way with poppets and amulets. Before I even knew it, a wish escaped me that someone who'd truly appreciate all Deidre's brilliant qualities would come into her life. And here I'd been scolding Heather for psychic meddling!

Still, I found myself humming a tune from *Gypsy*, "*Lucky, you're a man who likes children, that's an important sign...*"

I gave my head a good shake and forced myself to pay attention to the conversations around me. Fiona was holding forth on her theories of raising children. Although she was herself childless, Fiona got to practice her ideas on her beloved grandniece, Laura Belle. The self-possessed little girl, whose morning glory eyes and reticent speech gave her an unusual grave beauty, fostered with "Aunt Fifi" for most of the year.

"Let each child be taught the beauty of all living things. And respect. Even insects deserve respect. Take Grandmother Spider, for instance, weaver of fate, bringer of fire to the Navaho, and let's not forget Robert the Bruce, inspired by a cave spider. We Scots revere spiders for their persistence. Spiders are our friends."

"Not in my kitchen, they're not," Phillipa muttered.

"I confess to having squished many a spider friend hanging around my cellar workroom. Although they do give the place a certain Disney-like aura," I whispered. "The Wicked Stepmother's inner sanctum."

"Okay, are we going to share our wishes, or what?" Heather demanded. "Frankly, I've never believed that keeping it secret adds any potency to a wish. So I'll say it right out—I wished for a perfectly wonderful dog-loving, helpful sort of person who cooks divinely to show up at my door looking for a home. And pretty darned quick, too. The only home-cooked foods we're having these days is whatever Dick grills. Thank the Goddess for grilling men—and take-out, of course. The Walrus and the Carpenter, Rick's Cafe Casablanca, Chuck's Catering—they've been keeping us from wasting away."

"Oh, the trials of the witch and famous." Phillipa, who cooked with ease and inspiration, smiled smugly.

"Speaking of trials," Heather said, "I guess everyone knows that Cass has been called to jury duty?"

"She's certainly been *kvetching* about it in my kitchen," Phillipa said. "And when did any personal secrets come as a surprise to you lot of witches? So I might as well tell you that *my* wish involves a slim volume of poems published by a discerning university press. I'm visualizing a kind of moss green cover—I suppose suede is out of the question. Perhaps deeply-textured grass paper or pressed leaves. Deidre?"

Deidre sighed, a small resigned exhalation that all of us heard with quiet attention. "I just wished that my life would be less of a struggle, if you know what I mean. I shouldn't complain, I know. I have my children, and they're good kids, most of the time. Just the usual high jinks, and a bit of a problem with Willy since Will died. Poor grades and so forth. But they're healthy as young fillies. And I have a reliable au pair and a doting mother-in-law to help care for them. I like my work, especially coming up with new designs, and the shop seems to have made its own market niche. Finding time for everything has never been my problem, as you know. But, with all of that, I'm...I don't know...I feel like the Wizard of Oz, a big show of activity with nothing much behind it. Anyway...I left it up to the Divine Cosmos to simplify my life and give it a shot of joy."

Fiona beamed agreement. "It's always best to frame our wishes so they're open-ended, leaving the details to Spirit. We can never imagine the surprising ways things will work themselves out for the good of all."

"And your wish, Fiona?" I prodded. "If it's not too secret."

"As if we don't know," Phillipa whispered.

"Oh, nothing special. Just a little rhyme for Laura Belle, you know. Now, Cass, I hope you don't want to get out of that jury summons, dear." Fiona adroitly skirted the subject of herself and her heartfelt desire to shelter her grand-niece forever. "But if you do, I have this little Hecate spell. Works best at the dark of the moon, of course, since Hecate is Queen of the Night. My supply of rue is getting low, though. I'll need to get a refill on that."

"No, no—thanks anyway, Fiona. Hold off on Hecate, that's strong stuff. Not that I wouldn't like to know how to work it. Always good to have a decent banishing spell up one's sleeve. But I guess I've decided to go for it. Joe will be Goddess-knows-where, but Heather's offered to take in the doggies."

"You're probably going to land smack in the middle of that disgusting murder in Wareham." Deidre took another tiny stitch. "Marie and Therese Reynard. Beaten, raped, and murdered in their own home by two depraved drifters."

"Allegedly murdered by the two depraved drifters," I interrupted.

"Oh, they have the right guys, all right. The cops picked them up the same day. They still had the money from the Reynards' bank account, almost $21,000. And the girl's locket. One of the guys had it in his pocket, probably grabbed it as a souvenir," she continued. "Marie and Therese were found asphyxiated. That poor man came home and discovered their pitiable bodies, battered and abused. Albert, is it? He owns two French restaurants, in Hyannis and Chatham. They say he had a heart attack right then and there. Just a slight one, though. Recovered enough to attend the candle vigil, then went right off his head, sobbed all through the hymns." She held out the pillow cover she was working on and inspected the letters critically. *Twinkling stars and candles bright, Faeries guard you through the night.*

"Please say no more," I begged. "I don't want to sully my mind with details—just in case."

"Well, don't let those brutes get away on any damned technicality, Cass." Deidre stabbed her embroidery with a tiny needle. "You know, I heard that they took the girl upstairs and..."

I put down my glass and covered my ears with my hands. I'd read the same reports as Deidre, of course. And heard the same rumors. Particulars of a heinous crime were supposed to be kept under wraps but somehow, in Plymouth County, certain juicy details would leak out, perhaps something a neighbor saw, or careless words spoken by the bereaved families. I would just have to let go of the ugly reports and speculations and bathe my thoughts in the blue-white light of Spirit.

After a moment, when I could see that Deidre's mouth stopped moving, I uncovering my ears and took a thoughtful sip of wine. "This will be looking at murder in a different way than we usually do. No arcane spells from Hazel's book, no skulking around to look for clues, no personally wrestling with killers—just pure facts presented in the forum of reason."

"A pleasant change," Phillipa agreed.

"The problem of evil in the world is always a challenge," Fiona said. "No wonder that Christians were driven to invent Satan. Someone to blame, rather than having to look inward for the real source. Oh, not just Christians, of course. The worst impulses are in everyone, absolutely everyone, no exceptions. Usually well hidden. Sublimated, we hope. Under control."

"Until Dr. Jeckle drinks that foaming cocktail," Phillipa said.

MABON, THE AUTUMN EQUINOX,
SECOND HARVEST OF THE YEAR

CHAPTER FOUR

An agitation of the air,
A perturbation of the light
Admonished me the unloved year
Would turn on its hinge that night.

– Stanley Kunitz, *End of Summer*

A few weeks later I reported to Brockton Superior Court, where I sat around all morning with a disparate crowd of citizens in the jury assembly room. Several names with their allotted numbers were called to the grand jury pool, none of them mine. At lunchtime, the beefy bailiff, Della Fortunato, sent the rest of us home. We were instructed to return the next day.

The second day was a repeat of the first, except that now people were called for the petit jury pool, trial jurors. But not me.

That evening, our circle celebrated Mabon, when equal day and night signaled the end of summer. Because this was the Sabbat that ushered in the Libran sun sign, I felt particularly empowered. In fact, I felt a thrill of anticipation, for which I could not account. Mysterious events were moving toward me on the hidden rivers of fate. Even clairvoyants can be surprised, I reminded myself, especially about their own lives.

Again we were holding the Sabbat at Heather's, the weather being fine, the evening graced by a great, gold harvest moon. Deidre took her turn as priestess, wielding her hand-painted, yellow-handled athame. None of our August wishes at Lammas had really come true—yet—but Lammas wishes were asked to manifest by Samhain, and might well take longer. We resolved to be patient. Heather renewed her urgent need for a housekeeper. Phillipa revealed that a small literary publisher was still dickering over her volume of poems. Deidre complained about mean kids at school causing Willy, who was not making a good recovery from his dad's death, to feel even more miserable. She was very tempted, she said, to give the little bullies "a bit of a buzz."

"Allow the Cosmos time to restore harmony among Willy's classmates," Fiona counseled, taking the familiar Navajo medicine bag out of her reticule and sprinkling each of us with a pinch of corn pollen. "Meanwhile, I'll hum on it."

On the third day, I was finally called into the courtroom. I was so nearly asleep over my paperback, *Brother Cadfael's Penance*, I barely recognized my own name and number. There were fifty or more of us in the petit jury pool, assigned by number to seats in the spectator gallery. Although exemptions had been covered in our answers to the summons, Judge Mortimer Lax gave us one last chance to declare that serving would be a personal hardship, since the trial for which we'd been called was expected to last three weeks or more. Mothers of young children, caretakers of elderly parents, a few small business owners, and sole supporters who wouldn't be paid by their employers could still fade away—and did.

From those of us who remained, potential jurors were selected by lot. Mine was the tenth name chosen. I was suddenly wide awake, fingers crossed on both hands, humming my wish (that useful trick taught by Fiona). Now that I was here, I really wanted to serve. Those who hadn't been selected were required to hang around as well. Some of us jurors would surely be excused, and replacements from the pool would be needed.

Judge Lax explained that the co-defendants of the State of Massachusetts versus James Robert "Jim Bob" Farrow and Walter "Tookie" Lovitt were charged with capital felony, murder, kidnapping, sexual assault, assault, burglary, robbery, and larceny. In other words, the state was throwing the proverbial book at this pair of degenerates. (*Alleged* degenerates!) As my friends had warned me, I'd drawn the most sickening case of home invasion to occur on the Massachusetts scene in recent memory. I wondered what the difference was between burglary, robbery, and larceny, making a mental note to question Stone. Or would that be considered discussing the case with others? Oh, well, with my notoriety in the annals of local crime, I'd probably be bounced shortly anyway.

Voir Dire. "To speak the truth." That was when the prosecutor and the defense attorney got to chat with us jurors. Each of us was asked several routine questions and then a few questions more specific to this case. If our personal biases and history fit the questioning attorney's needs, we were on. If not, we could be excused for a stated cause, or without cause being specified, since each side was allowed a limited number of peremptory challenges.

Some of the questions were general, and some nonsensical. Prosecutor Stan Steemer wanted to know, if a juror could choose, what role she would like to play in the trial. I said "bailiff," although I really would have preferred being the judge. Steemer scowled warningly, as if I had made a joke. He was a small man with long eyelashes and a tip-tilted nose, who appeared to compensate for his boyish cuteness by adopting a pencil mustache and a furious demeanor.

Other questions were absolutely apropos. Attorney Roy Laratta for the defense team asked, "Have you, or any member of your family or a friend ever been the victim of assaultive behavior by another person?"

Answering that question should definitely have been the end of my jury stint. For the past few years, my whole life has revolved around violent crime (which made me wonder if something about my eccentric psyche might have been attracting sinister stuff, even this horrific trial.) I've had more than my share of run-ins with psychopaths. They've tried to bomb me to smithereens, poison me with hemlock brownies, burn me at the stake, and drown me in the icy Atlantic. But I could hardly go into all that detail. I mean, how much time did the court have to listen to the Saga of the Circle and the Perils of Cassandra, the Crusading Clairvoyant?

So I reported incidents that were matters of police record. Possibly Judge Lax would have remembered the hemlock poisoning case, which had come to trial in Plymouth County. In any case, I had been only one of several victims—one of the lucky ones. Steemer actually smiled for the first time in these proceedings, apparently pleased to accept a juror whose history suggested she'd have little sympathy with these particular defendants.

If the defense attorney had any sense, I was certain he'd toss me back into the jury pool like a menacing piranha. But Attorney Laratta, whose low forehead and thick black hair was reminiscent of the days of the pompadour, merely asked me about my herbal business, my marital status, if I'd ever been divorced, if anyone in my family had been treated for mental illness. (*Dear Aunt Gladys Moon, merely eccentric, if you asked me.*) And how I would regard the expert testimony of a psychiatrist? Last, he asked whether the experience of being poisoned at the Presbyterian hospitality hour or thrown off Plymouth Pier in December would make it difficult for me to weigh all the evidence in an impartial manner.

"No," I said firmly. (I'm a Libran, after all.)

He gazed at me thoughtfully. Soft brown eyes and a slight pout—*I'll bet he's beguiled many a jury with that disarming face.* Laratta was no inexperienced public defender fresh from his bar exam but a well-known criminal lawyer. Because this was a high profile case, he'd had been appointed as a special public defender along with Henrietta Sharpe, a civil rights expert, both attorneys known for their zealous defense of criminal clients and some notable acquittals. Ms. Sharpe (who preferred to be called Hank Sharpe) wore a severe chignon and a khaki pants suit, the mannish effect subtly offset by a glimpse of black silk cami and her leopard-skin, stiletto heels. She sat at the defense table making notes on a yellow legal pad and tapping one of those jungle shoes, her straight brows drawn together in concentration. Although she did not question me, she had skewered others about their experiences and prejudices.

My sixth sense kicked in for an instant, and I saw that Laratta, who was a Plymouth guy, knew rather a lot about me. And whatever he'd learned had led him to some favorable conclusion. He believed his strategy, whatever it turned out to be, would reach me. He smiled pleasantly, then turned away. Ms. Sharpe looked up and nodded coolly.

Prosecutor Steemer, no poker face, registered serious disbelief. But Steemer had already accepted me, so too late to quibble now. He and his second exchanged glances. The assistant, Thom Hazzard, whose salon-styled hair and slick monochromatic outfit made him look more like a game show host than an attorney, dove into his copious notes, looking, no doubt, for whatever they had missed about me.

I wondered myself what Laratta was up to.

In the face of overwhelming evidence of their guilt (everyone knew the details, despite a gag order being in place) the defendants had pleaded "not guilty." The question about mental illness and psychiatric testimony strongly suggested some insanity or irresistible impulse strategy might be afoot. The most Laratta could hope for was to lighten the inevitable sentence from *life without the possibility of parole* to *life with periodic reviews*. And I'd assured him that I would listen to expert testimony with interest and respect. You'd think anyone would, but when one of the other prospective jurors had stated that psychology and psychiatry weren't real sciences, Laratta used one of his peremptory challenges to dismiss that person.

So, thanks to crazy Aunt Gladys, who predisposed me to be sympathetic to mental illness, or thanks to Fiona's humming magic, *I was in.*

Yes, I'd got what I wanted—to be stuck here for three weeks. Or more. A regular martyr to the justice system. I'd be lucky to get out by my birthday in October. Sometimes I hardly know what drives me to get myself into situations like this—some perversity of character, I guess.

I'd thought that jury selection (twelve jurors and two alternates) would be completed by early afternoon, and I'd be sent home to rest and reflect until the trial commenced. Foolish me. *Voir dire* took the entire day and most of the next morning. The implacable Fortunato told us to report back right after lunch. Opening statements would begin immediately.

With a dead serious demeanor that belied his boyish features, Prosecutor Steemer, wearing a dark navy suit with subliminal check pattern, a white shirt, and a dark red tie, stood up to begin his opening statement.

We jurors cast covert looks at the two defendants.

"Jim Bob" Farrow was a slight man with mean little eyes and a shabby beard that looked as if the moths had been at it. It partially covered the red birthmark on the left side of his sallow face. Perpetually tensed, he appeared ready to spring out of his chair with hooked claws. "Tookie" Lovitt was a hulking brute, squarely built, and muscular with the look of a sub-human wrestler—shaved head, cruel smile, snake-tattooed hands and wrists hanging out of his jacket. Despite Laratta's obvious wardrobe coaching, the defendants didn't clean up well. Not even a Neanderthal mom could have loved these two.

Looking at us with an expression suggesting sincere regret for having to put us through these grim details, Steemer began to reconstruct the crime practically minute by minute.

After parking Lovitt's Chevy a distance down the street which curved along the Wareham shoreline, Farrow and Lovitt had been watching the sprawling, pseudo-French, villa, waiting for Albert Reynard to leave. About seven-thirty, Reynard departed in his Mercedes and headed for his Hyannis restaurant. Shortly thereafter, the two men broke in through the kitchen door. It was presumed that Marie Reynard and her daughter were still sleeping and heard nothing until they were awakened by the terrifying presence of the two men in their bedrooms. Lovitt was armed with an AK-47 assault rifle, Farrow with a 498 Marine combat knife. At that time,

Therese may have tried to escape or use her cell phone, because she'd been beaten and tied to her bed. Meanwhile, Marie was hustled downstairs to prepare breakfast for the intruders while everyone waited for the banks to open. Possibly she was promised that no harm would come to her daughter if she cooperated.

At this point, Steemer paused and shut his eyes as if in pain. Then he seemed to get a grip on his emotions. After consulting his notes, his gaze moved from juror to juror as he continued his reconstruction of events. We were transfixed. And yet, I found the earnest, pompous little prosecutor rather unsympathetic, although the crime was certainly heinous.

Around ten o'clock that morning, "Jim Bob" Farrow had accompanied Marie Reynard to the Wareham branch of Rockland Trust, where she withdrew $21,000, almost everything in a joint savings account. This large cash withdrawal, the "anxious" expression on Mrs. Reynard's face, and the "menacing" appearance of Farrow "hovering" at her side had worried the bank teller, Faith Rodriguez. As soon as Rodriguez could leave her window, the teller attempted to alert bank manager Wendell Jordan about her suspicions. Engaged in an adversarial meeting with a dissatisfied but important client, Jordan had waved her away. The teller had then called the Reynard home, just to allay her own fears. When Mrs. Reynard answered, she'd assured Rodriguez that everything was just fine and she should not under any circumstances involve anyone else in her queries. At noon, the teller went to lunch. When she returned at 12:55 P.M., Jordan was free and Rodriguez explained her concerns. Such a large cash withdrawal, nearly closing the family's joint account, was unusual, Jordan agreed. But he knew the Reynards. Checking the computer records, he confirmed that Marie Reynard had other savings accounts in her own name that held considerably more, as did Albert Reynard's "Chez Reynard" business account.

Still, Jordan was uneasy enough to call Mrs. Reynard about 1:15 P.M. Responding as she had to Faith Rodriguez, Mrs. Reynard told the manager in no uncertain terms that everyone at the bank should leave her alone and not contact anyone else on her behalf. The manager took two more meetings with clients initiating reverse mortgages but found he was still disturbed about the uncharacteristic Reynard withdrawal. Torn between Mrs. Reynard's insistence and his own gut reaction, he tried to locate Albert Reynard by phone at each of his restaurants. Having failed to contact Mr. Reynard, at 3:15 P.M. Jordan decided to call 911. Two officers were dispatched to the bank branch to discuss the Reynard transaction with Rodriguez. Both the teller and the manager related the substance of their calls to Mrs. Reynard and how the woman had insisted almost hysterically that no one else should be involved. The teller described Mrs. Reynard's voice on the phone as "sounding funny, like she was going to burst into tears or something." This led the officers to speculate that the presence of a "small menacing man with a sparse beard that didn't quite hide a birthmark" who'd accompanied Mrs. Reynard might indicate that some kind of hostage situation going on at the house. The officers decided to investigate quietly, without sirens.

At 4:05 P.M., Plymouth Police Headquarters got a panicked 911 call from Mr. Reynard, who had just come home to find his wife dead on the living room floor. The two officers, already on their way from the bank, arrived within a few minutes. They found Mrs. Reynard, trussed and asphyxiated, in the family room. Mr. Reynard gray-faced, clutching his chest, doubled over with cardiac pain, was lying at the foot of the stairs, clutching his cell phone. While one officer called for back-up, a crime scene team, and an ambulance for Mr. Reynard, the other searched the house and found Therese's body. She, too, had been asphyxiated. It appeared that she had been sexually assaulted, as well, probably by Lovitt while Farrow and Mrs. Reynard were at the bank.

At this point in his narrative, Steemer lowered his eyes as if the mental picture he'd conjured up was too painful to bear. Several moments ticked by—not one cough or restless shuffle broke the silence—before he ended his presentation on a brisker note.

An APB was put out for Farrow, with the description provided by Rodriguez, noting that he might be traveling with a companion. As a murder suspect, Farrow was presumed armed and dangerous.

A man answering Farrow's description was spotted by an off-duty police officer at a gas station off Route 3 heading north. Farrow was buying a carton of cigarettes while Lovitt pumped gas into the Chevy. Patrol cars stopped the Chevy a few miles down the road. Most of the cash extorted from Marie Reynard was found in the vehicle. Subsequently, fingerprints at the Reynard home were identified as Farrow's and Lovitt's. There was not a shred of doubt that these two men were guilty as charged, and the state would be asking for sentences of *life without possibility of parole*.

Steemer sat down, sighed deeply, and rearranged his notes. It had been a theatrical presentation but effective. Not one day into the trial, every one of us jurors might have been tempted to vote "guilty."

Judge Lax declared a short recess. As we stirred out of our spellbound state Thom Hazzard eyed us jurors with speculation; he made a few notes on his legal pad.

After the break (during which one of my fellow jurors, a tough-looking contractor named Heller, took a couple of illicit drags of his Marlboro out the window of the jury room and was reported to the bailiff by another juror, a pleasant-faced nurse) we shuffled back to the jury box. Laratta stood up, buttoned the jacket of a charcoal gray suit that was nowhere near as spiffy or well-tailored as Steemer's crisp navy, and sauntered over to address us. The late afternoon sun reflected off his brilliantined pompadour. I really wondered what he could possibly say to mitigate the completely damning picture of the crime that Steemer had drawn.

Laratta smiled pleasantly, taking his time, and launched into a description of the common elements in the background of these two "boys." As children, they'd both been shuffled through a series of foster homes and subjected to repeated sexual and other abuse. As soon as they'd reached their teens, they'd run away from state care. Subsequently, Lovitt had served time in a juvenile facility for beating up an intrusive social worker at the church where he'd found shelter. By the time he was released at age eighteen, he'd built up his body with weight-lifting and even experimented with steroids smuggled in by a guard. Soon after, Lovitt had enlisted in the Army and served in Afghanistan, as had Farrow, although the two men never met until a year or more after they'd both been discharged.

Lovitt had been given a general discharge for constant brawling, Farrow, a medical discharge because of mental problems. Farrow soon began living on the streets, until finally he'd become too noisy and incoherent for the local police to tolerate. After a suicide attempt at the county jail, he'd been sent to Bridgewater State Hospital for evaluation.

Farrow and Lovitt had met and become friends at a halfway house for recovering mental patients. Farrow had been diagnosed with schizoaffective disorder, which is linked to both schizophrenia and bi-polar disorder, and had been stabilized by medications prescribed by the State Hospital psychiatrist. Lovitt was on probation, ordered by the court to abstain from steroids and live under supervision while undergoing outpatient anger management therapy for assaulting his girlfriend. Their shared experiences in foster care and in the Army had drawn them together. Laratta would show that both men were suffering from post-traumatic stress disorder for which they had received only intermittent treatment. In their mentally fragile state, they had become obsessed with the idea of making a fresh start on the West Coast. And for that, they needed a cash stake.

Lovitt and Farrow had believed the Reynard house was empty when they entered it that unfortunate day in May. Upon being discovered by Marie and Therese Reynard, they'd demanded cash, and Mrs. Reynard, having little ready money on hand, agreed to make a withdrawal at her bank. Meanwhile, she'd offered to make the men breakfast, and had done so. When it was time for the bank to open, Farrow and Mrs. Reynard had driven off in her Lexus. Left alone with Lovitt, Therese had become hysterical and violent. Lovitt had tied her to the bed for her own safety, and in the process her clothing had become disarranged and there had been some bruising. The evidence would show that no semen had been found on or in Therese's body.

After receiving the money from Mrs. Reynard, the two men had tied her up to prevent her calling the police immediately. Both women had been alive when Farrow and Lovitt left the house and drove off in Lovitt's Chevy.

The sympathetic story that Laratta had woven from the facts of the case was wildly different from Steemer's, especially the defendants' claim that they hadn't killed the two women. They were dead, weren't they? Tied up, terrified, assaulted, and asphyxiated. Looking at the sheer sleaze exuded by Farrow and Lovitt, I found it was easier to believe the worst about them, that they were cold-blooded, lying murderers, and I bet others had come to the same conclusion.

Immediately, I felt a stab of guilt for my own snap judgment—based on what? Horror over the tragedy and disgust with the slimy appearance of the two defendants? No, that wouldn't do. I'd have to talk myself into a more objective frame of mind. Listen to the evidence without prejudgment. Be like Athena, goddess of wisdom, ever impartial and fair.

If only that pair of degenerates didn't look so gruesome. Farrow's cruel little eyes. The hulking tattooed hands hanging out of Lovitt's suit jacket.

CHAPTER FIVE

Whoever fights, whoever falls,
justice conquers evermore.

– Ralph Waldo Emerson

As soon as I arrived home after my first day as a juror, I hurled myself against Joe's enveloping warmth to dispel the aura of those chilling opening statements. A monstrous crime had been perpetrated against the Reynard family. Mother and daughter had been beaten, robbed, assaulted, and murdered in their own home. My protective skin has always been a little too thin for comfort. I ached for the parent Marie unable to protect her child, the agony of their last hours.

"I'm not supposed to discuss the case with anyone," I warned Joe. Actually, I was dying to spill the day's dramatic events to a sympathetic listener.

Scruffy and Raffles milled around my legs, trying to wedge themselves between Joe and me. *Hey, hey, you're home, Toots! What a bum long day with this furry-faced guy. He didn't even remember our noon biscuits. I'm starving.*

Me, too. Me, too. Not being the alpha dog, Raffles was prone to repeating himself in order to capture a little attention.

Pushing away the wedge of aggrieved canines with my foot, I maneuvered closer to my rock of comfort. They took the hint, finally, and plunked down on their kitchen beds with heavy sighs of complaint. But in the midst of Joe's reassuring hug, my peripheral vision registered the well-worn, tightly packed duffle bag standing in the corner near the kitchen door. He felt me stiffen; I felt him shrug.

"Wouldn't you know, sweetheart, I got the call this morning. Captain de Greif asked for me especially."

I pushed away from the seductive comfort of Joe's arms and looked him in the eyes frostily. "De Greif? Isn't he the one who got too close to the testing site last time you guys were on one of your anti-missile missions?"

"See—that took your mind right off your day in court, didn't it?"

"Answer the question, please," I insisted.

"Yes, yes, the same de Greif. But we're not going up against the government this time. At least, not our government. I'm flying to New Zealand to meet the *Esperanza*. We're headed to the Southern Ocean Whale Sanctuary to confront the Japanese whaling fleet."

"Jumping Juno! How can they be whaling in a sanctuary? Isn't that illegal?"

"They're calling it a scientific study, for which they're entitled to kill a self-appointed quota of a thousand whales including fifty of the endangered Humpbacks."

"All right, lay it on me. Just how do you plan to stop the slaughter, Sir Galahad?"

Joe could not hide a grin of pure pleasure. "We're going to chase them off the edge of the world, sweetheart."

"Oh, sure. Well, do give me a call when you end up in the hospital or a Japanese brig. Do they even have hospitals in Antarctica? You may have to leave voice mail—no cell phones allowed in court." Despite my cavalier tone, for some reason I was more worried than usual about this expedition, but I really didn't want to weigh down the departing hero with my dour intuitions. Instead I concentrated on wrapping him in an even more protective light.

"I promise you I'll be fine," Joe said. "The younger men do all the real jousting."

"Sure they do." Time to let go of the argument before I made us both miserable. I sank into the kitchen rocking chair with a sigh, flanked by the two resigned dogs. "You know, honey, I could really use a glass of wine right now. The opening statements were chilling and, or course, conflicting. And we hadn't even been given our notebooks yet. We're supposed to get our notebooks tomorrow."

"But you took notes anyway?"

"Well, I happened to have a memo book in my lovely Italian leather bag. Can you imagine that Laratta for the defense is claiming that the two depraved maniacs who committed this crime are victims themselves. According to Laratta, Lovitt is frequently overwhelmed by irresistible impulses due to excessive use of steroids. And both men are afflicted with post traumatic stress disorder caused by their stints in Afghanistan. Laratta is also asserting that the two villains are *only* guilty of burglary, robbery, and larceny—not kidnapping and murder. That the two women were alive when the defendants left the house." With a sudden flash of guilt, I clapped my hand over my mouth—my big mouth.

"I'll forget I ever heard that," Joe assured me, turning to pour a robust Pinot Noir into two glasses waiting on the kitchen table. Not our everyday slug-of-wine pressed glass tumblers, but our best stemmed crystal saved for special occasions. "But I wonder how the prosecution plans to prove the kidnapping charge?

I restrained myself from explaining that Marie Reynard had been driven by a knife-wielding "Jim Bob" to her ATM and forced to withdraw funds under threat to her daughter. Meanwhile, seventeen-year-old Therese was back at the house being raped by "Tookie." Those horrid, soulless men! I leaped up and shook my hands and feet to dispel the negativity still clinging to me.

Joe, who'd seen this little dance before, didn't even raise an eyebrow. He said it resembled the tarantella, a dance supposed to mimic the frenzy caused by a spider bite, originally to cure the sufferer.

Yes, I thought, *shaking off the horrors was decidedly healing.*

"What about those Greek dances? Do they have some power or meaning?" On my trip to Greece to meet Joe's family, inspired by many glasses of ouzo, the men had danced up a storm.

"Ah, yes," said Joe, a faraway look in his eyes. "Hard to explain. Victory, independence, freedom—something like that."

And sexy, too, I thought. *All that macho posturing can be very stimulating.*

Speaking of Greek prowess, after draining my glass of wine in a few needy gulps, I noticed at last that we were surrounded by a rich meaty fragrance with a hint of Metaxa emanating from the oven. Ah, the farewell feast. "Hey, guys—good news! I believe we're having beef with mushrooms *a la Grecque*."

Two sets of ears perked up. Until Joe came into my life, I'd given up beef for ethical reasons. Scruffy was thrilled at the return of red meat (humanely and organically-raised, of course) to our table. I doled out the postponed pats and head scratches. "But I guess you two are going to have to stay with

Aunt Heather tomorrow. Won't it be fun to see Honeycomb and your other pals?"

Suffering stinkweed! Are we going to be stuck with that pack of tick-infested mutts again? Ack, ack, the stuff they eat over there tastes like bark and twigs. Boarding with the Devlin's ménage was not Scruffy's idea of a good time. *And besides, that blonde bitch won't give me a rec.*

Raffles' mother, Honeycomb, seemed never to have forgiven Scruffy for his part in her indiscretion. Better things had been expected of the pedigreed golden retriever therapy dog than in impromptu mating in my pine woods. Heather had been quite cross with me as well as with Scruffy. But it had been Honeycomb's first heat, and she'd kept it her little secret until it was too late to lock the gate.

We put aside the subject of the trial, which I was sworn not to discuss anyway, to enjoy our dinner. The Great Goddess had blessed me with a man who knew his way around a kitchen, for which I was eternally grateful.

After the last of the aromatic beef stew had been licked off their dog dishes, Scruffy and Raffles fell into a rapturous pre-bedtime nap, completely forgetting to complain about tomorrow's dire prospects—incarceration at the Devlin manse.

It was more or less the same with me. Content with Joe's hearty dinner, much red wine, a romantic walk on the beach under that radiant harvest moon, and a satisfying interlude in a secluded sandy cove, I forgot to worry about his departure and my new role as Madam Justice. And I continued to forget when we went home to bed and continued the wordless conversation of love.

The trouble was, we had to get up at the crack of dawn, as the expression goes, to get Joe off to Logan in his perpetual rented car, the dogs off to their martyrdom, and me off to another day of *Law and Order*.

Although I was prepared to refuse modestly when offered the post of jury foreperson—at least, to refuse *the first time*, like Julius Caesar when offered the crown in Rome—no such suggestion was ever made by my fellow jurors.

We'd gone around the conference table in the jury room, giving our names and professions. "Cassandra Shipton, herbalist."

"Hey, I know you! You're one of those trespassing witches from Plymouth, always running to the cops with lies about the neighbors," declared a frizzy redhead with the formidable build of a lady wrestler.

Wanda Finch, just my luck. "Yes, dear, I know you, too. Engaged to Iggy Pryde, aren't you?" The pig farmer was a former nemesis of ours and a perpetual threat to the environment. It was when we were investigating the chemicals illegally dumped on his property that Wanda had threatened Heather and me with a rifle. "Small world, Plymouth."

I felt the sidelong looks from other jurors. Wanda had succeeded in pigeonholing me as an eccentric troublemaker, certainly not foreperson material.

Besides, without very much discussion about it, one man clearly stood out as destined to be the popular choice—possibly because he was so handsome in a devilish way, with unruly dark hair, a day's growth of beard, and dangerous eyes. Hugh Collins had the kind of looks that a gal immediately feels in her lower chakras, if she's not on her guard. Nevertheless, something about him put this gal's psychic teeth on edge. "Horse trainer," he'd described himself. Instantly, in my mind's eye, I saw him slapping one of those wicked little whips against his thigh. Maybe he'd galloped over me in a former life?

The man simply exuded authority. *Ex-military*, I thought. *But maybe I should cut him a break. Judge no man until you've walked a mile in his L.L. Bean work boots.* When it came time to elect a foreman, the new owner of Fresh Meadow Farm, the burned-out Churchill stable, would be quickly nominated and seconded by the predominately female jury. I could see the scene as if it had already occurred. I live a lot of my life that way—balancing the actual present and the envisioned future, easier perhaps for a Libran than those born under other sun signs but still conducive to feeling rootless in reality.

I admit to having trouble with names. But I deny it's age-related, even if I am a grandma now. Because I've always been a bit scattered when meeting a room full of people—too many psychic impressions at once addles the brain cells, I find. So, in my own little lavender notebook, not the one provided to me by the court for trial notes, I wrote down everyone's name, profession, and whatever I'd inferred about them from our brief exchanges.

Thus...

Jurors:

Hugh Collins, horse trainer, W.Va, attract. black Irish, prob. foreman

Wanda Finch, Plymouth farming Finch fam. , armed & dangerous

Brooke Morgan, realtor, Talbot's catalog type, Heather relative?

April Rayne, hair stylist, never go there, finger-in-electric-socket style

Mildred Woolrich, retired bank manager, pals with Patty Peacedale

Ellen Heany, trauma nurse, nice healing vibes

Kurt Heller, builder—strong, squat, silent & sullen
Ernie Byrd, antique auto restorer, voluble gallant
Ralph Dunbar, Afro. teacher middle sch., "they call me Mr. D"
Byron Moody, unemployed, "published poet," check with Phil
and me, Cass, herbs and potions to go!
Alternates:
Anna Grimassi, retired from Children's Services, tough, defensive
Harry Drudge, Walmart associate, gray visage, ill-fitted

Alternates had the unenviable assignment of listening to all of the testimony and then getting dumped when deliberations began. Unless, of course, one of us jurors failed in some way. Grimassi and Drudge would be like understudies waiting in the wings for one of the stars to break that proverbial leg.

I was still searching for an appropriate phrase to describe Harry Drudge when I sensed Ernie Byrd leaning to read over my shoulder. Quickly, I clapped my memo book shut and slipped it into my bag. Taking out the new "official" notebook, I opened it to a blank page and moved a fraction away. Ernie constantly spewed out fulsome compliments to any luckless female who didn't get away in time. His courtly manner and rather twisted lips made me distinctly nervous. "A beautiful car for a beautiful girl," he'd said, running his hand suggestively over the fender of my nearly new Everglade Green RAV4 when we'd been out in the parking lot leaving for the day. Coming from him, "beautiful" took on an uncomfortably sticky feel, but Ernie probably thought he was being suave.

What a motley crew! I supposed every jury was like that, but all I really knew about juries was portrayed by the cast of that old film *Twelve Angry Men*. After all, *motley* is just another word for *colorful*. Perhaps that's the way it should be, diverse experiences bringing many points of view to the search for truth.

But, honestly, did I have to be stuck for weeks in the company of that loudmouth *Wanda Finch*? What could I possibly have done in a former life to deserve this karmic aggravation?

CHAPTER SIX

Come away, O human child!
To the waters and the wild
With a faery, hand in hand…

– W. B. Yeats

While I was driving home, my cell phone played its tinny tune, *On a Clear Day You Can See Forever.* Not being agile enough to talk to the hand at my ear while negotiating a curvy road, I pulled over to a grassy bank on 3A to answer. Maybe it was Joe, I hoped. I felt that familiar throb in my heart, a little catch of excitement in my throat. This guy of mine could always make my pulse dance.

But it was only Heather.

"As long as Joe's gone off to save the whales and your dogs are all comfy in our kennels, why don't you grab a few things at the house and move in here?" I considered that idea longingly for about three seconds—the Morgan mansion had some lovely, luxurious guest accommodations—before she went on to say, "We can have a nice old chat about your impressions of those two creeps—what are their names? Farrow and Lovitt? Guilty as sin, aren't they? Then let's watch the news and see what the press has unearthed about them. I've made a special Eye-for-an-Eye candle we can light."

Eye for an eye? I wondered what scary symbols Heather had sealed into *that* waxen work of art. "Oh, gee, Heather, that's very tempting, but...." I strained my brain for a decent excuse.

Like the answer to a prayer, *call waiting* popped up on the little screen. In my mind's eye I could see Freddie tooling along in her red Porsche Cayenne S, extremely sporty despite the two child seats in the back. "But, alas, I'm expecting to hear from Freddie any moment. *Oops, there she is.* Gotta go now, *call waiting.* Thanks for the doggie day care. Guess I'll leave the pups at your place tonight and pick them up tomorrow after court. Bye!"

"Where are you right now?" I asked Freddie after I'd switched to the second call. "Route 3 South. Feel like some company?" My daughter-in-law's voice was music to my ears. Jazz, that is—sassy and full of surprises.

"You and the twins?" I hoped.

"No, dear. Just me. The twins are at home with their impeccable British nanny, Miss Minerva Sparks, and I'm on my way to Otis Air Force Base. But technically, I don't have to report until tomorrow, and I'd much rather stay at your place than bunk in some decrepit military barracks, you know what I mean? *Ugh.*"

"Otis! What's up?"

"Oh, just a little assignment I agreed to take on. Not for the base itself. *Don't ask, don't tell.*"

"Okay. You're not the only one with a strict protocol, dear. I can't talk about the Reynard murder case either. I'm just on my way home from a long day of jury duty at Brockton Superior Court."

"Yeah, hon. I know. And bursting with testimony you're unable to discuss, I don't doubt. I guess we'll just have to be content with reading each other's minds."

"Such an inexact science."

Freddie laughed, as musical a sound as the laughter of an opera ingénue. "Speak for yourself, *Mother Shipton*. See you in fifteen."

During the rest of my ride home, I mused on the maze of secrets in which we found ourselves. First and foremost, Freddie was doing the odd covert job for the CIA. Not long ago, the Company had discovered her psychokinetic talents, which included addling delicate machines and remote viewing. Their interest in psychic powers, however, was embarrassing in some quarters, so it was kept very hush-hush. They'd even recruited my son Adam into the occasional *Above Suspicion* scenario: Mr. and Mrs. Harmless Tourist. Then, Joe was embarked on this aggressive and perhaps illegal mission for Greenpeace in Antarctica. Added to that, my own buttoned lip on the tragic particulars of the Reynard murders. Not only were the jurors supposed to avoid discussion, the judge had imposed a gag order on everyone. *As if!*

With so many subjects off limits, what would my daughter-in-law and I find to talk about?

My gorgeous grandtwins Jack and Joan, of course.

For our improvised supper, I warmed up the leftover Beef a la Grecque with an ample side of buttery egg noodles and tossed a mixed greens salad with big chunks of tomato, sweet bell pepper, red onion, and chopped, fresh herbs—still thriving in late September's sun. It was amazing what svelte

Freddie could consume without ever retaining an ounce of fat. Ever since our first memorable meeting when she turned up on my doorstep wanting to become a witch, she'd always been a hungry gal. Maybe it was an appetite-for-life thing. Or maybe her psychic talents revved up her metabolism. When I hugged her, I could feel a veritable burst of electrical energy that emanated from her lithe frame.

Although it was undeniably peaceful with no dogs whining for a share of our food, I had to admit I missed the big shaggy rascals anyway. Still, I thought it would be good for those pampered, protein-packed canines to run with Heather's pack for a few days. I smiled inwardly, thinking of how vociferous Scruffy's complaints would be when he came home. He was not fond of the nutritionally-balanced dry dog chow served at the Morgan manse. The Morgan housekeepers had often livened up the daily fare with goodies from the kitchen (Captain Jack's fish heads had been especially prized by the canine crew) but there being no housekeeper in residence at present, Heather would be maintaining their strictly scientific diet.

We drank quite a lot of Spanish Shiraz with our dinner and reveled in the minutiae of the twins' newest accomplishments. Joanie, who was as fair and fragile as her Aunt Cathy, nonetheless had been gifted with her mom's agility. She'd had already taken her first steps while Jackie, although inheritor of his dad's tall muscular frame, was still hanging on to chairs and falling down on his well-padded bottom. They both jabbered away to each other in a language that they alone appeared to understand, tossing a few *da, la,* and *ma* words to appease us grown-ups from time to time.

"But the other day, Joanie quite clearly demanded *more* and banged her sippy cup on the high chair." Freddie refilled our glasses. "And Jackie does a quite decent *grrrrrr* when we're playing with his Pooh Bear. I think I'm being perfectly objective when I declare they're both absolutely brilliant."

"And what about—you know...?" I asked. I noticed that the pepper shaker was slowly sliding toward Freddie, who quickly reached for it and seasoned the already-spicy beef. Although she tried to discipline (or at least hide) her psychokinetic abilities, they did tend to slip out when she wasn't paying attention.

"Oh *that*! Believe me, I've been on the lookout. I can't say I've seen any definite sign myself. But Miss Sparks has complained that Joanie must have fiddled with her nanny's iPod and made it go all static. Reminded me of when I was a kid. Used to get knocked around over the same sort of thing. I'd be accused of messing with my stepfather's car radio, which I never even touched, because it went crazy when I was in the car. Ruined the old pervert's ball game but brought in queer foreign stations, as if we were being bombarded by an active sunspot cycle or something." A shadow darkened Freddie's smile as she remembered her step-father's rage. "And more of the same when I was with the nuns, only verbal not physical."

"At least the twins will have a mom who understands and doesn't condemn these phenomena. And you'll be able to guide and protect them if there's trouble later. You know, like your accidentally zapping the computer clinic at school."

Freddie sighed. "And Miss Manson's car crashing after she threw me out of the class. But that's really why I sought your help and why we met. And it's through you that I met the awesome Adam, love of my life. But, yes, developing control is a mighty good thing. That, and keeping a low profile by staying out of casinos. Although, I must say it's mighty tempting to fool around with the big money slots, you know what I mean?"

"*Forget about it.* You're the guardian now, dear. Watching out for runaway magic in the kiddos. Along with everything else you'll have to watch out for. It's an awesome prospect. Do you think Miss Sparks will be up to handling any psychic shenanigans?"

"Well, she's no Mary Poppins, but she is pretty formidable. I can't see her being fazed by any situation that life might throw at her. Speaking of which, she told me she'd worked for the Reynards one summer."

I covered my ears with my hands. "Don't tell me, *please* don't tell me, for Goddess' sake."

Freddie grinned at me over her wine glass. Her smile was full of mischief but her curious amber eyes shone with a mysterious ageless wisdom. An old soul in a young nymph's body. As fascinating as Nimue. Well, she'd certainly fascinated my son.

"As if you could ever, ever *not* know *too much* for comfort," she said. "Don't worry. It can't be very important that my nanny was their nanny, sort of. The Reynards were honeymooning in Alpes-de-Haute-Provence at the time. Sort of a busman's holiday, checking out the local restaurants. The girl—Therese—was only twelve, so in need of supervision while her mother and new step-father were on their wedding trip. Her own father had died in a South Boston shoot-out. Adopted by Albert, so legally Therese Reynard. Miss Sparks was hired as a combination watchdog and house-sitter, which suited her just fine since she loves to reside near the ocean. That's why she came to us, despite being very much sought after in nanny circles. Hingham appealed to her."

Covering my ears didn't seem to work all that well. Interesting background stuff I wasn't supposed to know. *Story of my life.* I changed the subject to whatever Freddie was up to at Otis. Not that she had any intention of telling me, but my intuition is fairly keen, especially when I touch someone. Thus it was, when she hugged me good-night later, I got the clear image of a Freddie in remote viewing mode. There seemed to be photographs on the barracks wall, blow-ups of guys with swarthy skin and beards.

"You're not going to be chasing after terrorists," I demanded.

"*Leave off, witch-in-law!* You tuned right into my brain right then, didn't you? Poor Joe—how ever does he manage to live with *The All-seeing Eye?* Well...just keep in mind that this is a covert exercise known only to a few within the Company. Officially, the CIA's Stargate Project was something of a mortification and is no longer legally funded. But, unofficially the Company is still infatuated with so-called superpowers. That's why we're meeting off-site. So forget you ever pried into top secrets."

"I hope this won't mean you'll have to travel," I said. "Miss Sparks may be marvelous, but..."

Freddie grinned annoyingly. "Wherever I go, the twins will go with me. A great cover, don't you agree?"

I figured she was just teasing me—although she was on call for psychic assignments, Freddie's operational roles as an innocent courier (sometimes with Adam) had been few and far between. But right then, I vowed to myself that I would surround my grandkids with such an impenetrable sphere of spiritual light as would protect them from harm anywhere in the world. I'd speak to Fiona about that. She always came up with the most amazing spells. And no wonder. As a librarian and the Circle's official finder, Fiona either owned or had access to many an esoteric volume of magic. My personal favorite was *Hazel's Book of Household Recipes,* which had turned up at a Garden of Gethsemane church yard sale. Tucked between recipes for squirrel stew, calf's foot jelly, and mustard plasters, we had found some powerful magic spells, disguised as physics, prayers, or herbal preparations.

So I just smiled back at Freddie. "Remember, I'm older than you, dear, and I have better magic. *So watch it.*"

CHAPTER SEVEN

The pure and simple truth
is rarely pure and never simple.

– Oscar Wilde

In the days that followed, I learned that the real challenge to a juror was to stay awake in the afternoons. It was amazing that the sadistic, horrifying events in the Reynard home last May could be turned into such excruciatingly repetitive and dull droning as the testimony and cross-examination of police officers and forensic personnel. Laratta's constant objections to the smallest details were particularly mind-numbing. Not falling forward into a snooze was especially difficult after the rather ample lunches we enjoyed at local eateries in downtown Plymouth, having a whole hour and a half to relax and chow down.

The fascination of watching the two defendants squirm and glare, however, was enough to put a gal off her feed.

Relatives and close friends of the Reynards occupied the first two rows of the spectator section. Marie Reynard's mother, Therese's grandmother, dressed in unrelieved black silk, sat in front, right behind the prosecution's table but slightly to one side where she could be seen by the jury. She wept noiselessly into an old-fashioned, lace-edged hankie throughout the testimony.

How would I feel if the forensics being discussed involved my own immediate family? Watching her open grief, the injuries inflicted on the two women—Marie's battered mouth, Therese's bruised thighs and bloody clothing—I experienced her pain and anger in my own gut. Immediately, I looked away. *This is too much for someone with my thin skin. I should never have become a juror.*

Anna, who was sitting behind me, leaned over and whispered, "That's Madame Therese de Rochmont. Family has made a fortune in wine. Granddaughter named after Madame, poor baby."

Judge Lax glanced our way sternly. Anna inched away from my ear and sighed.

Albert Reynard, red-eyed and red-faced but unflinching, sat beside his mother-in-law and patted her shoulder from time to time. He looked straight ahead, resolute and grim. From Anna, I also learned that the man sitting behind Albert was Francis Reynard, his brother, and that Marie's sister-in-law from her first marriage to the late Marty Boyd was also in the courtroom every day. Rosalie Boyd Indelicato sat apart from others, her eyes wide and expressionless.

Just as I was longing for a cup of strong, black coffee, we were shown shocking photographs of the two women—talk about a wake-up call! Each picture was truly worth a thousand words of tedious forensic testimony. Electrifying and nauseating, the sight of Marie and Therese's abused dead bodies trussed up with duct tape made us sit bolt upright in our too-comfortable jury chairs. When the glossy 8 x 10s were passed around, silent tears ran down Ellen Heany's cheeks and Mildred Woolrich sobbed aloud. Judge Lax declared a fifteen-minute recess. As we filed out, I noticed Prosecutor Steemer suppressing a satisfied smile.

A mood of frustration and gloom was almost palpable in the jury room. Our breaks were supposed to be models of restraint. We'd been warned not to discuss the case with anyone, not even fellow jurors, until all the evidence had been presented. It seemed to me that others, like myself, were spilling over with reactions to the orchestrated presentations being given for our benefit. But we, the audience for whom this courtroom drama was being played, were expected to be as silent and circumspect as concert-goers—until the time came when Judge Lax would instruct us to begin deliberations. In our forced companionship, we had to come up with other topics of conversation—anything and everything but the Reynard case.

Wanda Finch and April Rayne the hair stylist were soon chatting away about the joy of big hair, to which they were both devoted. Wanda's was an explosion of frizzy red, April's a frosted "cotton-candy" confection.

Brooke Morgan hung on Hugh's every word. He had a slight but attractive Southern accent. Apparently, Brooke adored horses (and devastatingly handsome men).

Meanwhile I chatted with Byron and Ralph about poetry. Byron, whose dead-white skin looked as if he never saw the sun, was a Bukowski fan. Ralph, a cheerful endomorph, had canonized Wordsworth, hardly common ground. Personally, Yeats was my idea of a true poet. I could recite all of "The Lake Isle of Innisfree" from memory but thought this was probably not the time and place.

Mildred and Ellen hit it off, both devotees of Patty Peacedale's shawl ministry. They had brought copious knitting satchels from home and clicked-clacked away at their work, talking amiably. Harry Drudge sat beside them, his dyspeptic visage drooping into his gray shirt. I had the feeling he'd never make it to trial's end, but as he was only an alternate, justice would probably roll on without him. Drudge could have benefited from a shawl himself, but the two women hardly gave him a glance. Still, there was something truly magical about knitting healing thoughts and wishes into a garment that would later be wrapped around someone in need. I made notes on that for Deidre. Perhaps she'd like to try her own Wiccan version.

Ernie edged over to break up our poetic conclave and corner me. His effusive compliments soon began to get on my nerves, but Anna elbowed him out of her way to talk to me about local crime. Apparently she'd followed accounts of the Circle's escapades reported in the *Pilgrim Times*. Out of the corner of my eye, I saw Ernie approach Wanda and April. Maybe Wanda would deck him, I hoped. She certainly had the build for it, with biceps that would be the envy of any lady wrestler.

Leaning against the wall with his arms folded, Kurt surveyed his new companions with a perpetual sneer. Hugh Collins, who was being backed up against the same wall by Brooke, did his best to bring Kurt into the conversation. Kurt's chief interest in horses, however, was betting on them at the track—but he seemed to respect Hugh. I gathered that Brooke had sold Hugh Collins, a former West Virginia horse-dealer, the Churchill place and Kurt had done some work for him, repairing the burned stables.

"You've got your eye—and ear—on everyone, don't you, Shipton? Nothing much gets by you," Anna said. "Surprised the hell out of me that Laratta didn't dismiss you out of hand what with your being mixed up with those poisonings at the church. He must have some notion about you."

"For whatever reason, Laratta thinks I'll be be fair-minded," I said.

Anna studied me with a skeptical smirk. It was a relief when we filed back into the jury box and took our assigned places again.

What Laratta was trying to pull together as a defense soon became clear. His clients had been literally caught with the goods from the robbery, and the defense would stipulate to house invasion and robbery, but Farrow and Lovitt were not rapists; no semen had been found on or in Therese. They were not kidnappers; Marie Reynard had driven her own car willingly to the bank. And they were not murderers. Whatever caused the deaths of the two women had been neither premeditated nor intentional, according to the argument their attorneys were making.

Mildred Woolrich, seated beside me, wrote a line in her notebook and nudged my arm. I looked over. "If they died during a felony, it's still murder," her neat handwriting declared. She had underlined murder twice.

To bolster their feeble defense, Laratta's second, "Hank" Sharpe, questioned the medical examiner at length about the victims' health. Did he realize that Marie Reynard had a heart murmur, and that Therese had once fainted after a soccer match? The jurors stirred in a wave of disbelief as this alternate theory of the crime was offered by the desperate defense team, who were, after all, only court-appointed attorneys. As Sharpe strode back and forth in a slim velvet jacket and brown slacks, it seemed as if, not only the jury but even Farrow and Lovitt looked uncomfortable, perhaps at being defended by a woman—or could they finally be showing fear, imagining the trial's inevitable outcome? At least they weren't facing execution in Massachusetts. I didn't think I could have been a juror if the death penalty had been on the table.

Anna leaned forward again. "Fee, fie, foe, fum...I smell a manslaughter plea to come," she whispered.

"Shhhhh," whispered Mildred Woolrich, elbowing *me* in the ribs.

Judge Lax glared at us for the second time.

Despite Sharpe's attempts to drum up doubt, the forensic testimony offered by the plodding medical examiner confirmed that the women had been smothered, Marie in the living room with a butterfly-embroidered yellow silk pillow and Therese in her bedroom with a hypoallergenic foam rubber bed pillow. Obviously the two felons had not wanted to leave witnesses.

But, somehow, I could not quite make up my mind to dismiss Laratta and Sharpe's defense entirely. At least not until I'd heard the rest of the evidence. Both sides must be carefully weighed. Things were not always what they seemed. *Innocent until proven guilty*. The golden rule of law applied even to these two degenerates. No reason to rush making up my mind.

Maybe that's what Laratta had known or sensed about me. *The Libran thing.*

CHAPTER EIGHT

I was to taste in little the grief
That comes of dogs' lives being so brief.

– Robert Frost

The third day of the trial, a Friday, court was recessed until Monday. Joe was still en route to New Zealand, incommunicado. So I drove straight from Brockton to Heather's place, where I planned to cadge supper and bring home my doggies for the weekend. As soon as I arrived, however, I realized that if any sort of meal was going to be served, I'd better pitch in to cook it.

Heather was in full battle mode, pacing up and down the grand new kitchen in a safari suit from Nordstrom's, her long bronze braid swinging. This wing of the mansion had been remodeled after being bomb-blasted along with Heather's former housekeeper. It was now resplendent with warm Mexican tiles, handsome dark wooden cabinets, and impressive restaurant appliances. Cactus and other spiky-leaved green plants flourished brilliantly on the windowsills. Heather banged her fist on the green-marble-topped island, scattering a small array of tools she used to etch her hand-crafted candles. A pot of candle wax was melting over barely simmering water in the steamer. I glanced in. The dye chip had been added. The brew was mighty dark, and it smelled of some herb I couldn't readily identify, rather an acrid odor, like tannin. Agrimony, perhaps. Magical herb for seeing.

"Okay, Heather—what's up?" I asked in a fairly neutral tone.

"Bastards!" she exclaimed, taking down two cut-glass tumblers from the liquor cabinet and sloshing in healthy double shots of Jack Daniels. "Ice?"

"Yes, please. I'll get it." I opened the freezer of her enormous Sub-Zero refrigerator and filled the ice bucket waiting beside it. "So, tell me, what's the problem?"

"Dick's had two American Staffordshire Terriers dropped off at the hospital with ugly fight wounds."

"Pit bulls." I tasted my whiskey gingerly. It *was* rather heartening after a long day of murder and mayhem. "According to the AKC, they're two different breeds, and it's pit bulls who are trained for the fighting ring."

"I don't like to call them that. They've had such a bad press by that name, as if they were, for Goddess' sake, *killers*—I prefer the name American Staffordshire terriers. If they're trained correctly, they're perfectly sweet and gentle."

Big if, I thought. "There have been some incidents," I said tentatively.

"Don't *you* start. There *have been some incidents* with every breed you can name." Heather fixed me with her no-nonsense gaze. Where canines were concerned, she would countenance no common prejudice. "The kid who brought in those badly mauled dogs was some skinhead, skittish and evasive, who dumped the poor animals on the floor of the waiting room and literally ran out the door. Maury thought he recognized the boy, but we haven't had a chance to verify that yet. It looks as if someone on the South Shore has got himself a dog-fighting operation going. The kid was probably supposed to finish off those poor animals and chuck them somewhere—Miles Standish Park maybe—but, I'm guessing, he didn't have the stomach for it."

"And the state forest is so deserted this time of year. Even if Maury remembers where he saw the kid, there's not much to go on. The kid could claim he found the dogs in that injured state and dropped them off at the vet's like a good junior citizen."

Dick's holistic practice was growing fast among upwardly mobile residents of the South Shore, so he'd brought in an associate to help at the Wee Angels Animal Hospital, Maury Irving, who'd been a veterinarian with the Army for twenty years. Maury was a compact man with the deceptive slight build of a lightweight boxer, gentle with animals but somewhat reserved with people.

"Couldn't those two pit bulls...eh...*American Staffordshire Terriers*...have just got into it on their own?" I asked. "Maybe the kid ran off because he didn't want to get stuck paying the bill."

"Dick says there are scars and partly healed old injuries that make their condition consistent with a couple of fighting dogs who've been in the ring more than once." Heather checked the melting wax with a thermometer and added another dye chip. *Dark and darker.*

"So then, why don't you tell me what you're planning to do while I whip up a little dinner. I'm sure you're feeling much too upset to cook. Will Dick be coming home to eat? What about Maury?" Already I had my head in the other side of the refrigerator, looking for edibles. *Ah, a lovely large fillet of salmon. I'll have that on the table in short order. Nuke some spuds. Sautéed peas with onion. Some kind of salad? This wheel of Brie looks perfect.*

"You go, girl. We could all use a good home-cooked meal around here. Dick brought home that salmon, and I haven't the faintest. Maybe he was thinking of grilling it later? He'll be delighted, I'm sure. I'll just give you a clear field and go feed the doggies. Your two are not the greatest eaters in the world, are they?"

"Depends," I said. "But you haven't answered my question. What's with this candle business?"

"Oh, I just thought, you know, maybe I could flush out the bastards who are running those dog fights with this candle discovery thing I learned about."

I took out the salmon, the Brie, and some frozen peas and laid them on the counter. "Where do you keep the potatoes and onions? What discovery thing?"

"In the pantry. It's a spell I got from this Salem witch I've been corresponding with on the Internet. He's a flight attendant, and he's picked up a good deal of myth and magic in various places."

"I don't really trust the anonymity of the Internet." In Heather's marvelous old-fashioned pantry, I found crocks of potatoes and onions along with a lovely bowl of ripe, almost over-ripe, tomatoes on the counter. And many tins of fruit as well. I decided on Dakota figs in heavy syrup. *Yum.* Dinner was going to be a cinch.

"You'd be wise to check out any spells you're thinking of brewing with Fiona first," I called out over my shoulder.

"Yeah?. Well, maybe. Okay, I'll leave you to it, then." Heather drained her whiskey, turned off the heat under the melted wax, and strode out to the garage where she kept bins of perfectly balanced, nutritious dry dog chow and some canned stuff supposed to be easy on the kidneys. *Poor mutts!*

Maybe I could deflect the discovery spell, whatever that was. Knowing Heather's crusade against animal cruelty, it was probably more of a "search and destroy" mission. She'd surely never rest until she found those criminal promoters. Probably I should try to help, loathe as I always was to resort to clairvoyance. Mulling over this moral dilemma, I seasoned the salmon with scallions, Dijon mustard, and herbed crumbs and slipped it into a hot oven. Meanwhile, I microwaved the potatoes and began to sauté the peas with chopped onion. I sliced the tomatoes and dressed them with salt, garlic, basil, and olive oil. There were loaves of French bread stacked like logs in the freezer; one of these went into the oven when I removed the fish.

By the time Heather got back from her dog-feeding chores and Dick stamped in from the *Wee Angels Rescue Wagon*, supper was ready and the kitchen table set. A big teddy bear of a man, when Dick hugged Heather, who's a tall gal herself, she nearly disappeared. Maury came in after Dick and took in the supper scene with a glance. "Looks good," he said. "I see the Devlins have got themselves a new cook." His smile was sweet, but it never quite reached the sadness in his dark eyes. *No*, I said to myself. *Don't go there. You don't want to know.*

"Say, you're not looking for a job, are you?" A broad smile lit up Dick's face as he inspected the fare, while Heather took two bottles of a robust Medoc out the walk-in "wine cellar," opened one expertly, and filled all the glasses.

"Tempting." I said. "Unfortunately, with my present judicial responsibilities..."

"And her one-woman crime watch," Heather added, pushing aside a vase of yellow tulips to make room for the second bottle of Medoc. "But keep the faith, Dick. I've called on the Cosmos for the perfect housekeeper, and he or she will surely arrive before Samhain."

He rolled his eyes at me. "Come on, Maury. You'd better plan to chow down with us. Looks as if Cass has conjured up a feast here. You can wash up in the lav under the stairs." Dick, moving quickly and gracefully for such a big man, headed upstairs, I assumed to change out of the green scrubs he was wearing.

"So, you're going to get out that weird pillow of yours and have a search for my villains?" Heather asked when Dick and Maury had gone.

"How did you know about that damned pillow?"

"You're not the only one who reads minds, you know," she smirked. "And don't think you're going to save those scoundrels. Whoever's in on the dog-fighting, I'm going to fix them for good and all.

"How do you mean 'fix'?" Heather's spell work often veered toward the sinister side. And in her youth, she'd done a stint with animal activists, breaking into laboratories to free test animals—chimps, dogs, and cats. What would she not do with magic if animal well-being was at stake?

"*Fix*. Sort of like, *hex*, but not quite. I do have my ethics, you know."

"Yeah, sure. And I'll help you with a search, but I'd like to wait until this trial is over so psychic impressions won't get mixed up in my poor little brain."

"Cass, if you're obsessing over that open-and-shut verdict, you're just wasting your talents. What if more dogs are being maimed or killed while you dilly-dally with your murderers?"

Speaking of obsessing, Heather was well on her way. *Time to change the subject.*

"Say, Heather, is Brooke Morgan any relation of yours? She's one of my fellow-jurors. Perfectly sun-streaked, tawny blonde wearing Ferragamo flats and swinging a Hermes handbag. Dresses like a Talbot catalog."

"Oh, *Brooke.* Sure, she's a cousin several times removed. Don't you remember that it was my cousin Brooke who knew the Norse ship's captain and got the lot of us invited to the captain's table? Divorced. Works as a realtor but doesn't really have to. Resides in Duxbury—Snug Harbor—and keeps an apartment on Commonwealth Avenue. *Her* great-great grandfather was in the Triangle Trade. I don't know which was worse, her branch of the family trading slaves or our branch trafficking in opium. *Behind every great fortune there is a crime.* Someone said that, maybe Balzac. Brooke feels it's never too late for love or too early for gin. I would not introduce her to Joe, if I were you."

"Well, thanks. I'll keep that in mind. But your well-heeled cousin seems to have taken a fancy to our foreman, Hugh Collins. She sold him that burned-out Churchill horse farm. Handsome devil."

"He won't be able to ride fast or far enough. And Brooke is very horsy herself. Rides to hounds in Virginia wearing pink velvet. *The unspeakable in pursuit of the inedible,* as Oscar Wilde so aptly put it. I would disown her except that every year when I hit her up for a donation to Animal Lovers, she comes through very generously, even for a Morgan. She'll vote to convict for the maximum sentence, you know."

"She will? Why? How do you know?"

"Well, for one thing, those two are obviously guilty, and for two things, the wealthy are made uneasy by heinous crimes perpetrated against them by low-class thugs. And Marie Reynard was very wealthy indeed. The de Rochmonts are a big name in French wines. The Reynard brothers must get a pretty hefty discount on the excellent wines in their restaurant's cellars. *Wine Spectator* Award for the past three years."

I knew I shouldn't listen to gossip about the Reynards. Nevertheless, I said, "Madame Therese de Rochmont has been in court every day. The murdered girl was named after her grandmother."

"She'll have those murderers' heads in the guillotine or die trying. A formidable old lady, so I have heard."

~

"Cass is serving as a juror on the Reynard trial," Heather told Maury as I placed an enormous Talavera platter of Salmon Dijon à la Cass on the table. "But she's not supposed to discuss the guilt of those murdering bastards."

"I haven't been following the trial," Maury confessed. "I'm afraid I avoid the local news. Murders, rapes, fires. Different victims, but always the same sad news. Too violent an entertainment package for my taste." He helped himself to everything except the salmon. I remembered now that Maury was a vegetarian as Heather often wished she were. *Good move*, I congratulated myself, serving that Brie along with the French bread. I wondered about his years in the Army, hardly a non-violent career choice.

"You'll be wondering how I could have served in the military," he continued, picking right up on my thoughts. "Dogs, horses, even mules—they all need medical care wherever they're posted. VETCOM is responsible for animal disease and prevention for the entire Department of Defense. And we had watchdogs duties, too, if you don't mind the pun—food safety inspection, control of certain biological threats. Whether military or civilian, medical personnel see the results of violence every day. I don't need more of it served up to me at six every evening to know it's out there."

"That's maturity, Maury. Or empathy. Maybe you feel the victims' pain too keenly," I said. "Whatever. As for me, I find myself drawn into local concerns as if it's my personal mission to see justice done. It's a bit like being an evangelist, I guess. Compelled to rout out sin."

"So, being a juror must be right up your alley. How do you like it so far? I understand that most people try to get out of serving." He reached for the French bread and dipped it into the tomato oil on his salad plate.

"It's different. Intense but dull, for the most part. The jurors seem to me to be an ill-sorted bunch, but it's early days yet. Perhaps we'll work together like a well-oiled machine when we get to deliberations." At the same time I said that, it came to me that we'd never be in deliberations together. I didn't know why. Something...something would happen.

"Cass, you've got that funny look on your face." Heather filled my glass with wine as if proffering a restorative. "Are you feeling all right?"

"Sure. Just someone walking on my grave, I guess."

"Happen to you often, does it?" Maury asked with his solemn smile.

"Often enough. Speaking of local crime, what about Heather's suspicion that there's a dog-fighting ring nearby?"

"It's more than a suspicion," Maury said. "Dick and I both looked those dogs over and came to the same conclusion. The way a pediatrician might zero in on child abuse. Dog fighting is a nasty business, and we don't want it here."

"Just let me find the people who are running the show," Dick said in his booming voice. "I'll close them up pronto."

"Cass can locate them for us," Heather said confidently. "And I'm making discovery candles."

"Ah, I've heard of your clairvoyant powers." Maury looked at me the way people do—unbelieving but worried that it might be true. "You see into hidden places and events."

"Reluctantly," I said. Detective assignments from Heather always had a way of going awry somehow, but with a crime as vile as dog-fighting, I knew I'd have to give it a try. Now, where in the world had I hidden that psychic visions dream pillow this time? One of my wilder prototypes, it combined a potpourri of visionary herbs that turned out to be too potent to market. I was a bit afraid of laying my own head on it again, and I'd created the thing. I felt a twinge of sympathy for Dr. Frankenstein.

During the rest of the meal I assiduously avoided any discussion of the Reynards, and afterwards I brought my dogs home directly, amid much coughing and complaining.

My superior canine scenting skills detect a whiff of salmon. Salmon is a natural dog food. Fish oil gives a nice finish to coat of fur, you know. Got any salmon left for a loyal and deserving pal?

Raffles bounced around the back seat with excitement. *Fish! Fish!*

I supposed I'd have to open a tin of the stuff when I got home.

CHAPTER NINE

Love and scandal
are the best sweeteners of tea.

– Henry Fielding

I was airing out the kitchen from a particularly pungent incense concoction, an aromatherapy test gone wrong, when Phillipa drove over the following afternoon, Saturday, to share a pot of tea and keep me company. Wearing a wide-brimmed black hat and black cashmere shawl, she was carrying a basket redolent of molasses, ginger, cinnamon, and a whiff of nutmeg. Leaning in my open window, she smiled brilliantly, the smile that made her sharp features suddenly beautiful. "Trick or treat?"

"Looks like treats to me. And you look for all the world like the neighborhood witch come to pay a pre-Halloween call." I opened the kitchen door and put the kettle on to boil.

"It takes one to know one, dearie. How's the trial going?"

"Oh, you know. *The banality of evil*. The horror of it hangs around my heart like a heavy weight. Those two nonentities, that hideous crime."

Unpacking dark spicy hermits and gingerbread witch cookies from her basket, Phillipa said, "Dick and I have dined at Chez Reynard of Hyannis—that's the one run by Albert. Francis handles the Chez Reynard Aussi of Chatham. I don't know if he's part owner or only the manager. The cuisine in Hyannis was innovative and meticulously prepared, and the wine list was to die for."

"Yes, but was the food *tasty*? Never mind. Don't tell me. It's better if I don't discuss the Reynards at all. This stuff you've brought certainly looks delicious. What kind of tea do you fancy today? Want to try my Wise Woman Blend?"

"No thanks, dearie. I'm wise enough already. Just plain Earl Grey is my cup of tea. The food was very tasty indeed, as you put it in your peasant fashion, and rather expensive. Two people who like their wine are going to be nudging a hundred and fifty or more."

She watched me carefully as I hotted the pot, added spoonfuls of Earl Grey loose tea, and poured in near-boiling water. I was using the Chatsford teapot she'd given me one Christmas. Herbal pattern. And real china tea cups. Seeing nothing to critique in my tea-making routine, she nibbled a witch thoughtfully. "I wonder if Reynard wasn't overextending himself somewhat by opening that second restaurant in this bastion of thrifty Yankees. Oh, it's all right in the summer when the tourists swarm in, but we dined at Chez Reynard in early April, and the place was half empty."

"Hush with the Reynards, will you! Oh, I do love hermits!"

Scuffy's nose nudged my knee. *Hey, don't forget me, Toots.*

Me, too. Me, too. Raffles flopped down beside his sire.

I put a slice of candied ginger in each of our cups and poured in the hot tea "Try this—you'll like it," I promised her. "The thing is, Phil, I have a real *hunch* that the trial won't get as far as jury deliberations. But just in case, I'm trying to follow protocol."

"Hmmmm. Does that mean I shouldn't tell you what else I've discovered about the Reynards? And if you feed one more of my handcut ginger ladies and Jamaican hermits to those two animals under the table, I swear on the Cauldron of Cerridwen that I'll never bring you another basket of goodies."

Hey, Toots—don't listen to that spoilsport. We canines don't get nearly enough sweet stuff.

Sweet stuff! Sweet stuff! Raffles nudged the back of my knee hopefully.

"Too much sweet stuff will rot your big beautiful teeth," I said.

"You're talking to the dogs now, I trust," Phillipa said. "So, anyway—here's what I heard at the Myles Standish Free Library's Cookbook Club where I was giving a presentation on my *Native Foods of New England.* Remember that one? Penobscot Shepherd's Pie made with ground moose meat and fiddleheads? I feel it's important to introduce some recipes with one or two ingredients that will prove to be impossible to buy at the supermarket. Confers a touch of class. Gives food critics something to get their teeth into, so to speak. But, I digress."

"You certainly do." By now, I admit, I was indecently curious to learn whatever tidbit Phillipa had picked up at the cookbook club meeting.

"Yes. Well, back to the meeting. Winona Synge, who teaches domestic science at Silver Lake High School, told me that Reynards' three and a half-million-dollar estate—Chateau Marie—with ocean views and extensive manicured grounds is *on the market*. Rumor has it among ladies of the club that real estate taxes on the property, which are shockingly high in that exclusive part of Wareham, have not been paid this year."

"On the market? Before or after the murders?" I couldn't help myself. The question just popped out of my mouth of its own volition.

"I'm not sure, but I think the house may have been advertised in early spring, so possibly just before the home invasion. Might actually have inspired those two swine. A multi-million-dollar price tag must have made the house appear to be a succulent plum ripe for the plucking." Phillipa tasted her slice of tea-soaked candied ginger. "Say, this is really good, Cass."

"But you're not sure. I mean, about when the house was put up for sale."

"Perhaps I misremember and the place went up for sale right afterwards. That could be. Reynard wanting to rid himself of tragic memories, and all that. But who would want to buy a house that was the scene of two such grisly murders?" Phillipa frowned at the very thought and poured herself a second cup of tea. I passed her the jar of candied ginger.

"Someone relocating here from the West Coast. The real estate agent will have played down the lurid aspects. You know how they are. Just close the deal and run. If the buyer is troubled with weird manifestations later, she can always have the place exorcised and blessed," I said.

"Not all exorcists are created equal. Maybe Dee's friend, Bishop Whatshisname, who confessed that he sees dead people, might be able to do the trick. He had a certain force of soul, don't you think?"

"Bishop Aiden Guilfoyle," I said. "Dee sees dead people, too. I wonder what she'd make of the crime scene."

"I thought you didn't want the Circle's interference in your vestal deliberations." Phillipa raised a winged black eyebrow.

"And every one of you has gone out of her way to fill my ears with local tittle-tattle!" I said crossly. "Ignoring your gossip had been like trying to unring a bell."

Phillipa laughed merrily. "You're Cassandra the clairvoyant, my dear. *No way* you're going to keep your judgment unsullied by extraneous information. But never mind. I won't say a single other word about the Reynard case. In fact, I'll change the subject. So, tell me, what do you think of these hermits? I soaked the raisins in dark rum for three days."

Oops! Was that a hiccup I heard under the table?

CHAPTER TEN

What beckoning ghost along the moonlight shade
Invites my steps, and points to yonder glade?

– Alexander Pope

"Cassandra!" It had been ages since I'd heard it, but I recognized the soft, soothing voice of the doyenne of St. Rita's House, a shelter for battered women. It was Sunday night, and I was relaxing on the sofa in my living room, watching *The Ghost and Mrs. Muir*, my cell phone nearby in case Joe should break security and call me. (*Fat chance!* Greenpeace special ops were held sacred by my husband. Something about the Greek warrior ethic.) The pups were sacked out on the windowseat, rump to rump. Occasionally Scruffy would lift up his head *pro forma* to check out the driveway. How often the most peaceful moments of my life seem to attract interruptions!

"Serena! So nice to hear from you again." As if I didn't know that I was about to be conned. Like Heather with her abused animals, Serena Dove was a fierce and fearless advocate for abused women, and she would tap any shoulder when help was needed.

"It's been too long! You must come over to St. Rita's for lunch one day soon. And bring your admirable daughter Becky. Katz and Kinder, isn't she? Family law? A fine old respectable firm. We've consulted with Attorney Kinder from time to time. But right now, I confess, I've been at my wit's end with one of my clients. Then I thought of you. It's exactly the kind of problem you're so good at unraveling." I imagined the face at the other end of the phone line. The wiry gray hair, the sweet, comforting smile, the shrewd bright eyes. I really didn't have time for Serena's problem clients right now.

"Oh, gee, Serena. I don't know how much help I can be. I'm serving as a juror in a major criminal case at Brockton Superior. I'll be at court all this week, and perhaps for weeks to come."

"Then I'll get right to the point, my dear. I need a safe house for a gal who's being battered by her dead husband."

"Serena, that's just not possible."

"So I would have believed had I not seen it happen with my own eyes. Her name is Ashling Holmes. Ashling Malone as was. We tried a prayer vigil for Ashling, but that didn't prevent hymn books from flying around the room. So then we thought maybe a recitation of devout poetry would calm the devilish thing. But his mischief just got wilder. Gerard Manley Hopkins took a real beating. Sister Mary Joseph, our visiting psychologist, suffered a black eye from John Donne, and the poor girl herself was concussed by Hildegard Bingham We tried bedding her down in the chapel, and for that bright idea we got ourselves a broken stained glass window. The Magdalene window, very dear to my heart. Do you know how much it costs to repair stained glass?"

Holy shades of Amityville! I wasn't too thrilled at the idea of broken windows in my dear little saltbox cottage either, albeit they were only plain glass. "You did say the husband is *dead*?"

"Archibald Fennimore Holmes. Famous poet, drunk, and womanizer. Not so well known, a closet batterer. Perhaps you've heard of him?"

"I think Phil might have mentioned him. Neo-formalist poet Boston Brahmin. How did he die exactly?"

Serena was silent for several long moments. "Fell down three floors in the stairwell of their apartment building. He was Professor of Victorian Literature at Harvard University, his alma mater."

A vision of my own first marriage flashed before my eyes. Gary staggeringly drunk, and me trying to get him up the stairs without both of us falling. *I was on the wall side without a banister, and I was slipping, his vomitous breath in my face.*

"Apparently, Archie's ghost is an unforgiving one. But why do you think Ashling would be safer with me? And what about *my* safety, by the way."

"The thing is, this evil spirit seems to be bypassing the traditional Christian safeguards such as a silver cross and the Good Book. Thank the Lord I remembered that you guys have your own banishings, protective spells, herbal amulets and such. So I thought, if St. Rita isn't doing the job, why not give the Mother Goddess a shot?"

"Very ecumenical of you, Serena."

"Well, now that I'm no longer a nun, I can go for situational spirituality as I see fit."

"Sounds as if you have a poltergeist on your hands. Has there been much damage?"

"At St. Rita's, just the incidents I mentioned. The other manifestations seem to be aimed—and I do mean that literally—at this poor girl. There's been a fair amount of bruising, too, from spectral pinching. We can readily imagine what species of bully Holmes was in life, how he behaved toward those he perceived as weaker. Ashling is surely well rid of that lout.

"Ashling is an unusual name."

"She's an unusual gal. A wraith. But gifted, very gifted."

"Gifted in what way?"

"Levitation. You know, Saint Teresa herself levitated when in rhapsody."

"*Levitation!* Hey, Serena—are you saying that this Ashling has been floating around the halls of St. Rita's?" Levitation is a form of psychokinesis, Freddie's specialty. But Freddie had never demonstrated that she herself could defy gravity, just the gravity of small objects within her purview. I sincerely hoped neither of my two precious grandkids would ever carry inherited psychokinesis to such heights.

"Ashling has her episodes pretty much under control except for the nights. Generally, she ties herself down before sleep and that works."

"But you yourself have witnessed Ashling in flight?"

"Oh, no, dear. Let's not exaggerate. I would hardly call it *flight* exactly. But I have seen her feet leave the ground when she was walking down the aisle in chapel. I could hardly believe my eyes. I even scheduled an emergency check-up with my ophthalmologist. And he confirmed that my eyesight is 20/20 with my current lens prescription. So then I questioned Ashling on the matter—gently, you know—and she admitted to the phenomenon. The Lord, she claims, is the wind beneath her wings. It's her feet, though, actually."

"Okay, let me see if I have this picture straight, Serena. You have a client named Ashling Holmes who's able to levitate with the help of the Almighty and who is being harassed by the ghost of her late husband, a fairly well-known poet?"

"Yes, that's about it. So naturally, *you* came to mind."

"Yeah. *Something weird, and it don't look good. Who you going to call?*"

"Well then, *will you do it?* Will you take her in for a few days and see if you can sort out the ghost, at least?"

"Serena, I really am so very tied up with this court case."

"And there's one more thing you should know, Cass. Before you decide. Ashling has an affinity for animals as well. They love and trust her at first sight. She'll be right at home with your two little fellows."

A glimmer of an idea was tracking through my brain. Could this be the Cosmos' notion of an *au pair extraordinaire*? But first we'd need to get rid of Ashling's *Ghost of Husband Past*. I'd consult Fiona on that.

"You don't say. Do you happen to know if she can cook?"

Serene knew when the fish had taken the bait. "A lovely light hand with pastry and bread," she crowed. "Archie—may his soul rest in peace, the sooner the better—had been accustomed to the haute cuisine created by his mother's French chefs, so Ashling had to master *le cordon bleu*, poor wee gal."

I sighed. "Suppose I visit you tomorrow right after court adjourns. We'll just meet and talk, no promises."

"Just wait until you taste Ashling's scones."

~

"Fiona, do you know anything about exorcising a poltergeist?" The film had ended with Gene Tierney and Rex Harrison wafting off together into the mists of time.

Still early enough to call Fiona, who was something of a night owl anyway.

"A poltergeist can generally be traced to a disturbed young person in the household," Fiona said. There was a pause while she took a sip of something. A Scotch toddy, I imagined. "I have some books around here somewhere." I heard the sound of a stack of books sliding to the floor. "Yes, here we go. I just put my hand on them. *Exorcism for Dummies. The Seven Spells of Highly Effective Exorcists*. Oh, but it's this pamphlet I like the best. *A Common Sense Approach to Poltergeists.*"

"You mean that the victim is the perpetrator?" I asked. "This victim happens to be a *protégé* of Serena's, a young widow. Abused *from beyond the veil*, so the story goes."

"My, my, how interesting! But that's a simplistic diagnosis, my dear. It's true, though, that the girl's own energy may be at the heart of the phenomenon. Has she exhibited psychic energy in any other aspect of her life?"

"*Has she ever*! But we'll get into that later. What about guilt? Could she be punishing herself for some fancied sin?" *Giving Hubby a little push, maybe?*

"What do you think she did? Murder her husband?"

"*Cut that out, Fiona*."

"Just a guess, my dear. A psychically informed guess."

"I'm only guessing myself. But her husband was a bully and he did die in an accident at home."

"Well, you know what they say, Cass. *Most accidental murders happen in the home.*"

"Yes, Fiona. Sure. But back to my original question. Please consider this an emergency. I may have this young woman from St. Rita's coming to stay with me. She's afflicted by a poltergeist whom she believes is her husband, a poet of some reputation, and not only for his poems."

"I understand, my dear. If I were you, I'd start out with a mugwort and sage bath. After that, a simple banishing séance ought to do the trick. Would you like me to participate?"

"I thought you'd never ask. *Of course*, I need your help."

"Let's see...we'll need blessed thistle, dragon's blood, and unicorn root."

"Unicorn root?" My knowledge of herbs is fairly encyclopedic, but every once in while Fiona would come up with a folk name that was news to me.

"Chamaelirium luteum. Sometimes called starwort. Those three are traditional, but personally I like to add a pinch of rue. I do hope you have everything on hand, dear!" Fiona's voice betrayed a rising enthusiasm for the task.

"Yes, I even have starwort. Garlic and silver bullets as well, in case of vampires. *Eye of newt and toe of frog.*"

She rattled right on. "Garlic is popular for exorcisms, too, dear. Speaking of silver, we'll do negative rhymes as well. So appropriate for banishing a poet."

"Negative rhymes?"

"Unrhyming rhymes are especially powerful."

"Such as?"

"Silver. Purple. Orange. Month. Only four words in the English language for which there are no rhymes."

"I don't mean to be argumentative, but how exactly do you propose to rhyme the unrhymable?"

"*Un*exactly. When do you want to have this séance? Traditionally, Sunday is best for exorcism, but I rather like Tuesday for banishing."

"When you're dealing with a poltergeist, the sooner, the better."

"Tuesday, then. But you haven't even made up your mind about the girl yet, have you? What's her name?"

"Ashling."

"Ahhh."

"What do you mean, *Ahhh*, Fiona?"

"A beautiful woman in peril, that's an Ashling."

"I'm going to St. Rita's to meet her tomorrow after court adjourns. Then we'll see."

"I rather think you won't be able to resist the challenge. So, I'll arrange some neighborly care for little Laura on Tuesday night and be there with bells on."

After we hung up, I wondered if she meant *bells* literally. You never knew with Fiona.

~

"*We're all in our places with sunshiny faces*," Wanda Finch sang softly as we filed into the jury box on Monday morning.

"Except Harry Drudge." Even when she tried to whisper, Anna Grimassi's voice carried clearly beyond the jury box.

"Hey, that's right! Where's old Harry?" Ernie Byrd peeled his attention away from watching April Rayne's curvy body as she settled into her chair. Her big, big hair was going to make it difficult for him to see past her, but maybe he didn't care.

Judge Lax tapped his gavel twice and gazed at us reprovingly. I was reminded of middle school in my youth with Miss Toothacher monitoring the halls.

"Poor guy," Ellen Heany whispered. "Didn't you hear? Harry Drudge died on the job at Walmart Saturday night. He was a greeter."

"One of those gray guys who loom over the entrance with scary smiles," Anna Grimassi explained.

There was a general sucking in of our breaths. Most of us hadn't known of poor Harry's demise.

"Ladies and gentlemen of the jury," Judge Lax intoned in a commanding voice that resounded off the courtroom paneling. "I'm sorry to have to inform you that one member of your jury panel is no longer with us. Harold Drudge passed away over the weekend. Inasmuch as he was an alternate juror, one of two, and we are a week into this trial, we will continue without him and hope that the rest of you remain in the best of health throughout the balance of your service. Mr. Steemer, are you ready to resume?"

The prosecutor's face shone with boyish enthusiasm as he called George Entwistle, lead detective in the investigation of the Reynard murders. Most of the jurors were already taking out their official notebooks and pens. Kurt Heller, his arms folded, made no move to take notes, however, and April Rayne appeared to be searching through a shocking pink, plastic handbag in vain.

George Entwistle didn't fit the image of a detective, but then neither did Phillipa's husband Stone, who looked more like a distracted professor at a boys' school, *Mr. Chips* perhaps. Entwistle, on the other hand, could have been one of those Norman Rockwell doctors, kindly and practical. I wondered if they knew each other, and if it would be kosher to ask Stone what he thought of Entwistle.

The detective's testimony occupied the entire day, with time out for our long lunch break. Steemer took Entwistle step by step through every facet of the crime, the same events the prosecutor had already outlined dramatically in his opening argument. Entwistle presented his version of the home invasion based on everything the detectives had pieced together from the testimony of Rodriguez and Jordan, evidence collected by the crime scene team, and the forensic report.

When police officers had entered the Reynard home in response to Albert Reynard's panic call, they'd discovered him collapsing with a heart attack near the body of his dead wife. The officers called for an ambulance and back-up, then searched the premises. They found Therese's body, tied to her bed. The next to arrive had been Entwistle and his partner, the detectives who'd caught the case. Marie Reynard's body showed no obvious signs of battering except a bruise on her mouth and a circular mark around her right wrist, Entwistle testified. Therese, however, had several facial and body bruises and her clothing was torn in a manner suggestive of sexual assault. After securing the crime scene, Entwistle had summoned the medical examiner and the scene-of-the-crime crew.

An APB had gone out describing a small man with a beard covering a red birthmark who was wanted for questioning in a home invasion and murder. Soon afterward, a call had come in from an alert off-duty policeman who'd sighted a man answering the suspect's description with a male companion at an Exxon station. The policeman had even taken a surreptitious picture of the two with his cell phone, which he forwarded to the officers in charge for confirmation. One of the two men in the photo looked like the police artist's sketch of "Jim Bob" Farrow, drawn from the bank teller's description. A nearby patrol car had been directed to the scene, and, after a quick chase, the two officers had forced the Chevy off the road and apprehended the suspects. Most of the money Marie Reynard had withdrawn from Rockland Trust had been wrapped up in a jacket in the Chevy's trunk. "Caught red-handed," is how George Entwhistle described the scene.

A police line-up had been hastily arranged, in which Faith Rodriguez positively identified Farrow. Following a night of non-stop interrogation at the station, Lovitt and Farrow, somewhat the worse for wear, had admitted to breaking in and robbing the Reynard women, each blaming the other for planning the crime. "Jim Bob" owned up to forcing Marie Reynard to withdraw a large amount of money from Rockland Trust, leaving his partner to guard Therese at the house.

Laratta's cross-examination brought out that the two men had confessed to robbing the two women but nothing else. When the defendants learned that the victims were found dead at the scene, they'd insisted on "lawyering up," as Entwhistle put it.

Both men had persistently claimed that they were innocent of rape and murder, even before Laratta showed up to take over their defense. Like a small pebble thrown in a pond, this denial of guilt had sent a ripple of disbelief through the jury box. Mildred Woolrich tut-tutted, and Brooke Morgan made an audible scoffing sound. Ralph Dunbar sighed, and Wanda Finch stifled a snort. There followed an uncomfortable shifting of bodies in chairs, and someone behind me ripped out a notebook page and crumpled it up.

I studied the two defendants, looking for a glimpse of the truth or a nudge from my intuition. Farrow was fidgeting, his feral expression furtive and trapped. Lovitt slouched in his chair, hulking and belligerent. My gaze moved away, drawn to the two rows of Reynard relatives, their intent eyes and grim faces. Therese de Rochmont, with tears running down her face, was wrapped in a black lace shawl, her back as straight as Queen Elizabeth's. Albert Reynard looked exhausted and gray; his thin lips were blue, a contrast to his brother Francis, red-faced and stalwart. How I wished I could read auras, that electric surround that reflects every physical and emotional impulse of the body.

The jury's shuffle of unrest had earned us another reproving glare from the bench, but by then it was past four, so Judge Lax decided to adjourn. Again we were admonished not to discuss the case, just when it was obvious that we really wanted to voice our feelings of incredulity loudly to one another in the parking lot.

Striding beside me as I hurried out to my car, Hugh Collins was muttering under his breath, whether at the suspects' refusal to confess fully or the rapid clip-clop of Brooke Morgan's expensive heels trying to catch up with him, I couldn't be sure. Dogged gal, that Brooke. No wonder, though. Hugh really had a film star's charisma, some attractive unshaven outlaw type, James Dean for grown-ups, not the sort of man who appealed to me. Always that beguiling smile, but I sensed a coldness underneath. His eyes, I thought, betrayed a certain disassociation from the rest of us. Possibly I was prejudiced by the warmth of Joe's Aegean-blue eyes—just thinking about them made my knees weak. *Oh, where's my wandering Ulysses tonight?*

All I wanted for myself at that moment was to return as quickly as possible to my kitchen rocking chair, a large tumbler of wine, and the hope that Joe would break radio silence (or whatever) to call his lonely wife. But I'd promised to stop by St. Rita's and meet the levitating Ashling.

In case I would, after all, take on this challenging girl, I decided to run home first and pick up Scruffy and Raffles. Dogs are so very sensitive to ghostly phenomena, my two would be better off spending the night in Heather's *ménage.* My explanation was a tad brief—"I'm expecting a girl with a ghost tonight"—but Heather welcomed us warmly anyway. Scruffy, however, was less than pleased by this turn of events.

Thanks a lot, Toots! Some fine way to treat a loyal companion! Dumped for another night in the flea hotel with nothing but kennel sweepings for dinner.

Dinner! Dinner! Raffles danced into the dog yard with innocent enthusiasm.

"Better borrow a cross from Patty Peacedale," Heather advised. "I think you're supposed to hold a big silver cross in front of you and say some *Begone* stuff."

"Fiona promised to help me," I called back as I jumped into my RAV4.

"Oh well, then," Heather hollered out the door. "That specter won't stand a ghost of chance."

CHAPTER ELEVEN

And I have asked to be
Where no storms come,
Where the green swell is in the havens dumb
And out of the swing of the sea.

– Gerard Manley Hopkins

St. Rita's had the look of a gray fortress, complete with spiked wrought iron fencing and a formidable gate that was kept locked at night, the better to discourage stalking spouses. The battered women's sanctuary had once been a convent, and the shelter's guardian angel, Serena Dove, had once been a nun. The aura of their former lives, however, remained in evidence. The parlor was still dominated by an ornate, gilded Bible on an oak stand (in emergencies, Serena used it for *sortes biblicae*) and a statue of St. Rita with the thorn of her martyrdom stuck in her forehead, arms outstretched in the bow window. A gold-framed painting of Jesus as the Good Shepherd hung over the marble fireplace. Archangels supported the mantel. Renaissance cherubs appeared as andirons in the fireplace.

Serena welcomed me with a firm embrace for one who appeared so fragile and ushered me into her private apartment, once the sanctum of St. Rita's Mother Superior. Tea had already been prepared and was waiting for us. We sat opposite one another in ornately carved chairs with red cushions. Serena's wiry gray hair appeared a little wilder than usual, but her smile was as warmly reassuring as ever.

"Goodness, here we are again," she said genially. "Embarking on another rescue mission together. And I'm so very grateful for your help."

"Ah, well, Serena, I haven't absolutely agreed yet. I'd like to meet Ashling Malone before committing myself to rescuing her. And I do want your assurance that this will only be for a few days."

"Of course, of course. I've asked Ashling to give us ten minutes or so before joining us for tea. Last night was blessedly quiet, I'm happy to report. No evidence of spectral high jinx, so Ashling got some much needed rest." Serena poured me a cup of robust Irish tea and one for herself. "I'll be glad to take the girl back into our care if only you can exorcise that husband of hers."

"The unruly ghost. Some husbands will just never admit that it's over when it's over, but this one is grasping for his wife right out of the grave. Surely you tried to lay him to rest yourself?" I asked. "It seems to me that the Catholic Church wrote the book on exorcism. And St. Rita herself is a patron saint of impossible causes."

"She is, and I did indeed try to rid us of the hooligan poet. With the aid of Sister Mary Joseph, whom as you know is a very forceful person. I wanted to be certain not to do anything that would disturb the balance of Ashling's mind. That whole *Begone ye unclean spirit, power of Satan, infernal dragon* thing can get fairly intense."

"Didn't work, eh?" I sipped my tea. It was excellent, just what I needed after a hard day in the jury box.

"No, we were not successful, as demonstrated the following night in the chapel when a silver candlestick crashed into my Magdalene window. Most upsetting. The women whom we shelter here are already in a nervous state, and that flying candlestick was enough to send them into hysterics. Perhaps I should have called for a priest after all."

"If we can't manage on our own, my friend Dee knows a bishop who specializes in exorcism. Bishop Aiden Guilfoyle."

"Bishop Guilfoyle." Serena's shrewd eyes were thoughtful. "Sister Mary Joseph mentioned him as well. Has a bit of a reputation with spectral phenomena, doesn't he?"

"Yes, so I've heard." Actually, the bishop had confided in us that he himself had been troubled with the so-called *glamourous* powers—that he'd often been visited by visions of the dead. So the Church decided to make use of him as an exorcist and keep quiet about the rest of his questionable abilities.

There was a soft knock, and the heavy oak door of Serena's apartment opened. The young woman who entered so quietly had pale blonde hair tied back loosely with a ribbon. Her eyes were downcast; the dress draped on her thin frame was ankle-length, some amorphous shade between tan and gray. I glanced immediately at her feet, which were bare and appeared to be firmly in touch with the handsome Persian carpet. There was something of the Pre-Raphaelite heroine about her. The plate of scones in her hand might have been a jeweled chalice or a gypsy tambourine. I shook my head to rid it of such fanciful notions. Scones were scones, and these looked really good.

"Cass, I'd like you to meet Ashling Malone Holmes. Ashling, this is Cassandra Shipton, the kind woman who's offered to help you with your problem."

Ashling smiled wanly. Her eyes were an unusual shade of gray, thickly fringed in blonde lashes. "How good of you, Mrs. Shipton. I do hope I won't be too much of a bother."

One couldn't help but warm to this delicate creature, bare blue toes and all. I smiled. "Call me Cass, dear. Actually it's Ms. Shipton, although I am a Mrs. My husband's name is Joe Ulysses."

"Sit down, Ashling," Serena said with brusque cheeriness. She poured a third cup of tea and set it before the girl. Ashling passed the scones around before perching on an uncomfortable-looking oak side chair. The scones were freshly made and meltingly good. I realized that I was quite hungry, and it was getting on toward dinnertime. Time for a quick decision. I consulted my intuition, and the vibes seemed to be affirmative.

"Delectable scones, Ashling. I can't promise anything for sure, but I'll try my best." The girl still looked unsure. I assumed my trustworthy-aunt demeanor. "And I have knowledgeable friends to help me. So if you wish, when you've finished your tea, gather your things together and we'll be off to my house for a few days. I have a lovely empty guestroom under the eaves where you can stay. I also have two rambunctious dogs. They're boarded out tonight, but they'll be home tomorrow. I understand you've a skilled hand with animals."

She smiled a faraway smile and gazed through one of the long dark windows. "I trust animals, and they trust me, Ms. Shipton. Such lovely innocent souls." Then she turned those strange fringed eyes toward me. "You're very kind to take on me and my troubles."

Soon after, Ashling wafted away on her slim bare feet to pack her satchel, which, not surprisingly, would turn out to be a tapestry carpet bag, very romantic.

"Does she ever wear shoes?" I asked Serena. "It's mighty cold out there. *We've had our afternoons of golden leaves. Now for the black and wild October Eves*."

"I have instructed Ashling that she absolutely must wear shoes when she goes outdoors. Especially at this time of year, she'd catch her death. Do you know whose poem you're quoting there, Cass?"

"Quoting? Oh, don't tell me." I didn't even know from where the words had come.

"Yes, yes, dear Cass, that's early Archie Holmes. Your mind works in wondrous ways, my friend. Levels beyond levels."

CHAPTER TWELVE

From ghoulies and ghosties
And long-legged beasties
And things that go bump in the night,
Good Lord, deliver us.

– Scottish Saying

I was glad to see that Ashling had indeed slid her narrow feet into shoes, even those insubstantial ballet slippers. The girl said little on our drive home along 3A, just stared out the window at the passing houses and autumn-gilded trees and glimpses of blue-gray ocean. Once she asked me if I thought ghosts could follow people. I replied that ghosts were usually associated with a particular locale, but sometimes—rarely—they did haunt a person rather than a place. Time and distance, I explained from my own instinctive knowing, meant nothing to the unquiet dead. Then I thought I shouldn't have said that, so I added a few soothing words about how we could and should help those who have passed away to release the cares and concerns of this life. I felt no need to drag Satan into it. Exorcism is a perfectly simple and natural way, I said, of reassuring the dearly departed that it was time to move on.

It seemed oddly quiet without Scruffy and Raffles to greet me, and something about the girl's aura made the silence more intense. I found myself chattering nervously while settling Ashling into one of my guestrooms, the one I thought of as the "girls' room" with rose-patterned wall paper and ruffled white Cape Cod curtains. As she gazed out at the cold gray Atlantic, her tender profile was very like my mental image of Elaine the Lily Maid.

When I suggested she take a brief rest while I made dinner, she turned and smiled. "Thank you. It's lovely and peaceful here. What a wonderful home you have, Ms. Shipton. It smells of all my favorite spices and others that I don't recognize at all."

"Cass," I reminded her again.

Soup, I thought. *What this girl needs is a good dish of chicken soup.* Obviously, my motherly instincts were kicking in.

~

If there's one thing no *herb wyfe's* larder should be without, it's chicken soup stock, preferably homemade, stored in the freezer for just such emergencies. Soon I had the anti-anxiety, good-for-what-ails-you, oodles-of-noodles, aromatic golden potion ready to bolster up my guest—with a robust salad and French bread on the side. She ate daintily with no discernible appetite. I don't think I've ever seen anyone take smaller bites, except maybe my ethereal daughter Cathy.

With no dogs to pester us, it was a quiet supper. I confess to watching Ashling covertly as she helped clear the table, so I could swear that her feet (now bare again) never left the floor. And nothing untoward disturbed the kitchen—no flying plates or restless salad tongs. *So far, so good.*

A little stack of wood was ready near the fireplace. I made a small blaze, just enough to cozy us while we had coffee and molasses cookies. At first Ashling had glanced around fearfully as if half-expecting her demon husband to assault us at any moment, but when no spectral effects shattered our serenity, she relaxed and, at my prompting, spoke a little about the late, great poet.

"I'd just turned nineteen when we met. A junior at U. Mass on a scholarship and a shoestring. Archie was so far above me, such a literary genius, I could hardly believe he'd even notice me, let alone want me for his girl, his wife. He was forty-seven, in his prime. Personally I thought he was incredibly handsome, even though his friends razzed him about his waistline and his receding hair. I saw from his book-jacket photos that he'd once had a mass of dark curls. But to me, his new higher forehead suited his profoundly intellectual nature even better. And he was so virile, so masterful, although sometimes I'm afraid I failed him as a lover, and he would be angry with me for weakening him. Then there was the drinking, of course. He explained to me that all poets are followers of Dionysus, it just goes with the Olympian territory. Perhaps all that wine did aid him to court the Muse, but after a drinking bout with his friends, he could become quite irritable. And Archie had so many fascinating friends, life with him was like hosting a perpetual literary salon. Sometimes I did wish, though, that they'd do their philosophizing and critiquing and drinking and eating and throwing up and passing out somewhere other than our place. We had a lovely apartment, high up, overlooking the Charles River, old-fashioned tall windows, beautiful moldings, but it wasn't really big enough to..."

"...to function as a poetry hotel," I finished the sentence for Ashling when she faltered. She'd drawn quite a portrait of

Achibald Fennimore Holmes. I only wished she herself could see it. *What an ass he must have been*, I thought to myself. But I could remember being besotted with my own big blond ex-husband Gary Hauser even after he began to drink too much and make our lives generally miserable. It takes time for a gal to take a good cold look at her Mr. Used-to-Be-Right.

A log blazed up in the fireplace the way they sometimes do, then rolled off onto the hearth. We had an exciting few minutes shoveling up the sparks and coals. Meanwhile, I found myself with many still unanswered questions, so I decided to push things a bit.

"If it's not too painful, tell me about that last night, the night of Archie's accident." I patted Ashling's hand, and I could feel the tension traveling through her body. Or was it guilt? But then, I thought, perhaps I was predisposed to thoughts of guilt or innocence because of my present involvement with the home invasion murders in Wareham.

It was as if a veil came down over her eyes, those soulful gray eyes. "It was all so awful, so awful. One of those terrible literary evenings when everyone gets wasted and rails loudly against the bourgeoisie because one of them got a disappointing review by a critic who was known for her vile, lowbrow taste and lack of poetic sensibility. The *London Review of Books* it was. Pauline Hatchett had slashed to pieces Archie's last book, *The Colossus of Me*; *New and Selected Poems*. The shouting and profanity just went on and on..."

"And you were...where?"

"In bed. I was so exhausted, and I had a backache. From the baby, you know."

"*Baby?* You were pregnant?"

"Yes, five months, but I lost it. A boy it was, too. I had thought Archie would be so pleased."

"But he wasn't pleased?"

Ashling didn't answer, just went on relating the events of that fatal evening in a monotone. I felt sure she'd told the same story in the same words many times.

"Finally, they straggled out onto the street about four-thirty. Archie was at the top of the stairs, reciting another limerick about Polly Hatchett. I came to the door to remind him that the neighbors had been complaining about his late-night recitations in the hallway. He turned, his back to the railing. I walked toward him. His hands...he brought his hands up into fists like a boxer. I'm sure, though, that he didn't mean to punch me in the abdomen. When he'd done that before, I'd explained to him that he was hurting his own child. I just think those quick motions he made right then, a sort of *one-two*, and the little dance with his feet threw him off-balance. He lurched backwards and toppled over, down the stairwell." Ashling shuddered. "I'll never stop hearing that terrible scream."

"Whatever happened, you mustn't think it was your fault." I admit my instant reassurance was biased. There had been times during my first marriage when I'd been used as a punching bag myself. "I mean, if you stepped aside to avoid Archie's fists or even pushed him away from you, and he happened to lose his balance...well. The instinct to protect one's unborn baby is basic and powerful—one doesn't think it out, one simply reacts." At least, I hoped this fragile young woman hadn't actually given her drunken poet an intentional push. Not that he didn't deserve it, but it wouldn't do for Ashling to go through life carrying a backpack of guilt.

Guilt or innocence—sometimes it's a very fine line between them. Especially if a Libran is drawing it. It wouldn't surprise me if Librans turned out to be the cause of more hung juries than any other sun sign.

My thoughts zoomed back to those two degenerate thieves whose fate would be in the hands of us twelve jurors. Which reminded me, in turn, that there could be other motives besides self-defense that might induce a wife to seize her chance.

"Did he...are you... was there life insurance or something like that?" I poked at the fire, just to keep it glowing until we went upstairs.

"Archie didn't believe in insurance. None of that betting against one's self for *him*, he used to say. We'd been living on a generous allowance from his trust, but those funds reverted to the rest of the Holmes family upon his death. If there had been a child, of course..." Ashling's voice trailed off in a sad smile, gazing into the sputtering fire. After a moment, she collected herself and continued. "Our son was stillborn the week after Archie's accident. His library might have been... there were a number of first editions...but he left all those to Harvard, along with his letters and manuscripts. They'd promised him a little bronze plaque, you know."

"What about fine furnishings and art works? No *Antiques Roadshow* thrills in your apartment? I'm guessing the Holmes family may have gifted Archie with a Hitchcock chair or two, perhaps a Chippendale desk. And the Fennimores, didn't they collect Impressionists? You didn't happen to inherit a little Renoir, did you?"

Ashling laughed, the first time since I'd met her. "Archie didn't care for the Impressionists that his mother adored. He preferred primitive masks and so forth. I've already sold those to a dealer. I think he may have got a bargain, but I did need a few dollars to keep going. As for the furniture, originally it included a number of quality heirlooms but I'm afraid those items were battered far beyond *distressed* after the constant partying. Even Good Will hesitated to take some of the pieces I donated. Then there are royalties, of course—but serious poetry never seems to make much money, does it?"

"What about Archie's parents—are they living? Won't they see to it that you have a decent allowance, if only to honor his memory?"

"His father—Harrison Winslow Holmes, Bank of Boston, perhaps you've heard of him?—passed away a year earlier, and Archie's mother, Fanny Fennimore—well, I shouldn't complain, but....Somehow she blamed me for Archie's drinking, for his death, for the miscarriage. No way was she going to provide for someone who'd destroyed her son's life. Her attorneys pushed me to sign papers—I hardly knew what they were. Oh, one was the literary thing. Fanny insisted on being Archie's literary executor. I guess I'll have to get a job as soon as I figure out if I'm good for anything." Ashling looked down at her hands, turning the thin gold band around and around her slim finger.

"Of course you'll be *very good* at something. I'm sure of it. As soon as this trial is over, I may be able to help you find..."

I never did finish that thought. An eerie coldness swept through the room, and it seemed as if several light bulbs blew at once. There was a fearful crash in the kitchen, which I found out later was my 10-inch cast-iron frying pan hurling itself off its hook by the stove. Ashling screamed, and the glowing embers in the fireplace seemed to jump up and down.

"Ceres save us!" I threw my arms outward, little fingers pointing toward the inexplicable cold draft. "Cease and desist! *Out! Out of here*, I say!"

Luckily, I keep my rowan wand on the mantel. (In truth, I rarely use it except on formal occasions—rowan is the "witchwood" of divination but it also protects against spells and elementals.) I whipped the wand out of its blue velvet sheath and held it out in front of us like a sword. The quartz at the tip seemed to glow with intense light.

"Listen up, Archibald Fennimore Holmes, you're *dead, Dude,* and it's high time you were *gone* as well."

One of my stone Inuit carvings bounced off the mantel, narrowly missing my head. I whirled around toward the fireplace, fencing with the wand, and shouted, "I have *good news* for you, Holmes. Now that you're *deceased*, you have become your poems, you have become your admirers." (Was that Auden I was quoting?) "And now for the *bad news*. We're not going to put up with your spectral shenanigans any longer."

Another Inuit carving came flying my way. Maybe my wand needed recharging. I might have to bring in reinforcements to banish this rowdy fellow. "Ashling, hand me that fireplace broom," I said to the pale, shuddering girl. That broom was my besom, well soaked in cinnamon oil to drive away negative spirits. Ashling, who had been cowering in the corner beneath the parson's cupboard, put forth a trembling hand and unhooked the small broom from the fireplace, pushing it my way without leaving her sanctuary.

Brooms—besoms—are richly magical, made for sweeping away the evils of this world. Remembering a conversation I'd had with Fiona about the laying of unfriendly ghosts, I dropped the broom on the floor between my feet and did an impromptu jig over it. Fiona had said that stepping over a broom would prevent a noisy spirit from causing a disturbance. Of course, Archie had already caused the disturbance, but maybe he could be persuaded to vanish into the thin air from which his destructive energy had materialized. I improvised a few more steps. Then I caught sight of Ashling staring at me in bewilderment. Not everyone understands the magic of spontaneous dance.

"It's a way of communicating with the departed," I explained breathlessly. "If you wanted to actually have a talk with Archie, we'd lay the broom in the doorway." I gestured toward the front door which opened directly into the living room—a wide-board pine door, the outside painted cranberry. It was rarely used; in New England, the front door was traditionally relegated to visiting clergy or departing dead bodies.

"Oh no, no, *no*," Ashing screamed, putting one of my herbal pillows over her head. *Sage and several kinds of mint. Good choice for promoting calm and good cheer.* But it didn't seem to be working as well as it might. The girl was trembling like a mouse in cat country. Perhaps the thought of actually *talking* with the husband whom she may have helped with a slight shove into Summerland was just too intimidating.

"Okay, okay. I'll just give him a quick sweep out of here, then." The old front door creaked and groaned at being awoken from its slumber for anyone less than a visiting prince or pastor. It opened inward, revealing the nicks and notches of earlier, rougher times, scars not quite masked by coats of paint. I picked up my broom in a cloud of cinnamon scent and vigorously swept the air, the windows, the floor and ourselves, always moving the vibrations in the room out the door. The October night was moonless with a skittish wind that pulled away to the west whatever ghostly vibrations I was pushing out the door. Quickly I slammed it shut and threw the wrought-iron bolt.

There! It was blessedly quiet at last.

I replaced my two Inuit pieces on the mantel. "I think that did it, Ashling. We've probably heard the last of Archie—for tonight anyway." At least I hoped so. *Sometimes the magic works...*

Then I purified the rooms and us with sprinkles of salt water (I get mine right from the nearby Atlantic) explaining what I was doing and why to my wide-eyed guest.

"Oh, like holy water. That's what my mother would use," Ashling said.

"Yeah, like that," I agreed.

Regretting our after-dinner coffee and its shot of caffeine, I made a pot of kava tea to calm our nerves before we ventured off to bed. "I've never been visited by a poltergeist before," I confided in Ashling as I dispersed the wood embers so that the fire would be settled for the night. *Perhaps I should consult Deidre*, I thought. The youngest member of our circle, always so prolific with magical arts and crafts, had acquired her ability to see the dead only recently. But those few specters who had appeared to her had all been victims of murder. My only spectral visitor was occasional and invisible, the welcome spirit of my grandma, always soothing and loving. This was, after all, her home of many years, and I was the granddaughter to whom she had entrusted her herbal legacy, so it was not surprising that she lingered here with me.

Sipping her tea, Ashling continued to hug the sage and mint pillow to her abdomen. I imagined how she must have looked when she was swollen with child. The terrible disappointment and heartache she must have felt—and the anger! Allowing myself to feel her emotions empathically, I had something like a psychic inspiration. I felt sure that it was her own anger drawing the noisy ghost. The poltergeist wasn't exactly Archie, per se, but some elemental being, like the whizzing and whispering "strangelets" we'd encountered on the beach in Bermuda. Fiona had called them spawns of darkness, guardians of the veil between worlds.

"Ashling, I believe these manifestations might come to an end," I said, "if you could find it in yourself to let go of your anger and forgive Archie."

She looked at me unbelievingly. "But I'm *not* angry with Archie. I *loved* him."

"It's possible to feel both love and anger for the same person. Would you be willing to undergo a forgiveness ritual—it might help you be rid of this scary stuff that's been happening around you."

She looked at me with those mythic gray eyes for a long moment, then nodded, barely.

The truth was, I hadn't a clue how to organize a forgiveness ritual, but I'd bet my besom that Fiona did!

As we turned in for the night, me to my first floor bedroom and Ashling to the guest room upstairs, I glanced back to make sure she was steady on the stairs and not fainting. And she was steady, sort of. In fact, her bare feet seemed to be skimming the stairs, hardly touching the wood. I blinked my eyes to clear them. Did I see what I thought I saw?

With Ashling and her troublesome ghost foisted off onto me, no doubt the staff of St. Rita's would be getting their first good night's sleep since the levitating girl had descended upon them.

That Serena was going to owe me for this *big time.*

CHAPTER THIRTEEN

The jury, passing on the prisoner's life,
May in the sworn twelve have a thief or two
Guiltier than him they try.

– William Shakespeare

It was barely six-thirty when I called Deidre the next morning.

Surely the mother of four young children had to be up and about very early, I reasoned.

"Holy Mother, Cass. Do you know what time it is?"

"Don't you have to get the kids off to school or something like that?"

"Oh, I'm *up,* all right, but I'm right in the middle... Never mind. It must be important, so lay it on me."

"Serena Love talked me into giving shelter to a young woman who's being haunted by her dead husband, a well-known Boston Brahmin poet. We had a hell of a night. He raised the Old Nick with my stuff. I threw everything I had at him. Finally, he thumped off, or whatever it is ghosts do. Only I still have jury duty today, and I have to get going. The dogs are at Heather's, so no problem, but I'm loathe to leave this gal alone in case the ghost returns. So I thought...I wondered if you...where you have some expertise in that field."

"But I don't even *like* poetry," Deidre wailed. "Don't ever tell Phil, though. She'll think I'm a hopeless mundane."

"I didn't say that the ghost *recited* poetry. I merely said he *was* a poet before he transcended to that great poetry venue in the sky."

"Oh, good. When you said it was a night of hell, I thought that he must be one of those poets spouting *spindrift and spume* poems."

"No, I believe he wrote conversational stuff about his failed loves and dysfunctional family. When he was alive, that is. Now he's just doing what ghosts do...you know. Chilling the flesh. Crashing about. Casting heavy objects hither and yon. Delivering the odd spectral pinch. That sort of thing."

"And you need me for what? A specter-sitter?"

"You've got it. Please, Dee! Poor Ashling is beside herself. Which reminds me. Guess I ought to mention that, according to Serene Love, Ashling sometimes levitates. Like St. Teresa."

"Ashling? That wouldn't be Ashling Malone, by any chance?"

"That was her maiden name. She's Ashling Holmes now. You know her?"

"The Malones are, like, distant cousins of Will's. And a name like Ashling—you remember it."

"How many cousins do you guys have?" Deidre's husband, a fire fighter, had died of heart failure while trying to rescue another one of his cousins, Sister Mary Vincent, from a burning convent. It seemed as if every Irish name anyone mentioned in Plymouth would always ring the relationship bell with Deidre.

"Our cousins are legion, my dear. Big families. For which we give thanks to the Lord and to the rhythm method of birth control, Catholic roulette. My own brood is small by comparison to most of the Ryans and their kin. I suppose, then..."

"*Oh, great*! You're a doll, Dee. I'll be leaving here at a quarter of eight. Could you possibly be here by then?"

"Ashling...imagine that. Did I hear you say she *levitates?* Like with a broom or something? I always thought that was an invention of the inquisitors and fantasy authors. Betti will be here this morning to care for Annie, and she stays until I get home from work, looks out for the other three after school. I *was* going to get a jump on decorating the shop for Samhain, but I can let my assistant Hal make a start. I've already outlined a plan. *The Last Harvest and the Faeries' Feast*."

"Sounds gorgeous, Dee. So, is that a yes?"

"Sure. And what is it you want me to do, exactly?"

"Keep Ashling safe."

"I'll bring amulets, then."

"Amulets? Like your Venus of Willendorf?"

"Not this time. Willendorf is too beneficent for special ops. I've worked up some powerful little carved black teak pendants to protect against dark forces of the elemental kind. Since our Bermuda cruise. Well, you know."

"Never go walking out without your amulet?"

"Right. And you can bet that Santa is going to bring one of these black teak babies for each of you."

"That'll be a first for the jolly old guy."

"Before St. Nicholas was a saint he was a Pagan god, dearie. *Gotta go*."

~

Deidre's new Aurora Blue Mazda3 pulled into my driveway at precisely 7:44. A time manager *extraordinaire,* Deidre was the exact opposite of Fiona, who was perennially late and not the least bit upset by it.

My own relationship with time was always a tad optimistic, never taking into account the unforeseen traffic event and/or a run of red lights. Dependent as I was on split-second timing, I didn't allow the moss to grow under my wheels as I raced to Brockton.

I could have saved my tires the trouble. With no explanation from the redoubtable Della Fortunato, my fellow jurors and I were left to hang out in the jury room long past the time we usually filed into the courtroom. The more we pressed Fortunato, the more firmly she crossed her wrestler's arms and zipped her lips. "The judge is conferring with the attorneys in chambers," was all we could worm out of her.

Once the free doughnuts and coffee had been ravaged, most of us behaved as restlessly as caged chimps. Even placid Mildred Woolrich picked up the pace of her knitting to Sorcerer's Apprentice speed. Ellen Heany, who usually gave off kindly, healing vibes, was compulsively clicking her pen, clucking her tongue, and tapping her foot. A neurotic rhythm section all by herself.

I read my Cadfael paperback and kept an eye on everyone else. There was an unease crawling up the flesh of my arms, I didn't know why. These sensitivities happened to me often, even when I wasn't having a genuine clairvoyant spell. The trouble was, they didn't explain themselves. What I needed was a decoder ring for the whim-whams.

Kurt Heller opened the window. He stuck his head out, hunched his shoulders in a peculiar way, and drew a few puffs from his Marlboro before Fortunato got wind of it. She stormed into the jury room and banged the window shut again as if she wished his head were still in it.

Hugh Collins, usually a model of classic carriage, was slumped in his foreman's chair, looking exquisitely bored, his closed eyes shutting out the hopeful gaze of Brooke Morgan, elegantly suburban in full Talbot's regalia. I found his blasé pose annoying, along with the man himself, I couldn't have said why. Even more so than the sight of April Rayne nervously chipping bright blue polish off her nails.

Wanda Finch and Anna Grimassi were huddled in the corner, exchanging ribald jokes, I guessed, from the timbre of their low laughter, while Ralph Dunbar, his round face shining like a cannonball beneath the overhead light, concentrated on a *Times* crossword puzzle, which he was rapidly filling in with a pen. *Show off!* He seemed more at ease than any of us. Byron Moody scowled furiously into his small leather notebook and jotted down a few words.

He caught me glancing his way and leaned forward confidentially. "This trial, it's been an inspiration. The talons of the law sinking deeply into those boys, with not a scintilla of thought given to the hellish cesspit from which they may have emerged."

That sounded like a mixed metaphor to me, but what did I know? "I believe we're only supposed to consider present crimes not prior traumas," I said.

"If you ask me, we're not supposed to use our sensibilities at all. Everything is simply black and white to *them.*" Before I could inquire as to the elusive identity of "them," the poet continued eagerly. "Do you think your friend Phil Stone—you mentioned her at lunch last week—might be interested in joining us at our poetry venue, the World's End Cafe & Bookstore, for our monthly session? As our featured reader, of course, although we also have an open mike session for walk-ins. A couple of performance poets, a few slams, and some very powerful free verse. Blows your mind, man. Excellent bagels and muffins, by the way. I encourage people to buy something. Man, those bookstore people are nice enough to let us perform and everything."

"Gosh, sounds great. I'll mention it to her, Byron. She's a pretty busy gal, though." Deidre's phrase "a night in hell" surfaced in my mind. Still, you never knew. Phillipa might revel in this kind of thing. With my luck, she'd probably drag me along. But I felt quite cheered to think about something besides the invisible crawlies I was experiencing, so I smiled at Byron warmly.

"Do you happen to be familiar with the poetry of the late Archibald Fennimore Holmes?" I asked.

"Alas, poor Archie, I knew him well," Byron said without a scintilla of irony. "What a tragedy, what a loss to literary Boston. Who knows what masterpieces he would have produced had he lived?"

"How true!" I intoned respectfully. "Did you ever happen to—ah—attend any of his legendary soirees?"

"What great times we had!" Byron reminisced with glistening eyes. "A generous host, a beautiful sensibility."

"And were you there the night he...of the accident?"

"Sadly, no. I'll always wonder if there was anything I could have done. I feel something was not quite kosher about that terrible calamity, if you know what I mean." Byron paused to scribble something in his leather notebook, dashed a tear out of his eye, and continued. "I daresay his little wife came into quite an inheritance. Boston elite, you know."

"Really! Well, I will speak to Phil about that Café thing," I said. Evidently Byron Moody knew little of his squandering hero's true worth.

He brightened. "And you come, too, if you like, Cass. Love to have a genuine non-writer in the audience. You'll probably enjoy experiencing this piece I'm composing on the trial. It's really intense, man."

Before I could frame a suitable demur, Fortunato loomed in the doorway and gazed around the room solemnly.

"They've all gone to lunch, so you jurors may as well do the same. Be back here at..." she consulted her wristwatch ... "one forty-five *sharp*.

"Hey, Fortunato, we're entitled to an hour and a half," Kurt complained loudly. "We don't have to be back here until two."

Fortunato scowled blackly at the nicotine-deprived juror. "Yes, you do, Heller, because I say so. The judge expressly ordered that you lot be in the jury room and ready to take your places *before* two. So don't even think about giving me a hard time."

"Let's all go to Fred's Fast Fresh Fish on the dock," Anna suggested. "They'll serve us right away, and we'll have a chance ..." She glanced at Fortunato's retreating figure and lowered her voice. "...to compare notes about what's going on here."

"I don't think we're allowed to," Mildred quavered uncertainly.

"Put a sock in it, Mil," Wanda said. "Good old Fred's. The *4F* we call it. Every damn thing on the menu is fried. Sounds like a wicked good plan to me."

~

Soon we were crowded around a red-and-white-checked table with bottles of beer and plastic baskets of fish 'n chips or fried clams, as chummy as we'd ever been. Buxom, red-haired Wanda Finch leaned forward and continued to hold forth, but her booming voice was somewhat quieter than usual. She'd recognized the reporter and photographer team from the *Patriot Ledger* who were sitting at a small table by the wall; the reporter was talking on her cell phone. The shocking crimes against the Reynards had not only attracted the attention of local news but also national media. For all we knew, any one of the other patrons might be a reporter. "Here's what I think, gang," Wanda said. "Those attorneys are working out some kind of deal, and naturally we're going to be the last to know."

"Wanda and I believe there's a plea bargain in the works." Anna Grimassi smirked knowingly.

"You mean, we're all going to get out of here, maybe even today?" Byron Moody was hopeful. "With the thanks of a grateful Plymouth County," Byron continued his fantasy. I wondered how this turn of events would affect his poetic inspiration of the talons and the cesspit.

"You're full of crap, Wanda," Kurt Heller scoffed. "What kind of agreement could those guilty scumbags hope to get?" He lit a Marlboro, ignoring horrified looks from his companions and nearby patrons. The waitress hurried over, but before she could reach us, he'd stamped it out under the table. The air around us, however, reeked of tobacco. Brooke Morgan waved it away with her hand, making a little moue of disgust.

"If I were Steemer, I'd never agree to a plea. I'd trust the jury would bring in the only possible verdict," Mildred Woolrich said mildly. She gazed at the last full-stomach clam in her basket and speared it with her fork. "*Guilty*! Any reasonable jury would convict those two sleazebags of premeditated murder in the first degree."

"The defendants have been holding out against that murder charge," Ralph Dunbar reminded us. "It's possible they're now going to admit their guilt in the deaths of those two women in return for a reduced sentence."

I found that somehow startling and wrong. The uneasiness I'd felt earlier was returning and settling on my stomach. Or maybe it was the fried clams.

Ernie Byrd, who'd taken care to seat himself where he could lean across April Rayne while reaching for salt or ketchup, suddenly seemed to tune in to our conversation for once. "Those two Reynard women—no one really knows how those boys got themselves in the house. They might have been *invited*."

"*Invited? I don't fucking think so!*" Anna slammed her beer bottle on the table dangerously. "If it were up to me, I'd throw those two lowlifes into a cell for the rest of their lives whether they confess or not."

The *Patriot* reporter looked up. She whispered something to her companion with the camera.

Byron's body language bristled with disagreement at Anna's outburst, but he folded into himself and pressed his lips together.

"Keep it down, Anna," Wanda warned. "*The walls have big ears here*. It will be a good thing if the trial does end today, so I won't have to deck that prick Ernie."

"I'm surprised at how mean-minded some of you people are," Ellen Heany said. "If we voted right this minute, I personally couldn't find it in my heart to say it was *murder*. I mean, the woman had a heart murmur."

"Don't tell me *you* fell for Laratta's smoke and mirrors," Mildred looked at her new friend with an amused smile. "Why, he's no better than a snake oil salesman. It's a good thing you're a nurse, Ellen, and not the loan officer in a bank."

"A trauma nurse learns a great deal more about human nature than a buttoned-down banker ever does," Ellen replied hotly. "Those poor misfits never killed anyone!"

"Damn it, listen up all of you." Hugh narrowed his eyes and hit the table with his fist. His bottle of beer toppled over, but he caught it almost instantly. *Excellent reflexes!* "This is specifically the kind of loose talk I'm not allowing you to have. So you'd better knock it off."

"Hugh's in charge, you know," Brooke added, mopping up the spill with her napkin. "And I, for one, am going to conduct myself according to the rules the judge outlined for us."

"Oh, *bollocks* who's in charge," Wanda stage-whispered. "I'll say whatever I want to say. And I agree with Anna one-hundred percent. Those lousy bastards ought not to be allowed to plea bargain their way out of life without parole. I only wish Massachusetts still had the death penalty."

"Hey, Finch, why don't you shut it and give us all a rest." Kurt bristled with disgust. He was not a big man, but from his brush hair cut to his gnarled fists, he exuded hostility. "We elected Collins boss, and whatever he says fucking goes."

"What is this, a clip from *Twelve Angry Men?*" Ralph asked. "Cool it, Wanda. You, too, Kurt. And Anna. Let's try to get through this jury business with a modicum of dignity." He spoke firmly as if to an unruly class, but his ready smile took the sting out of his authoritative tone. *I like his style—too bad he's not the foreman instead of Pretty Boy Floyd there*, I thought.

"You wouldn't want to be responsible for a mistrial, now would you, ladies?" Ellen asked. "I think we are all aware there's a nosy reporter over by the wall. If it got back to the judge that you've been spouting *guilty verdicts* before we've heard all the evidence..."

"This conversation is over," Hugh said in a tone that was not loud but thoroughly chilling nonetheless. "Check please," he called out to our waitress.

~

Thanks to our irate foreman, we did get back to the court before two. It took a little time to elbow our way through the media crews hanging around the courthouse steps, but it wasn't until two-thirty that the judge summoned us to the jury box.

The courtroom, which had been filled with Reynard relatives and onlookers throughout the trial, was even more packed this afternoon. Every reporter who'd ever looked in at these proceedings seemed to be crushed into the press box, hanging on whatever the judge would say next. Only one pool photographer was allowed to take still pictures *sans* lights in the courtroom, so the rest of the cameramen were massed outside.

It was as we jurors had suspected—for us, the trial was over. An agreement had been reached between the attorney for the defense and the prosecutor. Judge Lax dismissed us with a very graceful speech about the importance of jury duty and his personal appreciation for our service. We filed out, back to the jury room. I felt deflated somehow, and apparently so did the other jurors. It was like leaving the theater after a film noir matinee—back to the too-bright real world.

"Hey, Fortunato, what's the story here?" Kurt demanded. "Did Farrow and Lovitt admit to the murders? How long they going to get? It can't be long enough to suit me."

Fortunato was impassive. "If you want to know what happened, I suggest you watch the six o'clock news, Heller." And she would say no more.

Out in the parking lot, a biting wind and wild rain were slanting in from the northeast. Sea gulls were screaming their way inland, never a good sign. Everyone was in a hurry to dodge the press and get into their cars. Good-byes were perfunctory, but there was one incident that chilled me even more than the piercing wind. I brushed by Therese de Rochmont, Marie's mother, as she was being helped from the courthouse by Rosalie Boyd Indelicato, Marie's sister-in-law from an earlier marriage.

Grasping my hand with a strong claw grip, Therese de Rochmont looked me savagely and said, "You know, don't you. I've been watching you, and you know this is all wrong. So what are you prepared to do about it, eh?"

"So sorry. You must forgive Mama. She's upset," Rosalie explained as she urged the old lady toward a shiny black Lincoln.

The reporter from Fred's spotted us and sprinted our way, trailed by her photographer, crying "*Mrs. de Rochmont, Mrs. de Rochmont, how do you feel about today's developments? Do you think Lovitt and Farrow got what they deserve.*" A burly driver opened the back door of the Lincoln and whisked the two women inside.

Therese de Rochmont's white face peered out at me as they drove way at the stately speed of the Queen Mum's limousine. The photographer snapped a few pictures, then the pair ran around to the front of the building to assault the emerging attorneys with more pushy questions.

The ghostly image of the woman's face, the feeling of her fingernails digging into me, the note of urgency in her quavering voice, stayed with me all the way to Heather's. But the cold aura of that strange incident was dispelled when Scruffy and Raffles jumped joyfully into the RAV4. There is no one like a dog for clearing the air of gloomy thoughts, and two dogs are even better.

Heather invited me to stay, of course—*have a drink, do a little magic* (whether that meant hexing dog-fighting thugs or cooking another dinner for the Devlin crew, I didn't linger to find out.)

"I got to do this exorcism thing with Fiona tonight," I said. "How about tomorrow, instead. Probably a better day for finding that dog-fighting ring anyway. Mercury rules tomorrow."

"Yeah—wacky Wednesday. Communication, divination, skill and cunning. Perfect. Come for lunch," Heather said, then paused, possibly remembering that she no longer had a cook. "We'll do Japanese take-out," she exclaimed brightly. "I have some bottles of excellent sake."

I would have to find some place safe to leave Ashling, I thought. I did want Heather to meet Ashling, but at a more fortuitous time. Not while Heather was lighting her weird homemade candles and I was consulting my psyche about the evil business of dog fighting. Hard to believe it was happening in our own peaceful Plymouth. Perhaps I could drop the girl off with Fiona, if the two of them hit it off together all right tonight. What a good idea! No spectral husband would dare harm the girl at Fiona's enchanted cottage.

"It's a date," I said. It felt good to be a free woman again, no longer a martyr to civic duty. "I'll bring my chopsticks."

CHAPTER FOURTEEN

Spirit whose work is done! spirit of dreadful hours!

– Walt Whitman

Serena wasn't exaggerating about Ashling's effect on animals. My two rambunctious characters burst into the house full of *we're-home-again* energy, then stopped short, instantly taking in the intriguing scent of a delightful stranger. They pushed right past Deidre with hardly a rec—she was curled up on the sofa embroidering a pillow cover—and ran straight toward Ashling's frail form standing hesitantly in front of the bow window. As they bolted across the room, Ashling folded herself into a dog-high crouch and allowed the two dogs to adjust to her presence, offering her hair and hands to their eager noses.

The girl! The girl! Raffles bounced around her gleefully, ecstatic with her newness.

Hey, Toots—did she follow you home? Can we keep her? She smells good, like cookies. Got pretty decent vibes for a non-canine. Knows just the way to scratch my ears. It was clear that Scruffy, as well as his offspring, was easily smitten with my visitor. Even after she rose to her feet (which I noted were shoeless) and perched on the window seat, they jostled each other to sit next to her and took up guard on either side like bookends.

"And what are your names, big guys?" She drew up her bare blue toes under her long skirt and went on to have a kind of soothing whispered conversation with her eager worshippers, an arm around each dog.

While this love-fest was going on, I had a chance to share the trial's end with Deidre. "We must try to catch the story on the six o'clock news," I said. "I don't even know what was agreed upon today, can you imagine? But what about your day? Any manifestations?" I noticed that she was wearing the teakwood amulet on a thin leather thong around her neck. She saw me noticing.

"Ashling's got one on, too," Deidre said. "Should keep the spectral high-jinx down to a dull roar."

"But did you *see* anyone, Dee?" I pressed the question.

Deidre kept her eyes on the embroidery. "Maybe, maybe not. A transparent *thingie* I wouldn't even call a man—more like a gremlin. Ugh. I whacked him away with your broom—very effective that broom. What have you got on it?"

"Cinnamon oil. Your gremlin may be a manifestation of unconscious anger, not a true ghost." I didn't say *Ashling's anger*, but I saw that Deidre got the gist. "If I'm right, we should be able to exorcise the poltergeist with a simple forgiveness ritual."

Her new friends had not distracted Ashling from taking in my meaning. "There's nothing to forgive, Cass—Archie was the love of my life. How could I ever be angry with him? Those few little incidents I mentioned—well, every couple has their minor disagreements."

I raised my eyebrows at Deidre without comment. I'd already told her what Ashling had let slip, Archie's penchant for punching his pregnant wife.

"Dear Cousin Ashling, you must know that I truly understand how you feel," Deidre said softly. "After all, I'm a widow, too. I realize that it may seem like a betrayal to remember the truth of those 'few little incidents.' The more you feel that Archie's death has released you, that a burden has slipped from your shoulders, the more guilt you'll feel. And guilt makes grief sharper and more hurtful. Believe me—I'm aware of these things."

"I would never call my life with Archie a burden, never! Archie was a genius, you know," Ashling insisted. "You have to make allowances for genius. He was tortured by his immense talent. And he tried to tolerate my strangeness, he really did. I'm such a misfit. Naturally he was upset no end when I...when I...you know...floated a little."

"Well, a woman can't be tied down all the time," I said defensively. The poor girl had needed acceptance not criticism. I mean, how hard could it have been to tolerate a few paranormal incidents? Thank the Goddess that Joe took such things in stride, as a real man should.

"And you were the *most* sympathetic wife, Ashling. *A woman of valour, who can find her? For her price is far above rubies,"* Deidre soothed her cousin with Biblical proverbs, legacy of her Catholic childhood. "But now, I think we can all agree that Archie must rest in peace." She turned to me, out of Ashling's line of vision, and winked. "Then everyone else can be at peace, too. So, what's a forgiveness ritual, anyway, and how do you combine that with an exorcism?"

"Who knows? But I bet Fiona can come up with something terrific. Remember how she shooed away those black imps on Bermuda!"

"Yeah, she's probably carrying a pamphlet about it in her reticule." Deidre smiled in her old mischievous way, a good thing to see. She held up the pillow cover she was working on. A faery godmother looking remarkably like our plump friend Fiona was scattering stardust from a green reticule. *Magic Is Afoot* read the lettering. "Everyone needs a Fiona in her life, just to set things right, don't you think?"

"Goddess bless her," I agree.

~

After Deidre had gone home, I turned on the news. Ashling was no more concerned than Scruffy and Raffles about the Reynard home invasion case, so she offered to take them for a walk outdoors. "Not far," I warned. "That wind is stronger here than inland, you know." I had an image of the rootless Ashling sailing off over the Atlantic like a pale balloon. "And please wear some sturdy shoes!"

The trial's end was the lead story locally and a feature of the national news. A plea bargain had been reached, the details of which had been only partially leaked to the press. The evening news anchor, Audrey Hodge, whose lined face and down-to-earth manner testified to her long experience in local affairs, reported that Farrow and Lovitt had agreed to plead guilty to second degree murder in exchange for life with the possibility of parole after 25 years. Hodge affirmed a rumor that Hank Sharpe, as part of the agreement, had requested that consideration be given to their serving those sentences in a medium security prison work farm in Chillblaine, Massachusetts. Stock footage of the new prison farm showed a bucolic setting with fields of waving corn and free range livestock. *Nice work if they can get it*, I thought. The judge had taken this request under advisement and would deliver his decision at sentencing. The mere twitch at the corner of Hodge's mouth suggested what she thought of this mollycoddling. I did like this woman.

No one among the Reynards had agreed to be interviewed except Francis, Albert Reynard's brother, who acted as the family's spokesperson. Standing at the end of his brother's driveway, the handsome French-style villa obscured by stone walls and massive plantings, he addressed the gaggle of TV reporters, expressing the family's satisfaction with the result of the trial and the "closure it would bring to this tragedy."

In a month of Sabbats. Not to Madame Therese de Rochmont, I said to myself. Mama de Rochmont wasn't going to be satisfied with mere "closure" as those two confessed murderer/rapists trooped off to feed pigs in Western Massachusetts.

My instincts were proved accurate a few days later when a lavish gift of de Rochmont wines was delivered by a uniformed driver to my kitchen door with a note written by an arthritic but still bold hand. *My Dear Miss Shipton. I'm told you have powers to divine the truth. I wish you to know that the whole horror of the deaths of my Marie and Therese has not yet been revealed. The guilty deserve punishment commensurate with the crimes. Please help me to find justice. Madame de Rochmont.* Poor thing. I wondered if she was in the throes of early dementia.

When I mentioned the gift to Heather, she insisted that I read her every label over the phone. There was a moment of awed silence. Then she said, "Wow. These are special occasion wines, Cass. Exquisite, I don't doubt."

"I'll save them for our next celebration then. Maybe when Joe gets home safe from his mission to the Antarctic."

"De Rochmont should thaw him out, all right. There's nothing like a noble red wine to build up the blood."

"Yeah," I agreed. "But I'm not exactly sure that's what Mama de Rochmont has in mind. The plea bargain seems to have tied up all the loose ends in the crime. The guilty will be punished—perhaps not as severely as she could wish. Madame may have preferred that the murderers be sentenced to the guillotine rather than 25 years of hoeing corn in Chillbaine."

~

Fiona "with bells on" was not a mere figure of speech. As she bustled through the door in her new Irish coat sweater and fulsome Macdonald plaid skirt, I could hear a faint tinkle coming from somewhere in the vicinity of her trainers, which were moss green and almost a match for the old green reticule she brought with her, her magic grab-bag.

Not surprisingly, Ashling took to Fiona's calm maternal manner immediately and became visibly more relaxed and less fearful. I explained the problem of the poltergeist and my forgiveness theory as gently as I could without rousing Ashling's spirited rebuttal. Fortunately, with Fiona, you didn't have to dot all the i's and cross the t's. She got it in one.

"And along with our little ritual tonight to ease Ashling's heart," I added, "we ought to say a few words of power for her future as well. She'll need some kind of employment now that she's single again. I have some ideas, but they're only of a temporary nature."

"Ashling, what a lovely name! Looking for gainful employment now that you're alone in the world, are you? Being a single woman again can have its compensations, you know. Even without a cat like my adorable Omar, it's possible to be alone without being lonely. I've been many years a widow myself—Goddess rest Rob Ritchie's soul—and I have to admit there's a peacefulness of heart in not having the constant care of a husband to humor and cosset. Depends on the husband, of course. Some are more high maintenance than others. And then there's never having to explain what you spent and why you spent it. Speaking of money, Cass will have some ideas about your future employment, rest assured. I couldn't count how many young women like yourself she's helped to sort out their troubles. You can trust her with your memories, my dear—all of them, past and future. Did you know she's a clairvoyant? No? Yes, indeed." Keeping up a comforting stream of chatter, she ushered Ashling into the living room where I'd made a cheerful small blaze in the fireplace.

They sat together on the sofa, while Scruffy and Raffles vied to place themselves within leaning distance of their new love object. Fiona continued. "You must put yourself in my hands entirely—perfect trust and perfect love. That's the Wiccan way, my dear. Now I'm just going to anoint your lips and wrists with essential oil of rose for loving forgiveness, and your ankles with basil and sage for anchor and balance." As she spoke, Fiona whipped tiny flasks out of her reticule, seemingly without even looking at the labels. She also brought out her medicine bag decorated with Navaho symbols. I could see that this was going to be an eclectic spell all right—part Wiccan, part Shamanism.

"Then I'll bless you, my dear, with a pinch of corn pollen for harmony, which is much the same as beauty. Oh, goodness me, Cass, there's one other herb we need.. I keep forgetting to replenish my herb chest. Herb of grace, you know," Fiona continued. "Grace and forgiveness go hand in hand."

"Never fear. The complete herbalist here." I hurried downstairs to my workroom. Joe, who threw himself enthusiastically into do-it-yourself home projects between his Greenpeace assignments, had rebuilt the old cellar. The gloom of this former catacombs had been dispelled by a bright, uncluttered laboratory look. I bypassed Joe's florescent lights, however, in favor of my dear old green-shaded single-bulb lamp still swinging over the rocking chair I favored for my ruminations, and rummaged through the pine shelves where Grandma used to store her jars of home-canned foods. There were several packets of dried rue between rosemary and sage; I brought a few upstairs.

Fiona lit cinnamon and myrrh incense sticks and gently drew Ashling to her feet (which were bare, of course) so that they were standing face to face. As she sprinkled a circle of rue around Ashling, the two dogs sat up suddenly, noses twitching, and Raffles howled.

Hey, what are all those big smells she's putting on the new girl. Getting nervous here. Scruffy looked at me anxiously.

"Just stay still and be quiet." I said, taking my place beside the girl.

Ashling looked at me with a hurt expression.

"Talking to the dogs, Ashling," I explained, as I'd had to explain many times before. "Rituals can be a bit fearsome to canines."

Hey, it's not that I'm afraid, Toots. It's the kid here who's getting his collar in a twist. But a sensitive canine can only take so much nose overload, you know.

"Yeah, yeah. Well, if it gets to be too much, you two can skedaddle upstairs to the blue room."

"Don't be alarmed, Ashling," Fiona said. "Cass talks to her dogs, and vice versa. That's something you don't get much of with a feline. Omar tends to keep himself to himself. And *now*..." Fiona drew forth her athame from the old green reticule; the ritual knife was a wicked looking Scottish dagger... "we'll cut this Mr. Hyde out of your life *for good* with a magic blade." *Yes, and a bit of dark power as well.*

Fiona drew herself up into a fearsome glamour. I'd never know how she did it, but as I had observed many time before, she'd metamorphosed herself into a tall and regal goddess figure, or tricked us into seeing her that way. For a moment,

I almost thought I saw an owl on her shoulder—but, no—*not possible*!

A very faint *who whooo* sounded somewhere in the room.

Scruffy and Raffles started and took off up the stairs. Just as well, in case the poltergeist got active.

Ashling drew back just a bit. "Mr. Hyde? You don't mean Archie, do you?"

"You will never lose the man of your dreams, my dear. But the nightmares will cease."

"Oh. How did you know about the nightmares?"

"I can see them in those shadows under your eyes, my dear."

Fiona cut a mean swath with that Scottish athame as she quickly cast a circle so that we could work "between the worlds." I stood in awe, and I was not alone. Ashling, anointed with oils, sprinkled with pollen, surrounded by incense, and encircled with rue, her gray eyes huge with wonder, stood as still as a sculpture and never moved a finger or toe.

The poltergeist did not *go gentle into that good-night*!

Such strange clankings and groanings, scratchings and squeakings, rumblings and raspings had never been heard before within the walls of my small house—for a half hour or more we endured a ghostly Bedlam manifesting around us. Upstairs, Scruffy howled like his ancestor the *ur*wolf, and Raffles followed his sire's woeful lead, a Transylvanian duet if ever I'd heard one. But Fiona never faltered until the last rat-squeak, dragging footstep, clattering chain, and distressed doggie had fallen into silence.

"There!" she said with satisfaction as peace finally descended. "I think we may have seen the last of that black upstart. And now, about this lovely young woman's future..." Fiona drew from her ever-present reticule a pen—it was an actual quill pen made from what looked mighty like an eagle feather—and a small bottle of dragon's blood ink that I recognized from an earlier ritual. When it comes to *Semper Paratus*, the Coast Guard can't hold a candle to Fiona.

"I'll need parchment. Or pure linen paper, if you have it," she informed me imperiously.

I ran to my office, the former borning room next to the kitchen, and brought back a sheet of my best Crane stationery. Fiona eyed it critically and nodded approval. She laid pen, ink, and paper on the coffee table, thought for a moment, then wrote in her neat librarian's hand words that neither Ashling nor I could quite decipher though we strained to read upside down.

"I'm writing this in Gaelic, my dears," Fiona explained. "An excellent language for magic, I've always found." She folded up the paper into a bird shape and asked Ashling to spit on it. After which, she consigned the spell to the glowing embers in the fireplace. It flared up in a spirited fashion, then subsided into feathery ashes.

Fiona, too, slowly faded into her everyday pudgy librarian self, as she opened the circle. After taking a moment to purify her athame with the symbols of the four elements—smoke and fire, water and salt—she stuck it into its sheath and tossed it back into her bag with a sigh of relief. "Wow! After that work-out, I could sure use a slug of Scotch." She sank gratefully onto the couch.

I opened the parson's cupboard where Joe kept his stash of "medicinal" spirits and poured each of us a healthy belt. I was rather surprised that Ashling downed hers without hesitation. Possibly those years in the Holmes literary salon had given her a taste for the hard stuff.

Personally, I'm a great believer in the earthy comfort that food gives after a night of spiritual adventure, so I left Fiona to reassure Ashling while I made a stack of grilled cheddar cheese sandwiches with a dollop of chutney on sourdough bread and a pot of robust Assam tea. Cautiously the dogs crept downstairs, sniffed the air, and were satisfied that peaceful vibes had returned. I let them out onto the porch where they availed themselves of the pet door (installed by Joe) to run outdoors and commune with the night.

"I am feeling a wee bit peckish," Fiona admitted as she wandered into my kitchen drawn by the sizzle of butter and the whistle of the kettle. As I flipped sandwiches, she whispered in my ear, "I thought I'd give that power spell a bit of theatrics, you know, Cass dear. To ratchet up the placebo affect."

"Placebo? In spellwork?"

But before I had a chance to follow this quirky trail of "Fiona logic," Ashling appeared, looking a bit giddy and disoriented. I glanced at her bare feet. They seemed to be safely in touch with the tile floor. Was it too much to hope for that Fiona's forgiveness and exorcism spells had quieted the girl's penchant for levitation?

"Where have those big guys disappeared to?" Ashling asked.

"Outdoors for their mid-evening ramble. You can let them in, if you like. They're very fond of toasted cheese."

I watched out of the corner of my eye as she glided to the back door.

"Yes, she's quite grounded," Fiona confirmed. "For now. If you think it might help, I have a magical stone with grounding power—merikanite obsidian, Apache tears it's called—in my reticule."

"Of course you do," I said. "Let me borrow it for a few days. Flights of fancy are all very well, but we don't want them to get out of hand."

Fiona drew out a marble-size smoky brown stone that had been polished and was half-transparent when held up to the light. "Semi-precious," she said.

"Aren't we all."

CHAPTER FIFTEEN

aru-dake-no-sake-o-tabe-kaze-o-kiki

Finish the last
of the sake,
hear the wind.

– Santoka

It had been a few years now since we five initiated our circle, inspired by a wildly eclectic course in women's studies given by Fiona at the Black Point Branch Library. Yet it was only recently that I had begun to keep a real Book of Shadows and not just a volume of formulas for herbal products. Of course I kept the herbal thing, too, but mostly as a supplement to the Shipton family manuscript crammed with shaky fading ink recipes that I'd inherited from Grandma along with her seaside saltbox home.

"Cass's Book of Shadows" (affectionately known as CBS) was devoted to notes on spiritual experiences and magical spells, past, present, and future. It existed as a fat green notebook and was also stored in my computer, thus doubly insured. I wrote up the exorcism ritual that Fiona had concocted. A gal never knew when she might need to put an end to some *I-shall-but-love-thee-better-after-death* relationship.

Following my Wednesday luncheon at Heather's, several new notes were added, one of them heavily underlined. "Do not attempt a clairvoyant vision after consuming a surfeit of sake."

The idea had been to have a quick lunch, just Heather and I, followed by a serious finding session aimed at uncovering a dog-fighting ring supposedly operating in Plymouth. Upon reflection, however, Heather had realized that it was nearly my birthday, and Joe was off somewhere in the Antarctic on a Greenpeace mission to protect the Southern Whale Sanctuary. So being my dear friend, she'd seized the opportunity to arrange a birthday party with other dear friends to celebrate (and hasten) my advance into mid-life crisis.

Vehicles were inconspicuously parked behind the three-car garage, now a kennel for Heather's several canine companions, and the circle was assembled before I even arrived. To their credit, no one leaped out and screamed "surprise!"—but surprised I was! Had I known, I wouldn't have shown up in faded jeans and an old Greenpeace sweatshirt of Joe's bearing the legend, "You Can't Sink a Rainbow." Thanks to Phillipa, however, my sandy hair was sporting a stylish shoulder-length cut by Sophia's Serene Salon, and my face was subtly brushed with her recommended mineral powder makeup. And thanks to Joe, I was wearing my Athena coin earrings. So at least from the neck up, I was party ready.

Having promised Japanese food, Heather had hired a Boston catering firm, *Samurai Sushi,* to lay out a sumptuous Asian spread on a wicker dining table in her conservatory amid vigorous palm plants with jungle-size leaves and discarded chew toys. The *de rigueur* raw fish and sticky rice morsels were artistically arranged for our delight. Showy but insubstantial.

Thankfully, the chef, accomplished as a surgeon with his flashing knives, also whisked together a shrimp stir-fry and a pork sukiyaki at table woks. This is what I thought of as "the real meal." A decorous girl assistant brought heaping bowls of rice and tiny jugs of sake to the table.

Magical work was put aside while we feasted and toasted with innumerable thimblefuls of warm rice wine. Heather, in a quilted jacket embroidered with a five-toed dragon, worn over black silk pants, kept pouring the sake with a liberal hand.

Naturally there were the usual quirky birthday gifts, bestowed with the customary hugs, laughter, and tears.

Fiona gave me what she called "a traveler's grimoire," a narrow thin book bound in crimson suede. Inside she'd penned (more of that dragon's blood ink?) a few simple chants and rhymes for a safe journey, leaving the rest of the pages blank "for you, dear Cass, to keep your own magical notes and reflections during your trip."

"My trip? Am I going somewhere?"

Fiona smiled that infuriatingly knowing smile. "Someday, somewhere, somehow, my dear."

"That Samhain trip to Bermuda was enough excitement for the present, thank you very much, Fiona. But I'll treasure this lovely grimoire."

What was she sensing? Before I could start brooding, however, Deidre presented me with a silver bracelet inscribed with runes. I'd have to look up those meanings later—Goddess knows what well-intentioned magical mischief she was up to!

Heather's gift was a handmade Libran candle, with tiny scales of justice, silver keys, five-petal Rose of Venus, and a diminutive opal ring embedded in its pale-blue-fading-to-soft green wax, Libran colors. "Wow, that's not a real opal, is it?"

Heather merely winked.

Phillipa had made the gorgeous birthday cake, my very favorite dense chocolate decadence. "But that's not my real gift," she said. "For your birthday treat, I insist on taking you to lunch very soon—as soon as you can tie down your flying nun with an appropriate guardian. Where do you have her stashed today?"

"Ashling's returned to St. Rita's. She needs a few days of retreat before she takes on the world again. As I explained to Serena Dove, I believe that Fiona exorcised the dead hubby, or whoever the poltergeist was, and now everything should be peaceful and calm, except for the levitations. And after all, the staff at St. Rita's are mostly ex-nuns, therefore unfazed by the odd miracle. So...where are you taking me?"

"I thought it would be great fun for us to visit Chez Reynard and see what's cooking with the fox family."

"Oh, groovy," I said. "I wonder if it's really good manners for a jury person to visit the scene of the bereaved, so to speak."

"Oh, stow those Libran ethics," Phillipa said.

On the face of it, ordinary birthday gifts. (Well, "ordinary" by our standards—perhaps a bit outré to more mundane gals.) But as it would turn out, some of them had a fateful connection to future events. The first hint of magical hi-jinx would be that lunch with Phillipa, if I'd only known. I often wished that my clairvoyance could kick in a bit sooner—like before I got myself into another tragic muddle.

But this was my birthday party, a rollicking afternoon of free-flowing sake and the wicked laughter of women who haven't run out of anecdotes about their ex-husbands yet. It was after three when the chef's slim helper had cleared away and packed their van, which was decorated with a fierce samurai warrior brandishing an antique sword. One thing you could say about Heather—she didn't do things by halves.

"All right then," said our hostess. "Let's get at it."

A box of handmade candles was produced from its hiding place amid the conservatory greenery. There were thirteen of them in shades of deep purple to purplish-black, with various symbols of discovery embedded in them—a doll's glass eye, a tiny magnifying glass, a charm-size silver telescope, a dowsing pendant, crystals for scrying—and even a miniature tarot card, The Star, to enhance psychic insight. She arranged them in a pentagram shape on the now-bare conservatory table, and lit each one with a whispered prayer. We were very quiet watching her. Well, most of us were quiet. In Fiona's case, silence was punctuated by the occasional soft snore.

"Now if you will all please hold hands around the table, I'll say this discovery prayer my internet pal in Haiti sent me," Heather said.

Phillipa nudged Fiona, who started up, and we all complied. There was a heavy perfume to those candles, and I felt myself succumbing to their fragrance and wavering lights. Gazing fixedly at any light, whether from candle, fireplace, or crystal reflection, always put me in danger of a trance. *Uh-oh*, I thought, just before I fell into darkness.

Most times, a clairvoyant trance for me is like viewing a very short film, but a few times I find myself wandering within the scene like a dreamer, only in a place more realistic, less amorphous than a dream. This time I was part of a feudal Japanese scene. As I peeked through a screen with other maidens, a giggling gaggle of them, I witnessed some kind of scuffle going on in the courtyard. I could hear men shouting. The language was transparent to me, as if there were a translator in my head.

The men were crouched around a ring of stones, betting on a fight, an agonizing battle between two Akita dogs. One man in voluminous silk robes was seated separately on a dais, another man standing beside him held a scroll on which he was making marks with a brush. There was something familiar about those two men who held themselves apart, but before recognition could fully click in, I was bolted out of the trance.

Not for the first time, I woke with a bottle of smelling salts under my nose and Fiona's warm arm around my shoulders, her silver bangles tinkling, a comforting sound, like tiny temple bells.

Real trances induce nausea, which I've learned to overcome by sitting straight upright and opening my eyes wide. Usually. Didn't work this time, though. I had to dash to the powder room under the mansion's broad staircase so that I could upchuck my birthday repast. *Too much sake,* I concluded. *Way too much.* I still seemed to be reeling. I kept a steadying hand on each tiled wall of the little lavatory until the floor stopped undulating. Not only did all that rice wine make me ill, the Japanese fantasy it inspired had made the vision obscure and unreadable. Except that there was *something* familiar about two of the principals.

Added to the sins of a sake-soaked vision, I'd been totally grossed out by the sight of two healthy dogs mauling each other for the delight of a blood-thirsty Japanese audience. No wonder I'd lost my lunch.

I came back feeling pale and weak to face the concerned faces of my friends. And their curiosity. "Did you see anything? Do you know who's organizing the dog fights?" Heather demanded.

"In a word, no," I said. "Too much Japanese joy juice, I guess. Fiona, why don't you have a go with the dowsing crystal? You always were our best finder. The thing I do is sometimes not so easy to decipher. Two of the Japanese men I saw looked familiar but I can't quite put my finger on *who.*"

"Just give me a wee moment," Fiona said. She pushed Heather's candles out of the way, careless of their pentagram formation, and drew forth her dowsing pendant from beneath her shirt and cardigan. "I do believe I may have a map of Plymouth in my bag," she muttered as she peered into the miraculous depths of the green reticule. "Yes, yes, here it is. A bit antique, but it will serve."

Phillipa and I exchanged glances. "How fortuitous," she mumbled. "Just happens to have it handy."

Fiona ignored us and laid out the map with Deidre's help. It was indeed an antique map. We would have to superimpose our current knowledge over the old post roads and cow paths.

After warming her crystal pendant between her hands, Fiona swung it experimentally over the map, talking soothingly the while. "O, guiding spirit, is today a good day to ask for your wisdom? Swing right for yes, left for no."

The lazy circle being described by the pendant gradually evolved into an energetic swerve in the "yes" direction.

"We are making an important search today, dear spirit. Any light you can shed on our quest would be most welcome. We are looking for the site where evil men have been hiding a dog-fighting facility. Animals are forced to fight to the death for the entertainment of gamblers. We must put a stop to this cruel slaughter. Please show us the way."

We hovered around the table as the pendant in Fiona's plump hand began to swing in a gentle circle over the Plymouth map. It seemed like forever but was only a few moments before the circle narrowed to an arc that pointed again and again to one area of Plymouth. Heather put a light pencil check against the place that seemed to be the pendant's goal.

Fiona lowered the pendant and rested her hand as the rest of us began peering at the marked map. Heather fetched a new Arrow map from her cozy little study, and we began arguing over how to translate the ancient to the modern.

"Now that's North Plymouth there, near where the Wampanoag Deli is now," Deidre said as she used her finger to trace a path on the map, "so this must be the old Boston Road, and down here we move south."

"No, Dee, you're way off." Phillipa leaned over the two maps, looking back and forth as her hair fell forward, shimmered like shook satin. "You've got to zoom inland to arrive at the place where the pendant was pointing."

"Here's the old Morgan property," Heather cried in excitement. "Much of it was sold off by the Captain's descendents, but at one time we owned all this...and this. It's almost as if the dog-fighting facility is not that far away."

I looked over Heather's shoulder. *The light was beginning to dawn over Marblehead.* Elements of my vision cleared a little in my sake-soaked brain. I began to recognize certain features.

"The Morgan place was a vast estate then," I said. "Now you're down to a mere twenty-seven acres or so, right?"

"Right," Heather said. "So? Spit it out, Cass."

"Well, if you look at the new map, right down here on what used to be the Morgan holdings, you'll find Fresh Meadow Road. And what's on Fresh Meadow Road?"

"Holy Hecate!" Heather cried. "Fresh Meadow Farm. Horse training and boarding. And naturally they have kennels, too, for the stable dogs. What a perfectly secluded situation to house a clandestine operation. It's all been rebuilt after the fire, too. Who knows what's inside those buildings now?"

"Also," I said hesitantly. "I believe it was Kurt Heller who did the work. And Hugh Collins owns the farm. Collins and Heller were both on the Reynard jury with me. Collins was our foreman. I have to admit he had a kind of macho authority, and he's certainly attractive if you like the untamed Heathcliff type, but still I got those icy cold vibes. Now I think the two men in my Japanese vision might have been my intuitive attempt to finger Collins and Heller, only all that sake I drank veered me off the mark."

"Perhaps we should alert Stone to our suspicions," Deidre said. She was seated cross-legged on a floor cushion, her short blonde curls shining under the overhead light, her busy little fingers stringing chakra beads on thongs. Never an idle moment for Dee!

"*Oh, no, you don't*!" Phillipa replied instantly. "*I'm* not going to tell my poor befuddled detective that Cass has had a Japanese vision and Fiona dowsed a practically prehistoric map to find a modern dog-fighting operation. What is this... some episode of *Medium* that you're dreaming up? I'll need something just a bit more like down-to-earth evidence before I lay this one on him."

"Yes!" Heather agreed—too quickly. "Cass and I will just have to sneak in there and make an undercover video."

"Hey! Hold up there, Heather. What do you mean '*Cass* and I,'" I objected. "How do you suppose we're going to sneak into a working stable without alerting the grooms and causing a ruckus among the animals?"

"Just a minute...I feel a brainstorm coming on." Heather tugged at her long bronze braid as if trying to ring a bell in her brain. We were respectfully silent, waiting. Finally, she jumped to her feet and cried, "Brooke! I'll get Brooke to case the joint and tell us when the coast is liable to be clear!"

"But your cousin has the hots for Hugh Collins." I pointed out the obvious flaw in Heather's scheme. She was undeterred.

"I'll put it to her, woman to woman. Cousin to cousin. Morgan to Morgan," she stated firmly.

"Blood, after all, is thicker than wine," Fiona cried, leaping to her feet, sake cup in hand. "So let's raise our glasses to the downfall of this dog-fighting thing!"

I thought perhaps I had had quite enough sake for one day, but Heather filled our cups all round again, so we joined in Fiona's impromptu toast.

"Bagpipes!" Fiona declared with a ladylike hiccup. "This is a moment for bagpipes, if ever there was one. I think I have Rob Angus's bagpipes somewhere in the cellar. I ought to get them out and practice some of the good old Scot war songs."

"Ceres save us," Phillipa muttered.

"I'm very fond of *Amazing Grace*," Deidre said. "It was played at Will's funeral, you remember—quite stirring. The Firefighters Bagpipe Brigade. Nice lads from way over in Western Massachusetts. Firefighters are a really close knit community."

"It might need tuning, though" Fiona continued on her own train of thought. "I seem to remember that my darling Omar disappeared for hours the last time I played *Scots, wha hae wi' Wallace bled.* I finally found him on my neighbor's doorstep huddled down with his favorite catnip mouse."

"A very sensitive soul, that Omar," Phillipa said.

CHAPTER SIXTEEN

She loved me for the dangers I had pass'd,
And I loved her that she did pity them.

– William Shakespeare

Feeling somewhat knackered from the excitement of my party and the subsequent zeroing in on Hugh Collins and Fresh Meadow Farm, I was ready for a ladylike collapse on the sofa when I got home late that afternoon. But then Joe called to wish me a happy birthday and tell me all the innovative ways he'd like to deliver his wishes in person. Immediately I felt perkier, even sultry. After a few minutes of sexy love talk, we finally got around to exchanging the news. His wasn't good. Not from my perspective, anyway.

Somehow the *Esperanza* hadn't managed to engage the Japanese whaling fleet despite numerous passes over the Southern Whale Sanctuary and the assistance of a surveillance plane from New Zealand. Perhaps the information Greenpeace had received was skewed. Their expedition's timing might have been off-beam. Captain de Greif intended to make another tour around the Sanctuary—those whaling bastards were out there somewhere! This time they would follow the krill, marine shrimp that are the whales' main food. Full speed ahead to save the Humpbacks!

I groaned. "So that means you won't be home for *ages*—right?"

"Well, it will *seem* like ages when I'm missing you so much," Joe said diplomatically, "but it will really be only another two weeks or so."

"Two weeks! Two more weeks of dangerous encounters!"

"Just to keep things in perspective, sweetheart—remember that this is my job, we haven't actually encountered the enemy yet, and I'm being well paid for my time."

"Yeah, I suppose. *A man's got to do what a man's* etcetera. I guess I'll just have to carry on without you."

"Carry on with what? Aren't you still on jury duty?"

"Oh, that business. That was all settled last week. The defendants pleaded guilty to second degree murder in exchange for a deal, and we jurors were dismissed with thanks. So now, you know, it's just *same old, same old.*"

"Now *that* I don't believe. What have you really been up to?"

"Not too much, honestly, honey. Serena sent me a young woman in need of an exorcism, and Fiona helped me with that. Ashling Malone Holmes. Isn't that a pretty name? She's a dead-broke widow, poor thing, and she has another problem, too. She levitates."

"Levitates? Okay, lay it on me. I believe everything."

"You've heard the expression, *walking on air*? Well, it's a rather extraordinary sight when you witness it with your own eyes. They tell me St. Teresa had her light-footed moments, too, so I guess it's considered more of a mystical rapture than a sign of the devil. Parapsychologists think it's a form of psychokinesis. You know—like the psychic energy that makes Freddie able to reprogram slot machines and screw up delicate machinery. I'm just grateful that Freddie has never been afflicted with Ashling's problem. You'll probably meet Ashling and see for yourself, if you ever get home."

"I can hardly wait. Well, as long as you keep *your* two feet on terra firma. And what's next? Why do I have the feeling you're up to something else?"

"That's called ESP, honey. Heather has a little project for her and me over at Fresh Meadow Farm."

"The stable that burned down last year?"

"The very same. The Churchills sold out, but the new owner has rebuilt the premises, so we hear."

"And..."

"And what?"

"You and Heather are going to take riding lessons?" I could hear an infuriating chuckle in his voice, barely suppressed.

"Not exactly. Just a little investigatory work. Nothing risky, you know—not when compared to your high seas jousting," I reassured him insincerely with some satisfaction.

"*Jesu Christos*...what's going on?"

"The details will just have to wait until you get home, Ulysses." And no matter how he argued and pleaded, I would say no more. Let him worry and fret for a change!

~

I did lie down later on the sofa, but, even though I dabbed my wrists with lavender scent and my head rested on soft sage-and-mint pillows, I was much too keyed up to rest. And so were my canine companions.

Hey, Toots! It's been mighty dull around here today while you were out partying. We canines need exercise to keep our muscles toned, you know. So, how about a little squirrel stalking in Jenkins Park?

Scruffy bounced around the living room with annoying energy, stopping occasionally to flip my arm up with his nose.

Squirrels! Squirrels! Raffles hopped up on the windowseat and gazed longingly at the woods.

Clearly, I was outnumbered and outflanked. Wearily, I dragged my body into the kitchen and shrugged into the old green lumber jacket hanging by the back door. "The next time I go out for the day, I'm going to drop you two off at Plymouth Pets Day Camp. I guarantee the camp counselors at PPD will see that you mutts get all the exercise you could possibly want."

Camp! Camp! Let's go to camp!

Muzzle yourself, kid. That place is for wimps and retards, not real he-man canines like yours truly. Those exercise freaks make you run after some frigging beach ball till you drop in your tracks. Humph.

I listened to their mutterings with an inner smile while I clipped leashes to collars and pulled on my mud boots. Scruffy had never been a fan of group games, and to tell the truth, neither was I.

I grabbed a canvas tote, in case—I never knew what goodies I might want to harvest in the woods. At the very least I might get some pine cones to use for kindling.

The odor of wet earth and decaying leaves, pine resin and tree fungus—the particular perfume of October in the woods—was as much of a pick-me-up as a nap might have been. When we were far enough into the interior of the park, I let the two dogs off leash to romp away their excess energy, while I harvested some dandelion and goldenseal roots. Although it was getting late for sporting with squirrels, who were sensibly tucked away in their burrows as day drew to a close, Scruffy succeeded in raising a flock of black ducks off the interior wetlands, the discovery of which had saved the park from development a few years ago. Raffles was enraptured by the flutterings and squawkings, and Scruffy adopted a definite swagger as we headed for home and suppertime.

While the dogs wolfed down their dinners, which included some tasty leftover salmon, I ducked my head into the office to check my email. There was a thank-you note from Serena with a reminder that Ashling was still destitute and in need of employment where her particular eccentricity would not be a problem. Serena said she knew I would want to help poor girl, as I always had helped others in the past, and she promised to pray for me.

Oh, well. There really was no weaseling out of one's karma, and mine was to help those who came to me in distress.

"Thanks, Serena," I typed in reply. "I need all the prayers I can get right now, and so does my guy Joe, who is at this very moment crusading in Antarctica to divert Japanese whale killers. I will look into something for Ashling, but while I'm at it, why don't you get the girl some ballet lessons? Just think what a nice surprise she'll be for some jaded dance instructor."

Then another thought came to me, *bang*, out of the blue. What about putting the squeeze on Ashling's in-laws, that tight-fisted, mean-spirited family of rich Yankees? I typed a hasty email to my oldest child Becky, a family lawyer at the well-respected firm of Katz and Kinder, asking her to look into the matter of an allowance for Archibald Fennimore Holmes's widow. It was only right and fair. Maybe Becky would think of a thinly veiled judicial threat to shake some money out of the Holmes' family tree. As I was typing, it occurred to me that Becky and I hadn't actually talked in ages. Two weeks anyway. It would be good to catch up and find out who she was seeing these days. I wondered if it was still Attorney Johnny Marino whose stocky build, square jaw, and intense dark eyes reminded me of Joe, although a less open and accessible version.

Still in a bit of gastric distress from my birthday lunch, I made myself a cup of fennel and mint tea and nibbled a few common crackers, then went back to the computer when a half-formed thought I'd had earlier came to full consciousness. Heather! She needed someone to replace Captain Jack, and Ashling was a wonder with dogs as well as a decent cook, judging by those feather-light scones and Serena's reports of her culinary prowess. Well, I'd be hearing from Heather soon enough when she was ready to sneak into Fresh Meadow Farm. I would broach the matter then, if we weren't running for our lives.

Meanwhile, a little advice from my daughter-in-law might be in order. I could only hope that my email was secure and not the subject of some government probe, I thought, as I typed a note to Freddie. "Heather and I need to get into a place where we suspect the owner is hosting an illegal operation involving canines. Call me on cell!"

Well, the speed of modern communication is a magic all of its own. It seemed as if I had hardly hit *Send* when my cell phone played its tinny tune, and there was Freddie herself, demanding to know what I was getting myself into this time.

I explained it all from the appearance of the injured pit bull at Dick Devlin's emergency room to Fiona's dowsing out the location of the dog fighting ring, and everything between. Even in my condensed version, this took a few minutes, during which Freddie could be heard to whistle, sigh, and groan at various junctures of the story. Then I told her about Ashling's strange phenomena as well. Might as well make a full report of all my current conundrums. "So...what do you think?"

"*Thinking* has nothing to do with 'our thing', as the Mafia would call it," Freddie said. "So let me just hit the highlights. First, I'm desperately worried about you two sedate Plymouth matrons hopping over some paddock fence in the dark of night and running into a pack of fight-trained pit bulls. You'll need really reliable surveillance first. Do you really trust this Brooke person?"

"She's Heather's second or third cousin."

"Flaky like all the Morgans? *I rest my case*. Let me try a spot of remote viewing, at least. There are dudes in special ops who think I'm wicked good at that stuff. Maybe I can send you a plot plan of the premises."

"Oh, thank you, dear—that would be grand."

"What I really want to do is to raid the place with you. But Minnie—*Minerva,* I should say, she hates Minnie–has been called home to England for some family crisis, *she says*, and I'm stuck here on my own with the Terrible Twins. So I'm not free to be your Gal Friday, and we're both screwed. Because *you're* not going to be any help in the child care department while there's a wrong to right or a crime to solve."

"But Miss Sparks will return, won't she? She seems to me to be a real old-fashioned nanny, right out of the storybooks."

"Sure. She even carries an umbrella, but thank God she doesn't levitate with it. Yes, as soon as the monarchy is saved, or whatever Sparks is up to. Her cousin she's so worried about was the deputy dressmaker to Herself, and is now a retired pensioner."

"Really? How cool is that! Anyway, okay, do the viewing thing. I have every confidence in your abilities. Speaking of which, have *you* ever tried levitation?"

"No, thanks. I have enough trouble controlling the stuff that just happens to me naturally, you know what I mean?

Speaking of which, would you like me to have a talk with poor dumb Ashling about that very subject—control."

"Hmmm. Good thought. Maybe when things quiet down, the three of us can get together." *One levitates and the other bends metal objects*, I observed to myself. *Sounds like a fun lunch.* Thoughts of the Mad Hatter tea party flitted through my mind.

CHAPTER SEVENTEEN

But screw your courage to the sticking place
And we'll not fail.

– William Shakespeare

An aerial photograph of the property and a scan of Freddie's remote viewing results arrived the next day by express overnight mail. "Photograph courtesy of Big Brother in the skies," she wrote. Freddie's own shadowy map sketched and labeled the buildings of Fresh Meadow Farm as she saw them in her mind's eye. There was a long driveway through acres of pine and oak, with many riding trails winding their way through the woods. In the center of the property was a vast clearing in which office, stables, paddocks, and both indoor and outdoor arenas were situated. A kennel was located to the left of the paddock area, screened by a stand of pines. The house, former residence of the Churchills, was set back from this area of activity. But Freddie's sketch also showed another, hidden area beneath the indoor arena.

Freddie penciled notes on her sketch. "Ignore this discrete kennel beside the paddocks—pure window dressing. It's the cellar under the indoor arena that reeks of darkness and death.

Ugh. Shadows of a holding pen and a fight arena. My best guess—this is your target. For Goddess' sake, watch your step."

How does she do it? I wondered. And then, warily, *Can I rely on this? Just how accurate is her view?* Surely the CIA wouldn't be employing Freddie's talents if she were not the real deal. As her mother-in-law—and friend—I should believe in her abilities and be grateful.

I called Heather. "I have something helpful from Freddie," I said. "What do you hear from Brooke?"

"Well, didn't I have a time convincing my obdurate cousin to get on board!" she exclaimed. "But *finally* she agreed to help us take a look, 'if only to shut you up' she said. Brooke still fancies that treacherous lout, but not if he's guilty of animal abuse. She's a Morgan, after all. Anyway, Brooke has learned that the two live-in stable hands will be taking the horse trailers to West Virginia next weekend to pick up a pair of fillies who are to be boarded and trained at Fresh Meadow. That will leave only Collins himself on the premises, and Brooke is going to make him an offer he can't refuse—dinner with some rich prospective clients. She figures the coast will be clear from about eight to ten, perhaps longer. Saturday night. Be here by seven."

"Oh, well. We may as well get this over with. What can I bring?"

"Nothing. I have everything. Pen lights, wire cutters, lock picks, video camera, flask of brandy, and some treats for the dogs laced with sleepy-time pills. Got them from Dick, unbeknownst of course."

"Dick doesn't know what you're doing! How are you going to just take off like that?" I was constantly amazed at what Heather could get away with—and a little envious.

"I told him we're having an outdoor Wiccan thing. Dark of the moon and all. Dick never questions stuff like that. It's Maury I have to watch out for, but I don't think he'll say anything."

"Maury knows we're going out on a mission?"

"He was there when I mentioned our outing, yes. We were at the hospital having a look at one of those poor savaged American Staffordshire Terriers. We don't know her name—if she had one—so we tried calling her by different names. She seemed to respond best to Wendy, so Wendy she is. We're calling the other big old bruiser Captain Hook. A bum front leg and an attitude. Some loathsome creature had filed Wendy's teeth down to little nubs. Maury says that's because she was probably used as fight bait by those sons of bitches. I wanted to bring Wendy home, but Maury is still testing her temperament. She cowers when anyone approaches her, which is not a good sign. Dick told me that sometimes Maury brings a quilt into Wendy's pen and naps with her so she won't be afraid. You know Maury never says much, but I detected a certain skepticism when I said we were going to have a dark of the moon circle on Saturday night. A sort of lifted-eyebrow and smirk thing. Then he said, 'don't get caught,' which would be a strange remark if he had believed my story."

"Indeed it would. Do you think he'll mention his suspicions to Dick? As I recall, you did promise Dick that you would stop breaking into facilities to rescue animals."

"Yeah, but I specified laboratories. *Always leave a loophole*, that's my philosophy. And besides, I don't think we'll be rescuing any slavering fighters on Saturday night, so I won't actually be breaking my promise. Just a little video tape of the facilities, and we're out of there. If you're looking for a good cardiovascular exercise, I always say there's nothing better than a little spurt of danger. Gets the old ticker pumping and jumping."

"I think I'll stick with fast walking the dogs," I said. "Okay. See you around seven on Saturday then. Commando black is what's being worn this season, I presume?"

"You got it."

Saturday was still looming darkly on my event horizon when Phillipa took me out in her slick BMW 5 for that promised birthday lunch at Chez Reynard in Hyannis. The new car was jet, of course. What other color would Phillipa choose? I determined not to tell her anything about my "mission impossible" with Heather, but like so many promises to myself, my resolve didn't last long.

This birthday fete generously arranged by Phillipa turned out to be one of those fateful experiences that almost makes a person credit the notion that "everything happens for a reason," which in my saner moments I do not believe.

Despite not having a reservation, we were seated immediately at quite a nice table overlooking the ocean, testimony to it being a slow day in October, *sans* tourists. Personally, I'm happy with any table—provided it's not near a door, especially the kitchen door, or out in the middle of the room, or too low to cross one's legs, or facing a bar with the video in full bloom. (I try not to be fussy.) So I appreciated the perfect setting and the waiter who simply gave his name as Louis, with a French accent, and took Phillipa's wine order without chatting us up.

After the amazing Pouilly Fumé had been opened and poured, and the birthday toast made, I blurted out the unwelcome news that Heather and I were going to try to gather some video evidence at Fresh Meadow Farm.

"Oh, sweet Isis. Don't tell me *anything* about it."

"For Goddess' sake, Phil. We'll have to rely on Stone to carry our investigation forward, once we have gathered the proper evidence."

"I don't want to know. *And I don't want Stone to know.*"

"Surely we can't close our eyes to something so purely evil in our midst."

"*I* can, dearie. And I have just one word of advice—*don't get caught*."

"That's what Maury said."

"Maury? Does that mean Dick knows what you're up to?"

"No. They're very different guys. Dick just takes everyone and everything at face value, the least suspicious of men."

"Well. Heather lucked out there. At last."

"Yeah. Fourth time never fails, as she puts it. Dick is a perfect teddy bear. Maury, on the other hand, seems to have a sixth sense when it comes to those minor subterfuges that keep peace in the home."

"Good thing he's not married," Phil said. "Have we ever tried to fix him up with anyone?"

"*Not* a good idea. He definitely isn't blind-date material."

"How intriguing. I must get to know him better." Phillipa turned her attention to the menu. "Let's each get something different so that we can swap and compare."

"So that you can cadge recipes, you mean. Or is it a review you're writing?"

Phillipa blushed discretely under her olive-gold complexion and adjusted her black paisley scarf with the kind of artistic touch that I admire but can never quite manage to imitate. "Whatever. For appetizers, why don't I order the Escargot Montmartre and you get the Chesapeake Bay

Oysters Coquilles. Then you'll have the lobster puff pastry thing and I'll have the Dover Sole Francais...it says here that it's flown in fresh daily...unless you'd rather the sole?"

"Oh, go ahead and order for us both. This is your ballgame, after all. Just don't order anything raw for me. Cooked oysters, right?"

"Absolutely. Drenched in cream. You'll never know those babies were once living beings."

"Drenched in cream? In that case, I'd better have the Dover sole. That Lobster Napoleon must have a zillion calories."

"Then we must have salads, too, for balance. Why don't you have the Avocado, Beet, and Arugula Salad with Chevre Tartin, and I'll have the Warm Belgian Endive with Spiced Pine Nuts."

Louis had the good sense to bring us extra plates and serving spoons, and we were soon sampling our way though haute cuisine heaven. By the time I was loosening the top button on my raw silk slacks, and Phillipa was perusing the dessert menu, word must have got around to the front office that a guest who'd ordered so much food at lunch plus a full bottle of wine might be writing a restaurant review on an expense account.

"Uh oh," Phillipa said. "I believe that's the proprietor sidling over this way."

I looked up startled into the beaming face of Albert Reynard. I hoped he wouldn't recognize me as one of the jurors who had listened with rapt attention to the details of his wife and step-daughter's dreadful murders. Apparently not. His expression remained studiously cordial.

"*Bon jour, Mesdemoiselles*, and welcome to Chez Reynard. I hope you are finding everything to your satisfaction?"

"*Mais oui*," Phillipa assured him. "Service has been impeccable, and the food superb. Especially my companion's Dover sole. Delectable."

"*Très bien, très bien, Mesdemoiselles*. May I offer you, then, a complimentary selection of our desserts...perhaps with a cognac?"

"*Merci beaucoup*, Monsieur Reynard. That would be most agreeable," Phillipa said in a tone that suggested she was used to this sort of VIP treatment, as probably she was. Albert Reynard spoke a few quick words to Louis, then made his way to the other few tables where guests were lunching.

Louis brought us two dessert plates, two forks, and a variety of desserts artfully arranged on a palette-shaped serving plate with a decoration of chocolate "paint brushes." This was followed by two snifters of cognac, and some extremely fragrant black coffee in a silver pot. The cups were demitasse.

"Wow," I said. "I don't know where I am going to put all this, but I'm certainly going to try."

"It's a bit over the top," Phil admitted, "but after all, it's your birthday, and Joe is—Goddess knows. Where is Joe exactly?"

"Antarctica," I mumbled through a forkful of chocolate-raspberry gateau. "This is to die for..."

"Not bad," Phillipa admitted, after digging in her own fork.

It seemed impossible, but somehow we managed to polish off the sweets, the brandies, and the coffees. After Phillipa had paid the check, we waddled to the door and were met again by the generous proprietor.

"Exquisite, Monsieur," Phillipa murmured, putting out her hand.

Monsieur Reynard gallantly lifted her slim fingers and kissed them. "*Au revoir, mademoiselle*"

I took a step back, but not far enough. He took hold of my hand and lifted it to his lips. I gasped. I reeled. I nearly fainted. "*Merde, merde*," I gasped.

"*Si désolé, Monsieur. C'est le brandy*," Phillipa murmured and rushed me out the door into the revivifying October east wind.

"What in Hades happened in there?" she demanded. "You behaved like a veritable Victorian damsel in distress. Has no one ever kissed your hand before?"

"Wait. I don't want to throw up," I moaned. "Just get me into the car and I'll explain everything. Do you have any smelling salts?"

"Do I look like Fiona? She's the only woman in the Western Hemisphere who is still carrying smelling salts." Phillipa clicked open the passenger door of her BMW and gently ushered me inside. "Try tucking your head between your knees," she advised.

As she got into the driver's seat, she clapped her hand to her forehead—the realization struck home. "Smelling salts! You're asking for *smelling salts? Don't tell me* you've had some sort of vision."

"Poor Grand-mère de Rochmont," I moaned, my voice muffled by my knees. "No wonder she was so upset."

"*Will you tell me what's going on*!" Phillipa demanded as she raced north on Route 6. "It was the kissing thing, wasn't it? I'd forgotten how impressionable you are to touch."

"Not always, or I'd be locked up. It's not easy being me, you know." I sat up. I was beginning to feel nearly normal, but steely with resolve.

"I know it isn't, girlfriend. So...why don't you lay it on me."

"Albert Reynard. What a fraud that bastard is. Well, the heart attack was probably the real deal. Maybe he had no idea how traumatic it would be to put a pillow over his wife's head. And the daughter's, too, I don't doubt. *Step*-daughter. He must have walked in on the opportunity he'd only dreamed about. His wife trussed upon the floor, maybe even unconscious. Marie had a great deal of money. Someone told me that. Was it you? No, I think it was Heather. All the time I was a juror, none of you would stop filling my ears with gossip about the Reynards, even though you knew I was under oath not to read or talk about the case."

"Oh, stop complaining. You can't deny you were curious and you were listening, for all your show of putting your hands over your ears. But what you're saying, it's incredible. And odious. Are you certain?"

"Of course I'm not *certain*, Phil. When have I ever felt absolute confidence in my own beastly visions? But unfortunately..."

"...they've usually been spot on." Phillipa finished my sentence. "Oh, this is utterly deplorable. Beyond the pale. A talented restaurateur murdering his wife—and that poor young girl—for money. Well, I guess he may have over-extended himself when he opened that second place in Chatham, Chez Reynard Aussi."

"Maybe Marie refused to finance any more of Albert's grand schemes. Madame de Rochmont may know."

"*Ah, quelle tragedie*," Phillipa said with fervor. "Now, I'll never be able to dine there again—one of my favorite restaurants, too. So you have concluded that those two miscreants who stood trial...who confessed to the murders...are *not guilty*?" Phillipa edged through traffic on the bridge while I gazed into the misty distances of the canal.

"Oh, they were guilty, all right. Of everything *but* murder, just as they always maintained. Home invasion, larceny, probably rape—with a condom, no traces. Only one thing they didn't do. They did not kill those two women. But who would have believed that? So they confessed to get a better deal. Because a jury verdict of first degree murder would have put them away forever. But second degree murder carries the possibility of parole. And in a way, they were guilty. *Felony with death resulting*. No need to feel sorry for those two."

We were silent awhile as Phillipa eased through traffic onto Route 3 North.

Finally she said ruefully, "And I had to take you right into the lion's mouth for lunch!"

"Fox," I said. "Fox's mouth. Reynard the fox. Do you think his brother knows?"

"Why don't you arrange for him to kiss your hand, too, so that you can have another nifty vision. And by the way, what exactly did you see?"

"I saw Reynard looking down at Marie. Her eyes were closed but she was breathing. I could see her breast rising and falling. I saw his face, that little twist of his lips. Did you notice how thin and blue his lips are? Fish-like."

"No, that hadn't occurred to me. Haddock or mackerel? So then what happened—in your provocative little vision?"

"Trout, I think. Then he took a pillow from the sofa and knelt over her. I could see the pillow very clearly," I said, shuddering at the memory.

"And that was it?"

"That was plenty."

"Okay...what are you going to do now? Or should I say, what are *we* going to do. Do you want me to tell Stone. Probably ruin his career, but hey! Justice must be served."

"Not yet. Better we should cause Reynard to reveal himself."

"Oh, a bit of spellwork, then," Phillipa said.

"You bet. It's what's worked for us before."

"Who knows? But it does seem to concentrate the cosmic forces for truth, justice, and the Wiccan way, doesn't it? We'll get the circle together as soon as possible. Well, right after your little escapade at the Farm. With a *murderer-most-foul* in our sights, we can't wait until the next Esbat," Phillipa said, her expression grim and determined. "Perhaps Reynard will have another cardiac episode, a nice fatal one, and save us the incense and incantations.

"I'm not sure that speculation is kosher for Wiccans. Sunday then. My place, where we can be perfectly private, worse luck."

"And when exactly do you expect the return of your crusading husband?"

"Soon, but not that soon."

Phillipa sighed. With a friend as close as she is, I can never tell if I simply know her that well or I'm reading her mind, but that sigh spoke volumes. A wistful envy. If only Stone were a traveling man instead of an Earl-Grey-by-the-fireside type. When a husband travels, a wife may roam—who knows where? I often sensed that rootless place in Phillipa's psyche. A desire not to settle.

"Beware of what you wish for," I said.

"Oh be quiet, you witch."

CHAPTER EIGHTEEN

We saw the risk we took in doing good,
But dared not spare to do the best we could
Though harm should come of it.

– Robert Frost

There *was* something to be said for being able to stride out of one's house dressed in full commando garb, even to the black knitted cap pulled down over my ears, flashlight and cell phone hooked to belt, without having to explain my intentions or justify my mission to a curious husband.

On the other hand, canines can be curious—and insistent—too.

Hey, just a flea-hopping minute there, Toots. You can't fool a canine's superior intuitive nature, you know. You're up to something exciting tonight. I can smell adventure a mile away. So let's get outta here—I 'm good to go. Scruffy did his best to block my way through the back door. He's a big dog with a significant rump, but I'm used to pushing him aside, when the need arises.

Good to go...good to go! Raffles danced around, clueless but ready for anything.

"Sorry, fellas. You've had your dinners, you've had your good run in the woods, now your task is to guard the house until I return." *If I return* was the thought that thrust itself unbidden into my consciousness. *Maybe I should call someone? Naw. Phil knows, and I can count on her to keep tabs on police reports tonight.*

Heather ran out of her house before I could park my car. Surprisingly, she was wearing a bright blue parka. She jumped in and ordered me to drive away. "I don't want Dick to catch sight of you in that jewel-thief outfit."

She struggled out of her parka and threw it onto the back seat of the RAV4. Underneath she was wearing a slim leather jacket, turtleneck, and wool slacks—the all-black outfit had a definite Nordstrom's flair. There was a silver flask in a black leather case clipped to her belt, as well as a pen light and a cell phone. Over her shoulder she carried a flat leather tool bag. Pulling out a black beret from the pocket of her jacket, she fitted it over her hair, although her long bronze braid still hung down her back.

"Cool," I said, turning out of her circular driveway. "Got the video camera?"

"My cell phone. Whatever evidence we photograph will be sent immediately to my PC."

"*O, brave new world*," I said. "My cell is only a phone, a plain ordinary phone."

"Well, Cass, we've entered a new millennium, you know. Witches must move with the times. You'd think we were still getting around on brooms, to hear you talk."

"Salvia divinorum."

"Are you speaking in tongues, dear?"

"Salvia divinorum is one of the herbs that gave some early herbalists the sensation of flying through space and time. A hallucinogen. Recently resurrected by resourceful youngsters."

"You don't say! Do you have any? Why don't we all try it!"

"Yes, I do say. Yes, I have some. And no, we won't all try it—are you taking leave of your senses?"

"Sometimes, Cass, you are no fun at all."

"Still, when you need a partner in crime, *who'ya gonna call*? Just have a look at this great stuff my daughter-in-law sent us."

I nodded toward the folder I'd tucked between the bucket seats. Heather pulled it out and studied the contents with her penlight. Inside were the aerial photograph and Freddie's remote viewing map.

"Freddie says the dog-fighting facility is in the basement of the indoor ring." I whizzed along Route 3A. Every mile was bringing us nearer to our target, and I was feeling decidedly edgy.

Still perusing the maps, Heather said, "Where do you think it will be safe to park?"

"Look in the aerial photo. See that little oblong building and parking lot near Fresh Meadow Farm on Route 3A? That's one of the Finch farm stands. Closed for the season. We'll park in their driveway. It's only a few hundred yards from there to the Collins property, so we can walk in. The dogs will bark, but no one's at the farm tonight, right?"

"Right. I checked with Brooke only moments before you arrived. Hugh was already at her place drinking single-malt whiskey with some rich racing types."

"And the grooms?"

"On their way to West Virginia. We're safe as houses."

"Sure we are. So...all we have to do is...break into the indoor ring...take photos of the set-up and the dogs, if there are any...and get out."

A peeling red and white sign on a post, *Finch's Farm Fresh Vegetables and Fancy Fruits,* loomed out of a slight mist that had risen from the damp earth. I checked my rear view mirror. No cars on the road in back of me. Turning the RAV4 into the farm stand's driveway, I parked on the shadowed side of the building.

Various cardboard signs in the dusty window touted freshly picked sweet corn, vine-ripe tomatoes, pure local honey, and u-pick apples. A white board tacked over the door was crudely lettered in black paint. *CLOSED FOR THE SEASON—SEE YOU IN APRIL*

We jumped out, closed the doors as quietly as we could, and crept past the Finch establishment down the road toward the two huge boulders that marked the entrance to Collins' driveway. It was eerily silent, no sign of life anywhere. A dignified black-and-gold plaque hung from wrought iron hooks near the entrance. *Fresh Meadow Farm. A Boarding and Training Facility. H. Collins.* The ghostly mist rose around the sign and the surrounding woods.

"Where did that fog come from? This is like a blasted Stephen King story," I whispered as I followed Heather down the well-packed earthen road. It appeared to be swept clean of dead leaves, probably by a constant stream of vehicles coming and going. *And horses.*

"Don't get paranoid, Cass. It's merely some guardian spirit watching out for us," Heather assured me. "Druid cloak of invisibility, and all that. But do watch your step. Mucho manure."

"*Too late.* My sneakers are already plastered."

"Well, scrape it off on something. We can't afford to leave tracks," she whispered briskly.

I grabbed a dry stick and scraped away at the stuff, hopping after my leader.

It was a quarter mile before we arrived at the clearing. Unlike the dark entrance road, there were bright spotlights everywhere revealing neat white buildings with green shutters, new stables replacing the burned-out ones, and numerous paddocks. Freddie's map, now memorized, proved to be a Goddess-send as we crept silently but confidently toward the indoor arena.

Although we tried our best not to make any sound, somewhere in the stables, sensitive horses heard us and whinnied nervously. In the kennel beside the paddocks, dogs took up the alarm, but not with any great anxiety. Short, sharp barks. *Pro forma.* Once we had gained the dark side of the arena, we stood very still in its shadow and listened intently. There was no human sound anywhere, and even the animals were quieting down.

The arena was new also. I could smell raw wood on the stairs and railings, fresh paint on the exterior.

"Let's try that bulkhead," Heather whispered. "Bet it enters directly into the basement." She was already moving toward the slanted doors, jiggling them. One side opened easily, and there was a hook-and-eye arrangement on the corner of the building to keep the door from falling back. Heather hooked it, and we crept down several cement stairs. There was a damp fetid smell down there that got stronger as we approached the inner door, the one that opened into the cellar.

End of the easy part. That inner door was securely locked, possibly of the dead-bolt variety. Locks are not my forte, but they're putty in the hands of some of my practiced friends. Fiona, for instance. And Freddie. Now it seemed that Heather, too, was undaunted.

She opened her tool kit and took out what I imagined was a lock pick, probably left over from her former glory days of breaking into laboratories to liberate test animals. She fiddled and fiddled, while I grew increasingly uneasy.

"Say, Heather...what's that scratching sound inside, do you think?"

"Wait a minute, Cass. I almost have this, I think." Heather concentrated on her task to the exclusion of all else, but I was increasingly disturbed by sounds inside the cellar. A snuffling, shuffling, squeaking, scrabbling sort of noise.

One of those killer dogs!

Just as that thought bounced up and hit me, the lock snapped open.

"Ah ha," Heather breathed, and with that she put her hand on the brass doorknob.

"*Wait! Heather, wait!*" I commanded. "*Don't open that door!* One of those ferocious pit bulls is right inside the door. Can't you hear him? He must have been left loose to guard the premises. He'll kill us. Well, one of us, anyway. And then, how will I explain your sad fate to Dick?"

"American Staffordshire Terrier," Heather corrected me.

She opened the door.

CHAPTER NINETEEN

I'm a lean dog, a keen dog, a wild dog, and lone;
I'm a rough dog, a tough dog, hunting on my own…

– Irene MacLeod

My heart sank to my manure-encrusted sneakers.

Then I realized, through my haze of fear, that ingenious Heather had only opened the door a tiny crack and she was braced against it opening any further. But in that narrow space, a dog's long claws were trying to dig his way through, the better to tear out our throats. He was openly snarling now, not a pleasant sound. And his entire muscular bulk was attempting to force the door with methodical thumps of his burly shoulder.

"Help me hold this door, will you?" Heather said calmly. She took something odoriferous out of her pocket. It smelled like chopped liver left out at room temperature, possibly for days. She pushed the soft ball through the door and clapped it shut.

"This won't take long," she said, and sat down with her back to the door, waiting. I sat on the bottom cement stair whose freezing dampness easily penetrated the bottom of my black jeans.

"What was that?" I asked. "Sleepy-time fudge?"

"You bet. Fast acting, but it won't hurt the little bugger a bit."

"What if he doesn't eat it?" I whined.

"I'm betting he will. They keep those fight dogs lean and mean. He'll be too hungry to refuse a yummy treat." Heather checked her watch, a black Sea-dweller Rolex. "Let's give him 10 minutes. I have 8:02—what do you have?"

I glanced at my Timex. *Takes a licking and keeps on ticking.* "8:05. I sure hope Hugh Collins hasn't finished his dinner yet."

"At Brooke's? Have no fear. My cousin is devoted to a long cocktail hour. They'll probably just be staggering into dinner now. Okay, we'll give the doggie until 8:15 to fall into a snooze. While we wait, let's say a little protection ritual. Here's one of Phil's that I know by heart.

Light divine surround me, keep me safe from every danger,

Make my form invisible to any harmful stranger."

I added,

"*Guardians of the north and south, guardians of the west and east,*

Lead me from the ravening ways of evil man and savage beast."

"Amen. Good one, Cass," Heather said.

"That's Phil's, too," I said.

"She sure can come up with them. A good rhyme rings the psychic bell, don't you think?"

"Yeah. Maybe she was a Druid bard in a former life."

"I wonder what I was," Heather mused.

"Some warrior queen, I suspect."

We lapsed into silence. While we sat there, I tried to visual a protective sphere of spiritual light. This is easier done when one is at home in one's rocking chair than when one is about to face a rapacious pit bull. I hoped my spiritual armor didn't have too many holes in it.

Heather glanced at her watch again. "The big fellow should be dozy by now—let's go."

She pushed the door.

And pushed.

And heaved.

The pit bull, now slumped down behind it, made a fairly heavy doorstop, but Heather managed to wedge herself through. I followed, gingerly. The dog was snoring and drooling. The nasty stench of a neglected kennel assailed us as we stepped over the fallen guard.

"Ugh! How long will this guy be out?" I wondered softly.

"Don't know," Heather replied. She reached into her tool bag, pulled out two medical masks, and handed me one. I put it on gratefully. "Differs with different dogs, could be fifteen minutes, could be two hours."

"Oh, swell," I said. "Let's get on with it then. I suppose they clean this place up before fight night, don't you? A stink like this could be bad for business."

"Try to breathe through your mouth," Heather said.

"I'm afraid to take a step. How about a little light over here?" I suggested.

I expected the thin brilliance of a penlight, but Heather had found the main switch and snapped on floodlights that illuminated the entire arena. She started at once to shoot video with her cell phone. Several dogs who had been crammed into carrying cases began barking and snarling—a ferocious racket. Outdoors, horses in the barn and even dogs in a distant kennel added their nervous protests, but I could hardly hear them in the confines of the cellar. Off to one side of the carrying cases were two pens, one with a worn-out looking female nursing a brood of puppies and the other housing a urine-soaked golden retriever whose coat was falling out leaving bare patches.

Heather was swearing in disgust as she video-taped. "*Shit, shit, shit.* The Goddess is going to get you for this, Hugh Collins!"

The fighting area itself was a deep earthen pit ringed with benches and chairs. Dark stains bore silent witness to its murderous use. For someone like me, always sensitive to vibrations and visions, the experience of being in that cellar was an overwhelming nightmare. Clouds of blackness swarmed over me, buzzing like bees.

"Heather," I moaned. "I have to get out of here or I'm going to faint. If I collapse, you'll have to drag me out."

"I know, I know. Wait just a minute. I just want to get this...and this." Her phone camera turned toward the two canine pens. "That retriever must be the bait dog," she muttered. "I'll see Collins in Hades for this."

I was doubled up, struggling not to vomit, when I heard a feeble sound near the door, a cross between a whine and a snuffle. I whirled around and saw the guard dog struggling to stand, dragging his hind quarters.

"Uh oh," seemed to be the only warning I was able to utter.

Heather glanced over. "Okay, we're out of here," she said in a low tone, slipping off her leather jacket. "Get on the other side of me and move slowly *slowly* toward the door. *It will be all right.*"

I did as I was told, and we crept forward, step by craven step, until we were almost at the door. As we passed the light switches, Heather reached out to click them off.

"Oh no," I wailed.

"Just hang onto my belt," Heather said. She turned on her penlight to illuminate our path, but it definitely wasn't up to the task. We could barely see the door. Or the dog.

Just then, the shadowy pit bull seemed to find the strong muscles in his back legs. He stood facing us, lowered his head and raised his upper lip in as frightening a snarl as I hope never to hear again in this life. I was sure he was only a few seconds away from springing toward Heather's throat. Or mine.

The woman was made of iron. She never flinched once. As gracefully as Xena hurling a javelin, she tossed her leather coat over the dog's head, a perfect maneuver that both blinded him and gave those massive jaws something to savage.

Which he did, snarling like Cerberus, the mythical triple-headed dog of Hades. We jumped out the cellar door and slammed it shut. With admirable presence of mind, Heather had snapped the deadbolt into place again. It clicked audibly as it locked. We dashed up the cellar stairs, unhooked the bulkhead door, and let it slam down into its frame.

I took another look at my Timex—we'd been in that reeking basement just over fifteen minutes, and yet it had seemed like hours.

The horses and dogs were still making a clamor in response to our encounter with the guard dog. "Don't worry. They'll quiet down once we've gone," Heather puffed beside me as we jogged out to the main road.

"What's going to happen when Collins sees your coat back there?" I hardly had breath to continue my train of thought, that surely Collins would ship the dogs somewhere else and clean up all evidence of dog fighting. "I certainly hope he won't be able to identify you as the intruder."

"Yes, that could be a problem." Heather, who was in much better shape than I, seemed to have her second wind and was running easily and gracefully while I stumbled along beside her. "But I'll wager there won't be a whole lot left of my jacket by the time Fido Fierce gets through taking out his frustration on it."

"If Collins… realizes… that his game is up…," I gasped, "he'll cover…his tracks before…this horror can be exposed by the law," I explained my fear.

"That bastard may get rid of the living evidence, but the place is still obviously a fighting arena. And he'll never be able to erase all traces of blood. I think we've got him good and proper. We'd better. Otherwise I might be tempted to take stronger measures."

I really didn't want to know what Heather had in mind. And anyway, we had reached the safety of the farm stand. I had to stop right there, however, and lean over trying to catch my breath, but Heather just kept jogging in place as if we were out for a pleasant evening run.

"Home free," she gloated.

"*What the fuck are you two doing here?*" An angry husky voice shouted at us from the shadows of the building. A stocky form with a wild head of orange hair stepped out holding something in her hand. It was Wanda Finch.

"Hi, Wanda," I said, rather breathlessly still, as I stepped in front of Heather. "Remember me, Cass, your jury mate?"

"You're damned right I do. But what I want to know *right now* is what you and your partner in crime think you're doing on my property?"

"Does *biker girl* think we're after last year's rotting tomatoes?" Heather whispered behind my back. She'd stopped jogging and was now doing her cool-down stretches.

"Be still, will you," I muttered.

"What's that? What's that?" Wanda strode forward to where the faint aura of the single streetlight brought her into view. Her expression was menacing, and she was toting a baseball bat!

"Hey, Wanda, take it easy. We mean you no harm."

"Take us to your leader," Heather said in her stranger-in-a-strange-land voice, still having her little joke.

"You're not helping." I stepped backwards onto her foot to make my point. Then I stepped forward to meet Wanda. I'd decided to try a new gambit. The truth.

"Listen, Wanda. This is important. Can you keep a secret?"

Heather kicked me in the back of my shin, but I ignored her.

"Depends. You girls having some kind of secret rendezvous out here?" Wanda snickered nastily.

"Here's the real deal, Wanda. We heard there's a dog-fighting operation at the Collins' place, and we wanted to have a look for ourselves."

"No shit! Just like you had a *look for yourselves* at Izzy's farm, trying to make out that he was dumping chemicals or something?" Wanda raised the baseball bat threateningly. It was true that we'd got her fiancé Izzy Pryde of Pryde's Pigs into a passel of trouble a couple of years ago, but somehow he'd lied and bribed his way out of prosecution. Still, the woman obviously still bore me a grudge. Perhaps because paying for the clean-up had caused her fiancé to postpone their nuptials. Rumor had it around town that the Finch-Pryde alliance was washed up.

Heather sighed. I heard her reaching into her leather case, rattling something. *Pepper spray? Stun gun?*

"Please, Wanda. Let bygones be bygones, and give us a break here. This isn't about us. This is about some poor dumb beasts being slaughtered for entertainment right under our noses." I always believe in appealing to a person's better nature, even when in doubt that she has one.

Wanda brought the baseball bat down onto the gravel driveway with a mighty thud, causing a geyser of pebbles to erupt. She narrowed her eyes. "I got a dog," she said. "A sweet little rascal, he is, too. Lord Nelson, I call him. Purebred English bulldog."

"I bet Nelson looks just like his mistress," Heather said in a low tone. I noticed she kept well in back of me though, for all her brave repartee.

Luckily, Wanda hadn't heard a thing. "I don't hold with dog-fighting," she continued. "So I'll tell you this, gals. Third Friday of every month, there's a steady stream of pick-ups heading up that road of Collins's. I've heard stories at the Wander Inn, too—been invited to come and watch the fun, even. Don't have the stomach for that kind of sport, though. Maybe...maybe it would be good to break it up. For the poor old dogs, you know. Not for you two snoops."

"Thank you, Wanda. Can we call on you, if we need a witness?"

"You do that, and you'll be fucking sorry," Wanda said. "That Collins—he's a cold bastard, snooty and stuck on himself, thinks he's too good for us ordinary folks. I don't plan to get on his wrong side. Us being neighbors and all. You just go and do your sneaking around by yourselves. Got a policeman friend, don't you?"

"Eh..." I stalled. I sure didn't want to bring Stone Stern into Wanda's gun sights.

Just then Heather's cell phone rang. It played a few tinny bars of "Born Free," really startling in the shadowy, silent parking lot.

"Oh, dear," Heather listened to the excited voice. "Well, don't worry. Cass and I are just leaving. No, we're okay. Yes, it was a regular bloody shambles, all right. Thanks, Brooke." She clicked off. "We'd better get out of here."

"Collins?" I asked.

"Left the party early. Apparently he's got some kind of silent alarm connected to his cell phone. Warns him if there's a break-in."

Wanda laughed meanly and slapped her thunder thighs.

"A word of warning, sisters. He keeps a Glock 34 competition pistol in his glove compartment. Showed it to me once. Claims to use it for target practice at the Plymouth Gun Club. You two better hop on your ponies and vamoose."

"Thanks, Wanda. If you change your mind and want to be a witness..." I said. Wanda scowled blackly. "Anyway, we're out of here."

Heather and I jumped into the RAV4 and took off down 3A in a splatter of gravel.

"I hope to Goddess that villain doesn't destroy all his dogs because of this," Heather said grimly as I sped home through the darkness.

I was silent for a moment, saying an inward prayer of gratitude to whatever guardian spirit had got us out safely from that repulsive cellar.

"When the law gets into Collins' establishment, the animal control people are going to recommend that the dogs be put down anyway," I reminded her. "Fight trained pit bulls...American Staffordshire Terriers, I mean...are not considered good candidates for retraining and placement in a normal home."

"Yeah? Well, I will take every one of those fellas, and they'll be fine, just fine. You should observe how well Wendy and Captain Hook are coming along under Maury's care."

"Then you'll have to talk fast to take those fighters into your shelter when this whole thing busts open."

"I can do that," Heather said. "If that poor little Golden lives long enough, I want her, too. And I've got a cousin at

City Hall, keeps me legal with the dog pack at home." She reached into the back seat, grabbed her bright blue parka, and slipped into it.

That reminded me. "I sure hope there's nothing about that leather jacket you used to baffle Killer Dog that will identify you to Hugh Collins. We could have a bit of a problem there."

Heather was silent, not a good sign.

"There wasn't anything, was there?"

"I'm not sure," she said finally, "what I might have had in the pockets. I mean, there really wasn't time to check. I had to act fast, you know that."

"Oh, shit," I said. "If there was something, what would it be?"

"Hmmm. I'm thinking. Might have had a credit card receipt from the gas station. I'm not quite certain. Or one of the shelter's business cards."

The more nervous I got, the more my foot rode the gas pedal. I forced myself to slow down to the speed limit. Immediately, the car behind me honked with impatience.

Heather put her hand out the window and gave him the finger. Not the usual road-rage finger, but the witch's wand finger, the small pointed one.

The driver dropped back a car length, as well he might.

"You mean, the card on which is printed, *Animal Lovers Shelter, a no-kill refuge for dogs and cats, Heather Morgan Devlin, Manager* with address, phone number, and cell phone?" I demanded.

"Not my cell. But the rest of it...pretty much as you say."

"*Jumping Juno*! You know, Heather, I think the time has come for you to warn Dick what you've been up to this evening. Just in case Collins shows up, with or without his Glock, and makes trouble."

At that moment, I was driving into the circular driveway of the Morgan manse, and out came the very man himself. He looked worried and seemed to be in a hurry.

Heather rolled down her window. "What's up, Honey?"

"It's Joe. He's been trying to reach you, Cass. I guess...now don't get excited. He sounded all right. Cheerful, you know. But he just wanted to give you an update on his expedition. So you won't worry."

A thousand scary scenarios tumbled through my mind. The curse of a vivid imagination. "He gave you a phone number?"

"Yes, honey, he did. But he said not to get anxious, he's getting the best of care. He's in the New Zealand Memorial Hospital, Floor 6. And he asked me to remind you that there's a time difference."

CHAPTER TWENTY

My wish is to ride the tempest, tame the waves, kill the sharks;
I will not resign myself…

– Trieu Thi Trinh

Practically pushing Heather out of the car, I drove home at fever pitch. As soon as I got inside, I rushed Scruffy and Raffles onto the porch where they could avail themselves of the pet door. Then I dashed into my office and checked world time on my computer. Nine o'clock my time was two o'clock in the afternoon in New Zealand—*the next day*! How can that be? The mind staggers. But still, a decent hour to call.

The nurse who answered at the Orthopedic Surgical Center was not a gold mine of information. *Your husband is in stable condition. It's a tibia fracture. I'm sorry, I don't know how serious. He's still being evaluated and treated. Yes, I'll have him call you as soon as he returns to his room. Room 666. Did I say something funny, M'am?*

It was three frantic hours (five in the afternoon New Zealand time, midnight in Plymouth) before Joe called back. How reassuring it was to hear his voice!

"Sorry, sweetheart. I know you've been worrying. I just couldn't get away sooner. They've had to put my leg in a cast, dammit. *Plaster fixation*, they call it. It's the most conservative treatment."

"Good. I'm in favor of conservative medicine. But a cast! Does that mean you'll have to stay there for weeks and weeks? Oh, how damnable is that!"

"No, no. Let's concentrate on the upside, sweetheart. At least it wasn't an operation and a metal pin in my leg."

"Oh, sure, the Pollyanna outlook."

"You bet. Although I never read that blasted book. But here's the deal—the company is going to arrange for me to be flown home on a suitably equipped airplane as soon as the doctors here are convinced there's no infection or other trauma, just a nice clean fracture. I've been warned I may have to wait as long as two weeks, though. But not on this floor. I'll be in a rehabilitation wing on the first floor. That will be good. It's spring here, you know, daffodils and the whole works. Nice to get outside. But I'll have to use crutches, of course, until the cast is removed."

"Never mind stumping through the tulips. How long exactly before they release you?"

"Depends on the X-rays. When the fracture shows healing."

"Joe, how in Hades did this happen? Don't you recall promising me to stay on the ship and out of trouble when you encountered the whale killers?"

There was a long pause while my beloved assembled his palatable truths and outright lies. Not that I wouldn't have done the same myself. "I did for the most part. But then the captain of the Japanese whaler tried to imprison the guys who'd confronted him. Just young volunteers, you know. And none of them could understand what the Japanese captain was shouting. Well, what can I say? It looked as if our kids were going to get beat up and thrown into some foul brig on a rusty old whaler. So..."

"So..."

"I got into it." Joe said this in a matter-of-fact tone, as if, *what else would you expect?*

"What exactly does that mean?" Honestly, a gal could have quite enough of this macho bullshit.

"As it happened, our cook on the *Esperanza* spoke Japanese. He's a physics professor—Haruo Sato—who volunteers for Greenpeace on his sabbaticals. I pulled Sato out of the galley and into a skiff. We rowed over and boarded the whaler."

"Rowed? What kind of seas were you in?"

"Calm enough. The other guys had the motor boat. So anyway, Sato bowed and asked politely what the captain planned to do with our colleagues. The captain lectured Sato for several minutes. I don't know what he said, but his tone was harsh and Sato looked flushed and miserable. Then a couple of sailors came up, making rude gestures that threatened to flip Sato over the side. Well, what could I do? Before we were done scuffling, I got knocked down and someone jumped on my leg. When they realized that they had really injured me, they decided to send the whole crew back to the *Esperanza*, so that was all to the good. Moving into the skiff hurt like blazes, though."

"Where the hell was Captain de Greif while all this was going on?"

Joe chuckled wryly. "Shouting for Sato and me to come back with the skiff. Sadly, we couldn't hear him. He was glad enough to get the crew back, so that was that."

"What about the poor whales?"

"The *Esperanza* will stay to hassle the whalers. De Greif plans to discourage the killing with all means at his disposal.

That's why I had to be air-lifted back to the hospital in New Zealand."

"Ceres save us! I guess I should be glad you're still in one damaged piece. So I'll postpone scolding until you get home, honey. And I hope this means you'll be given a good long time to rest and recuperate."

"Hey, sweetheart, I won't be completely incapacitated, you know. Just because my leg's in a cast..." Joe's voice lowered to that sexy range that does something melting to my second chakra.

"Love will find a way," I said. "After all, your other parts are working, aren't they?" And more in that vein. Eventually we hung up, with Joe promising to call the next day between bed baths and other fun procedures.

Well past midnight, but I couldn't sleep. I'd let the dogs into the bedroom just for the comfort of their quiet breathing. I lay with a cold cloth scented with sage oil on my forehead, a cup of chamomile tea on the night table, and sandalwood incense smoldering in a lotus burner, while I made a mental list of magical matters pending.

I soon realized that the number of serious issues on my agenda was far too complicated to be retained in the brain of a woman whose short-term memory was fast becoming frayed around the edges. And we were planning our emergency ritual for—*horrors!*—tomorrow night here at my house. Well, I would just have to pull myself together right now. There were crises that needed to be resolved. I would not allow myself to faint and fail like a Victorian heroine; I would get my magic spells organized!

I cast the cold cloth aside and dragged myself over to the small maple desk that had once been my grandma's. Recently I'd had the occasion to mix up some dragon's blood ink, and I'd grown rather fond of it. Now I used an old-fashioned quill pen to jot down in crimson letters the formidable to-do list for Sunday.

1. Healing magic for Joe's tibia fracture.

2. Safe flight home as soon as possible.

3. The arrest of Hugh Collins for promoting dog fighting, preferably before he went after Heather with his Glock.

4. A clean up of Collins' operation, with Heather taking charge of the dogs' rehabilitation.

5. Exposure of Marie and Therese's real murderer, Albert Reynard, ideally revealed by himself.

6. And let's not forget poor little Ashling Malone needs a job and a home.

Feeling that I had fought the good fight (or, I was *going to*) I headed back to bed. But first, I pulled my grandma's shawl out of the closet and wrapped it around me. It enveloped me in the clean scent of lavender and the warmth of memory, and soon after, I fell into the deep sleep that calms the anxious heart.

CHAPTER TWENTY-ONE

Mistress, there are portents abroad of magic and might,
And things that are yet to be done. Open the door!

– Elizabeth Jane Coatsworth

Deidre arrived first, looking like Red Riding Hood in her peaked red wool hat, a work basket over her arm. "Merry meet! Samhain is in the air," she exclaimed. "That old thin veil is parting, and I've been seeing things again. Holy Mother! I don't know if I'm going to like this new *crazy business* at all. It's just like one of those *I-see-dead-people* TV shows. Bishop Guilfoyle called it a 'glamourous power.' *Give me a break*!" Deidre rattled on as if she might be slightly high. I wondered if she'd been having a few too many "drops of the Irish" in her tea.

"Sit down and relax, Dee. You could ask the good bishop for an exorcism."

Deidre perched on the edge of a kitchen chair and hooted. "Not on your life. I have no intention of falling back into the paternal fold, my dear. But don't you want to know *who*'s been haunting me?" She reached into her basket for a cushion-cover, flower faeries, and laid it on the table to admire. Letters of pink and green were being embroidered beneath a garden scene. *Faeries are flowers that never fade.*

Deidre seeing another ghost! Sometimes those who've been murdered simply refuse to rest in peace. A mad idea raced through my thoughts. "Don't tell me, let me guess. Did the specter you saw bear any resemblance to Marie Reynard?"

"Therese, I think. Young, beautiful, lingering on this plane for justice, just like that drowned bride last year. Obviously, something must be done about her death and her mother's. Even if we're the ones who have to do it." Deidre's small sharp needle pierced the fabric decisively.

"*Tell me everything.* Any element might be a key."

"Eh, later maybe," Deidre said, for just then Fiona puffed in the back door on a wave of cold October evening. She was wrapped in a tartan cloak, lugging her reticule, and sporting a brand-new walking stick topped with a silver coyote head. Coyote, wily shapeshifter, was one of her totem animals.

Heather strode in right after, carrying the moldering Book of Shadows Fiona had found at a library sale. It was covered in leather so old, it had turned purplish-black, and anything that touched the cover was marked by its dark silken dust.

"Merry meet, my dears," Fiona cried with great good cheer, silver bangles clattering as she hugged us in turn. Two round spots of rouge on her plump cheeks put me in mind of a Kewpie doll. A crochet needle and two pencils were stuck in her coronet of carroty-gray braids, marking this as one of her more addled days.

"Where?" said Heather, holding up our precious reference. "Fiona said this was the one for tonight's work. *Hazel's Book of Household Recipes* is a tad too cautious."

"I've set up an altar in the dining room this time," I said. "I thought we might need the table. I'll have some ginger tea ready in a minute." After hotting the pot, I put in several slices of candied ginger as well as bags of Asian tea. China tea cups (pottery mugs always got a raised eyebrow from Phillipa) were set out on the kitchen table.

"An owl has come to visit us at the library," Fiona recounted with breathless drama. "Owls are spiritual teachers, you know. I've named her Blodeuwedd and invited her to make a home in that great old oak at Black Hill Point."

"Blodeuwedd?" I asked the obvious.

"Celtic flower goddess who was turned into an owl. Rather the opposite of the frog and the prince, don't you think?"

Sometimes trying to follow Fiona's train of thought made me feel a bit lightheaded.

"You speak owl?" Deidre inquired, beginning to embroider with green thread.

Fiona hooted a few rather authentic-sounding owl calls. Moments afterwards we heard two thumps upstairs, as Scruffy and Raffles leapt off the twin beds and racing downstairs from their retreat in the blue guest room.

Where's that feathered freak hiding? Just let me find the hooting little bastard. I'll take him out for you! Scruffy began to root around the corners of the room, snarling menacingly.

Take him out! Take him out! Raffles danced after his sire. A new game was afoot!

"I'm surprised at you. There's no owl here, there's just Fiona," I said sternly.

"No offense, Fiona. She's just talking to the dogs again," Heather explained wearily. "We're all agog at your feathered messenger from the Cosmos."

"None taken," Fiona said. "Cass's rapport with her doggies is a joy to behold. Omar doesn't exactly talk to me, but he listens more intelligently than many humans, I find, and I bet Cass feels the same."

"Present company excepted," I said.

"Oh, goodie, here's Phil," Deidre sprang up to hold the door open for Phillipa and the picnic basket she was toting.

"For cakes and ale," Phillipa said, "after the work." The fragrance of exotic dried fruits, sweet rich spices, and savory cheeses wafted past our noses as she opened her basket and set out her goodies. Scruffy and Raffles interrupted their search to sniff the kitchen counter.

"Cass, will you get these beasts out of here!" Phil commanded. Her tone was severe but a cookie in each hand descended to dog-nose level and was speedily accepted.

"Okay, you two. Back upstairs," I ordered. "You know how you despise incense."

Frankly, Toots, I prefer a nicely rotted fish. So good for my handsome coat. That stinky incense stuff gives me a headache. Scruffy trudged back to his retreat, pained resignation in every step.

Stinky stuff! Stinky stuff! Raffles pranced joyfully after his leader.

Coats were deposited in my office, and we all trooped into the dining room, where I'd cleared the buffet to set up an altar with a purple damask runner, candles of various colors, crystals, salt water, incense, my crimson-lettered list, bouquets of mums and colorful leaves, and our traveling triptych of Hecate. Heather deposited her book on the dining room table, which I'd closed up to its smaller size to leave room for moving around.

"Ugh," Deidre whispered, eyeing the decrepit volume. "It looks like something that might have belonged to Snow White's Wicked Stepmother."

We lit candles, invoking the spirits of the four directions and offering a divination bouquet of incense: frankincense, sandalwood, lavender, and cinnamon. I cast our circle with my athame, a plain jane dagger with a carved wood handle, blackened with age, that I'd found in my grandma's gardening basket when I inherited this cottage by the sea. Purified and blessed, of course, as Goddess knows where it had been—cleaning fish, for all I knew.

Healing was our first work. Heather's bloodhound Trilby was ailing—Lyme disease—and Wendy, the traumatized pit bull, was still cowering away from people and other dogs, although Captain Hook was becoming cautiously social with the kennel staff. Fiona's suitor Mick Finn, the Plymouth Fire Chief, was in hospital suffering from kidney stones. I included Ashling Malone as well. The poor pale widow looked like a wraith in need of a strong iron tonic. We added those four names to Joe's already lettered on my dragon's blood healing list.

After we'd held hands and released our prayers to the Divine Source of All Healing, it was time to face up to the evil in our midst. I admit that I felt a little Dianic thrill of the hunt, even while reminding myself of our high-minded objectives.

Ours is an unstructured circle; we took all the time we needed to view Heather's cell phone video of the dirty business going on beneath the neat white buildings with spanking green shutters at Hugh Collins' showplace horse farm. Phillipa agreed to show the video to Stone. It would be a tricky business, however, for her detective husband to find a legal cause to investigate Fresh Meadow. As if we needed reminding, Phillipa pointed out to Heather and me how entirely illegal had been our foray into Collins' hidden activities.

"What were we supposed to do?" Heather demanded. "Allow more dogs to be mauled and discarded in the woods like poor Wendy and Captain Hook?"

"*Wendy?*" Phillipa lifted one slim black eyebrow.

"One of those beat-up pit bulls the Devlins rescued," I muttered. "American Staffordshire Terriers," I corrected myself, glancing at Heather's frown. "It's a sweet name, really. Poor little thing has hardly any teeth. The bastards filed them down to nubs so they could use her as bait dog."

"What a heartless sod," Phillipa said.

"The thing is, we need to put on our little pointy black hats and spellbind that 'heartless sod' so that the whole disgusting business comes to light," Deidre said, stabbing the Book of Shadows with her little finger. "It isn't as if one of the dogs is going to call the SPCA. So I guess it's up to us."

"Right," Heather agreed briskly. "Now—do we have anything in this grimoire that will blow the roof right off that indoor arena? And take Hugh Collins with it?"

"Now, now," Fiona admonished in a mild reasonable tone. "Spells always work better when the explosions are left to the Cosmos to ordain."

"It's doable," I said. "Not the blow-up hex, though. Think of the possible collateral damage. Innocent civilian animals might be injured. So what we want is just a sensible *put-your-own-head-into-the-noose* kind of spell. But we also need something very similar for Albert Reynard." I related my vision of Reynard kneeling over his barely conscious wife and pushing a pillow over her face to stop her breathing. The horror of remembering what my third eye had seen must have made me a little green around the gills, judging by the concern in the faces that surrounded me.

I'd told them all before, naturally, but I couldn't remember if everyone had heard the whole story, complete with the case of expensive French wines presented to me by the grieving matriarch in hopes that I would help her to find justice. It seemed clear enough that Madame Therese de Rochmont wanted the truth at all costs, and I felt she deserved that. Perhaps she suspected her own son-in-law (not the degenerate home invaders) of complicity in the murders of the two who were closest to her heart.

"We ought to break open some of that exquisite burgundy tonight," Heather suggested. "Might help the spell, you know."

"It must have been a money thing that bothered Madame de Rochmont," I mused. "I wouldn't be surprised to learn that Marie was contemplating a divorce, leaving Albert high and dry in bankruptcy court with his two French money pits."

"Those 'money pits,' as you call them, are both very fine restaurants," Phillipa declared. "Oh well, I suppose he might have been wiser not to open the second Chez Reynard Aussi when the first one hadn't really got off the ground, except with the summer tourist trade. Clearly, he is over-extended. Or was. He'll surely be in better shape if he sells that million-dollar property he's inherited."

"Three million," Deidre corrected. "Their joint property is listed for three million five. By the way, it's still called the Chateau Marie. Albert sure married himself a cash cow when he got that de Rochmont heiress. And the girl." Deidre sighed. "Did you all hear that I saw another specter, and we think it was Therese? Only lasted a few moments. I could see right through her, and if you don't think that's unsettling! Her hands stretching toward me as if imploring that I do something. I'll tell you, it gave me quite a turn when I realized that she was holding out a rosary, and the beads were dripping this viscous *stuff*. Holy Mother! Somehow I sensed that she'd been through a bad time with that step-father of hers. I suppose most of the estate would have been Therese's, if she had lived."

Fiona had been absently listening and humming while she paged through the Book of Shadows. Now she muttered, "*Ah ha*. The very thing."

The rest of us were immediately hushed as if the Oracle of Delphi had just woken from her sleep.

Fiona looked up at me with her round gray eyes shining behind the little half-tracks. "Cass, dear, do you happen to have any *Salvia divinorum?*"

Heather smirked. "Going on a little journey, are we?"

"Not us, dear. Hugh Collins. Albert Reynard. And Kali, we will need Kali-Ma to perform this spell," Fiona said. I could see her drawing herself up into a full-fledged glamour—an aura of unquestionable authority. She marked her place in the decrepit dusty book with a faded, raveling indigo ribbon. "There! This one!"

We all leaned over the yellowed parchment, breathing in its familiar musty smell. Phillipa read the recipe aloud.

That the Truth May Be Revealed

All praise to dark, divine Kali-Ma who aids us
to reveal the hidden crimes of the heart.
After casting your circle, you will light three candles: Purple, Gold, Black.
You will anoint your bodies with oil of rosemary and mint for power and protection.
You will burn herbs of divination, dried Salvia Divinorum and Dragon's Blood.
You will breathe incense of myrrh.
You will pass a Tiger's Eye through the smoke three times.
You will hand the Tiger's Eye from one to the other.
You will name the ones whose secrets you seek seven times.
You will raise a cone of power and release the spell to Kali.
So Mote It Be.

"Wow!" Deidre breathed. "This is, like, high magic. Can we afford to get ourselves in this deep?"

"Can we afford not to?" Heather said.

Deidre continued her whine. (Having the odd ghostly visit must really be getting on her nerves.) "I mean, didn't we start out this circle of ours just wanting to celebrate the ancient holidays and bring something of the feminine divine into our lives?"

"Yes, but then Cass involved us in her blasted visions and the next thing we knew, we'd become a psychic posse, suburban Wonder Women," Heather reminded her. "But all that's beside the point now...what about those poor dogs?"

"Dogs, yes. But also that tragic mother and daughter, murdered so that Reynard could fund his failures," I said. "Also I'm worried about targeting two different situations—won't that weaken the spell?"

"Not at all! We simply must infuse the spell with twice as much spiritual power," Fiona declared firmly. Already she looked two inches taller, imperious as an ancient queen.

"Wait here. Chant to Kali or something. I'm going downstairs to collect the ingredients," I said.

"Does anyone have a tiger's eye?" I heard Heather asking as I departed to the cellar with an empty apple basket.

"Oh, it's right here somewhere in my bag," Fiona replied. "Actually I brought one for each of us to keep. More powerful that way, don't you think? We can all eyeball it every morning and refresh our intention."

I smiled and went to fetch the Salvia, Dragon's Blood, Myrrh., and essential oils of various herbs. Upon consideration, I threw in a head of garlic as well. I thought about all the spells that all the women throughout the ages had secretly concocted in their kitchens. Surely each one added her own special touch to insure its potency. Like a recipe for chicken soup, really. No two ever tasted exactly alike. And in this case, for this cause, my psychic soup would contain a few bulbs of garlic. What's good against vampires might protect us from human devils as well.

CHAPTER TWENTY-TWO

All the familiar horrors we
Associate with others
Are coming fast our way:
The wind is warning in our tree
The morning papers still betray
The shrieking of the mothers.

– Philip Larkin

Looking around at the intent faces of my friends, I couldn't help but wonder if they, like me, carried that tiny seed of doubt in their inner selves—*does this stuff really work?* We were organizing one of our more elaborate spells, and a double whammy as well. Not our first get-the-bad-guy magical campaign, but we'd never really know *for sure* that it was our spell and not pure chance that had brought these villains down. But we were always careful to avoid anything that remotely resembled a hex or curse—Goddess forbid! This was Plymouth, Massachusetts, after all, home of the puritan ethos not voo-doo enchantments.

We followed the Book of Shadows' arcane directions to the letter, intoning the double charm seven times. *Hugh*

Collins, let your wicked ways come to light. Albert Reynard, reveal your evil murders to the world. All the while, passing our tiger eyes through the heady incense that filled the room.

This time, we focused our energy by chanting the many names of the Goddess, our slow shuffle around the room building up speed along with our invocation, until we were dancing around the grimoire and singing out the litany. When it got too much to bear, I signaled, we threw our hands skyward—and practically fell back to earth ourselves.

By the time we finished our intricate spellworking that Sunday, we were fairly well exhausted. *Especially me,* I thought, with everything that had gone on the past few days. That disastrous kiss on my hand at Chez Reynard and the ugly vision that followed. The terror of breaking into Fresh Meadow with Heather of the madcap schemes. Joe's dangerous exploits and the anxiety of being separated while he recuperated from his latest mishap. And now this almost-dark-energy effort to bring justice into balance. *Whew!*

Raising the cone of power had been a divine experience, though.

Which was exactly what Heather said. Before we got into our spellwork, she had expertly opened some impressive red wine from the de Rochmont cache, applying my old wine-opener with her usual vigor. Now she gave the wine a rapturous sniff, then filled stemmed glasses all around "Divine! I felt the power surging in all my seven charkas, and then some! Now let's get grounded with this really fine wine."

In the respectful silence that accompanied the first taste, I heard an unfamiliar sound outside the dining room windows, a kind of stumbling, crashing noise. "What's that?" I peered from the candlelit room into the darkness beyond the panes of glass and saw nothing. I looked around at the others; they, too, had heard the clatter.

Without another thought, I ran into the kitchen and out onto the porch, where I glimpsed a bundled-up figure pushing his way through the lilac bushes beside the garage. I could hear the dogs rushing downstairs, so I banged the kitchen door shut before they could follow me. I don't know what I thought I could do—tackle the guy?—but nevertheless, I dashed out the door into the yard.

"Who's there? What do you want? Show yourself!" I heard Fiona right behind me calling after the departing figure. I stopped and turned around to ask what she had seen. Instantly I sprang back as I saw that Fiona seemed to brandishing a long, thin rapier! It looked deadly sharp as the light from the house glinted off its shining steel.

Of course. That stick. Coyote, you old trickster!

"Fiona, for Goddess' sake," I cried angrily. "Put away that thing before you take out someone's eye." *Like mine!*

Heather and Deidre were still inside, trying to see through the dining room windows, but Phillipa had rushed out after Fiona.

"Fiona, what in Hades have you got *now?*" she cried crossly. "I really thought that when Heather tossed your pistol overboard from the cruise ship, that would be the end of your being a walking armory."

Fiona stuck the blade back into its sheath and smiled with infuriating aplomb. "A true Scot never goes out without her weapons, my dear."

Was it only I who detected the plural? But I had other matters to worry about at the moment. "*Who was that*, do you think? Someone spying on us? I sure hope whoever it was didn't hear us too clearly." The unknown person had disappeared beyond the garage into the woods. "Especially while we were working up that Kali spell against Collins and Reynard. My reputation with the neighbors is questionable enough."

"Hey, Cass! Reality check," Phillipa reminded me. "I doubt very much that trespasser was just a local busybody. More likely, an unknown intruder, perhaps no more savory than the two who invaded the Reynard home."

"Cass, dear, do you have any reason to suppose that either Hugh Collins or Albert Reynard has guessed that we're on to him?" Fiona asked.

The moonless October night was suddenly colder. I shivered. "Heather may have left a business card in the pocket of her leather jacket. The one she threw over the pit bull's head when we escaped from that cellar. Then there's Reynard. Do you suppose he might have heard about Madame de Rochmont's interest in me?"

There had been something familiar, I realized now, about the figure that ran away in the night—the shoulder, the way he hunched, like a football player huddled over the ball. A memory was tugging at my consciousness but it just wouldn't come up into view. *Damn!*

"Listen." Phillipa held up her hand. "Is that a car starting up? Just beyond those pines?"

"Hard to tell," I said. "Being near the water always plays tricks with sound. Anyway, he'll be long gone before we can run up there."

After a few more pointless moments outside, we went back into the house where I had to face my two frustrated canine companions.

Hey, Toots—what's up here? Why did'ya leave us cooped up here with the ladies? No fair, keeping all the fun for yourself! Some dangerous stranger was out there in the dark, you know. We canines, with our superior senses, could have run him down for you in a heartbeat. Scruffy barked sharply at me with his best alpha dog stare.

Run him down! Run him down! Raffles scratched at the kitchen door hopefully. This was the door that Joe had recently sanded and refinished, installing a bright new deadbolt lock. He would not be best pleased to find it marked up again.

"Pipe down, you guys. Cut that out, Raffles. You two will get plenty of chances to chase around tomorrow."

Oh, yeah, sure. When there's nothing out there to run after but ratty squirrels. Alpha dog stalked off to his kitchen bed and plunked himself down with a deep accusative sigh, closely followed by his ever-faithful offspring. Raffles even managed to emit a small echoing moan. *Ratty squirrels. Ratty squirrels.*

Depositing two conciliatory cookies on their beds, I bustled into the living room to light a fire and dispel this gloomy development. There were aromatic apple and pungent pine logs to burn, and I threw on some branches of dried sage as well. We drank the de Rochemont wine (even I could tell that it was a superior vintage indeed) with cautious toasts to the ultimate success of our efforts. And we ravaged the sweets and savories that Phillipa had brought in her basket. Sugary stuff is positively medicinal after experiencing a touch of the weird.

"Cass, you must have some idea," Deidre said. "You're the seer. Gaze into the firelight or something."

"I can't turn it on whenever I want to. I'm not some blasted light switch," I whined. Really, I got tired of their thinking that my clairvoyance was on call. "If it were that easy, wouldn't I have known the moment Joe got himself in trouble? But no, I hadn't a clue until that phone message from New Zealand."

"The art of clairvoyance is more accurate when it involves strangers," Fiona declared. "Emotions often cloud the third eye. Except in the case of a death, of course. If Joe had passed through the veil, you'd have known, because he'd have come to say good-bye before departing for Summerland."

"Thanks for the comforting thought, Fiona." I gazed at the fire sourly. Fingers of flame rose and fell. Bits of ember flickered into the chimney. Pine especially was liable to spark. Breathing in the scent of apple, pine, and sage, I felt peace entering my spirit. Quiet thoughts fell upon us, and no one spoke for several minutes.

Then someone spoke. *It was me.* I heard myself say, "I know who that was." *Did I?*

"Well, who then?" Heather demanded.

I was still listening to myself as if to a stranger. "Kurt Heller. I believe it was Kurt Heller." As my conscious mind had caught up with my intuition, I'd realized that there'd been something quite familiar about that figure and the way he held his body in a half-crouch. The way he'd looked trying to take a puff of nicotine at the jury room window. Or maybe it was a simple psychic flash. Actually, it didn't make any difference how that *knowing* had arrived in my brain. I felt quite confident now of the rightness of my pronouncement.

"Kurt Heller was a member of the jury panel I was on, and he's a pal of Hugh Collins. I believe he was the contractor who rebuilt Fresh Meadow after Collins bought the place," I said with great conviction, as if the thought had not just occurred to me: *builder—new building.*

"So this Heller probably planned the indoor arena with the secret dog-fighting facility in the cellar." Heather had been eagerly following my train of thought.

"Yeah, but his showing up here tonight is a real worry, Heather. You must have left that Animal Lovers business card in your jacket pocket after all, and Collins found it. He's probably connected the dots between Heather and me and the rest of you by now. Everyone who reads the *Pilgrim Times* must know what we do. That story about how we discovered leaking barrels of toxic chemicals that had been dumped at the pig farm, for instance. And before that, the missing family—well, we found the girl alive anyway. Even one of the women on the jury, Anna Grimassi, recognized me. Collins probably sent Heller here tonight."

"We're infamous, all right—thanks to you, Cass. But how could he possibly know we were meeting?" Deidre's round blue eyes looked skeptical.

"Uh oh," Heather said. "I wonder if our intruder was the guy who turned up at the Wee Angels Animal Hospital earlier today. Asking if we had a pit bull needed a home. Ha, ha—*as if!* Poor old Wendy is spooked by everyone except Maury, and Captain Hook is still having socialization issues. Besides, I didn't like this Heller's eyes. Or his smile, either. *Cold, cold, cold.* So I gave him the bum's rush, as my dear mother would have called it. But then I jumped into the old dog car and came along here. He could have followed me—for what, do you suppose?"

Heather's "old dog car" was a lovely Mercedes sedan whose windows were perpetually sticky with dog drool.

"Could be to spy on us, or could be something worse," I said gloomily. "I *told* you it was a mistake to break into the Collins place."

"Yes, but you went right along, so don't get all righteous now that we're caught out," Heather said testily. "Oh, if that was Heller, the bastard probably wanted to get his hands on Wendy before we guessed what those scars were. Which Dick figured out as soon as he laid eyes on her."

"Ladies, ladies," Fiona remonstrated. "We must look upon this *visitation* tonight as a Goddess blessing in disguise.

It may signal the beginning of the end for Collins and his vile business, had you considered that? Mark my words, his control over events is unraveling even as we speak. We don't know how and we don't know when—that we have to leave up to the Divine Forces of the Universe. *Time wounds all heels.*"

"Ah, Kali, the Cosmic Avenger," Phillipa crowed. "May She work in Her usual dark, devious, dangerous ways."

"Yeah, and may those two blackguards find themselves hoist with their own petards," was Deidre's *amen.*

"A petard," said Fiona, "is a small bomb or someone breaking wind. I like the idea of the bombardier blowing himself up in the air, don't you?"

"Fiona, do you really know everything?" Phillipa asked.

"No, no, dear, of course not," Fiona replied modestly. "But what I don't know, I can certainly access."

"A computer search?" I suggested.

"Not necessarily," she replied with an enigmatic smile.

Later, when we got to the strong-black-tea stage of the evening, I broached the subject of Ashling to Heather. "A young widow looking for employment, rather a shy nature, needs sheltering for a time. But I've been told by Serena Dove that she's a fine cook, and I can testify myself to her affinity for dogs. Ashling Holmes. Lovely, ethereal young woman. A bit fey, though, I have to admit."

"Hecate preserve me, what exactly do you mean by 'fey,' Cass," Heather asked, rather suspiciously I thought.

Deidre chuckled. "Ashling Malone Holmes is a distant cousin of us Ryans. I've heard she's a treasure. Always rises to the occasion, you might say."

"Well, yes, there is that. I have to say the girl is subject to the odd levitation episode," I said, then hastened to add. "But it used to be worse. She used to be plagued by a poltergeist, who might have been her ex-husband, the drunken poet, but Fiona and I managed to show him the door. The door between the worlds, that is."

"So this is the cosmic answer to my call for a housekeeper? Another weirdo for my collection of eccentric housekeepers?" Heather complained.

"It's so hard to get decent help these days," Phillipa said, winking at me.

"This would just be temporary," I assured Heather, "until Becky figures out a way to shake an allowance out of her late husband's Boston Brahmin family. Like getting blood from a stone statue. But Becky can be very resourceful in a good cause."

Heather smiled suddenly in her dazzling patrician way. "A good cause, you say? Well, then, I guess I can give this Ashling—what kind of a name is Ashling anyway?—a chance to manage the Devlin ménage. We are in desperation mode these days. You don't even want to know what we've been eating, Phil."

"Down to your last tin of Beluga? I shall have to bring you one of my care packages," Phillipa said. "Vegetarian, I presume?"

It was a sensitive point with Heather that she hadn't yet succeeded in giving up free-range chicken and wild-caught fish. "Maury is our only true vegetarian," she admitted.

"Fiona tells us that the name Ashling means *beautiful woman in peril*," I said. "A bit light-footed, but very much in need of someone to watch over her."

"If she can manage to reach poor spooked Wendy, I won't care how much she floats around the place," Heather said. "Easier for her to reach the top shelves, I suppose. That butler's pantry has those eight-foot-high china cabinets."

I felt really good about foisting Ashling onto Heather. Just as she could be counted upon to champion any animal cause, after one look at the abused widow, Heather would surely take the girl under her protective wing. Ashling, after all, was in just as much need of TLC as Wendy.

CHAPTER TWENTY-THREE

How else can I explain
those rainbows when there is no rain,
it's magic.

– Sammy Cahn

Joe's homecoming a week later quite took my mind off our *reveal-yourself-you-bastard* spell and the mysterious intruder I believed to be Kurt Heller. Since Joe wouldn't be able to drive his customary rental, I had the grueling task of finding my way to the Arrivals gates at Logan Airport. He'd been entrusted to the care of airport special needs personnel, and they were waiting for me at the curb, Joe in a wheelchair wearing his usual nautical pea coat, with duffle bag and crutches in tow. His Greek cap was set at a jaunty angle, and his Aegean blue eyes were as arresting as they'd been the first time I'd encountered them in Jenkins's woods. *Even beat-up and in a wheelchair, he's still a hunk*, I thought.

Things being as they were, our embrace lacked its usual steaminess, but how wonderful it felt just to hold him close and inhale his familiar scent, like herbs on a summer hill. And I was partial to herbs. Surely everything that had been going wrong would be all right now. The man carried with him that macho air of confident power that's both comforting and annoying to a woman. I wondered if he had that same reassuring affect on nervous Greenpeace volunteers as he had on me. They certainly must have believed he would leap to their defense in a heartbeat. Not that Joe would be doing any leaping in the near future. Still, I felt safer and more secure with him beside me.

"I didn't really need that wheelchair," he assured me as soon as I was weaving my way out of the Logan maze. "I can manage just fine with crutches."

I glanced at his right leg stretched out under the dashboard. The cast had a bluish look.

"What happened to all those autographs? Did you wash them off?"

Joe looked at me sharply. Wondering, no doubt, if I could "see" what had been written there. I gave him my Mona Lisa inscrutable smile.

"The crew, you know, couldn't resist doodling on all that white space. Not the thing to show off on a plane, however."

"Racy stuff? There were girls, then, on this expedition?"

"A couple," he admitted.

I let it go *for now*. "I'm glad to have you home in one piece, cast or no cast," I said. Perhaps my tone was a little too heartfelt. Knowing me as he did, Joe figured I'd got myself into hot water...again.

"You'd better catch me up on what's been going on, sweetheart. Or should I say, how much mischief have you been stirring up? Start with the trial...it ended with a plea bargain, you said? *Not with a bang, but a whimper.*"

So I filled him in on all the seamy details I hadn't shared while he was in hospital in New Zealand. "I didn't want to worry you," I explained, "*but here's the real deal...*"

It took much of the drive home to unburden my conscience of everything he didn't know (and wouldn't have approved of if he did.) How my new suspicions (and visions) about the murders had evolved after the trial had been stopped short. Madame de Rochement's appeal to me for justice. I told him, too, about being called in by Serena Dove to help Ashling, the destitute widow soon to be employed by Heather, and the impromptu exorcism organized by Fiona to rid the girl of her dead husband. Then there was the tale of Heather's crusade against dog-fighting and our "visit" to Fresh Meadow Farm. Finally, I mentioned the intruder who had been seen skulking around the bushes last week. By the time I'd finished the whole incredible saga, we were well past Quincy and Braintree, heading south on Route 3 for Plymouth and home.

From time to time, Joe swore or groaned at some detail, or asked irate questions, such as "Why in God's name did you have to break into a place full of killer dogs?" and "You mean you believe it's up to you to bring some damned French wife murderer to justice?" and "What the Christ was Heller doing skulking around our house? You should have let old Scruff loose to bring him down, and then called the cops to throw his ass in jail," and so forth.

"Scruffy agrees with you big time, but I didn't want him or Raffles to get hurt," I explained. "I guess to me, they're love objects, not guard dogs. But now I have you to be my protector."

"Oh, yeah—some protector with this bum leg. I wonder if Fiona has an extra pistol she can loan me during the emergency?" Joe said.

"Not just pistol, honey," I warned him. "Now she has one of those fancy-dancy walking sticks that conceals a wicked-looking rapier. Handsome thing, topped with a silver coyote. But you have a blade, too, haven't you? Some fishing thing?"

"Fillet," he said. "Not your regular commando knife. I guess you'll have to protect us by magical means. What is it you do—spells? Smudging? Sachets? Amulets?"

"All of the above," I said. "And don't forget the three arrows on the roof. Supposed to ward off evil attackers. Those I got from Tip, and he fixed them up there for me, too." Tip Thomas, a.k.a. Thunder Pony, was an expert tracker and a fund of shamanistic knowledge. We'd shared some wild adventures in the past, but now he was away at school, taking advantage of tribal grants to study Native American music.

I'd also crushed basil, marjoram, valerian, and elder into a powder and used it to bless the rooms with a light dusting of protection. I'd brushed negativity right out of the house with my cinnamon oil-soaked broom and tacked a sprig of rue to the bottom of the cellar stairs to dispel fears. Once in a while, when the whim struck me, I'd stroll the borders of my property sprinkling a salt blessing. In lieu of a griffin or dragon, we had a totem pole—eagle, bear, and salmon—at the top of the beach stairs, serving as our spiritual watchdog. It has been a gift to Joe from the grateful Native Americans on the Pacific coast whose forest Greenpeace had protected from big lumber interests.

I guess I've got us covered, I told myself. *Of course, that spell we concocted may stir things up a little.* I hadn't mentioned that most recent spell to Joe, because of its obvious dangers. *Time enough for that later, maybe.*

Besides, he'd really had enough excitement for one day. With an injury like a fractured bone, weakness is not confined just to the injured limb, but affects the entire body with an enervating fatigue. As soon as we got in the house, I insisted that Joe lie down quietly in the bedroom and allow me to bring him a tray of soup, toast, and tea. This was to be followed by a nap *to promote healing*, I explained.

Truth to tell, the little lunch and nap didn't go quite as planned when Joe insisted that I lie down beside him, and one caress led to another. *Gently, gently*, I insisted, but no one paid attention. We'd been separated for weeks, and we were too thirsty for each other to resist making love as best we could, considering the liabilities of a cast. That sweet beard of his kept teasing my skin—all over. For a timeless time, I thought of nothing at all but pleasure.

How do two porcupines make love? Very, very carefully.

We both slept, a good restorative nap, and woke refreshed, smiling foolishly to see each other across the pillows. Slanting in our bedroom windows, the afternoon sun shone through the crystals I'd hung there—sphere, heart, and sickle moon– scattering rainbows over our bed. They trembled on the white linens and on our faces and arms like faery blessings.

Quietly then, Joe told me how it had been for him to confront the angry Japanese whalers in the frigid Antarctic waters. The anger, the fear, the determination. Certainly a more impressive adventure than any of mine. Somehow, I always spilled my crazy stories first, while Joe was never in a hurry to tell of his own exploits.

Lunch had been light (but sweet), so we had an early supper in the living room, watching an old favorite DVD of Joe's, *The Hunt for Red October.* We sampled another of the de Rochemont red wines with parchment-wrapped "bandit's lamb" as the Greeks called it). Scruffy admitted to being glad that *the furry-faced guy is back again*, and lay under Joe's tray table, snout pressed close to the socked foot peeking out of the cast.

Raffles, of course, was glad at all times to see anyone—not the best resume for a watchdog. Scruffy tried his best to discourage his offspring's good nature, but Raffles remained affable and out-going.

Where did I go wrong? This crazy mutt thinks we're some bleeding heart golden retrievers. Scruffy growled softly at his grinning offspring.

Patiently I reminded the complaining Scruffy that Raffles' mother, after all, actually *was* a golden retriever, the redoubtable Honeycomb, a registered therapy dog.

Now, as Scruffy detected Joe's injury with his nose, he shot me a meaningful glance. *If you want me to clean up the furry-faced guy's hurt place, you're going to have to take off that big white thing he's got around it. We canines have a superior healing ability, you know.*

"Yes, I know, but it's already been cleaned by cute New Zealand nurses, so he's okay for the time being. Just concentrate on sending him healing vibes instead."

"I suppose you're talking to the dog again," Joe said. "What's he want to do now—take over as practical nurse?"

Maybe another piece of that lamb stuff would improve my healing skills.

"You've had quite enough lamb for now, fella."

"At least, I hope you're talking to that mutt and not me. I was about to ask for seconds," Joe said.

I refilled his plate and our glasses, put another apple wood log on the fire, and snuggled up on the sofa beside my "sailor, home from the sea." At that perfect moment, naturally my cell phone rang. I took the call in the kitchen so that Joe could watch the final scenes of the film, the fake explosion, the Red October cruising silently into the Penobscot River.

It was Heather in a mood of high excitement. "Phil tells me that the State Police are on the look-out for a steady traffic of vehicles arriving at Collins' place some night, especially on Fridays, which might indicate that a fight is scheduled. Frankly, I don't think that idea is worth a damn, do you? It's fairly rural there, so Collins will certainly spot the stake-out and cancel everything. I wouldn't put it past him to kill the dogs and bury them. Clean up the cellar. Destroy the evidence. I can't stand this waiting, Cass. I'm just beside myself. *I want action!*"

"Calm yourself, Heather," I said. "Remember that most criminals are too greedy or too stupid to cover their tracks adequately. Besides, we have that impressive spell in place, so I'm guessing Collins will make some disastrous miscalculation that will expose his operation. It's only a matter of time. Meanwhile, you'd better watch your own back, since we know that Kurt Heller has been sniffing around. You haven't noticed anything unusual, have you?"

"He'd better stay away from us. I've warned Dick and Maury to be on the lookout for some nasty Neanderthal skulking in the bushes. Of course, since I haven't told Dick about our little *adventure* the other night..." She paused. I could hear ice cubes clinking in a glass. Liquid courage, I didn't doubt. "I had to make up a bit of a faery tale about why Collins may have sicced Heller onto us."

"Maybe you'd better tell me exactly what you said, so that we'll get our stories straight. But I can't imagine how you dodged that bullet."

"I told Dick—and Maury, too—that we'd had a perfectly ordinary conversation with Wanda Finch about her neighbor's stables, during which *you'd* asked a couple of innocent questions about the dogs on the place and were there any pit bulls because *you* had a *friend* who was interested in buying a good guard dog. But Wanda must have got the *wrong idea* in her noggin, and thought that we were *investigating* or something, so she told Collins, and Collins sent Heller to intimidate *you*. And I might be next."

"Oh, thanks for making me the heroine of your pulp fiction. And did they believe that load of manure?" But I had to admit to myself that it was a plausible explanation. Heather's resourcefulness never ceased to amaze me.

"Dear Dick did, of course. He never questions me. But I detected a skeptical look in Maury's eye when I launched into my story. Still, I don't think he'll say anything."

"Speaking of Dick and Maury, what do they think of Ashling? Is she working out okay?"

"Oh, yes, I meant to say. She's a fine little cook of the Irish variety. I don't mean boiled-to-death cabbage, but contemporary Irish cuisine, all that fresh fish. Did us a lovely trout almandine. And the most delicate biscuits and whatnot that ever melted in your mouth. I must remember to invite Phil to lunch so I can have the fun of seeing her try to pry recipes out of Ashling, who hardly ever speaks, poor lamb. In many ways, she's like a wounded animal herself. I put her in the Wedgwood blue bedroom. I always think that blue is a healing color, don't you? Especially for head cases."

I knew that bedroom, actually a charming Victorian suite with an aura of serene luxury. Not too many housekeepers got assigned to such lavish quarters. Fanciful moldings with wreaths and cameos, a four-poster mahogany pineapple bed, chaise lounge, and a separate sitting area with an adorable ladies' desk. Tiny balcony overlooking the woods. The bathroom was all white marble with an enormous claw-foot tub. Lying in that bed, looking out at stone circle on the hill that Heather had created and the pine woods beyond, how could anyone remain depressed?

"Excellent choice. And what about that other little problem of hers? Has that given any trouble?"

"Oh, *that.* Light-footed is better than light-fingered, I always say. Dick never noticed a thing, but I wish you could have seen Maury's face when Ashling reached for a platter in the butler's pantry. Ha, ha."

"And the dogs?"

"You were right on there. She's got them all eating out of her hand, literally and figuratively. I'm almost jealous. Ashling is definitely a keeper. Which probably means I'm destined to lose her sometime soon, the way my luck with housekeepers goes. But honor is due, Cass."

"I'll tell Serena Dove. I guess I've cleared that marker."

"You owe her?"

"She sheltered Rose from that brutish Arab husband, you recall?"

"Right. I do now. Well, I'm very glad indeed to take Ashling off Serena's hands. I suspect there was a bit of consternation among the battered women when Ashling was lodged there with her poltergeist, whom I'm thankful not to have met, and her drifting about like a balloon lady. Say, how's Joe?"

"He's good. Gets around on crutches just fine. I think he's in need of a little home cooking and general cosseting, though."

"Aren't we all. Well, give him my love. And keep thinking of ways to stir things up with Collins."

"I think the cauldron's been stirred enough, Heather."

We'd hardly said good-bye when Becky, my oldest, called. She sounded tired.

"Hard day, dear?"

"You wouldn't believe it, Mom. Family court can really be the most stressful place. Sad and frightening cases. Abused children afraid to testify. Vengeful wives. Threatening husbands. The occasional outbreak of violence. But never mind that for now—I called because I have an idea of how we can pry an allowance for Ashling out of the Holmes family's coffers."

"I knew you'd think of something!" Even as I said that, I had an instant vision. I saw in my mind's eye a book with an eye-catching glossy jacket. "Is it something about a book?"

"Oh for god's sake, Mom. I wish you'd cut out that mind-reading thing! Yes, it's an idea for a book. A book that Ashling could write about her years with the late, lamented genius Archie Holmes. Oh, *not really*. I'm sure the poor girl would be glad to forget all about that bastard. But if the Holmes family should get *the idea* that Ashling is prepared to write a *tell-all* about her years with their precious Archie, only because she needs the handsome advance that any publisher might pay for such a literary expose, it's possible that her in-laws might decide to bestow a decent allowance on the girl after all. It's not as if the tightfisted old sods don't have the money."

"Isn't that just a little tiny bit like blackmail?"

"Yeah, but I bet it will work."

"I think you're right. But I'm not sure that Ashling would be willing to lie to her in-laws. I sense that the girl has her own honor code, and she follows it."

"All I need is Ashling's permission to approach the family about access to Archie's letters, papers, and manuscripts before they are consigned to the bowels of some Harvard library. They will, of course, inquire as to their daughter-in-law's interest, and I will explain that she's working on a manuscript in which several publishers have expressed an interest. A harmless little subterfuge that might turn out to be true, after all. Why shouldn't Ashling consider an autobiography like so many other widows of famous literary figures?"

"Or daughters. Sometimes it's the daughters who pen the really nasty stuff, under the guise of coming to terms with their childhood traumas. But your idea is truly brilliant. You're a genius, dear."

"Thank you, Mom. And don't worry, I'll never write about *my* childhood with Glenda the Good Witch of the West."

"It might put off Johnny Marino's tribe. I suspect they're all good Catholics."

"I love how you segue into my romantic life. So you probably want to know how things are with Johnny Marino?"

"Only if you want to tell me, dear."

"It's over, really over. And there's someone else's name on my dance card now."

"I don't suppose you'd like to tell me about him?"

"As if I ever had to do that! No, Mom, let's just see what you can come up with. But I will give you one tiny hint."

"Only a hint?"

"Yes," Becky said firmly. "And this is it. He's *not* an attorney. Because I'm sick and tired of attorneys. Criminal or corporate, they're all the same lying bastards. But Josh is the other end of the spectrum."

"*Josh?* Josh who?"

"Hey, Mom—sorry! I absolutely have to go now. I promised I wouldn't be late."

"Wait...wait...late for what?"

"*Blithe Spirit.* Can you imagine? An updated revival at the Colonial. Dame Judi Dench, so should be great. Listen, have Ashling call me at K & K tomorrow so I can explain, maybe get her to go along with the scheme. Bye!"

I found myself saying good-bye to a dial tone.

Well, I would just have a *good think* about Josh and see what I could come up with, given those several other senses that Fiona says we all have—sixth, seventh, eighth—what ever. Damn! I'd really liked Johnny Marino, too. He'd reminded me of Joe, only with a slightly darker side to his personality. And an excellent chef, too! Sexy men who cook are not that thick on the ground.

I went back to the living room to tell Joe all the news, but he was sound asleep, sitting up with his foot on the hassock, a dog on each side of him, like big, warm body pillows. Nevertheless, discipline must be maintained.

"Get off that couch, you mutts."

Scruffy raised his head and gave me one of his best alpha dog narrow-eyed looks. *Hey, Toots. I had to take care of the furry-faced guy while he's knocked out—that's the top dog's job. Now I gotta go pee.*

Raffles jumped down and shook himself. *Gotta go pee. Gotta go pee.*

The film had faded to credits. I switched the channel to New England news and let the dogs onto the porch so that they could dash through the pet door. My mind was still occupied with the mysterious Josh. *Blithe Spirit. Noel Coward. There was a writer who knew his clairvoyants. Madame Arcati, the bicycling medium. Got his title from Shelley, of course. "Hail to thee, Blithe Spirit!"* My free association was going into overdrive, but gradually the images on the TV screen took over and began to register in my brain, at first vaguely and then with intense concern.

A bundled-up blonde reporter, standing in front of an ornate wrought iron gate with gothic finials, was interviewing a police officer. I remembered her, always the gal sent out to be blown away by hurricanes, Heidi Hurt. She was pressing for more details about "the strange disappearance of Therese de Rochmont from her Chatham estate, *Beau Rouge,* which was well hidden from the cameras behind that intimidating fence. The officer said the investigation was ongoing and there was no comment at present.

As Heidi reviewed the story in bouncy detail, smile repressed but eyes shining, this morning at eight, when the housekeeper, Elsa Kitchener, had brought up Madame's usual breakfast tray, she'd found the bedroom suite in disarray as if there had been a struggle, its occupant missing. The elderly heiress of the de Rochemont wine dynasty was not to be found anywhere. The cars were all in the garage, the driver had not been called. After a quick search of the grounds by the housekeeper, and her husband, the butler, Maxwell Kitchener, the police had been called to report that the mistress of the estate had gone missing and it appeared that there had been an intruder. Several squad cars had arrived, and a more thorough search had taken place, both inside and outside the fenced property whose back lawns sloped right down to the ocean. Madame de Rochemont, Mrs. Kitchener had declared, was not senile and not in the habit of wandering about at night by herself. "And there you have it," Heidi concluded brightly. "Another potentially tragic mystery in ill-fated de Rochemont family. *Over to you, Harry.*"

I sat down heavily in one of the wing-backed chairs facing the hearth and stared into the blaze. Firelight reflecting off a bronze fireplace shovel dazzled me for a moment. A glaze came over my eyes, and I felt that I was zooming through the night like an astral traveler. A moment later, I came down to earth in a garden where I found myself standing near a small marble statue touched by moonlight. I recognized Dionysus, garlanded with grapes. The figure seemed to be placed at the edge of a garden of raised plots, possibly herbs. Nearby, an arbor was roofed by dark twisted vines. As I looked through the arbor, I saw another garden beyond, with topiary shrubs and marble benches. A man was lifting what appeared to be a door in the ground. He propped it open with a rake and picked up a blanket-wrapped bundle.

At that moment, the dogs began scratching at the back door, and I shot out of my vision as if from a cannon. Nausea overcame me, but I managed to struggle through to the kitchen and let in the impatient canines before they could damage the wood. Scruffy and Raffles ran inside to slurp long drinks of cool water. The kettle was still hot; I made a cup of mint tea with a slice of crystallized ginger and sat at the kitchen table sipping it until the queasiness that always accompanies my clairvoyant episodes passed. After a while, I went back into the living room.

Joe was still dozing on the sofa. The sports newscaster was enthusiastically reliving a local basketball game.

I returned to the kitchen, where the dogs had already settled into their beds. This was news I needed to share; I called Phillipa.

"I was just nodding off," she complained. "Having an early night for once."

"True friends are never supposed to say that," I said. "So wake up and listen. Therese de Rochemont is missing from her Chatham estate, and there were signs of a struggle in her bedroom."

"*Couldn't this have waited until morning?* She'll probably be found wandering in her nightie somewhere down the road."

"Madame de Rochemont is not senile. She's sharp as a dagger. And I saw something."

"*Saw?* As in, *you had a vision?*"

"Right. So tell Stone that she was wrapped in a blanket and probably thrown into some kind of covered pit or well near a topiary garden on her own estate."

"Do you want his superiors to think he's balmy?"

"Okay, just tell him what I saw, then, and let him do whatever he thinks is best. But I couldn't *not* tell him. Even though I know this isn't his case, since it's not Plymouth County. But he's the only law enforcement guy I know who might believe me."

"He's asleep, and dead tired, the poor baby. I'll tell him in the morning, I promise. So…what do you think happened?"

"I think Albert Reynard may have decided to shut up his insistent mother-in-law. If she talked to me—and, let's face it, trafficking with a clairvoyant is a desperate last resort—she must have talked to others about her suspicions. She just wasn't going to let her daughter and granddaughter's murders go unavenged. I don't doubt that she may have begun to harangue the district attorney. Just as he was congratulating himself on closing that nasty case successfully."

"Possibly you're right. There's the glimmer of a motive. But did you actually *see* who it was hauling around a body? If it was a body. Did you think you recognized Reynard?"

"No, I didn't see anything except a man's dark form. It was night, moonlight illuminated the scene. Do you remember how bright that moon was tonight? October. Some call it the Blood Moon."

"Okay, now you're freaking me out," Phillipa complained.

"And there was a statue. Dionysus," I continued. "So if there actually *is* a Dionysus to be found on the de Rochemont grounds, and a topiary garden, there is probably a body in a hole somewhere, too."

"Okay. I'll call you in the morning," Phillipa said. "Maybe Stone can at least inquire about the statue."

"And tell him to find out where Albert Reynard was tonight."

"This evening? Most evenings he can be found at the Chez Reynard in Hyannis, where I took you to lunch, remember?

Monsieur kissed you on the hand, and you flipped out? Honestly, I can't take you anywhere."

"What about the Reynard Restaurant in Chatham?"

"Chez Reynard Aussi?. I believe it's his brother Francis who runs that one. And I've heard some rumors that a certain unsavory element has been muscling in. I rather think the Reynard brothers have been sinking in a quagmire of loans, not all of them legitimate."

"Really! Well, Albert should be sitting pretty once his wife's will is probated."

"Hmmm. Let me look into that. If Madame de Rochemont was considering some sort of civil action..."

"*Let's get Heather!*" An inspiration had struck me. "Ask her if she knows anything about Madame de Rochemont's current legal affairs. Heather's the champ at that sort of local gossip. And after three disastrous divorces, she has a close personal relationship with her own law firm, the old, respectable Borer, Buckley, and Bangs. Especially Bartholomew Bangs, Esquire. Maybe he knows."

"I see you've roped me into another of your Nancy Drew episodes."

I laughed. "Nancy Drew meets Michael Myers of *Halloween.*"

"Speaking of which—it's Samhain in a couple of weeks. And I'm presiding."

"Perfect! Maybe the dead will speak to us," I said.

"I can hardly wait. Can I go back to bed now?"

"Okay. Talk tomorrow then. Early."

After we'd clicked off our cell phones, I heard the *clump, clump* sound of crutches, and Joe was beside me, looking concerned. "What's up? Has there been another murder?"

"Looks as if. In my mind's eye, that is. But as far as the police are concerned, at present it's a missing person case.

Madame de Rochemont.. I told you about her suspicions, remember?"

"And you're guessing she's been murdered? By that same French guy? *Tell me you're not getting yourself involved in this mess.*" Joe's warm blue eyes can turn rather frosty during conversations like this. And we've had more than a few of them.

"Relax, Joe." I tried putting his arms around me. He was about as relaxed as a steel support column. This was definitely the trouble with marriage. Having to explain your actions to someone else. Especially when you weren't one hundred percent sure of what you were doing. Nevertheless, I forged ahead. "I'm not exactly *involving* myself, honey. But because I know what I know, I'm trying to get some official law enforcement person involved. That would be Stone Stern, of course, the only cop who wouldn't think I'm absolutely bonkers. Not that he can investigate the events himself—*Beau Rouge* is not in his district. It's just that I have to *do something, tell someone*. So would you, if you were me."

His arms turned back into arms, and he knocked his forehead slightly against mine. "No use. I guess I'll never knock any sense into you. At least I'm home now with an excellent excuse to stay." He tapped his cast. "There's no way this French guy…"

"Albert Reynard," I murmured.

"…this *Albert Reynard* could possibly find out that you've been fingering him, right?"

"No way at all," I said. Still, I had a small uneasy feeling in the pit of my stomach. I turned away to make myself another cup of mint tea.

"Okay, that's good, then." Joe pulled himself over to the refrigerator and opened its door. Instantly the two dogs, who'd appeared to be sound asleep on their kitchen beds, sprang up alertly and joined him.

I could go for some of that lamb. Or a hunk of cheese. Or a bowl of ice cream.

Ice cream! Ice cream!

Joe opened the freezer and took out a half-gallon of caramel ripple. *Could it be that he heard those two beggars?*

SAMHAIN, OCTOBER 31, THE LAST HARVEST

CHAPTER TWENTY-FOUR

Now the veils of worlds are thin;
To move out you must move in.
Let the Balefires now be made,
Mine the spark within them laid

– *Lore of the Door*, Wren

Early the next morning, I hustled over to Phillipa's place for a conference. I found her watching the New England news channel in her *Architectural Digest* kitchen, her built-in "coffee system" already spitting out two cappuccinos. The fragrance of warm apple coffeecake wafted from a napkin-covered basket on her long marble table. I was glad I'd gone light on breakfast.

Phillipa looked at her watch. "You're so predictable. I knew you would be here at nine-the-latest. Do you know what's going on this morning?"

"No, what? Have they found the body?"

"Not a chance. But Heidi Hurt's camera crew caught Albert Reynard scurrying into the estate a half hour ago. I think they must have been camped out there since before dawn, poor sods. No doubt the cops had invited the old fox in to have a word. There's a chance I may be able to find out if Reynard has an alibi for last night. Stone has a friend on the Chatham police force, someone who owes him a favor."

The endless commercials began, and Phillipa muted the sound. We sipped cappuccino and nibbled the delectable coffeecake.

"Aren't they even looking for the body?" I demanded.

"My sense of it is that they're still treating this as a missing person case, or maybe, by some stretch, an abduction. The local police force, of course, will not want the FBI to get involved. I put a word in Stone's ear about the Dionysus statue, the arbor, and the topiary garden, and he'll try to bring himself to ask his Chatham buddy if there are such items on the grounds of *Beau Rouge.*"

"Have you called Heather?"

"Yes, and she's going to see what she can find out from Bartholomew Bang about any gossip concerning Madame's legal affairs. Apparently Bartie Bang, the old roué, is sweet on our lissome Heather."

"I wonder...well, we'll go over all of this with the others at Samhain. Are you all ready for it? Is there anything I can do?" My offer was a tad hypocritical, since when it came to arranging a feast and decorating for the holiday, Phillipa was a one-woman wonder. It would have served me right if she asked me to bring a pie. I had never made a from-scratch pastry without cursing, although sometimes the pesky stuff came out well after all. Especially if no company was expected.

Phillipa smiled, the smile that lit up her sharp features with an unexpected beauty. "*As if.* Just be prepared for a dynamic Sabbat. I've written some new, and if I do say so myself, *potent* invocations. Perhaps spirits from the Other Side will pierce the veil and liven up our ceremony."

"Gee, I'm all goose bumps. Are you sure I can't bring anything?"

"Just your broom," Phillipa said. "In case we have to fend off any strangelets."

~

That wasn't as weird a suggestion as it had sounded in a coffee-and-apple scented kitchen at nine in the morning. When we celebrated Samhain a few days later, storm clouds scudded restlessly across the night sky, with only occasional glimpses of the stars beyond. Unseasonable thunder cracked a distant whip. Indoors, while the hearth fire in Phillipa's huge fireplace spat and sizzled, the Samhain circle we cast had a brooding mood to it, whether in response to Phillipa's powerful script or just the general atmosphere of recent evils, it was impossible to tell. The candles we lit for our beloved dead flickered ominously, as if a dark-fingered breeze had infiltrated the warm room. Although no actual specters, ghouls, or strangelets appeared in our midst, there was a sense of *some-things* rushing and brushing around us.

Fiona had to step into the center of our circle and do some banishing maneuver with her hands (sweeping, thrusting, and gesturing aloft) before we could raise a decent cone of power and release our various worries, wishes, and healings to the Universe of Infinite Solutions.

When Phillipa opened our circle and we stepped back into the mundane world, the general air of relaxation and relief was more profound than usual.

"Hey, wasn't that chilly business—*eerie, dearies,*" Deidre said, shaking her hands as if they were wet. "I sure hope I'm not being the lightning rod for any uninvited *thingies*."

"Nonsense, Dee," Phillipa said. "You just never know what a Samhain ritual will scare up. Don't you agree, Fiona?"

"And wasn't that one a thriller!" Fiona reached into her reticule for sage oil to anoint her wrists, then offered the tiny bottle around the circle, as if it were a container of Tic Tacs. "Now, I wonder if our spellwork had anything to do with this business of Madame de Rochemont," she speculated.

We'd gathered nearer to Phillipa's copper-hooded fireplace for "cakes and ale"—or whatever feast our hostess would provide. The blaze seemed merrier now, highlighting Moroccan brass tables. Sleek, inky Zelda sprawled on a golden Afghan rug, yawning opulently. Outside, the October wind lived up to its mystique, howling and rattling the windows.

"Could it be that Albert Reynard is revealing his true self *by committing another crime*?" Heather mused.

"What a nasty, horrid thought that is!" Deidre exclaimed. "Talk about unintended consequences!"

"Maybe Heather has something there," Phillipa said, filling crystal liqueur glasses with *Strega*. "Here, drink this, Dee. It will put heart into you. Whoever said magic could be predicted—or governed? If a spell goes even a wee bit off target—whammo! collateral damage."

Deidre tasted the yellow liqueur gingerly. Hers was not an adventurous palate. "Whew! Strong...what's in this stuff, anyway?"

"Only two people in the world know the answer, and they're both named Alberti," Phillipa said. "*Strega* is linked to the Witches of Benevento, whom I can only assume were witches of good tidings, for the liqueur is said to have magical strengthening properties. Makes a good love potion as well. I can't tell you how much of the stuff I poured into Stone while we were courting."

"One of my late, lamented housekeepers, Lucrezia of the perpetual black dress, used to serve this liqueur to Cass and me," Heather said. "With a two-fingered hand gesture she thought I didn't see and a meaningful look in her eye. I didn't know at the time that 'strega' meant 'witch'."

"I believe she was warding off the evil eye," Fiona said. "Horns, you know. The other meaning is *cuckold*, which doesn't apply."

"Collateral damage is possible," I agreed reluctantly, ignoring the colorful digression. "The tragedy of Tristan and Isolde was caused by a misdirected love potion."

Phillipa passed around fragrant cheese pastries. I followed with a tray of pretty little morsels that she swore were called "faery cakes" in Britain.

"Oh, don't be such a wimp," Heather said. "This is a Wiccan circle, not an episode of *The Golden Girls*." She held up her glass to the light, admiring its shimmering yellow color.

"He'd committed two murders which were blamed on Farrow and Lovitt, *and they confessed*—so he was in the clear. If he'd kept a low profile from then on, he might have got away with it. But now..." Phillipa reclined on a silk-cushioned sofa. Instantly, Zelda leaped up beside her and allowed her fur to be stroked thoughtfully.

"Now he's put himself in danger of being discovered," Heather finished the thought. She was seated cross-legged on the floor by the hearth, the firelight shining on her long bronze braid. I envied the ease with which she could assume those yoga poses, then jump to her feet painlessly later. "But I agree with Dee—what a revolting development if we are responsible for any harm coming to that poor lady."

"Oh, Madame's been harmed, all right." Deidre put down her glass on a brass table. "You wouldn't happen to have a Diet Coke in the fridge, would you, Phil?"

"No, I would not. Drink your *Strega*," Phillipa said firmly. "Are you in communication with the old broad, Dee? What a useful talent!"

"No, Phil, I haven't been chatting with Madame. But I have seen her deceased granddaughter again, I regret to say. My unwelcome new gift, such a cliché—*I see dead people*. Just before I drove over here, not surprisingly. Samhain is the best time of the year for ghost-viewing as well as leaf-peeping."

"But nothing of Madame? Maybe I'm wrong, then. Could she still be alive?" I still hoped against hope for a less tragic outcome to the story.

"No, I didn't see Madame. Just the ghost girl, Therese, doesn't speak, but—I can't explain it—it's as if her presence, her demeanor, tells me things. Oh, I don't know. Maybe I'm just fantasizing. But she smiled and held out her arms, as if she were welcoming someone she loved."

"Yikes," Heather said. "Weren't you afraid it would be you?"

"No, you know how it is with ghosts…"

"No, how?" Phillipa asked. "My own knowledge of dealing with the dead is limited to saying Kaddish from time to time."

"Ghosts are not *there* for the living. They exist in another realm among similar otherworldly beings. Because of some unfinished business of their own, they have not moved on to a higher plane, and they linger in limbo until their spirits are satisfied. It's doubtful that Therese was welcoming, or even *seeing* me, except as a means of retribution."

"The grandmother, too, will not rest until the true murderer is punished," Fiona said in a lugubrious tone, somewhat mitigated by her tinkling silver bangles. "Even in life, she could not rest, and now the murdering son-in-law will never be free of her."

"Cripe," Phillipa said, springing up to pass around the sweets and savories again. "This is like something written by Poe. *The telltale whatzis*. Well, I for one am not going to be made to feel guilty. All we did, really, was to sprinkle a few herbs and call for justice. *We did not invite another murder*."

"The Cosmos has its own incalculable way of meting out justice." Fiona drained her thimble-ful of *Strega* and held out the glass. "Mmmm. May I have some more? Let's not brood, ladies. We did it. It's done. Life goes on."

"For some of us, it does," Deidre said darkly.

~

"How was the Halloween party?" Joe asked innocently when I swept into the house around midnight in my green hooded cloak. He was sitting in the kitchen rocker, his foot resting on a pine footstool, a mug of something hot that didn't smell like coffee in his hands.

"Yo ho ho and a hot rum toddy?" I countered.

"The sailor's remedy for whatever ails you. Have one. If you're not already too sloshed on witch's brew. Why do you look so worried? I thought these get-togethers were all *merry meet and merry part and merry meet again*."

Sure, if you don't fool around with magic, I thought but didn't say. "Oh, well, Samhain—Halloween—you know. Feast of the dead and all. The beginning of the year's dark half. It's one of your more sobering Sabbats. But it was good. Very good."

His expression remained unconvinced. "Do you want to know what was on the eleven o'clock news?"

"Something about the missing woman?" I asked eagerly.

"No. Something connected to your other little project, the dog-fighting ring."

"Oh, what...*what?*"

"Two women out walking last evening were attacked by a so-called *pack of pit bulls* running loose near Fresh Meadow Farm. The victims have been taken to Jordan Hospital with multiple injuries. It might have been worse if Wanda Finch hadn't been at the farm stand that's up by Fresh Meadow when the incident happened. Says she was cleaning up the fall display of dried corn and what-have-you when she heard the screams. Grabbed a rifle out of her pick-up truck, shot one of the dogs, and scared off the other. Finch says she saw only a couple of dogs, not a pack. It appears that they may have escaped from the Collins' compound—it's the only place with kennels in that area. And although Collins vigorously denies owning what he calls 'any wild dogs, pit bulls, or unlicensed mutts,' the incident has prompted numerous irate calls from neighbors insisting on an investigation. But the Fresh Meadow kennel, Collins claims, houses only hunting dogs—hounds, retrievers, and beagles."

"Well, well," I said. "That was downright careless of Collins, wasn't it? I wonder if some judge will issue a warrant to have a look inside Fresh Meadow?"

"Possibly. If there are enough complaints," Joe said. "But what about the other dog, the one that got away from Finch?"

"I can just imagine..." I started to say. The cell in the leather bag I'd just hung on my office doorknob sang out its little tune. "That'll be Heather. She must have just got home and heard about what happened." I removed my phone from the bag and opened it gingerly.

Heather was screaming as I put it to my ear. "*We've got to get that other dog before those crazy fools shoot it down.* Any excuse to *kill* something! Dick and Maury and I are going to go out there with tranquilizer guns and try to bring in the fella, see if he can be retrained."

"Calm yourself, Heather. It's no use trying to save that pit bull. In cases of severe dog bite, the court invariably orders that the dog be destroyed. Use that energy to call for an investigation of Collins."

"You see…*you see now what happens*. We try a simple little spell to get this bozo to expose himself, and the result is one dog shot to death and another hunted down like a wild animal."

"It's what Fiona warned us about tonight. When magic is invoked, there's no way of knowing the wider ramifications, no matter how carefully the spell is made. *Beware of what you ask for*…as the saying goes. Maybe I'm swearing off."

"Yeah, me, too. Well. Perhaps. Depends upon the circumstances. *Anyway*, first light, we're still going to try rescuing that other dog, if we can find him. I will speak up for the dog myself if it comes to a court case. I wonder if I could be appointed as a friend-of-the-court canine advocate? I bet Collins is in a nasty temper tonight, trying to figure out who to blame for those dogs of his breaking out."

"I just hope he doesn't blame us."

"Why should he do that?"

"Maybe because he knows it was you and your sidekick who broke *into* his place once and may have done the same again. So watch yourself. And call me when you get back tomorrow."

After I'd done my best to calm Heather and we'd said good-bye, I realized that I now had Joe to appease, and he was not a happy camper. "Let's go to bed," I suggested, always a surefire means of calming the troubled waters.

It took a while, but peace and harmony were restored. Not before a stern lecture, of course, on how to stay out of dangerous situations by the simple expedient of minding my own business. But kisses are an easy way of silencing the lecturer, and one thing always leads to another even sweeter distraction—rather the opposite of the Lysastrata strategy.

CHAPTER TWENTY-FIVE

If you go out in the woods today,
You're sure of a big surprise...

– "The Teddy Bears' Picnic," lyrics by Jimmy Kennedy

Considering all that happened next, I had to admit that Joe had a point in his MYOB philosophy. My karmic chickens came home to roost. Only, they were more like vultures.

Clairvoyance is of limited value to the clairvoyant—even when it's a matter of life and death, we are often clueless about the future of our own lives. So it was very much after the fact when I learned of a certain chain of events that led to dangerous outcomes for me.

One of our earlier interventions, the investigation into the Pryde Pig Farm, had resulted in Iggy Pryde having to pay an enormous environmental clean-up bill for the illegal chemical dumping he'd allowed on his property. The weight of debt and recriminations that followed had put a dent in the Iggy Pryde and Wanda Finch affair, with the eventual result of a broken engagement. At loose ends, romantically speaking, Wanda had been an easy mark for Kurt Heller to take out for a few beers so that he could pump her for information about the break-in at Fresh Meadow Farm. He may even have wondered if the tough redhead, Collins's neighbor, was responsible. But Wanda had spilled the beans about Heather and me going after the dog-fighting operation. "Fanatical crazies," was what she called us, and not for the first time.

That was merely confirmation of our involvement to Hugh Collins. He was onto us already anyway. Leave it to Heather to drop a jacket with her business card in the pocket at the scene of the crime!

After Collins realized that his dog-fighting operation had been permanently compromised, the dark-visaged, dark-hearted entrepreneur decided it was payback time. His next move had been to send his lackey to snoop on Heather and her friends, and Heller soon made the Circle connection. Unfortunately, we five were now rather infamous around Plymouth for our crime-fighting proclivity.

Given our ill-conceived break-in into the Fresh Meadow operation, Collins probably thought we had something to do with his two pit bulls getting loose and attacking the two women who were out for a walk near his place. It would have been logical to blame us. Having seen Collins' dog-fighting facility with my own eyes, it seemed unlikely that the dogs could have slipped out of that cellar. Unless one of the grooms who doubled as a kennel keeper had been careless when cleaning the pit bull pens. Dogs are generally expert in pushing open doors that are not completely shut, and some can even use their noses to lift latches.

However it happened, the Incredible Escape was not our doing (unless a touch of magic had been involved, after all) and I was grieved to hear that as a result one dog was dead and another was being hunted down. But Collins blamed Heather and me, as we found out later.

Nothing in my sixth sense alerted me that I was more vulnerable than I realized. It was as if Collins was operating on the Old Testament law of "an eye for an eye"—only he was thinking more along the lines of "a dog for a dog."

I've always loved our rambles in Jenkins Park. This newly designated conservation land, located on Route 3A between Phillipa's house and my place, was entirely wild and overgrown, but laced with narrow footpaths of least resistance where sneakers have trod for decades. The rest of the "park" was a dense tangle of great oaks and pines, thrusting saplings, fallen logs, twisted bushes, and the debris of countless windstorms, reminding me of a giant game of *Pick Up Sticks*. Some of the fallen branches, disfigured with toxic-green lichen, looked like monster arthritic hands with crooked fingers. Glimpses of the Atlantic peeked through the east border of the park. If cleared, it would have made a very desirable condo location, but the wetlands we had discovered there plus a nest of bald eagles had put the kibosh on that developer's dream.

Even in November, I make it a practice to carry my foraging basket when walking in Jenkins Park, for I often find useful roots, pods, cones, dried seeds, bayberries, and ritual woods to harvest. And I wouldn't dream of walking the old paths without my two canine companions. The park and the beach are our two special off-leash places where a dog can get a good run after a squirrel or a thrown stick. When Joe is home, he usually goes with me, but with his injured leg, he was still confined to the house when, two days after we heard news of the pit bulls' rampage, I went out walking with Scruffy and Raffles.

I'd found a hazel tree and, having given proper reverence to its sacrifice, I began to whittle away a few likely branches to make wands and dowsing forks. My "woman's knife," as

Tip called it, had been a gift from him—polished black wood handle with a decorative inset bloodstone, and the sheath beaded with shamanistic symbols for power and good luck. It was small, sturdy, and practical, perfect for the job at hand. The dogs had occupied themselves with treeing an insouciant squirrel, their front paws on the venerable oak where he'd climbed for refuge. They were barking gleefully, while I cut and trimmed two wands.

Suddenly, Scruffy leaped away from the tree.

Watch out, guys! I'm sensing bad trouble out there. And he's coming this way. Hey, I don't like this. I'm getting killer vibes. That crazy canine is looking for blood.

Scruffy pricked up his ears and drew back his upper lip, snarling in that barely audible way that is most menacing. Nudging Raffles down from the tree trunk, he paced back and forth on the path nervously, the fur on his back standing up like a long brush. Suddenly he stood stock still and braced himself in front of me and his offspring.

"Hey, Toots. Watch out…watch out…

I'd stopped what I was doing, laying the wands and the basket on the ground. I hadn't heard a thing myself, but Scruffy was alarmed, and that was enough.

Crash! Thump! Smash! A dog hurtled out of the bushes like a small wild boar, a compact body with a big white head. He dodged the braced, growling Scruffy and sprang instead onto Raffles' back, sinking his teeth into the vulnerable neck. Raffles screamed and tried to shake the animal off, bucking like a wounded horse.

Instantly, Scruffy jumped into the fight and grabbed the marauding dog's leg between his teeth, straining to tug him off Raffles. The attacker made a guttural sound of pain deep in his throat without letting go his hold on Raffles. He tried to free his leg, but Scruffy hung on, snarling deeply. I was screaming myself, of course, as I seized a sturdy fallen branch off the ground.

Standing over the mass of squirming dog flesh, I tried to bring my improvised club down onto the intruder's broad head, but I couldn't seem to get a clear swing that wouldn't knock out one of my own dogs. My cell phone was uselessly trapped in my pocket. My knife had fallen to the ground and was somewhere lodged in the pine needle carpet.

Finally, no longer able to bear Scruffy's tearing teeth, the marauder leaped off Raffles' back. Raffles yipped and dashed away, disappearing into the bushes. The other dog grabbed for Scruffy's throat conveniently situated below him where my dog was hanging onto the mangled, bleeding leg of the other. Scruffy ducked away, but just barely. The pit bull's teeth ripped Scruffy's ear and cheek instead. Scruffy let go his grip, and I brought the branch down on the wild one's cranium.

He shook his head, looking mildly dazed, but recovered too quickly. Scruffy backed away slightly, readying himself. The other dog came at him, big white head lowered, like some miniature raging bull, then quickly jumped for Scruffy's throat. I could hear myself screaming still. Just then I spotted the bloodstone in my knife's handle gleaming like a glass eye in the midst of the torn-up earth around the fighting dogs. I grabbed for it.

At the moment I raised the knife, Raffles dashed out of the bushes like a golden-brown streak of fury and butted the white dog's flank with his head. Scruffy leaped clear, but his front leg caught in a forked protruding tree root, and he yelped as he crashed to the ground. I brought down the knife and slashed at the attacker's neck. Blood spurting from his wound, the dog howled and ran away into the woods, his tail between his legs.

Hey, dumbledog, it's about time you showed. Where've you been, chasing chipmunks? And what kind of a maneuver was that? We're not goats, you know. We canines rip and nip, we don't try to butt the enemy into submission.

Scruffy was scolding from a prone position, still sprawled where he fell. Raffles limped over and licked at Scruffy's torn ear. Scruffy sniffed the wound on the back of his offspring's neck. I fell to my knees in the footpath with absolute exhaustion. The surge of adrenaline brought on by abject terror had drained away leaving me a limp blob.

You okay, Toots? I guess we finally drove that mad dog away, all right. He might come back, though. Let's get out of here.

Out of here! Out of here! Raffles was parading about like a prize fighter, making little moves toward the path to home. There was a bit of swagger in his prancing, reminiscent of his sire. I checked the back of his neck. Not too bad, and in a place that the pup couldn't reach to lick. As soon as I got home, I'd drench it with antiseptic. Heather kept me well supplied with a canine first aid kit.

Scruffy started out bravely to follow his offspring but cried out in pain when he tried to put his weight on his front left paw. The leg went right out from under him. That was a strain for sure, or worse.

"Stay, Scruffy. *Stay*, dammit. I'm calling for help." Holding the dog down gently to keep him from jumping up again, I dug out my cell phone and called Joe.

"Listen, honey. *Don't come out here.* There's some kind of wild dog loose, and he attacked our dogs. But it's okay, he's gone now. I whacked him with my knife and he ran away. Scruffy's not too spry at the moment, though, and I think we all need help."

"*Jesu Cristos!* Where the hell are you? I'll be right there."

"*No, no, you won't.* I just want you to call Phil. She's the closest. Tell her to bring a blanket so that we can carry Scruffy and to take some kind of a club as well. Just in case she encounters the monster. Tell her I'm at the place where the lady slippers always come up in the spring, and the fiddleheads. She'll know. I'd call myself, but I need to stay on guard, in case. After you've talked to Phil, call Heather and tell her to come out here with her tranquilizer gun right away. I'll need Dick, too. Or Maury. We have some injuries."

"You're all right yourself? Are you sure that beast isn't lurking somewhere nearby?"

"I'm okay, just shaken up a little. I think he's gone for good, but I'm watching out anyway. Scruffy can't walk. But I have a sturdy branch in hand and my knife, so we'll be fine. Now, please hang up and make those calls. Promise!"

"All right, all right. I'll make the calls," Joe said. His tone was angry but resigned. Oh well, I'd just have to deal with him later.

We clicked off, and I leaned over Scruffy to have a closer look at that ear. It was a miserable mangled thing; I sure hoped that Dick could sew it back together again. Now that I had a moment to think, I realized what must have happened. The first two fighting dogs may have escaped by accident, but that incident must have given Hugh Collins the idea of ridding himself of the living evidence of his crimes by dumping his canine warriors in likely places, preferably far from home, and combining the cover-up with a bit of payback. Tears ran down my cheeks. Raffles came and nuzzled under my arm that was stroking Scruffy.

"You did good, Raffles," I whispered. "A real chip off the old man."

Did good! Did good!

I didn't like the way Scruffy was looking, the eye turned toward me was somehow strange and vague. He was panting heavily but otherwise silent, not at all like himself. *Shock*, I thought. I stripped off my jacket and placed it over him. "You stay warm, little buddy. Help is on the way."

Before Phillipa could show up with her blanket and club, however, Joe stamped into our midst, blazing with righteous wrath. I should have known the inevitable reaction of a crusader would be to rescue his damsel in distress. I was too worried about Scruffy to scold my would-be champion.

"Hi, honey. We're okay. Didn't you have a hard time walking all this way?"

"It was fine," he insisted. "Oh, Christ. This doesn't look good, does it?"

"Yes. It doesn't. Is Phil coming?"

"She's going to drive her BMW to the nearest main road access and hike in with the blanket. Ten minutes, she said, and that was ten minutes ago. Hey...what was that cracking noise?"

"*Oh, Sweet Mother*!" I screamed.

The demonic white dog lunged through the bushes straight for Raffles!

Moving pretty fast for an injured guy, Joe lurched in front of Raffles. Lifting his crutch, he held it straight out toward the animal racing toward us, like Sir Lancelot at a jousting match. A direct hit to the chest. The white dog howled and dropped in his tracks. He appeared to be knocked out. Joe held the crutch ready to bash him on the head if he moved. The animal looked up with one eye rolling and lay perfectly still except for the panting. His paws were in the air and his neck exposed.

"He's given up," I said to Joe. "But watch him anyway."

"Yoo hoo," Phillipa called, running in from the main road. "Oh, Holy Hecate, what have we here! Looks like the last act of Hamlet. I guess you won't be needing this then?" She held up the baseball bat she was carrying, then leaned it against the big oak tree.

"Good, Phil," I cried. "Let's make a stretcher out of that blanket and get Scruffy out of here. He needs medical care right away. He needs Dick."

"I didn't have time to tell you," Joe said. "There was an emergency over at the Devlins when I called, and Dick couldn't be spared. Some kind of dog fight. Heather got in touch with Maury and told him to get over here to subdue your attacker before the law and the animal control people arrive. She wants Maury to protect the damned mad dog. I did have to call the cops, too, of course. I figured we'd have to report this incident if you want to implicate Collins."

"Yes, that makes sense. Dog fight at the Devlins? It's just what I thought. That bastard Collins is siccing all his killers on us. What about the tranquilizer gun?" I asked.

"Maury's bringing it. But this fella looks pretty tranquil already," Phil said. "Hit him with your crutch, did you, Joe?"

"Makes a very decent weapon," Joe admitted.

"Okay, I'd better get you and Scruffy over to Wee Angels now," Phillipa said. "Maybe by the time we get there, Dick will have sorted out the problems at their place. We'll need him to sew up that poor ear. Scruffy can't walk either, can he?"

"No, it's something with his left front leg."

Hey, Toots! Can't a guy get a bowl of cold water?"

Cold water! Cold water!

"All right, I hear you. You're going to have nice drinks of water very, very soon. Then that big doctor with the gentle hands is going to fix you up just like new, Scruffy. And give you something soothing for the pain."

I could see that Joe was frustrated that he couldn't help us with the improvised sling for Scruffy, who turned out to be a pretty hefty bundle for two women to manage, but you do what you have to do.

There wasn't room for all of us in Phillipa's BMW. Joe assured us that he would be fine going home on his crutch and would take Raffles with him. I handed him one of the leashes I had tied around my waist and told him which tube of medicine to squeeze on Raffles' wounded neck.

As we laid Scruffy on the back seat, I folded my jacket under him, having a fleeting thought for that impeccable upholstery. Normally, Phillipa wouldn't dream of allowing an animal into her sleek black beauty.

"I hope Maury finds that monster okay," I said, as Phillipa raced away from the road's shoulder with a mighty spurt of gravel.

"He will," Phillipa assured me. "He's a resourceful guy. Quiet but competent. I wonder if he wouldn't be good husband material for someone. How's the patient doing back there?"

"How can you think about matchmaking at a time like this? You're as incorrigible as Dee." I was hanging over the back seat, smoothing Scruffy's flank. I wished I knew how bad that leg injury was. "Scruff seems to be holding on okay, I guess. More alert, I think."

You're taking me to that bad smelly place, aren't you? I hate that. Pissy little cage, and they stick us with needles, you know. Haven't I suffered enough trying to defend you? Just take me home and I'll lick my own wounds, thank you very much.

"You can't reach your own ear, dummy. Not even a cat can do that."

Hey, Toots—no insults in my weakened condition. Where's that mutt?

"Raffles went home with Joe. There wasn't room for all of us in Phil's car."

"You're conversing with Scruffy now, right?" Phillipa said.

That damned kid has all the luck.

"Yeah, and he's feeling a little better, judging by the complaints."

~

Scruffy got even grumpier when he woke up after surgery and found his left front leg in a cast. *Hey, Toots, get this white thing off me...get it OFF me...I can't even walk right...and I'm gonna barf...Ugh, ugh, I feel like poop...this guy must be trying to kill me.*

And more in that vein.

"You fractured your leg, Scruff, just like Joe. Same side, too." I stifled a giggle, clearly a nervous response to our narrow escape. And the thought of my two guys hopping around together. "So just like Joe, you have to wear that cast on your leg until the fractur heals. You were very, very brave, and you deserve a medal, and I'm going to see that you get one. You can wear it attached to your collar. Bet Honeycomb will be very impressed."

Yeah, sure. That blonde bitch hasn't given me a rec since I knocked her up. I don't know what her problem is. She sure thought it was a good idea at the time.

"A female always reserves the right to change her mind. And change it again and again. Who knows how she'll feel when she sees that you've been wounded in action."

Phil rolled her eyes at Heather and Dick. "Cass still carries on talking to Scruffy just as if he's a person."

"They do seem to have some special sort of communication," Dick said mildly. He was still wearing his green scrubs, his bushy hair tied back into a pony tail. After the emergency at his own home, it was amazing how fast he'd pulled himself together and showed up here ready to perform as trauma room physician.

As Dick related the story while medicating Scruffy, another mysterious pit bull had appeared to cause havoc at the Devlins' place. He got himself into their dog yard and set about attacking one of the several canines always in residence at the Morgan mansion. In the fracas that followed, Honeycomb's chest had been scratched, and a new arrival, a boxer mix named Dempsey, had suffered a badly slashed eye. Trilby the ancient bloodhound had been frightened into the kind of collapse to which old dogs are prone.

Hearing the battle raging outside, Ashling had come running out and thrown herself into the fray without regard to bodily harm. She'd managed to corner the intruder with a floor mop, but Dick who ran out after her, not wanting to take any chances, had tranquillized the pit bull anyway.

Meanwhile, Maury and Heather had gone hunting in Jenkins Park for the other fighter, the one who'd attacked us. He'd been found easily enough after being severely winded by Joe's crutch and dripping a blood trail from my slash at his neck. Both pit bulls were now in recovery at the hospital, along with Trilby and Dempsey. Honeycomb's injury was a minor one, and she was at home in Ashling's care.

"Don't worry. The bad guys aren't housed anywhere near Scruffy's hospital bed. We have special quarters for the unsociables," Dick assured me. "Now what I'm concerned about, Cass, is that this cast will get bedraggled and dirty in no time, so I'm going to give you a cast protector with Velcro straps. Blue or red?"

"Blue or red, Scruff?"

"Dogs don't see colors the way we do, Cass," Dick said gently.

Gimme the bright one, Toots. Might as well make a fashion statement, here.

"I guess we'll take the red one, thanks, Dick."

"Okay, red it is. Now, how about a plastic hood to keep him from chewing at the cast with his teeth? It won't prevent him from eating and drinking, and my experience has been that dogs soon get resigned to wearing it. A good bit of insurance, in my view."

Hey, just a doggone minute here! No way am I going to wear one of those plastic buckets on my head! Think I want to have some dumb squirrel rolling around laughing his ass off at me?

"No thanks, Dick. Scruffy promises not to gnaw at this cast, even when it itches, right Scruff?"

Scruffy heaved one of those soul-searing canine sighs, hopped over to the exit, and sank down in a miserable heap in front of the threshold so that the door could not be opened without giving him a chance to escape.

I could take a hint. "Guess we'll take Scruffy home now, Phil. Perk him up with a little dinner. But just wait until Joe sees this—what shall I call it?—canine mirror image. Never mind, I'm just so relieved that Scruffy survived. What a terrifying attack! That beast!" I turned back to give Dick a grateful hug. "Do you think Scruffy's face and ear will heal up okay?"

"His cheek may be left with one of those intriguing dueling scars, but in the main, the ear will be in good shape," Dick said.

"*That beast*, as you call him," Heather said tartly as she strode into the surgery, "has been tranquillized and is resting in one of our private pens being looked after by Maury. Along with his buddy, the one who got into our dog yard and was routed by the incredible Ashling. And the other guy, the one that Finch didn't manage to shoot. Three rescues from the hell of dog-fighting. Five, if you count Wendy and Captain Hook. American Staffordshire Terriers get a terrible rep because of brutes like Hugh Collins. But I think there's a good chance we can rehabilitate the poor old sods. They're pretty marked up and obviously have had a rotten life. Until now."

"Heather dear, you know you're going to be forced by the courts to put down those fellas. Best thing, don't get involved," I warned.

"No one really knows that we've got those stray dogs, Cass. While the cops were all clustered around Joe getting the details, and you were racing over here with Phil, Maury and I tracked down the terrier and tranquillized him. Got him into the Wee Angels wagon with great discretion. So let's just say that the white dog you encountered disappeared after the attack. Same with the other two."

"But those pit bulls...eh...American Staffordshire Terriers...any one of them might be traceable to Collins' farm, might be proof that he's maintaining fighters for illegal games," I protested.

"No one wants Collins' hide nailed to the door more than I do, Cass. But not at the expense of one more exploited canine. These dogs of Collins' have led incredibly abusive lives, and now some of them are home safe with us. We're just going to find some other way to entrap the bastard."

"So I'm not supposed to admit that you've got outlaw dogs in custody? You've put me in a position where I have to lie, then?"

"Oh, *please!*" Phillipa's winged eyebrows rose in derision. "As if you never lied in your teeth to the law. Even to Stone, I might add. And frankly, I see Heather's point. If these brutes can be retrained by the Devlin crew and have a few good years, more power to them."

"Damn straight," Heather said. "If our circle is not for life over death, what are we?"

"Speaking of *death*, that animal could have *killed us*," I reminded her." You need to make quite certain that he'll never try to rip out someone's throat again—and if he remains a threat, you have to take responsibility for putting him down."

"I'll speak to that," Dick said. "*If he can't be retrained*... But I've never known a dog that couldn't be, so I'm hopeful." Heather's big, comfortable-looking husband, with his innocent eyes and charismatic warmth, inspired instant trust. I believed him.

But now, how were we going to put Collins out of business?

CHAPTER TWENTY-SIX

Oh, there are many things that women know,
That no one tells them, no one needs to tell;
And that they know, their dearest never guess.

– Roselle Mercier Montgomery

Stone was sitting at the kitchen table with Joe when Phil and I came in from the brisk November evening with a subdued and cranky Scruffy. Stone was wearing a moss green cashmere sweater-vest over a collarless shirt, sharply pleated chinos, and his scholarly metal-rimmed glasses. A china cup with steaming Earl Grey tea sat in front of him. Joe had on a raveling navy-blue fisherman's sweater and salt-faded jeans, a thick mug of aromatic coffee in his hand, his leg stretched out across the traffic lane.

"The odd couple," Phillipa murmured before going over to greet her husband with a kiss on the cheek. She smiled at him brilliantly; he took her hand, and a glow of warmth suffused his long thin face. "Errand of mercy accomplished," she said. "I trust that Joe has been filling you in on our excitement *du jour.*"

Curled up on his kitchen bed with a dog-desolate expression, Raffles looked up eagerly for his sire. Instead of being first in the door, however, Scruffy had limped slowly after us. He slunk over to his own bed and dropped onto it with utter exhaustion.

Stone and Joe enjoyed a good laugh at his expense. "Looks as if I've got some competition in the sympathy department," Joe said.

Scruffy growled his displeasure. Raffles, who was sniffing his sire's wounded ear and leg, backed off nervously.

"Cool it, Scruffy," I said, placing the water bowl within his reach. "Stone! I know word travels fast, but I confess that I'm a tad surprised to see you here already."

"Pit bull attack. Possibly I could make a case that this incident is linked to Hugh Collins having a peeve. Right here in my jurisdiction. Perfect!" Stone said. "Now I can go after the bastard as I've always wanted to do."

"You see?" Phillipa said, putting on the kettle for another boil. "Hugh Collins has *revealed himself*, wouldn't you say?"

"Unfortunately, the animal control people found neither hide nor hair of that brutal canine attacker," Stone said. "He seems to have disappeared into thin air. I hope he isn't holed up waiting for another go at you, Cass."

Phillipa and I exchanged glances. "I shouldn't worry," she said.

"He's out of harm's way, would you say?" Stone asked, with a rather direct look at the two of us.

"I wouldn't say, actually," his wife shrugged. "Or if I did, I'd say, leave the problem of confining the outlaw dog to the animal control officer and get on with nailing Collins."

"That's what I thought," Stone said enigmatically. "I'll wager the Devlins have had a hand in this. Dangerous dogs like that should be put down, you know."

"What's that heavenly aroma?" Phil turned her back on Stone, winked at me, and opened the oven door. "Ah. Pork Loin a la Ulysses? Gosh, Cass, you really lucked out with this guy."

"Watch her, Joe," I said. "She's only wanting to steal your Mom's Greek recipes." I peered into the oven over her shoulder. "Looks like there's plenty of herb roasted spuds, too. Why don't you two stay for dinner?"

"Got any more of that elegant de Rochemont burgundy?" Phillipa asked.

It was a surprisingly relaxed dinner, considering our earlier terrors. Phillipa sautéed some cubed butternut squash with garlic and black olives while I made a huge Greek salad with chickpeas, peperoncini, feta cheese, chunks of sweet bell peppers and tomatoes. The de Rochemont wine poured freely, and by the time we arrived at coffee and amaretti baked pears, I decided the moment has come to grill the friendly detective.

"What did you hear from your friend in Chatham?" I asked. "Any news of Madame's whereabouts? And by the way, must I keep calling him *your friend*? I think I might be trusted with the fellow's name."

Stone looked at me long and earnestly. "There's no way I can really get into their investigation of her disappearance, Cass. Just keep my ears open to the usual gossip and scuttlebutt. But I did speak to *my friend* about the layout of the grounds. Don Wolfe, a name you are never, never to repeat. We hung around together at the Academy. He's a detective now, with the State Police, Troop D, Yarmouth, by the way—patrolling Chatham. Told him I'd visited *Beau Rouge* on some earlier occasion and seemed to remember a statue of Dionysus near a topiary garden. He said, *maybe*, tight-lipped, as if he'd already got the word not to discuss details. But, just for you, Cass, I stuck my neck out a little farther. I said, there might have been an old well or cistern, closed up, somewhere near there. It could be worth a look-see."

"Oh, that's super, Stone. Will your friend dig into it, do you think?"

"Possibly. If he continues to be involved in the investigation."

"I'm pretty sure they *will* find Madame de Rochemont somewhere underground in the gardens of *Beau Rouge*," I said.

"And if that's true, I'm afraid they'll be calling *me* in for some close questioning," Stone said. "Cops are naturally distrustful of people who seem to *guess right* about the details of a crime."

"Or surely not distrustful of *you*," I said. I really couldn't imagine anyone being suspicious that such a gentlemanly detective could be guilty of bashing and burying a rich old lady. That would be like Lord Peter Whimsey coshing some decrepit dowager.

"If all else fails," Stone said, "do I have your permission to bring you into this, Cass?"

"Not on your life," Joe said.

"Of course," I said.

"A mad dog and a sadistic dog-fighting entrepreneur aren't enough for you?" Joe ranted. "Now you want to have some crazed killer find out you're pursuing him? Have you no sense of danger?"

"Joe...Joe..." Stone said in a placating tone of reason. "Cass's name will never go any farther than my friend Don in Yarmouth. It's just so that he can find that body, if there is a body, where Reynard has hidden it. It's all going to appear to be serendipitous."

"Just think, a wolf after a fox," Phillipa mused. "How droll."

"And how exactly can you guarantee Cass won't be implicated?" Joe demanded.

"Hey, I know this guy. Don's never going to admit to having a psychic source, believe me."

"It's on your head, then, if this gets out. You remember, I trust, how much trouble these two got themselves into last Christmas?" Joe jabbed a finger in the direction of me and Phillipa.

"Good Goddess, was that water cold," I exclaimed, recalling the bruising shock of my winter plunge into the waters off Plymouth wharf.

"I remember using my magical voice before I even knew I had one," Phillipa said. "I guess we all have more resources than we're aware of—until our backs are against the wall."

"Or we're hanging onto the Town Pier for dear life," I said. We smiled at each other, oblivious to the clash of male wills around us.

After a little more saber rattling, it was agreed that Stone would approach Don Wolfe with some additional background on his psychic source. And Phillipa would let me know if Stone's friend really did find Madame de Rochemont stuffed into a well.

News of our ordeal in Jenkins Park streaked faster than a meteor from Heather to Deidre and Fiona. The next morning, everyone in our circle was at my door for kibitzing and commiseration. And they all brought gifts, each in her own quirky style.

"What is this, some kind of shower?" I started a full pot of coffee. It wouldn't be Phillipa's Mediterranean brew, but there was something to be said for a good old-fashioned cup of American coffee, especially at—I glanced at my herb clock on the kitchen wall—only nine in the morning!

"You bet," Deidre said. "A Welcome-Back-from Danger Shower. How's poor little Scruff?" She settled herself on the padded bench under the bird-feeder window and took an embroidery out of a yellow workbag that matched her twin set.

"My two noble invalids are out for a slow, slow hobble through the garden with Raffles dancing circles around them. The pup feels like quite a hero since our encounter with Mad Dog, where he acquitted himself so admirably. Although Scruffy won't admit that."

"Cass is in her own little canine world again," Phillipa said, unpacking a basket of fragrant, still warm pineapple muffins. "Bromelain," she explained, enigmatically.

"Bromelain?" Deidre said.

"It's an enzyme in pineapple, making it the first fruit for stomach wobbles and bodily bangs and bruises. Trust me."

"Speaking of nutrition. And canines," Heather said, "you may wish to know that the unsociables are resting tranquilly in their new kennels, apart from the other animals. Enjoying some nutritionally-balanced decent dog chow. I really think they've been half-starved, poor babies. Poor nutrition does have a detrimental affect on animal temperament, you know."

"So does training to kill," I said. That "decent dog chow" would be the stuff that Scruffy called *twigs and bark*. I almost, not quite, felt sorry for the pit bulls. "Who gets the daunting job of feeding and exercising the brutes?"

"Maury seems to have a natural rapport with even the most nervous temperament, and Ashling, too. It takes time and incredible patience to retrain a fighting canine. We've named the three new fellows after the knights of the Round Table. The one we rescued from the Finch's shooting spree is Sir Bedivere, a survivor of every battle. The fighting dog that pervert Collins let into our dog yard is Sir Kay, the knight with a rather surly attitude. And the one you encountered in Jenkins Park is Sir Percival, who was raised in ignorance in the wilds but later, after training in chivalry, became a hero."

"What, no Sir Mordred? Your optimism never ceases to amaze me," Phillipa said. "But I have to admit that I'm impressed with your confidence. With Maury's healing touch, too. And Ashling, so frail, so intrepid."

Deidre looked up from her embroidery. "A very compatible couple, wouldn't you say?"

Heather and I groaned. But Deidre just grinned impishly. "I have a sixth sense about these things."

"Didn't I say?" Phillipa commented smugly.

"I wish you two wouldn't meddle," Heather said. "That could end up with my losing both of them, you know, in which case I'm going to be very cross."

Just then, Fiona breezed in, swept off her MacDonald tartan cloak and leaned her new walking stick against the wall near the back door. The silver knob, Coyote, the trickster, gleamed wickedly. I was reminded of Stone's friend Don Wolfe. And of Reynard, the murdering fox. Feeling suddenly faint, I had to shake my head and hands to rid them of negative thoughts and stamped around in a deosil circle.

"I'm glad to see you dancing again." Heather was wearing impeccable white wool slacks, a blue pinstripe blouse, and a navy blazer. In keeping with the nautical theme, she reached into her Nantucket handbag (plastic not ivory scrimshaw—*save the elephants!*) and brought out a carefully wrapped cylinder. "And this is for you, dear—designed especially for curing and courage." She removed the tissue surrounding one of her latest creations, a moss green candle with silver cobwebs and spiders imbedded in it. "Green for healing, spiders for feminine energy."

Fiona examined it approvingly. "Ah, the spider, emblem of the eternal figure eight, grandmother of storytelling and creation, spinning her web of illusion. A symbol of persistence as well. We Scots have been devoted to spiders ever since Robert Bruce was inspired by a determined spider while hiding in a cave."

Sometimes it was difficult to follow Fiona's fanciful leaps through myth and legend. And personally, I must admit I've found it hard to warm up to spiders. In fact, the sight of a spider in my cellar workroom was liable to give me the screaming meemies, as Joe had come to know.

"Thank you, Heather. The candle is lovely," I said. "Shall I light it now, do you think?"

Phillipa fished a pack of matches out of her black leather jacket and handed them to me. *Was she still sneaking cigarettes?* I gave her a *look* as I lit the candle. She smiled a Cheshire Cat grin and took the matches back.

"Mmmmm. It smells of sage. Really comforting," Deidre said. "Unless you're a turkey. Now look, I've brought you an amulet, and I want you to promise me to keep it with you *night and day*."

I opened the tiny embroidered silk purse. In it was an armadillo fetish carved from quartz. Very pretty, too. "What's the armadillo signify?" I asked. "Armor?"

"Spiritual protection, of course. Never go out without it. At least until all this business with Collins is resolved. And the law catches up with Reynard before he catches up with your psychic surveillance." Deidre took another tiny stitch in the pillow cover she was embroidering. *Harvest Home, corn and grain, All that falls will rise again.* "You could use some defensive charms right now."

"Okay, okay...*hush then*," I warned, nodding toward the door, where Joe and the dogs were coming back from their challenging walkabout outdoors. Phillipa stifled a giggle at the sight of Joe and Scruffy in their matching leg casts. Scruffy's was incased in the jaunty red Velcro thing that Dick had insisted that he wear. Pity there wasn't such a cover for Joe's cast, which was looking decidedly gray and bedraggled.

After greeting the assembled circle with a dashing smile and a half-bow (which nearly capsized him) Joe headed into our bedroom to "rest this miserable thing and check in with Greenpeace by cell phone." Probably glad to escape the highly female energy we five exuded when we were gathered together in one room, although Joe had the kind of male confidence that's was quite capable of dealing with any spillover of psychic vibes when the occasion called for it.

Toots, you gotta get this thing off me. It's all I can do to lift my back leg without falling over. My dignity as a French briard is suffering. Mature canines do not pee zig-zag and hop around like rabbits. Scruffy mumbled and grumbled his way toward his corner, took a desultory drink of water, and flopped down in disgust.

Like rabbits! Like rabbits! Raffles nosed Heather's slacks for news of the canine pack that lived at her house. She scratched him in the sensitive tail area, and he leaned against her blissfully. One had to give credit to Heather for being a dog lover who disdained all concern over dog hair and drool on her beautiful clothes—or for that matter, in her Mercedes. Those white wool slacks were beginning to look a bit worse for wear.

"This pup of Honeycomb's is coming along nicely," she said. "I wonder if he might be trained as a therapy dog like his dam."

Ha ha ha ha. Better watch out, kid. I've heard that they snip the balls off therapy dogs. Want them docile and so forth. Scruffy grinned for the first time since his injury, a canine version of the Clint Eastwood grimace.

"That's not true, Scruffy," I said. "At least, I don't think so."

Raffles sprang away from his new friend as if she were electrified and trotted back to his sire.

"What's not true?" Heather asked. "Do you really think that dog talks to you?"

"Is a male therapy dog always neutered?" I demanded.

Heather sighed. "It's so much healthier for all male dogs to have that procedure. No fear of prostate problems later. Aggressive tendencies nipped in the bud, so to speak."

Ha ha ha ha. Poor bastards.

"Castration is not an ideal way of preserving peace," Fiona said thoughtfully "You can bet your brooms, ladies, that my Omar is fully intact, including his elegant claws, which he often uses for *sortes biblicae* or its equivalent with some other good book. Males will be males, I always say. And females, likewise. Which reminds me that I haven't yet given Cass my little present." She reached into the bulging old green reticule from which she was never parted and brought out a moldy leather book, handing it to me with the reverence due a Shakespearean first folio. "Just a little something I picked up for you at the church."

We must have all looked at her with some consternation.

"Well, not the church *exactly.* The book table at Old Home Day."

"*Herbal Properties, Potions, and Poisons for Psychic Self-defense*," I read the title aloud.

"How alliterative," Phillipa murmured.

I turned to the title page. "*By Sarah Corey, Herb Wyfe.* The name sounds familiar. I hope Sarah managed to escape the hangman's noose. Being the village herbalist was a dangerous profession in earlier days."

"This fascinating old volume turned up at a North Shore Episcopalian fair." Fiona smiled modestly. Somehow antique gems like this always hid themselves under stacks of Steven King and James Patterson until Fiona came along to discover them. Her book sale prowess was legendary.

"The Salem trials came to an end when spectral evidence was discredited." Fiona warmed to expounding on the book's provenance. "Sarah may have benefited from the general amnesty of shame that followed. I'm guessing that she was a young relative, possibly a niece, of Martha Corey, who was hanged as a witch. Perhaps it was her psychic know-how that kept her safe. I wonder if she used a glamour to make herself invisible." She looked dreamily back in time through my kitchen window where a goldfinch and a chickadee were sparring for thistle seeds.

"Thank you, Fiona. Just what the doctor ordered," I said.

"Doctor Faustus, maybe." Phillipa continued her sotto voce ramble but was diverted by the ringing of the cell phone in her pocket. It played *Ding Dong the Witch Is Dead* which I personally thought was terribly bad karma but was her idea of a joke. She tilted her head and listened, her black hair catching and reflecting the light. "Oh, no. Oh, dear. Okay, I'll tell her. Bummer. So embarrassing for the poor sod. See you tonight then, darling."

The call ended; Phillipa looked up at our rapt circle of faces with a wry smile. "Sorry, Cass. Don Wolfe insisted that they search the filthy old well that's been covered up for decades, *ugh*, but no body was found, just a lot of moldy old junk. Apparently Don had some choice words to say to Stone about 'psychic friends' in general and you in particular. It's a good thing that Stone is as centered as he is. No amount of abuse is liable to knock him off balance. As I should know. But it is a tad embarrassing. I mean, how sure were you, Cass?"

"Sure enough," I said. "If not that old well, some other kind of pit, something not easily detectable but known to Reynard. Fiona!"

"Yes, dear?" Fiona was already taking her crystal pendulum out of her green reticule. She rubbed it against her coat sweater of many colors and held it up for inspection.. Its facets caught the morning sun streaming in one of the kitchen windows like a laser.

"No, no," I said. "Dowsing on a map won't do it this time. I sort of know where to look. I mean, I would recognize certain landmarks—the Dionysus, the arbor. We have to get in there ourselves and have you dowse the grounds with an actual forked stick. After all, in a way, we are looking for water. Maybe there was more than one well."

"Are you out of your bleeding mind?" Phillipa demanded.

"Now, now, dear," Fiona said. "Perhaps I can weave a glamour of invisibility around the two of us. I don't know if a glamour actually stretches, but I will try."

"It's not a crime scene, Phil," I defended my plan. "Not yet, anyway. Most of the police force probably believes that Madame has simply wandered away in a daze of dementia and will be found in some ditch somewhere, wearing a sable coat and satin bedroom slippers."

Deidre sighed. "Golly, I wish I could go with you. First you break into Fresh Meadow Farm with Heather, and now *Beau Rouge* with Fiona. You guys are having all the fun. I mean, I could use an afternoon off with Fiona, learning to be invisible. How cool is that!"

"Not exactly invisible, dear. It's more like being quintessentially unremarkable and unnoticed."

"Hey, Dee. Let's have a reality check here. Do you want your children to be visiting you *in Plymouth County House of Correction*," Phillipa nearly shouted.

"Next time, I promise you'll get in on the action, Dee," I soothed. "I'm sure we're going to have to do some more scouting around Collins place. But Phil is right, in a way. You have your young family to consider." My attention strayed back to the ancient herbal that Fiona had given me. I loved old recipes, so evocative. Never could tell what gems you might discover among them. Especially the forgotten lore of the village herbalist, usually a woman who doubled as an agony-aunt confidante, a midwife, and an abortionist. No wonder she was often suspected of being a witch.

CHAPTER TWENTY-SEVEN

Annihilating all that's made
To a green thought in a green shade.

– Andrew Marvell

Fiona's dowsing tool was a forked stick cut from a hazel wood tree, sacred to wells, springs, divination, and the development of wisdom. (She also had a hazel wand which crackled with creative energy for whatever work was at hand.) Instead of the MacDonald tartan cloak with the silver owl clasp, on this occasion she wore a shapeless green raincoat, much the same color as the reticule in which she concealed her dowsing tool. When she was traveling in a glamour of invisibility, she explained; tartans lacked the essential quality of being nondescript.

We had parked down the road, just out of sight of the imposing gate of *Beau Rouge,* which appeared to be unattended. *What, no police presence? Good for us, but what about the poor missing woman? Had she been put on the back burner so soon?* We rattled the gate, which proved to be locked.

Fiona took a set of passkeys out of her reticule, like something the chatelaine of a palace might have kept swinging from her belt. I looked around nervously as she clanked through her options, none of which seemed to work on the cumbersome lock.

"Blessed Brigid!" she exclaimed. "I never have this much grief from an antique lock. Oh, good. Here comes someone, perhaps the gatekeeper." She dropped the keys into her bag with a clatter.

An old man in a straw hat, carrying a rake over his shoulder, ambled toward the gate with slow dignity. His broad smile curved up like a crescent moon in his wrinkled round face. Ignoring Fiona, he peered at me through the wrought iron bars. "Madame de Rochemont not at home." He had a strong accent I took to be Mexican. I glanced around for help from my companion but almost didn't see her as she blended into massive dark rhododendron bushes flanking the gate.

"Yes, I know that," I said soothingly. Then, trying to adopt Phillipa's magical voice, I added. "Open this gate, please, and let us in."

Apparently I hadn't got it quite right yet, because the gardener turned the corners of his ample mouth downward and replied: "No one allowed in *Beau Rouge* without invitation, Miss. Mr. Kitchener away with police. He is the boss butler. You could speak to Mrs. Kitchener. She been expecting a girl help with the packing. You are Maria...Mary? Mary Corn?"

"No, I am *not* Mary Corn," I said, a tad sharply. "But I would like to speak with Mrs. Kitchener." If I could get as far as the kitchen, I might be able to have a look around the gardens afterwards.

Laboriously fiddling with the lock, he opened the gate, then thought better of it and clapped it shut again, frowning at me suspiciously. "I go and ask her. You wait here."

Some crows in a nearby pine commenced a noisy squawk-fest that drew our attention. "That cat again!" he complained.

"I say a thousand times, Mrs. K., don't let cat out of the house. She climb tree where crows nest." The gardener pushed open the gate a little, stepped out, and shook his rake at the tree.

Out of the corner of my eye, I saw (with some amazement) that Fiona was slipping through the barely open gate, right past the gardener. His attention seemed to remain fixed on the pine, as he threatened the invisible cat and noisy birds with his rake. Meanwhile, Fiona was moving like a green shadow down the circular driveway, where she seemed to melt into the foundation plants. When last seen, she was moving with surprising swiftness for a plump little woman lugging a reticule.

The gardener turned back to me. "You stay here, Miss. I go ask." He ducked through the gate and shut it after him but did not lock it this time. I would have to cool my impatience as he made his arthritic passage around to the back of the mansion. Should I wait for a chat with the housekeeper? And then what? Discovering I was not, after all, Mary Corn the packing lady, I'd be sent on my way. *No!*

I pushed the heavy gate and moved inside, pulling it closed again. The gardener would think we'd gone away. Or I'd gone away. I'd seen no indication that he'd noticed Fiona at all. *Honestly! That was so provoking!*

Now to find Fiona. Following her example, I moved into the shade of the foundation plants and scurried around the front of the mansion in the opposite direction from the gardener's route.

"*Hey, come back, you lady*. Come back! No permission to be in here. I call police. I call them now." So much for clinging to the coattails of Fiona's invisibility glamour. Instead of slipping through the garden like a transparent sylvan sprite, I was clumping along heavy-footed in my walking boots, being chased by the gardener, who was brandishing his rake, the wicked metal kind.

Imagine my embarrassment if I were arrested. Imagine Joe's concern, Stone's annoyance, Phillipa's wrath. I fled back to the gate, pulled it open a few inches and wedged myself through, completely chagrined. Ducking behind the rhodys, I tried to spot Fiona. Although she was nowhere to be seen, the gardener was very much in evidence, raking up a few imaginary leaves on the immaculate front lawn and keeping his eye on the gate. I stayed where I was, uncomfortably crouched amid prickly branches, rather than return to the car (fortuitously parked where my license number was not within sight of the gardener). I couldn't, after all, just drive off and desert my elusive partner. I waited and waited. Scratched and waited. Shifted and cursed and waited. Finally, the gardener disappeared inside the estate's three-car garage.

The coast is clear—now where is Fiona!

I glanced at my watch. How time doesn't fly when you're cold and uncomfortable! It seemed like an hour but was more like a half when Fiona finally reappeared.

She tried the gate. Spooked by me, the gardener had locked it this time. "Leaping Lord of the Greenwood!" Fiona muttered, fishing in her reticule for the passkeys. But just then, a horn sounded impatiently behind me, and I jumped out of the way, walking briskly toward the street as if I had simply been having a gander at the mansion, so lately in the news. Meanwhile, Fiona did her melting thing again, this time into the shadows of the fence.

The horn was still going strong, summoning the gardener on the run. I glanced back at the car, thinking this must be the butler returning. Well, no, not in that dashing red Mercedes roadster! And the face under the velvet cap's visor wasn't unknown to me. I'd seen that profile bending over my hand to deliver the deceiver's kiss. It was Albert Reynard! Just as I came to that realization, Reynard turned and caught me looking at him. His expression was perplexed. *He must be trying to place me*, I thought. *Where had he seen this bedraggled intruder before? And why is she skulking around his mother-in-law's mansion?*

The gardener came running to open the gate wide for the roadster to zoom into the inner driveway, the old man trotting after it. Reynard swung himself out of the small car and threw the keys at him. The gardener caught the keys, brushed off his pants, and bent himself double to fit inside the roadster; apparently it was his job to park it elsewhere.

Fiona stepped out of the bushes and eased her way out of the open gate before the gardener could return to lock it. We ran down the street to the safety of my RAV4 and hurled ourselves inside with breathless relief. I wasted no time in starting the car and driving off in a spurt of gravel.

"Good Goddess," I moaned. "That was the murderous Reynard, and I think he almost recognized me. If he remembers..."

Meanwhile, Fiona had caught her breath. "Eureka!" she crowed, when she could speak. "I found it!"

~

What Fiona had found with her dowsing tool was not water but the memory of water—an ancient cistern, abandoned and overgrown with grass. When her hazel dowsing tool had forked downward to earth at that particular place, she'd removed some of the grassy sod, which came up in blocks that appeared to have been recently cut. Under the sod was the wooden lid of an old-fashioned cistern. Knowing her time to be limited, she hadn't tried to pry up the lid but instead had hastily replaced the sod and brushed it over a bit.

Fiona, it seemed, knew quite a bit about these underground water storage tanks. (I wouldn't have been surprised if she'd pulled a pamphlet on cisterns out of her reticule.) She estimated the cistern's age at eighty-five years or more. It was probably made of concrete, eight feet in diameter buried ten feet in the ground, she told me as I drove home at top speed in a sweat of relief. The cistern's round vertical wall would be capped with a weathered oak lid. The tank had been conveniently located about twenty-five feet from the back door leading to the kitchen. At one time, there might have been a pump at the top so that the cistern need not be opened to obtain the water stored within, probably diverted from some nearby spring-fed pond located on the *Beau Rouge* estate.

When the cistern was abandoned in favor of town water, the pump must have been sheered off to make a level bed for a covering of sod. Thus the old cistern had remained completely hidden near an equally old grape arbor of thickly twisted vines. Inviting seating lined the shaded walls of the arbor. An herb garden of raised beds had been planted between the kitchen and the arbor, presided over by a small statue of Dionysus that have been intended originally to bless the grapes. Beyond the arbor, a brick walk led to the topiary garden and formal marble benches. Everything was much like my vision...except that I hadn't realized how close the scene was to the mansion's back door. I had imagined a closed pit. Don Wolfe had investigated a closed well of a much earlier vintage than the cistern, only it had not contained the body of Madame.

Fiona and I were now fairly certain that Madame was in the cistern. After our *Beau Rouge* adventure, we huddled over thistle mugs of steaming Lapsang Souchong tea in Fiona's parlor, plotting our next move.

"Reynard must have known about the old cistern," I said. "If he was careful about it, he could have removed the sod in blocks, got the old lid up somehow, and popped Madame's body inside. It's not great work to lay the sod back down and fluff up the grass a bit."

"I'm surprised the gardener didn't notice the disturbance," Fiona said, absently smoothing Omar Khayyám's fur. He stretched and arched his tail, then paraded up and down the coffee table, putting Fiona's tea tray in some danger. She opened her tin of shortbread and gave him a crumb. "More shortbread, Cass?"

"No, thanks," I said, eyeing the single dark hair stuck on the open tin's rim. "I'll call Phil now." Steeling myself for abuse, I tapped her number on my speed dial.

"Hello, Cass. I'm in the middle of a delicate sauce, here," was Phillipa's greeting.

"Okay, call me back when you've unchained yourself from the Viking. Fiona has had her eureka moment and located the body's hiding place. We think."

"Quick, just tell me where," she demanded.

"*Ding, dong, bell. Pussy's* not *in the well*...she's in the...." Leaving the sentence unfinished, I shut my cell phone and helped myself to more tea.

Phillipa must have whisked that sauce to perfection in short order. In less than a minute, my cell played *On a Clear Day You Can See Forever*.

"Where...where...where?" Phillipa demanded.

"In the cistern."

"What's a cistern?"

"An underground water tank used in earlier times. This one is not very far away from the back door leading to the kitchen. We're guessing that the location of the old well was known, with a picturesque roof that made it relatively easy for the detectives to check it out. Not so the cistern. It's completely covered with grass. But when Fiona poked around, she found that the sod had been moved recently because it was still cut into blocks, and the blocks had been replaced. Reynard had probably been told about the cistern, maybe even shown its location, by his wife or his mother-in-law. The poor old lady must be in there. You'd better tell Stone."

Phillipa groaned. "Do you really think that Don Wolfe is going to believe this one?"

"No, but the more he thinks about it, the more he'll be intrigued. He's a detective, after all, and he'll have to have a look. We're fairly sure we're right this time."

"Reynard won't get away with this murder. Some satisfaction in that," Phillipa said.

"Speaking of which, he saw me. Not Fiona, just me. Well, you know Fiona, the green shadow."

"*He saw you!* How?"

"I was just at the gate when he roared up to it in his cute red roadster and honked for the old gardener. I gaped at him, and he stared at me. I'm not sure whether or not he recognized me. Does it matter? I was just a luncheon guest at his restaurant."

"Unless…"

"Unless what?"

"Unless he's read one of the many, many news stories about your crime-fighting prowess in the *Pilgrim Times*."

"Hmmm. Well, I'll think about that tomorrow."

"Okay, Scarlett. But if we're right about this guy, he's murdered three women so far. I've heard that, after the first time, each murder gets easier to commit."

"So you will have a word with Stone?"

"Oh, yes. Of course I will. We can't leave de Rochemont in that cistern. Anyone who makes such extraordinary red wines deserves a proper burial."

"Ask him to give me a call if anything is found, okay?"

"Sure. One more thing, how will Don Wolfe know the cistern's location if it's so well concealed?"

"Fiona left her marker."

"Which is?"

"She just happened to have a flask of vinegar in her reticule. By the time Don starts looking around, the grass should be burned yellow in the shape of a pentagram over the old cistern."

"I'd like to have a proper look inside that reticule one day," Phillipa sighed.

I looked over at Fiona. She did not appear to be listening to my conversation. "Never look at magic too closely," I warned. "Talk later."

When I'd clicked off, Fiona laughed softly. "You're right, dear Cass. I like to keep a few surprises up my sleeve. And in the bag."

CHAPTER TWENTY-EIGHT

Be like the bird who, pausing in her flight
on boughs too slight,
feels them give way beneath her,
and yet sings, knowing she has wings.

– Victor Hugo

While I was waiting anxiously to hear about the cistern search, Becky called. "Success!" she crowed. "I've missed my calling as a shake-down artist."

"You've contacted the Holmes family about access to Archie's papers?"

"I sent a chill right through the blue-blooded veins of those Boston Brahmins. I told them that Ashling had acquired a literary agent who was dickering with Little Brown and Farrar, Strauss and Giroux over who would ante up the better advance on a definitive biography of Archibald Fennimore Holmes, renowned New England poet. I said that I'd been employed by his widow to request on her behalf unlimited access to their son's manuscripts, papers, and letters, including notes on an autobiography he had planned but never written. I didn't exactly say there were skeletons in the Holmes family's closet, but I certainly rattled their bones."

"And is there an interested agent? Or did you just..."

"Oh, please, Mom. I *always* cover my butt. I have a client in the middle of a distressing custody suit who's a literary agent with a very respectable New York firm. She was very pleased to do me the favor of discussing the prospect of a Holmes biography with Ashling. An intimate portrait of Archie the poet and the whole Holmes family, my client said, might actually stir up some real interest in publishing circles, particularly at Farrar, Strauss, and Giroux. Come to find out. Archie really had talked to an old Harvard buddy at Farrar, Straus and Giroux about publishing an autobiography, and rumor has it that the family was not amused.

"Wow...you don't say! Unfortunately, Ashling doesn't strike me as the writerly type," I said. "But never mind that, did you squeeze a few dollars out of tight-fisted *Mama* Holmes?"

"You're right, of course, Mom. Not only is Ashling uninterested in literary pursuits, but did you know that she's deeply dyslexic? Just putting a simple sentence together on paper baffles the poor girl. And she's certainly not a reader, even though she was surrounded by literary types during her marriage. It would be like Nora Barnacle writing a biography of James Joyce, *My Life as Jamie's Muse*. Hey, that's not a bad title, is it? And yes, your daughter has struck a vein of gold. Mrs. Fanny Fennimore Holmes has decided that Ashling should not be troubled with such crass commercial matters whilst deep in her grief over Archie. A very handsome allowance was proposed, and I offered to discuss the matter with her."

"Bravo, Becky! But now I wonder if this means that Heather will be losing yet another housekeeper?"

"Well, Mom, what do you expect? Ashling can hardly be required to sluice out the kennels when she becomes a merry young widow of means."

"Have you met Ashling in the flesh, or just talked with her by phone?"

"We met for coffee at the Starbucks around the corner from our offices. Some friend of Heather's called Maury drove her into town. I found her to be otherworldly to an alarming degree, wafting about in this sheer flowered dress that seemed right out of the thirties. She has the effect of making others rush to protect her, doesn't she? No wonder she ended up at St. Rita's."

"Maury is Dick Devlin's associate," I explained. "Good guy. On the quiet side. Did he join you for coffee?"

"No, he had business at Angell Memorial. Just made sure I was there to guide Ashling to a table. He was back to shepherd her into the car in less than an hour. Honor guard. Say, that reminds me of another queer thing I noticed about your young protégée. She floats."

"Does she? Whatever do you mean?"

"She's like one of those extraordinary ballet stars who glides over the earth as if she has wings on her heels."

"Just so, Becky dear. And I'm ever so grateful that *your* feet are firmly planted on the ground. Thanks so much for giving Ashling a hand."

"Sure, Mom. Whenever you need a little legal blackmail, I'm your gal!"

~

Ashling's change of fortune warranted a celebratory visit to Heather's.

Joe had his leg propped up on the antique sea chest that serves as our coffee table, a mug of the strong coffee he favors at hand, and a NOVA rerun about the bioluminescence of deep-sea creatures on the TV. Scruffy, who couldn't jump up on the window seat in his present condition, propped his head on one of its pillows and, like a regular dog in the manger, warned off Raffles from settling himself in their usual comfortable watching spot. Chins on the seat cushions, they gazed out the bay window together at wild November whipping the last of the curled brown leaves around the mulched herb gardens.

I'll stay with the furry-faced guy. That mangy crowd of curs gets on my nerves. I bet those dumb critters never saw a leg cast anyway. Better watch yourself, Toots. That wind out there sure is fierce.

Sure is fierce! Sure is fierce!

Distributing farewell kisses on foreheads, smooth and furry, I slipped away through the back door, well wrapped up in my windproof purple parka, and drove through the gathering clouds of the bleak autumn afternoon. A few hours with Heather might be just the ticket to cheer up a day like this. Providing, of course, I didn't discover Ashling packing her tapestry carpet bag.

Arriving at the Morgan Manse's circular driveway, I found Deidre's blue Mazda parked near the kennel-garages. *Of course!* As a distant cousin-in-law of Ashling's, she would want to help commemorate this financial coup.

Not surprisingly, Heather had insisted on rejoicing in Ashling's good fortune by opening a bottle of Veuve Clicquot. "Cass! Oh, good. What a wonderfully clever daughter you have! You must join us in the conservatory," Heather said, drawing me in the direction of looming potted palms, cushioned wicker furniture, and a sea of house dogs milling about. Deidre and Ashling were already there, sitting together on the wicker sofa. Ashling's bare feet were drawn up on the cushions. A good thing, because the conservatory floor was always chilly, not to mention strewn with dog belongings, chewed Mylar bones, pig ears, and other unsavory items.

With her customary finesse, Heather opened a bottle and filled four crystal flutes.

"All right, we're going to have a toast, but first..." Heather opened the French doors and shooed the restless dogs out into the November chill to relieve themselves and give us a few minutes of peace.

"Your daughter Becky has been a marvel! How neatly she pulled off this little coup—she's nearly as crafty as her mother," Heather said, hurrying on before I could comment. "And here's the very good thing for me! Ashling has decided to stay with us for the time being."

News that certainly relieved my aura of guilt! "Ashling, dear," I said. "How wise of you. No need to plunge into a new life until you're really know what you want to do or be. You've certainly been a goddess-send to this bunch."

"It seems as if Heather is always between housekeepers, doesn't it?" Deidre said.

I cast her a warning look. No need to go into details about those who had taken Ashling's role in the household formerly—fate had not always been kind to them. In fact, only Captain Jack had lucked out, reconnecting with old fishing buddies in the restaurant business.

"Good cooks always find good friends," I said, which was actually the text of a refrigerator magnet Phillipa had refused to paste on her SubZero double-door.

Ashling's smile was wistful and her gray eyes soulful. "I feel so at home here, thanks to Heather and Dick. And Maury, too," she said softly. "I love to cook for everyone, especially baking sweets and pastries. I love the dogs, dear furry little wanderers. I love this magnificent house and my beautiful Wedgwood room with the marble bath and that cute little balcony. And Heather insists that I must keep on drawing my generous salary even though Mother Holmes has decided to make me quite secure. So good of her, and I'm sure that's what Archie would have wanted."

A statement as wildly improbable as that made me feel that Ashing was continuing to block out memories of Archie's real nature. Perhaps she had even forgotten his vengeful poltergeist. O, blessed amnesia of the abused wife. I'd noticed that tendency in myself in glossing over the reality of life with my first husband Gary Hauser, that battering bum. He was sober now, of course, and gainfully employed at the Pilgrim Nuclear Plant, which was nice for the children. I was never one to hold a grudge, I thought, although if Gary should accidentally fall into one of those vats...*oh, well. Banish that thought*.

"We widows know what it's like to have to make our own way in the world," Deidre sighed, the twinkle in her eye at odds with her mournful tone. "Perhaps, sometime in the future, a knight in shining armor will appear on Ashling's horizon and sweep her away into living *happily ever after*. In fact, he may be closer than any of us imagine, just waiting in the wings, so to speak."

I knew that gleam. Deidre, the incorrigible matchmaker, had a scheme afoot.

"Hecate preserve us," Heather said, looking down that long road of endlessly interviewing housekeepers whom Fate would ultimately tap on the shoulder.

"Oh, I don't know if I could ever forget Archie," Ashling said. She eased off the sofa and almost floated around the room passing a basket of delectable puff pastry triangles. I was always tempted to glance at her feet—bare and blue-toed as usual. (Victorian mansions tended to frigid floors.) And those feet were barely touching the floor, as if she were a magical prima ballerina entering the stage.

The doors between the conservatory and the Victorian parlor blew open with a crashing bang that reverberated against the wall and threatened to break the glass panes. No wind from outdoors appeared to be involved; the outside doors were still closed tight.

Heather, Deidre, and I exchanged glances. "Is he back?" Heather mouthed silently.

Ashling looked up, startled, clutching the little cache of pastries to her frail breast. "What was that?"

"Oh, someone must have left a window open upstairs," Heather reassured her. "These old buildings have some weird effects." She opened the door to the "dog yard" and let in the horde of canines to clear the air of ghoulies and ghosties.

Deidre drew a wand of polished dark wood out of her workbag. I'd never seen that one before and made a mental note to question her about it later. Working quickly, she stepped out of Ashling's line of vision and described a pentagram in the air above us, muttering "Begone, blasted specter," then tucked the wand away again before the girl, feeling some vibration perhaps, wheeled around to see what was going on. Replacing the wand with an embroidery frame from her workbag, Deidre beamed at Ashling, a trace of her old mischief in her smile. The embroidery was a sampler bearing the legend *Forget-Me-Not* surrounded by small blue flowers.

Seeing something like a shadow over Ashling's shoulder, I shook my head to clear my vision.

"You have nothing to fear, my dear. May his spirit rest in peace," Deidre assured Ashling.

The girl sank down on a cushioned chaise lounge and unclenched her hands, placing the pastries on a wicker coffee table. The house dogs, rowdy with November energy, encircled her protectively, each one vying to lean against her.

Soon after, I went home to my own needy crew, leaving Deidre to contemplate her newest project—conjuring up a romantic partner for Ashling. If only Deidre would turn that marvelous but intrusive talent to finding a soul mate for herself. I'd been a single mom myself for many years, and I knew what fearful loneliness afflicted working women who "had it all" except for a guy to warm her heart and sort out garage mechanics.

CHAPTER TWENTY-NINE

O, thou, whose certain eye foresees
The fixed events of Fate's remote decrees.

– Alexander Pope

"It's high time I read the cards, don't you think?" Phillipa took out the Rider-Waite deck from a red silk bag that hung from her belt. That splash of red gave a note of relief to her all-black outfit, a cashmere scoop-necked pullover and corduroy slacks. "Perhaps the tarot will give us a sense of direction in this whacked-out season. I don't know when we've ever been so unsettled, between trying to get a leash on Mad Dog Hugh Collins and following the trail of Murderous Reynard the Fox. But probably our lives have been this weird before—and I just don't remember."

"You've blocked out our therapy-for-Dee cruise, then," I said. "And your own indiscretions." Reminders of past transgressions are what friends are for.

We were in her living room, reclining on apricot-silk-cushioned easy chairs and enjoying the blaze in her massive stone fireplace. Ignoring my little zinger, she topped up our glasses of an excellent Madeira. Phillipa knew how to give a cold, rainy afternoon in November her special touch of elegance. She pulled a Moroccan brass table to rest between us and placed the Queen of Swords on it as the signifier. "This will represent Madame de Rochemont—it's just the right card for an autocratic old widow."

"What I want to know is why it's been *days and days* since Stone tipped off Don Wolfe about that buried cistern and he still hasn't opened it," I complained.

"Because, my dear, Don has been assigned elsewhere—didn't I mention that?—and Stone has run out of options. There's no one else working on the Rochemont disappearance in whom he feels he can confide your cistern theory. Here—you shuffle."

I'm a feeble shuffler, and seventy-eight cards are a handful, but I did my best. A card fell out of the deck and winged into Zelda, who was reclining on her own silk cushion on the gray stone floor. The sleek black cat stood up, arched her back, eyed me with disgust, and stalked off to the kitchen. I reached for the card. "Leave it!" Phillipa ordered.

"You realize, don't you, that Thankgiving is just around the corner," I said, handing her the rest of the deck"

"And I'll be mighty thankful when we settle down to enjoying our blessings instead of dashing around town poking sticks into every wasps' nests on the South Shore. Before one of us gets stung by some killer bee."

"I think you've stretched that metaphor about as far as it will go," I commented.

"As the informal poet laureate of Plymouth County, I think I'm the best judge of that," she replied. Phillipa favored the Celtic Cross spread. She turned over two cards, the first to cover the Dark Queen, the second horizontal across to cross her. "Uh-oh," she said.

"Oh, why do card readers always do that *uh-oh* thing! You remind me of a mechanic looking under the hood of an ailing car." I leaned over and looked more closely. The cover was a guy turning his back on eight cups. The card laid across it was The Moon.

"The seeker is looking in the wrong place," Phillipa said, tapping the tarot card.

"Well, we know *that*!" I interrupted. "The question is, how to get him to look in the right place—the cistern."

"And crossing that is the card of hidden risk and secret foes. No surprises there. Sometimes The Moon can even mean danger to a loved one. Good thing Stone isn't assigned to de Rochemont, so I won't have to worry about him getting caught in the middle of whatever we've conjured up. Now let's find out what wisdom the rest of the layout will give us." Phillipa continued to turn over cards to complete the Celtic design, then studied them, sipping her tawny wine and scowling.

"Look at this! Behind these crimes is that dreadful grasping miser, the Four of Pentacles. That'd be Reynard. Then down here..." Phillipa laid another card on the table, beneath the Dark Queen. "The Devil, materialism in its ancient mythic form. So what else is new?"

"Keep going," I urged. "What's that brawl at the top?"

She took another sip. "Five of Wands. Violence, as you can see. Poor Madame has not wandered off on a senile toot. She's been battered and buried, just as you've insisted all along, Cass. Now, for what's ahead. Eight of Wands. Jolly good. Our quest moving along to a conclusion. This juggler of Two Pentacles indicates our own ambivalence over the pursuit of two desperate characters. And here's The Fool—that's how we're perceived, I fear. Then, Great Mother Justice on her throne—a perfect card for you, Cass. In this reading, it represents our hopes. And the final outcome, ah yes. The Chariot. Success! Victory!" Phillipa sat back and smiled that brilliant smile that lights up her face with beauty.

"What about the card that fell out of the deck?" I reminded her.

The smile faded. She reached out and laid it beside the Celtic Cross.

It was a skeleton in black armor riding a white horse. His banner was a five-petaled rose. And he appeared to be about to run down a woman and a child.

Death!

"Not always as bad as it looks," Phillipa said. "It could mean a complete shake-up. Destruction, yes, but also transformation. And there weren't any swords in this layout. That's a good thing."

Sure it is.

~

"What about that cistern?" I demanded. At least twice a day after our tarot session, I'd called Phillipa with this same question.

"Oh, sweet Isis, Cass! There's nothing anyone can do. If I've told you once, I've told you twenty times, there's no longer anyone connected with the de Rochemont investigation that Stone can nudge. This is not a new problem. As you know, our psychic flashes have never been popular with actual working detectives. Stone excluded, of course."

"I can't just let this go, Phil. I've got to do something," I said

"*Fine.* Just don't tell me what mischief you get up to next," she replied with some asperity. "I need plausible deniability."

"*Fine*," I echoed crossly. "See you around, then."

"Listen, Cass…" Her tone softened a bit. "You take care, now. Don't jump into any cauldrons your guardian angel can't pull you out of."

"What—*moi*?"

As we said good-bye, I determined that I wouldn't make any more whining calls to Phillipa. I would find another way to get the investigation moving. Perhaps I would just drive by *Beau Rouge* to see what, if anything, was going on. My old woven *Libra* handbag was hanging on the knob of the office door. Reaching in for car keys, I encountered a tiny silk purse that enclosed the quartz armadillo fetish Deidre had pressed upon me for "spiritual protection." And I thought about how Deidre had complained recently about always being left out of our investigative escapades. Just because she was the sole parent for four little ones. It really wasn't fair.

Also, it might be prudent for me to use a different car. That canny old gardener over at *Beau Rouge* might recognize my RAV4! I glanced at the herbal wall clock—just five, about the time Deidre would be heading home from her *faery shoppe*.

I called her on her cell. "Dee, honey, I'm thinking of having another look around *Beau Rouge* this afternoon. Care to join me?"

"Oh, goodie! I'll just phone Bettikins and see if she can stay to feed the kids. I don't think she'll mind. There's some big game on tonight, and she loves watching sports on HDTV. She's a fanatical football fan. And I fear she's indoctrinating the kids. I guess there's no escape from sports madness. Personally, I couldn't care less."

"Madness, indeed. Gary was always in a cold sweat because of some crazy bet he had riding on the game, but Joe would rather watch *Nature.* Can we use your Mazda?"

"Sure. I'll pick you up in about twenty minutes."

As we clicked off, I realized I'd be leaving my own dinner crew in the lurch. I put on my parka, threw the old handbag over my shoulder, and went to find Joe out in the garage, where he'd set up a workbench for his do-it-yourself projects. Simply having his leg in a cast didn't deter him from pursuing home "improvements" whether I wanted them or no.

He was engrossed in sanding a new banister he planned to install on the cellar stairs. The old one was unstable and dangerous, Joe had insisted. I'd said, yes, it did have a bit of a wiggle to it, but it would probably be fine for another hundred years. He'd merely smiled, that infuriatingly superior what-do-you-know-little-woman smile. *Oh well*, I'd thought. *He needs to feel useful. It's a macho thing.* "I'm using real mahogany," he'd said proudly. *It's just a cellar workroom*, I'd wanted to remind him.

Scruffy and Raffles were lying in the garage doorway, enjoying their before-dinner snooze. I stepped over them.

Hey, watch it there, Toots. We canines don't like being nudged about.

"Watch it yourself, Mister. If you want to be undisturbed, stay out of traffic lanes."

Joe looked up from his sandpaper with a startled expression. I put my arms around his neck for a hello (good-bye, actually) kiss. "Not you, darling. Scruffy. He complains when anyone looms over him. Dogs are very sensitive about being closer to the ground than humans."

Humph. Just because you humans can stand on your hind legs, doesn't mean you can walk all over us canines, you know. Or creep up on us when we're resting after a stressful chipmunk hunt.

Chipmunk hunt! Chipmunk hunt! Raffles woke up and shook himself clumsily, knocking against Scruffy's cast. A quiet snarl cautioned him to be more careful.

"Would you mind if I went out with Dee for a bit? She's just on her way to pick up some fabric for pillows, and she wants my opinion. I don't think we'll be gone much more than an hour or so. Do you want me to bring home some takeaway roast chicken from Forker's Turkey Farm?" Casually, I picked up a spade lying on the potting table and stuck it into my bag.

"Nope. Not to worry," Joe said."I'll get something easy out of the freezer when I'm through here. And feed the pups, too. You girls go ahead and mull over patterns to your hearts' content."

"You *are* a treasure."

"But what the devil do you need that spade for?" Joe glanced at the tell-tale handle sticking out of my bag.

"Oh, that. Yes. Dee promised me some iris rhizomes she's dividing. I thought I'd plant a stand of them in some of the borders. You know how I love purple flowers. Asters, heather, foxglove, lavender. Purple anything, actually. Now you be sure to rest that leg of yours when you get in the house." With a kiss and only a mild twinge of guilt, I left Joe to his mahogany masterpiece and went out into the driveway to wait for Deidre's car to arrive. For the first time, I noticed a few small holes between the bricks where I'd laid walks through the herb gardens. *Chipmunks, all right. Cute little buggers.*

CHAPTER THIRTY

Out of this nettle, danger, we pluck this flower, safety.

– William Shakespeare

It was dark by the time we reached *Beau Rouge*. Following the same plan that had worked before for Fiona and me, we parked Deidre's Mazda just out of sight around the curve of the road, and walked along the wrought iron fence..

"Holy Mother!" Deidre exclaimed, pushing at the gate. "Look at this! It's not even locked. I thought you told us that you and Fiona had a hard time getting in because the place was locked up tight."

"It was. I even borrowed her passkeys—she has a whole passel of them."

"I know. I can hear you clanking," Deidre said.

"Shhhhh!" I whispered. "For Goddess' sake, Dee, keep your voice down. There's a kind of bulldog gardener who guards the place. But I've a feeling that tonight might be our lucky night. We're due for a break on this case." I opened the gate a few more inches and eased inside, followed closely by Deidre. Wearing her peaked red hood and red Wellingtons, she looked like a woodland sprite, complete with mischievous grin. I congratulated myself on inviting her along—a hard-working single mom needed to do something *outré* once in a while. *Good for the soul.*

"There doesn't seem to be anyone around. Isn't that extraordinary!" Deidre murmured. "Almost as if you put a spell on the place."

"Pure luck, Dee. I'm not all that adept." I crept forward into the shadows cast by the large handsome house with its elaborate portico and ornate front door. No lights in front, but I could see a gleam in the back. Probably Max and Elsa having supper and watching *Wall Street Today*. I smiled inwardly at my image of the Kitcheners in the kitchen as I continued crunching forward on the gravel driveway around the other side of the house. I wanted to get to the kitchen garden without passing directly under the kitchen windows. A half-moon pouring light from its silver bowl was trouble enough.

"Where's the cistern?" My pixie companion stage-whispered and tugged at my sleeve. I put a finger to my lips and pointed toward the garden at the place that Fiona had marked for us. Imagine carrying a bottle of vinegar in that reticule! *Have Magic, Will Travel,* that was our incredible friend.

The five-pointed star burned into the grass was visible even in the faint moonlight. We crept forward, and I began cautiously working around the edges of the cistern where blocks of sod had already been cut and replaced to look undisturbed. I lifted the first one. Deidre pulled a lethal-looking pair of sewing shears out of her handbag and began working on the second.

"I'm hitting some wood thing underneath," she murmured.

"It's the cistern's old cap. Keep on what you're doing," I replied softly. I glanced at the kitchen windows and the back door. Everything appeared quiet and peaceful, so I went back to lifting up squares of sod.

A few minutes later, we had exposed the cistern's water-stained oak cover. I began trying to pry it open with my spade.

"What's this? *Who's this?*"

We both jumped up, startled out of our wits. A square dark figure seemed to have appeared out of nowhere. *Not nowhere!* I corrected myself. *From the garage.* I could see him stolidly planted in the door, the light silhouetting the square frame of his body while it masked his face.

Hearing shouts from the garage, the butler Maxwell burst out of the kitchen door waving a long French rolling pin like a baseball bat. "Is that you, Mr. Reynard, sir? Are these trespassers? Elsa, call 911 and tell them that we have nabbed two intruders."

A cruel flashlight shone in our eyes. "I know you," muttered Albert Reynard. "*I know I know you*! I've read all about you witches."

Deidre's bright boots appeared to be frozen to the ground. I grabbed her arm and hauled her with me back toward the corner of the house and the gate beyond.

"*No, Maxwell.* I'll handle this myself." Reynard spoke sharply to Kitchener. The man hesitated in the kitchen doorway, still holding his culinary weapon aloft.

"What are you two doing here," Reynard hissed. As he stepped into the light, I could see his thin lips twisted into a vicious scowl. His hand was rubbing his chest, giving him a Napoleon look. I held out both my little fingers in the traditional defense posture, and commanded "Cease and desist!" in my deepest, strongest voice. How I wished Phillipa were here! She was much better at the magical-voice thing than I.

"Get off this property and never come back or *I will kill you witch-bitches.* And I'll be within my rights. Self-defense against home invaders." His laugh was chilling. I was surprised that he didn't attack us, or send the butler and his formidable rolling pin to do the job.

Then *worse and worser*, behind Reynard, I glimpsed the rotund figure of the gardener running at full tilt, also from the garage. He was holding at the ready a lethal garden tool known as an edger as if it were a lance. Its sharp blade glowed under the garage lights.

"Ceres protect us! *Run!*" I urged Deidre. "Run as fast as you can."

I looked back to see Reynard holding the gardener back from following us and, no doubt, skewering one of us like a shish kabab. O*f course*, I thought as we dashed back to the gate, our footsteps heavy with fear. *He doesn't want the police to show up and investigate the damage. And find the body while they're at it.*

"Hey, Kitchener! Hey, Elsa!" I hollered back over my shoulder. "Look in the cistern! *Look in the cistern for Madame.*" The butler continued to brandish the long rolling pin.

I ran as if Cerberus the three-headed dog of Hades were at my heels..

But turned out that, once in motion, little Deidre could easily outdistance me, and by the time I reached the corner of the house, she was already leaping out of the gate. We raced toward the car, and she flung herself into the driver's seat, started the motor, and gunned it.

"Holy Mother! That was a close one," she giggled. "Do you think Maxwell will look in the cistern? Wow! I haven't had this much fun since we broke into that Q guy's house in Carver looking for bodies. Well, don't get me wrong—the murders were ghastly tragedies, and I mourn for those dear innocent victims. But going after that pervert was a real rush. Made me realize that all work and no play have been making Dee a dull gal."

"Talk about *Desperate Housewives*! Maybe you ought to think in terms of a new hobby. Or a new man."

"Are you kidding, Cass? I already practice every artsy craft known to woman and goddess. And as for a *new man,*" Deidre's little foot stomped down harder on the gas pedal."I have four children, two toy poodles, and Geronimo the Gerbil. I don't need a new *anyone* to pick up after."

I'd always felt that Deidre looked upon her late husband Will as just another one of the kids. He *had* been rather on the slow side, but a really good-hearted guy. What she needed now, though, was a real partner. Preferably sexy, strong, smart, and savvy. I tried to visualize that sort of lover for Deidre but in my mind's eye he kept looking like Joe, so I quit. *Let the Universe of Infinite Solutions handle this one!*

"I think you can slow down a bit now, Dee."

It would be a good thing, I mused as we rattled along Route 3 in the Mazda, when that excess energy always burning so high in Deidre was diverted into some sort of romantic sport instead of illegal trespass, and I should be ashamed of myself for involving her in such a potentially dangerous escapade. On the other hand, I did feel somewhat exhilarated myself.

"It *was* rather exciting," I admitted. "*Oops!*"

"Oops, what?" she asked, her tone suddenly sober. "What did you do?"

"Left my spade at the scene. Oh, well. No problem. I imagine the Fox grabbed it as soon as we ran out of there and used it to smooth over the sod to look as if nothing had happened. No way he'll want to call attention to that cistern by alerting the police. But it's not going to be easy. Surely the gardener has noticed Fiona's pentagram burned into the grass."

"What about those other people? The butler and his wife."

"I'm hoping that one of them cared enough about Madame to have a peek in the cistern, I said.

"Unless Reynard gets rid of them. Who's in charge there, anyway? With the old lady missing, I mean. Her daughter and granddaughter were murdered. Are there any other relatives?"

Suddenly a light went on in my sixth charka. "Yes…yes! Rosalie Boyd Indelicato! I wonder why I didn't think of her before. She's another in-law. Marie Reynard's sister-in-law from her first marriage to the late Marty Boyd. She seemed to really care about Madame de Rochemont, too. I wonder where she is, what she's been doing since the old lady disappeared? I should have tried to contact her before I dragged you into a life of sin and deception. Which, by the way, reminds me. Do you happen to have any iris rhizomes?"

"Iris? Rhizomes?—what for?"

"I promised Joe I'd bring some home. Lovely purple color, iris."

"We could stop at Finch's Floribunda on the way home. They'll have mums and spring bulbs and things. Always hoping we don't encounter Wanda."

"Or Collins. Fresh Meadow Farm is right next door." I remembered it well.

"Scratch that, then. Let's try Sachem Superfoods instead."

~

"Okay. I had to spend a tedious hour drinking Bart Bangs' inferior sherry to get all this," Heather complained.

I poured her another cup of strong black coffee. She'd brought Honeycomb with her, and the Golden Retriever was sniffing Scruffy's cast with a rare show of interest while Raffles galumphed around her in circles of great delight.

Hey, Mama! Hey! Look at me, Mama.

Honeycomb grabbed Raffles' leg and pulled it out from under him, causing him to topple onto the floor. If a dog could be said to giggle, he giggled and rolled on his back, waving his feet in the air, like a puppy. A very, very large puppy.

Get lost, Kid. Your Mama and I are conversing here. Scruffy barked twice sharply. Raffles rolled over onto his belly and put his nose between his paws dejectedly.

"Play nice, pups," I said.

Heather took a fortifying sip and continued. "First of all, the staff of *Beau Rouge* is not peering into the cistern because *they're gone*. The Kitcheners and the gardener—whose name, by the way, is Jesus Ramirez—have been given leaves of absence at half-pay. Apparently Reynard's regular attorney—Seth Bettencourt, surely you remember him, the wily old bastard?—did some fast talking that got Albert the Fox appointed Conservator of the De Rochemont estate because Madame, wherever she is or was, having wandered off without regard for her affairs, may now be considered incompetent to administer her finances and property. Meanwhile, the three servants have been encouraged to use this hiatus to seek new employment."

"Bummer. I feel as if we're back at square one."

"No, we're not. Light that Libran candle I gave you for your birthday and *think good thoughts*. Remember you asked me about Rosalie Boyd Indelicato, the late Marie Reynard's sister-in-law?"

"Yes. I had a bright idea that she might be useful, but I didn't know how to locate her."

"I found her." Heather could hardly suppress a gleeful grin.

"*You found her!* Great news, Heather! How? Where?"

"Oh, I have my connections, you know," Heather said airily. "After the trial, Rosalie and her husband Sal moved out of the apartment in Southie to a brand new mansion in New Jersey. Apparently Sal Indelicato got a promotion in whatever it is he does, which has something to do with waste management. Rosalie was very upset about Madame de Rochemont's disappearance, but she was immersed in the final preparations for her daughter Paula's wedding and wasn't free to rush back to Chatham. She has, however, been in touch with Chatham detectives working on the case. Or *supposed to be* working on it. Seems to me they've practically lost interest."

"Can she help us? Will she?"

"The answers are *maybe* and *maybe*. Bartie tells me that Rosalie could protest Reynard's being named sole conservator, petition the court for herself to be named guardian, which is a sort of co-conservator. She is, after all, as close a relation as that murderous son-in-law. So I have retained Bartie to contact Rosalie, explain the situation—well, not about the cistern, you understand, but the rest—and offer to file the petition for her."

"Great work! I wonder, now that you mention relations, do you suppose there is anyone closer than an in-law?"

"Well, as you know, Borer, Buckley, and Bangs were the de Rochemont attorneys, and Buckley recently assisted Madame to make a change in her will, the substance of which Bartie wasn't at liberty to say, but he did divulge that there's an elderly sibling and some cousins in Bordeaux where the original de Rochemont vineyards are located. No one in this country, though."

I took down the Libran candle from the kitchen shelf and placed it in the center of the kitchen table. It might have been my imagination, but the tiny scales of justice and silver keys imbedded in the pale blue-green wax seemed to wink with inner fire when I touched a match to the wick. I held myself back a little from focusing on the candle flame, however, because it only takes a few moments of concentration on a bright light for me to tune out of this world and fall into a trance. Sometimes it happens accidentally and triggers a clairvoyant vision, after which I feel ill and nauseous. So I've learned to be careful.

Avoiding the hypnotic flame, I suggested, "Let's zero in on that five-petaled Rose of Venus you've got in there and think about Rosalie getting an excellent result from Bangs' petition."

The softly hued wax gave off the serene, comforting scent of rose and myrrh. We spent a few minutes meditating on the Rose of Venus and Rosalie, a nice connection. We'd never actually met. I'd only seen Rosalie a few times in the courtroom in my short career as a juror and once in the limousine with Madame, but I felt she was someone I could broach with my insights into Madame's whereabouts. As a guardian, Rosalie could insist that the police open the cistern. Meanwhile, I would have to concentrate my inner forces on family matters—a beautiful Thanksgiving gathering, and the blessings of peace and safety for our circle and those we love—while I waited for Madame's body to be found and suspicion, finally, to fall on Albert Reynard.

CHAPTER THIRTY-ONE

Are you in earnest? Seize this very minute!
Boldness has genius, power, and magic in it.

– Jean Anouilh

"Remember the first Thanksgiving we spent together—at Dee's," I said. "You and I and Phil were all single at the time, and now look!"

"Don't forget, it's Deidre who's single this time," Heather said, "and we surely should do something about that, or what's the point of being witches?"

"Well, she does have the company of those four little ones," I said. "Although, as I remember my years of being a single mother, a person hungers for some grown-up love in her life. But it may take some time to find the right sort of family man who'll adore Dee and her kids and also be comfortable with the faery world she lives in."

"Yeah, just wait until he catches sight of those anatomically-correct dolls she makes for toilet training," Heather said reflectively. "And the voodoo poppets, although I don't think Dee's ever stuck a pin in a truly vital part, do you? And then there's the black mirrors she crafts so beautifully for skrying. And the occasional ghost sighting. Yes, there could be a problem matching up Dee."

"At least we don't have to worry about Fiona, who is always and forever a merry widow," I said.

"Still, as you say, we have burgeoned. There are almost too many of us to fit around any one table," Heather mourned. "Even without Phil and Stone."

"Not *almost*. There *are* too many of us."

"I've already invited Deidre and the kids, Fiona, and Mick Finn who's still smoldering around her. Ashling, of course. I'm depending on her to mastermind the sides, since Dick insists on deep-frying the turkeys. It's a macho thing that's replaced being king of the grill. And Maury, too, whose family are all on the West Coast. So why don't you and Joe join us? Don't worry about space—I'll rent something suitable."

Knowing Heather, I could only imagine what that would be—the round table out of Camelot, maybe. "Thanks, but I have my own entourage now. Adam, Freddie, and the twins, Becky and her new beau. As usual, I haven't met him yet but I've been given to understand that his chief attraction is that he's *not* a lawyer. Anyway, they're all planning to share the feast at *Chez* Shipton. And we've something to celebrate—both Joe and Scruffy will be out of their casts this week."

I'm bringing Josh, Becky had said, suggesting that I should figure out the rest on my own. She and her new guy had been going to see a performance of *Blythe Spirit* at the Colony Theater. I didn't know if that was a hint or my sixth sense finally kicked in, but in my mind's eye I saw Josh involved in the theater as more than a member of the audience. If so, Cathy must know; Becky would surely have shared that tidbit with her actor sister.

Sure enough, when I called Cathy and steered the subject around to Becky, I soon found out that Joshua Duvall was a member of the resident acting company at Trinity Rep in Providence. "Last of the resident companies, Mama," Cathy said wistfully. *Mama* was a new note, and she pronounced it in the Gallic manner. "Steady work. *That* must be a treat." Cathy and her partner Irene had scored some small film parts and the occasional TV walk-on or commercial. Between gigs, Irene worked as a bartender; Cathy, who was frail, usually stayed home, or sometimes filled in as a temp office worker at the West Coast office of Samuel French.

Irene got on the phone to say "Hi," and added, "Duvall has been in everything from *Peter Pan* to *Twelfth Night*. Becky says that he's going to do *Cabaret* next season. Did you know that Becky handled his divorce? Nasty custody suit."

"Becky has more fun keeping me guessing. There are children involved. then?"

"Not kids, Mama," she said, echoing Cathy's accent. "Two Papillions, Louis and Marie. Thanks to Becky, Josh secured visitation rights including sleepovers."

"Somehow this Josh doesn't sound like Becky's kind of guy." I was sorry I said that as soon as the words were out of my mouth.

"Leave her alone, Mama," Irene advised. "She's enjoying the glamour of it all."

"Yes, you're right. She's always been so sensible, so reliable, so organized. Maybe a romantic fling is just what she needs."

"That's what we think," Irene said.

Cathy said something that I couldn't hear. Irene laughed. A moment later, the fragile connection was broken before I could ask all the questions that were aching in my heart about Cathy.

~

Along with my cozy saltbox cottage, Grandma had bequeathed to me her copious notebooks filled with herbal lore, handed down by Shipton women for generations, reverently shelved in my cellar workroom. There was also one indispensable green book in which she'd written her personal recipes for Concord Grape Juice, Quahoag Pie, Herb Vinegars, Summer Pudding, Dandelion Wine, and so forth that I kept upstairs in the old borning room. While I was rummaging in my desk for that nostalgic book, I came across Freddie's "remote viewing" map of Fresh Meadow Farm.

What an amazing talent! I thought. *Too bad the CIA had found out about Freddie's abilities, though—sure can't trust their obsessive military mentality.*

The recipe book, neatly penned in ink bleaching to purple, was underneath the map. I thumbed through to find Grandma's Nine-Herb Stuffing. Sage, rosemary, parsley, thyme, tarragon, anise, marjoram coriander, cardamom—all in precise measurements that Phillipa would never work out, I thought with some satisfaction. I stuck Freddie's drawing in the book for a marker.

"Thoughts are things," as Grandma always said. It was as if thinking of Freddie's covert career had drawn her toward me, because the very next minute she called.

"How did it go?" I was careful not to be more specific on the phone. With Freddie involved, I was getting rather paranoid about the long arm of Homeland Security.

"Weird, Cass. Very weird. I sure will have to draw a line in the sand sometime soon. But never mind that now. I called to invite you to a just-us-girls lunch at the Siros, where I'll hit you up for some wild and crazy motherly advice, you know what I mean? And if the deal you're working on could use, say, a little push from my bizarre talents—like Uri Geller metal fatigue or a nice little virus—just say the word. Not now, of course."

"I got that," I reassured her. "Lunch sounds wonderful, dear."

"Right on. Also, you never did tell me how you made out with that little map of the farm that I drew for you. And I read in the papers that there's been some development in that murder thing where you were a juror. A missing old lady. We seem to have lots to catch up on."

"I'll come early, if that's okay, and visit with my darling grandkids. Warn Miss Sparks to stand back." Much as I had once felt some resistance to thinking of myself as a *grandmother* (in other words, *crone*), my first glimpse those two little beauties in the hospital had dispelled all such reservations. The most amazing uplift of love had filled my body, as if an invisible cord had attached husky Jackie and fair Joanie to my soul.

But I sensed that Miss Sparks viewed with some alarm any enthusiastic rush into her well-organized domain. On past visits I had noted that she cast a cold eye on what I believed to be perfectly appropriate gifts for Jackie and Joanie that I'd brought from Deidre's shop—mythic animals stuffed with protective herbs, troll and elf puppets, faery wings for Joanie and a Perseus sword for Jackie. I smiled to myself, thinking of the charming toys I'd been saving for this visit—cuddly white buffalos and winsome raven tricksters. Their soft cotton innards contained a few pinches of Fiona's corn pollen for the blessings of harmony and long life.

Aglow with anticipation, I arrived at Adam and Freddie's Hingham town house on 380 acres of the Wampanoag Country Acres, a gated community where I practically had to leave my eye scan with the guard as proof of identity. Freddie came out to meet me in the Visitors' Parking Lot, looking like a brilliant autumn leaf in her burnt orange turtleneck. The color blended perfectly with her amber eyes and spiked brown hair. The black skirt was mini, worn with thigh-high boots and a soft leather blazer. "Ms. Halloween of the New Millennium" I greeted her. A fragrance of sandlewood and something spicy that I couldn't identify surrounded us as we hugged.

Just as I'd thought, the twins loved their sacred buffaloes and pesty ravens, and, happily, Miss Sparks' sense of appropriateness was not disturbed a whit. "Birdie, birdie," Joanie crooned to her trickster, flying it around the room with her newly acquired toddling skills. Jack, still clinging to chairs, hugged his buffalo and babbled to his sister in their private language. With paranormal abilities on both sides of their DNA, I would bet that they'd have a telepathic connection for all of their lives. When they began to feel that they were different than others, they would need to be surrounded with the protection of uncritical love. Animals, for instance. Animals were so good at wordless allegiance.

"Shouldn't they have a real pet of some kind?" I wondered aloud. "Perhaps a savvy feline who would know how to keep little folk in line."

Miss Sparks gazed at me with chilly disapproval and uttered one damning word, "Allergies!"

"Oh, don't worry, Minerva," Freddie hastened to unruffle her nanny's fur. "Pets are *verboten* at Wampanoag. The Association rules!"

I couldn't help thinking how great it would be if Adam and Freddie bought a "real" house with a large fenced yard where pets would be welcome. But I tried not to invest my wish with too much magical energy. *Not fair!*

Soon afterward, my daughter-in-law tore me away from those two dear children so that Miss Sparks could feed them their nutritionally-balanced lunch while we escaped to Siros for grown-up beverages and carbohydrates galore. We sped away in her sporty red Porsche for North Quincy.

"I sure hope Joanie doesn't zap anything else while we're gone," Freddie muttered, negotiating traffic snarls with uncanny aplomb.

"Really? Has Joanie been showing signs of—you know—anything unusual in her aura?"

"Not in her aura, Cass. In the damned blender. Sparks likes to make healthful shakes with, you know, broccoli and other sneaky stuff, so that the twins will drink their vegetables all unknowingly, ha ha. Only the blender keeps misfiring and bubbling all over everything like the wicked witch's cauldron. And I myself have caught Joanie eyeing that glop with a glint in her eye—'mischievous intention', you might call it."

"Please, dear, no spectral evidence allowed at this trial. Give your daughter the benefit of the doubt and invest in a new blender. Some cheap, serviceable brand, so maybe it will work right. Joanie is far too young to be the cause of such shenanigans." A grandmother's bias, I admit. But it simply wouldn't do for a toddler, however adorable, to evidence paranormal powers, a family crisis never covered in Dr. Spock's excellent volume on child care. "Now tell me, what's up with your latest assignments? I believe I'm expected to sing for my supper. Or rather, skry for my lunch?"

But Freddie put off complaining until we were seated at a lovely table overlooking Marina Bay, drinking prosecco aperitifs. When our server, "Adolfo," had wafted away with our orders—spinach salads with gorgonzola, chicken piccata, and angelhair pasta—she leaned over and said one mysterious word, "pigs."

"Did you say 'pigs', dear?" The special glow that only the bubbly stuff imparts was beginning to relax my wise-woman demeanor. In fact, I giggled.

"It's not funny, Cass." Although no one was within earshot, Freddie leaned over and whispered, "They want to know if I can kill a pig."

"Kill a pig? How? Are you supposed to perform some kind of blood sacrifice?"

"Shhhh. Not with a weapon. By directing negative energy. Hexing them, as the mundanes might say. Practice, like, for 'neutralizing' enemies of the state. Psychic black ops. Talk about 'going over to the dark side!"

"Yes, but *why pigs?*" I was dumbfounded. *Kill a man with negative energy? When pigs fly,* I thought. *If that worked, a lot more women would be widows.*

"Pigs have hearts very like human hearts in size. A pig heart was transplanted in Poland—unsuccessfully— in the early days of cardiac surgery. Heart valves from pigs have been used in humans for a decade." Freddie leaned back and closed her eyes. "And I do have negative energy, you know what I mean. Used to have trouble controlling the vibes, but with your help, I've got a handle on those accidental zaps. And I've never spilled those little incidents in my past to the guy in charge. But he knows. He knows enough, anyway."

The prosecco wasn't doing it. Suddenly I was coldly calm. "What rank is this guy in charge?" I saw her hesitation and added, "It will just be between us, but I need to get a visual."

"General," she whispered. "Hard to believe, isn't it?"

"I guess I don't have to tell you that such a negative use of your powers would put you in the deep sh...—eh, bad karma—for several lifetimes," I said with my best maternal authority. Freddie was as dear to me as a daughter, and I wouldn't have her harmed by these military playboys who seemed to have no spiritual sensitivity. No conscience, as well.

"That's the thing. I do need you to tell me," Freddie said with uncharacteristic uncertainty. "You're my guru, after all."

"Good, then I'll tell you a few more things. The real reason that black magic rebounds threefold is not so much mystical as physical. The first harm caused by unrestrained negative energy is to dull your sensibilities and weaken your immune system. And when negative energy rebounds into your own life, it will inevitably affect those you love as well. Not in the sense of retribution, but simply as the natural law of contagion."

Freddie paled. "I've got to get out of this program. These people are downright scary."

"I'm sorry to be throwing a bucket of cold water again, dear, but this pig business is definitely out of bounds. Does Adam know?" I hoped I had instilled my son with something like my own value for life, but he, too, had been doing the occasional courier work for the Company.

"I haven't decided whether or not to tell him. Might be safer for him not to know, in case he might get, you know, all macho and interfering. What he does isn't James Bond stuff—it's a whole other trip, if you know what I mean. Just passes some guy a newspaper on a park bench somewhere in Europe, like, when he's at a show or convention for Iconomics. Adam doesn't even know what he's handing over, which makes me all kinds of edgy. Guess I shouldn't be telling you this. No sense both of us getting our panties in a twist."

"That's okay. I already 'saw' Adam in London last week. In my mind's eye, of course. Practically burned down the house lighting protective incense and so forth. I know the two of you only got into this because you're deeply patriotic, and that's to your credit. But, as you've discovered, every covert organization has its pocket of crazies."

"Amen, Cass. Speaking of crazies, isn't it a good thing that your pal Heather doesn't have a clue about the pig project!"

"Ceres save us! She'd be breaking into some government facility to rescue the pigs. And dragging me along."

~

Having burnished the house to a shining glow in preparation for the family Thanksgiving, I was assembling the dried herbs I would need for the stuffing when my cell rang. Messing about with aromatic concoctions in my cellar workroom always made me think of the wicked stepmother in Snow White.

"Shipton's Delicate Decoctions and Pretty Poisoned Apples," I answered.

"How do you know this isn't a call from the Neighborhood Witch Watch?"

"I have caller ID, Heather."

"A terrible thing has happened to Hugh Collins," Heather launched into her tale with a barely suppressed wicked laugh. "He's been attacked by an American Staffordshire Terrier."

"Good Goddess! Where? When? How?"

"Here. Last night. He broke into the hospital."

"Well, I guess he shouldn't have done that," I said. "Will he be okay?"

"Yes, but perhaps not as handsome. And he's threatening to bring charges against me for harboring fugitive canines, but I do think that when my attorney Bartie Bangs has a quiet word, Collins will reconsider. Nevertheless, I'll have to get the terriers out of town. There is an underground railroad for that sort of thing. Canine witness protection. In fact, I'm one of the way-stations."

"I'm not surprised. Why don't you tell me what happened from the beginning," I suggested.

So she did.

Two days ago, Stone, his partner Billy Mann, and a team of uniforms had swarmed into Fresh Meadow Farm with a warrant to search the premises for evidence of illegal dog fighting. Stone hadn't even told Phillipa of the raid for fear of compromising its mission. "For some reason, he was afraid that, whatever Phil knew, the rest of us would soon know as well. Can you imagine!" Heather said, with another deep, dangerous chuckle.

Although Collins had got rid of his pit bulls by dropping them off far from the Farm, probably out of a horse carrier, there was plenty of residual evidence. The blood-stained arena and the charred remains of canine bodies, plus the testimony of one of his grooms, had been sufficient for Collins to be arraigned at the Plymouth Courthouse. Having posted bail, he was released on his own recognizance.

In a rage of vengeance, Hugh Collins had broken into the Wee Angels Animal Hospital during the early hours of the morning on the day after the raid. His intention was to take a leaf out of Heather's grimoire and photograph the pit bulls he suspected her of harboring illegally—dogs that had once been part of his stable of fighters until he'd dumped them to get rid of the evidence. He was right about Heather's role as their rescuer. Wendy and Captain Hook, as she called them, had been cast off half-dead at the animal hospital by a scared teen aged boy who'd been paid to discard them in the state park. Sir Bedivere was wanted by the Animal Control Officer for attacking a woman on the street in Plymouth. His buddy had been shot dead by police, but Bedivere had supposedly disappeared, run away to parts unknown. In truth, though, he'd been secretly rescued and was being rehabilitated by the Devlins. The same was true of the white pit bull that Collins had chucked out in Jenkins Park, the terror who had attacked me and my dogs. Heather called that one Sir Percival—talk about a misnomer. Well, that was Heather for you! The fifth rescue, who'd been let loose in Heather's dog yard, was Sir Kay. A surly bunch of knights, if you asked me.

As luck would have it, the first of his former fighters that Collins encountered was Wendy, asleep in her pen with Maury curled up beside her in his khaki sleeping bag. He'd been working late at the hospital when she began howling in a despondent fashion, threatening to get the entire "unsociables" ward in an uproar, and so, as he'd often done in the past weeks, he'd decided to join Wendy in her pen as a comforting companion and get himself a few winks as well. Maury hadn't realized how exhausted he really was. His short nap turned into a fatigue-drugged dead sleep, which pleased Wendy greatly.

The pit bulls' quarters in the hospital had been clearly marked "nervous temperaments—hospital personnel only." Hugh had crept stealthily along that corridor toward the first pen, Wendy's. Other pit bulls began to stir and whine as he approached. Wendy bolted upright at the scent of the human who had so abused her and, when her fighting prowess waned, had even filed down her teeth so that she could be used as a bait dog.

"Good girl, good girl," Hugh had murmured, holding up his phone to snap her photo. Suddenly the long bundle of khaki sleeping bag in the corner had come to life.

"What the hell do you think you're doing in here!" Maury had exclaimed. Striding toward the pen door, he'd yanked it open, at which time a streak of yellow seemed to leap over his shoulder and onto Hugh Collins.

Collins screamed. Wendy mauled his face and defensive hands. Her teeth were only nubs, so she couldn't tear out Collins' throat, but her jaws were strong and her nails were sharp. Blood spurted everywhere. Maury grabbed the pit bull by the scruff and dragged her back into the pen. It had all happened in a matter of a few seconds.

After the ambulance had taken Hugh Collins away to be stitched up by a hastily summoned plastic surgeon, Dick, Heather, and Maury had conferred on the potential damages. There might be a lawsuit, although Collins would be on shaky ground, breaking in as he had done, and certainly there was a legal problem with harboring fugitive pit bulls.

"The only terrier that Collins really I.D.'d was Wendy. And Goddess knows, he's set her socialization training back to square one," Heather mourned. "So we've got to get Captain Hook and the three knights out of there immediately. One of those 'underground' stations, you know. Exeter, Rhode Island—quite a deserted woodsy kennel. I'll have the boys back as soon as the coast is clear, of course. But Wendy's in trouble. If it goes to court, Bartie Bangs will defend her—she's really the victim, not Collins. Or maybe I'll just claim she died of poison from sinking her teeth into that evil bastard. No way will I allow her to be put down. No way, *no way!*"

Heather was clearly on the edge of hysteria. I searched for a reassuring thought. "At least, Collins is out of business for good. I wonder what kind of a sentence he'll get."

"Vicks only got 23 months. Now that's a jury *I'd* like to have served on," Heather said darkly.

CHAPTER THIRTY-TWO

I am the ancient Apple Queen.
As once I was, so am I now...
Ah, where is the river's hidden gold!
Where is the windy grave of Troy?
Yet come I, as I came of old
Out the heart of summer's joy.

– William Morris

The pastry might not be as light and flaky as Phillipa's cool hands could conjure, but my sturdy apple pies were lined up in fragrant glory on the broad windowsill of my birdfeeder window, and the turkey was roasting to juicy, golden perfection, its rich aroma transforming Scruffy and Raffles into kitchen devotees, gazes and noses never leaving the big brown bird in the oven window.

In the midst of which, Phillipa called me on her cell. She and Stone were in Connecticut, celebrating the holiday with her brother Dan Gold's "blended family." She had talked his newest wife Paisley out of executing a Turkey Paella and was herself masterminding a bacon-wrapped French Roast Turkey with Truffle Stuffing and Vegetables *Provençal*.

But that was not the news. *The news* was Madame de Rochmont's body had been found in the old cistern after all.

After my parting cry of *Look in the cistern for Madame* to the loyal butler brandishing his long rolling pin, Kitchener's curiosity had finally overcome his anger at our intrusion. After the couple were given leaves of absence at half pay by the nervous fox Albert Reynard, who urged them to seek other employment, Kitchener and his wife Elsa had privatedly unearthed the cistern and recoiled in horror at the odor of putrefaction. Unsure what to do, the couple had contacted the new co-conservator, Rosalie Boyd Indelicato, who called the Chatham police.

"I'll tell the others," Phil said. "Happy Thanksgiving, Sibyl."

Joyfully and actively celebrating the removal of his cast, Joe was building efficiently small, ready-to-go fires for the fireplaces in kitchen and living room. His recovery came under the category of *mixed blessings*—no sooner was he off the sick list than he'd received his traveling orders. Now his old green duffle bag was packed and he'd be leaving Friday night for Medway, Kent, where the Rainbow Warrior was to lead an armada of boats protesting the controversial Kingsnorth Power Plant.

The dining room table was set with Grandma's best imported Blue Willow china and stemmed glassware, not my usual pressed glass tumblers. Two new high chairs were wedged between my old ladderbacks.. Decorating every room were bundles of corn shocks, families of corn dollies, swags of Indian corn, and bowls of shining apples in every hue from gold to deep russet. A glow of housewifely self-satisfaction suffusing my own apple cheeks. I was even wearing my "Fatal Apple" lipstick, a favorite shade.

It was a moment of deep thankfulness indeed!

Thankfulness that I actually had everything ready for our family feast in real not metaphysical time. Clairvoyants and other fae folk are troubled by a tenuous relationship with the actual world, especially Greenwich and its official clocks ticking off the moments of life. Yet here I was looking calm, collected, and well-organized. Whatever Becky had told her new boyfriend Josh about her "mother the witch," he would not be viewing the stereotypical frowsy disorganized crone. I smoothed down Grandma's chef's apron protecting my sage green cashmere sweater and leaf-printed skirt, enjoying a Zen moment of quiet contentment.

Ready though I was to meet Becky's new guy, I was glad Adam, Freddie, and the twins arrived first. Freddie always seemed to fill a room with her scintillating energy, and that went double with the twins.

Hey, it's the talcum kids again. They aren't as pesty as some smelly short people.

Short people! Short people! Raffles loved all children on sight. He appreciated their being on his level, easy to kiss and nuzzle.

Scruffy, however, was always a bit disdainful of little ones, especially those still in diapers or training pants. Raffles made up for his sire's natural reserve by cavorting around the twins with a welcoming nose and boundless glee. He made a good buttress for Jackie, who was still trying to get his legs to carry him upright. Joanie, who could toddle in her own forward leaning ballet style, always confident that there would be arms outstretched to catch her, made her light-footed way to Scruffy and plumped down beside him. She crooned something soft in his ear and put her arm around his neck. Suddenly, he didn't seem to mind.

"Be very careful of her. No pushing over or stealing toys," I warned Scruffy.

The look he returned was deeply scornful. *As if I didn't know how to behave myself.*

Behave myself! Behave myself! Raffles continued to offer Jackie a sturdy lean-upon.

Must be that French Briard blood, I thought. After all, they'd been bred to pull small carts. Although since Scruffy's cast had been removed yesterday, he was still walking a bit stiffly and painfully. Dick, the redoubtable holistic vet, had said it could be a touch of arthritis from the trauma, and it might very well heal itself in time. If not, he could try acupuncture.

No needles, no pins, no way! I ran into a needle-pig once, and that creeping pincushion had prickles as long as my paw. Ouch! Scruffy had pressed himself against the examination room door in an urgent let's-get-out-of-here posture He definitely was not a New Age canine.

Well, it had only been a day since Dick had removed the cast. I'd begin my own wintergreen therapy right after Thanksgiving. Scruffy had never objected to a soothing massage. Neither had Joe, for that matter.

A lecture in manners having been sternly imparted to both dogs, I turned to embrace my tall handsome son and slim, soignée "daughter."

"*Over the river and through the woods*," Freddie sang softly. "You're one of *my* blessings, you know. As mothers-in-law go, I lucked out."

Adam wanted to know what mischief I'd been brewing. With his green eyes and sandy hair, he was the child who looked most like me (only much taller, and with a classic physique) but when he scowled questioningly, I could see a flashback to my ex, Gary Hauser, currently employed at the Pilgrim Nuclear Power Plant. I shook my hands surreptitiously to be rid of that negative memory.

Opening the bottle of single malt scotch that Adam had brought to the feast, Joe looked askance at me, wondering how much of the current crime scene I would share. I winked at him, meaning *not much*.

So I said: "We're all grateful that the local law has finally put an end to that dog-fighting ring over at Fresh Meadow Farm. That's about it, dear."

"What about that missing old lady over in Chatham? Didn't she have some connection to the jury trial you were involved in?" Adam asked, helping himself from the array of cheeses and pates on the kitchen table.

Freddie, who knew about our attempts to get the old cistern searched, mercifully changed the subject to Adam's own plans. "Adam's got news, too. He's moving up the corporate ladder like a rocket. He'll be first among the many Iconomics V.P.s by next year if I don't screw up the deal, not being what you might call the ideal *corporate wife*, if you know what I mean." She chuckled wickedly. "But now he's, like, too terribly busy, what a drag! Can you imagine, he's got to hop on a plane to Chicago tomorrow morning, nose to the proverbial grindstone while the rest of the world is grooving over the long weekend! Not to mention that the awesome Sparks has flown the coop. Back to the ancestral digs in Merrie Olde England for a 'fortnight,' whatever that is. So I had this brainstorm. Why don't the twins and I stay over with you until Saturday? Or even Sunday?" Freddie paused breathlessly in her stream of consciousness delivery, and I jumped right in.

"Beautiful!" I exclaimed. "Joe's leaving, too, to join the Rainbow Warrior in Kent. I'll be thrilled to have you and the grandcutenesses to keep me company and help me cope with the leftovers!"

"It's two weeks," Adam said, ruffling her hair, worn today in soft natural brown curls rather than jelled spikes. Even her dress was feminine and floaty, but her platform shoes sported outrageous red heels. "A fortnight is fourteen days."

"I knew that," Freddie said, smiling up at him. "But doesn't it sound like it might be *much longer*? Especially to be without our incredible nanny?"

Adam grinned over his tumbler of scotch. "Now I wonder what escapade you two will get up to? And just for the record, if I'd wanted a corporate wife, I'd have looked up the Stepford Men's Club."

"*Escapades? Moi? Et tu mère sacreé? Impossible*!" Freddie reached into her copious tote bag, pulled out a couple of terrycloth bibs and proceeded to fit them over the twins' matching organic shirts with *Center of the Universe* imprinted on them. I busied myself with nuking the butternut squash casserole and tossing the salad.

After taking the turkey out of the oven to "rest" before carving, a move that Scruffy and Raffles watched with rapt attention, Joe was already subduing the mashed potatoes with brute strength when Becky arrived with Josh. Wrapped in a blazing new shawl of dramatic proportions, her shining asymmetrical haircut even more so, silver earrings dangling to her shoulders, Becky was breathless and apologetic for their late arrival, but I knew very well that it wasn't my well-organized daughter who had delayed the couple's entrance. She gave me a brisk hug and two bottles of dessert wines, a lovely amber muscatel.

Josh was shorter, older, darker, and had a lot less hair than his publicity photos, which just goes to show that the magic of the theater often begins in the dressing room. His dazzling smile had a charming sideways quirk, and his teeth had been bleached to California whiteness. Under the black Burberry trench coat tossed casually over his shoulders like a cape, he wore a gray raw silk blazer that was much too thin for November, but the long crimson wool scarf wrapped around his neck was halfway into December.

"Ah, the marvelous mother about whom I've heard so much, *La Belle Dame Sans Merci,*" he said, his accent pure Olivier, his voice deep and compelling. He took my hand and held it, not so much for a shake as for an intimate moment of sharing, having no idea, perhaps, of how much I would learn from his touch.

"Well, that's more sympathetic than Lady MacBeth," I said. "Welcome, Josh Duvall, to our holiday and our home. It's a delight to have you here, and I'm looking forward so much to hearing more about your life at Trinity."

Holding his hand for a second, I'd felt a swirl of conflicting emotions casting off in all directions like a fourth of July sparkler. Erratic and unreliable, but more dependent than controlling. I felt him looking deeply into the eyes of others, the better to see himself. I wondered how long it would take Becky to catch on to that.

Hey, Toots! Who's this bozo with our Becky, and what does he want with our turkey?

Our turkey! Our turkey!

Scruffy limped over to stand guard between the glorious aromatic bird and the newcomer. Raffles sniffed Josh's shoes with intense interest, then moved on to Becky's glamorous shawl and was rewarded with an ear scratch.

Becky introduced Josh to Joe, Adam, Freddie, and the twins, not neglecting the canine members of our family. "Scruffy and Raffles. These are Mom's dogs that I told you about," she said. "It's rumored that they talk to her."

"Must be a useful talent. I only wish my Louis and Marie could express their true wishes to the judge. At least, your fellows can tell you what's going on with them. Reminds me of an incident we had on stage with the dog Sandy in *Annie.*" Josh patted Scruffy and Raffles briefly on the head. Raffles rubbed against the new guy delightedly, layering his sharply creased black trousers with sandy-colored dog hair. Scruffy stalked off awkwardly to his faux sheepskin bed, a comfortable warm place near the kitchen fireplace.

"I was Warbucks, sporting a twinkling zircon tie pin and totally bald head." With a can-you-believe-this smile, Josh patted his less-than-lavish dark hair. "We had no idea what was going on with that mutt until he got onstage and threw up all his dog cookies. My first experience working with kids and dogs. And my last, I hope."

"Dogs never hide how they feel. Maybe that's why I find them so easy to understand. I hope you thought of a suitable ad lib," I said. Goddess knows what other eccentric details about me Becky had imparted to Josh to entertain him.

"Josh is very quick," Becky said proudly. "He distracted the audience in the cutest way."

Josh smiled modestly. "Just a matter of diverting their attention away from stage left. A simple magician's trick. Mercifully, Act Two ended soon after."

By way of distracting my own audience, I guided everyone into the living room where Joe filled drink requests and Freddie passed appetizers. Josh regaled us with more theater vignettes, name-dropping with abandon, while Becky gazed at him admiringly.

Freddie rolled her eyes at me.

"Ohhh, nice watch," she said, as Josh took a breath and reached for a bacon-wrapped Bay scallop. "TAG Heuer?" She touched it briefly.

He nodded, smiled appreciatively at the acumen of the diminutive brunette in the shockingly high red heels, and nibbled at the scallop.

"*Freddie*," I warned, wondering if that watch would ever run right again. "Would you like to get Jackie and Joanie into their chairs while we bring in the vegetable dishes. Becky, dear, you can help me, and when everything else is set, Joe will bring in the turkey."

"Shades of Norman Rockwell," Freddie said.

Except it was my gorgeous Greek hunk bringing in the heavy platter, not some overworked grandma.

And it almost was a Norman Rockwell poster! A charmed event. (I have to admit I'd put a little happy spell of my own devising on the gathering. Bunches of mint for blessings and good cheer, rose incense and rosy pink candles for love and happiness.). A normal, down-home, traditional picture of Americana. Except for the incident of Josh watching big-eyed as the carving knife slid down the table toward Freddie's tapping fingers.

"Old houses," I explained hastily "Always have to watch out for those slanted floors."

I was pleased to note that Grandma's Nine-Herb Stuffing was much appreciated, especially by our guest, a hearty eater. Scruffy and Ruffles, who had wisely positioned themselves under the high chairs, made out like bandit-raccoons on goodies dropped from the twins' trays, scarfing up everything except a rolling Brussels sprout that they declared to be non-food.

I'd zoned out for a moment, listening to Scruffy's dissertation to Raffles on the importance of avoiding all green things dropped from the table, then came back to the human conversation to hear Josh regaling us with anecdotes about his run with *Equus*.

"I played Dysart the psychiatrist, of course. And the most amazing youngster played the boy. Alan Strang. A young actor named Leon Luce.

A chill ran down my spine from my neck to my seventh charka. "Leon Luce? Somehow that name is familiar. What did the boy look like?"

"He looked like a veritable Puck. In fact, as I recall, he told me that had been his favorite role and had always brought him good luck.

"Good luck?"

"Apparently his performance in *Midsummer Night's Dream* had got him out of some dreadful school. I don't remember the details, but someone from McLean Hospital had sponsored his acting lessons."

Leon Luce, I thought. *Could it be? The name's similar. He'd have altered his name, of course. And his juvenile records would have been sealed.*

"As an herbalist, Cass," Josh went on, "you'd have been impressed with how much this boy Leon knew about herbs. At the time, I was having a cluster of headaches that no pharmacological remedy seemed to relieve. Until Leon gave me some tea that cleared my head completely. In fact, that marvelous *tisane* made me feel both lucid and energetic—a natural 'upper.' I was quite in young Luce's debt throughout the run of the play, as you may imagine. Leon prepared the tea himself from a recipe he'd got from his grandmama. I depended on him entirely. It's not always that one's colleagues in the theater will look out for one. Professional jealously runs rampant, I'm afraid. I remember one time—it was the Scottish play..."

"I think I may have met that boy," I interrupted Josh's train of appearances.

"Yes," Freddie agreed. "Turned us all off chocolate for quite a while, as I recall."

~

"You didn't zap Josh's watch, did you?" I asked Freddie later when we were out of earshot of the others.

"*Que, moi?* That expensive watch he's wearing is the Steve McQueen model," Freddie murmured. "So he must be doing rather well, for an actor, or he has a rich patron. But I liked Josh, I really did. Fun and gossipy, my favorite. A bit pretentious, though, if you know what I mean. Do you think he really met up with that nasty kid?"

"And lived to tell the tale, apparently. I wonder if Becky can find out what exactly became of the boy. Here I was thinking he was still in juvenile detention. Supposedly until he was twenty-one."

"What did you think about Duval's headache story?" Freddie asked.

"I think the boy we knew was quite capable of causing the headaches as well as curing them. Some controlled substance in that cure-all 'herbal' tea, I'll bet," I said. "An 'upper' indeed."

"Do you think it will last—Becky and Duval?" Freddie mused.

"Only until she gets impatient with mothering the genius," I said.

"Well, I still hope Becky has a groovy whirl with Mr. Right Now in the glamorous world of the theater while she's waiting for Mr. Forever to appear on her horizon."

Freddie and I often viewed family matters in rather the same light.

CHAPTER THIRTY-THREE

I know that I am restless, and make others so.
I know my words are weapons, full of danger, full of death.

– Walt Whitman

Soon after supper on Saturday night, we tucked Jackie and Joanie into the blue bedroom under the eaves, the new twin beds equipped with solid wood rails. Wind and rain drumming against the windows only made the room seem warmer and cozier somehow, with its flowered-sprigged walls and blue-and-yellow quilts. The night light threw a yellow star beam against the dark ceiling. Each child had chosen a beloved item from the small sea chest in the upstairs hall that I keep stocked with goodies for little guests. Jackie snuggled down hugging a stuffed wolf cub while Joanie's disconcerting amber eyes studied the faery godmother propped on her pillow. Handmade by Deidre, the doll looked mighty like Fiona, right down to the miniature green reticule. No pistol inside, however.

I had forbidden Scruffy and Raffles to sleep on the beds the twins were occupying, a rule they ignored as soon as I was out of sight. Since Jackie fussed if I closed the twins' bedroom door, eventually I had to shut both dogs in the rose guest room where Freddie would be sleeping later. After her stern warnings, Miss Sparks would never forgive me if dog dander awakened some latent allergy in her charges.

Hey, Toots! We canines are natural guardians of the young, you know. How can we watch out for bad stuff if we're locked away from our kiddos. I don't even think we have enough air. We may be suffocating in here. Ack..ack...ack.

Ignoring the vociferous complaints and scufflings going on behind the rose guest bedroom's door, I went downstairs to join Freddie for a quiet cup of tea by the fireside. Ginger tea with a shot of ginger brandy. I lit the Libran candle Heather had given me on my birthday. A burst of rose and myrrh incense filled the air. The opal imbedded in the wax winked mysteriously, as my birthstone is wont to do. The tiny gold scales of justice shone in the soft light. A few serene moments for adults to enjoy after a hectic suppertime with two toddlers, much as we loved them.

It was a good time for me to relate to Freddie the details of Hugh Collins' comeuppance, although she knew the highlights already, of course. "We tried so hard to resolve the situation without actually hexing the bastard—well, most of us did. You know Heather. She has to be restrained from going over to the dark side whenever it's a case of animal abuse."

"Mmmmm. Good tea, Witch-in-law," Freddie said, holding out her cup for a refill. "To my mind, there's a time and a place for a good old-fashioned curse—like, if it's personal and not some black ops for Uncle, if you know what I mean."

"Maybe. But keep in mind that a hex affects the sender as well as the cursed. Not so much a rebound, although that's the teaching, but more a diminishing one's own spirit." I topped up our cups with tea and brandy.

"Yeah, so you keep drumming into my head. But don't worry. I've no intention of going into the hex business. I have enough trouble just controlling my freak energy." Freddie sighed and sipped, nestled among the sofa cushions.

A few sparks flashed up in the fireplace like a small meteor shower. I tried not to gaze too abstractedly into the flames lest I slide into an unwanted fugue state, my own nemesis.

Suddenly Freddie sat bolt upright and put down her cup on the old sea-chest that served as my coffee table. "Hey…do you hear something?"

"Hear what?"

"Tapping. Like something tapping at the kitchen door," Freddie said.

"It's probably the ocean. A large body of water bounces sound waves in erratic ways." But I was already on my feet headed for the kitchen when I heard the crash of glass. *That was no misplaced sound phenomenon!*

I flipped on the kitchen light switch and felt a great hot throb of fear in my heart. Albert Reynard was standing there, wearing a strange floppy hat that was dripping water from the drenching rain. A neatly cut-out pane of glass from the kitchen door lay in pieces at his feet. In one horrid flash, I took in the crazed look in his eyes and the pistol in his hand aimed directly at me. My first and only thought was how to keep Freddie out of the kitchen and the sleeping babies safe from this crazy vengeful murderer.

Too late! Freddie cried "What's that?" and pushed right past me trying to block the kitchen doorway. "Oh, shit, who?"

"Albert Reynard," I said softly, stepping into the room beside her "Will you get upstairs to the children?"

"Yeah, sure," she said, moving directly in front of me again. "Get your cell phone, Cass. Call the police, for Christ's sake."

"Don't you dare do that, you stupid, stupid interfering bitch," Reynard said in a strange, cracked voice. He stared directly at me, almost ignoring Freddie. His eyes were wild and his skin had a queer look, pale as something left out in the weather. "If you make one move, I'll shoot this young woman in the stomach. I believe that's quite painful."

I froze. "Look, Reynard, it's me you're after. Let her go, and we'll talk, just the two of us." I thought longingly of the weapons I should have grabbed on my way to confront a crash in the kitchen. Grandma's rifle over the mantle (unloaded, sure, but a deterrent nonetheless). The rowan wand, sometimes so effective if pointed with an upsurge of energy. Even now the hilt of the biggest carving knife in the knife block was gleaming at me. So many weapons, and none within hand. *Damn and blast!*

All I had was my little fingers. I held them out, pointed as knives to ward him off. Reynard hardly seemed to notice.

"Talk about what? Thanks to you, that stupid Kitchener got the cistern opened. No one would ever have thought of that fucking old place if you hadn't interfered. Even the fucking police had given up looking for the old crone. Did you think you could ruin me and get away with it?" Reynard had the Gallic trait of talking with his hands. The pistol waved dangerously.

"Okay, okay, calm down now." I said, soothingly, trying to summon my magical voice, low and irresistible. But instead, my pleas came out rather squeakily. Possibly the voice still needed some work. Would logic work with a lunatic? "Your breaking in here will only make more trouble for you, you must realize that. There's no real proof, is there, that you put

Madame in the cistern?" I gave Freddie a shove with my hip and whispered, "Get the babies out of here."

"What we're going to have here, Ms. Shipton," the madman continued, "is a genuine home invasion, just like the one that relieved me of my wife and blabbing step-daughter. Did you know that my wife was going to divorce me, ruin me, because of some stupid complaint made by her stupid daughter? I couldn't allow that to happen..."

"Don't make your situation worse than it is already," I begged. "My husband will be back any moment, you know."

"Ha ha, you dumb bitch. I've been watching you. I know you're here alone with that brainless girl and her fucking kids." He waved the gun in the general direction of the upstairs. "If I leave no one alive..."

I felt a chill snake down from my neck to my spine. "You don't want to do this," I told the psychopath reasonably. "Why don't you just leave now before something terrible happens."

He smiled an executioner's smile at Freddie. "Go upstairs and bring down your kids, just like she said, young woman. Do it now. Maybe I'll let you leave with them."

Freddie dug me with her sharp little elbow and pushed me aside for the third time. "No way, you bastard," she said in a tone that crackled weirdly. I could feel a flash of heat emanating from her slight frame, sizzling and electric. She stretched out both her arms, palms up, toward Reynard and his gun. Was it positive or negative ions that robbed us of power? Whatever vibes were pulsating from her body at that moment, and especially from her hands, the hairs on the back of my neck were standing up. The air in the room seemed unnaturally still, the way it feels when the eye of a hurricane passes through. Reynard mouth quirked strangely. He raised the gun.

Ceres save us, he'll shoot her, I thought.

And he did.

A gun shot rang out deafeningly in the confines of the kitchen. There was a strange clanging sound. The two dogs barked crazily upstairs in the closed rose bedroom. I could hear Jackie begin to wail.

"Freddie," I screamed.

Then I realized that the largest frying pan on the pot hanger was ringing like a Buddhist chime. And Freddie was still upright.

But not Reynard.

He was clutching his chest with his left hand, the gun dangling from his right, his eyes glazing over with pain. "Help me, help me," he moaned. The weird flopped hat drooped over his eyes at a humorous angle, but we didn't laugh.

"What happened, Freddie? You're all right. Oh, thank the goddess," I cried.

"Looks to me as if this Reynard person is having a heart attack," she said in a calm voice. "Classic symptoms, don't you think?"

"I'll call 911," I said, but seeing the man who had threatened me and my dear ones suddenly weak and helpless, obviously hurting badly, I felt strangely reluctant to move.

Reynard crumpled over. The gun dropped from his nerveless fingers. I snatched it up off the floor.

"I don't think you'll need that, Cass," Freddie said with new authority. "Here, give it to me before you hurt yourself."

I did that. My knees were shaking, and my hands weren't too steady either.

But I managed to fish my cell phone out of the handbag hanging on the kitchen doorknob. I dialed 911.

"Cass Shipton. Shipton Cottage," I said. "We've had a break-in here. Albert Reynard forced his way into my house with a gun. But it's all right. Because I think he's had a heart attack, and he's all crumpled up now. Better send an ambulance. No, no one else has been injured. Yes, I'll keep the line open. No, we took that gun away from him when he collapsed. Oh, and call Detective Stone, will you? He knows…he knows…some things about Reynard."

"Good," Freddie said, sitting down in one of the kitchen chairs, the gun in her hand, her eyes never leaving Reynard who now appeared to be unconscious. "Do you think he's dead yet? I'm not feeling too well, Cass."

"This isn't his first heart attack, Freddie. He collapsed after he killed his wife and step-daughter. Made him look so bereaved and innocent."

"Yeah. I suppose…you don't think that I… I did send quite a jolt his way, if you know that I mean."

"You did what any mother would do, Freddie. You stood up to the man who threatened your children. If he was stricken, it was the Cosmos at work, not you. You do not have that ability," I assured my dear daughter-in-law without, I admit, a great deal of inner conviction.

"Jesus, I hope not," she said.

I thought about a pregnant Ashling facing her abusive husband on the stair landing. Perhaps all women have hidden powers that suddenly appear when their children are threatened.

I could hear the sirens coming down our driveway. I said, "We'll talk about this tomorrow. Everything looks better in the morning. Maybe it would be a good idea to get our circle together for a purification ritual."

"Yeah, awesome," Freddie said. "Better stop me before I give someone else a double whammy. The pigs will thank you."

CHAPTER THIRTY-FOUR

...it's funny now and then
How my thoughts go flashing back again
to my old flame.

– Coslow & Johnston

Phillipa was always our reliable source of information which we would have been denied through normal channels. Her husband Stone was ordered to look up his old friend Don Wolfe, a detective with the Yarmouth State Police, and have a chat. The de Rochmont murder was a Yarmouth case, and Albert Reynard, the alleged murderer, had been transferred to their charge.

Phillipa learned that Reynard had suffered a massive coronary but was recovering in Jordan Hospital's ICU, that he was under police guard, and that his brother Francis had hired Hank Sharpe to represent him.

I remembered Hank Sharpe from my days on jury duty. She might be a formidable criminal defense-attorney, but she would lose this case, I told Freddie. There was more than enough circumstantial evidence that Reynard had clobbered his mother-in-law and stuffed her into the old cistern. His motive was obvious. Madame de Rochmont's hysterical insistence that justice had not been done in the deaths of her daughter and granddaughter might reopen investigation into a case that had been closed for good with the plea-bargain "confessions" of Lovitt and Farrow. Reynard desperately needed the estate he'd inherited from his wife Marie, and her extensive securities and real estate holdings worth millions, to underwrite his failing Cape Cod restaurants. That would have been reason enough for him to silence Madame de Rochmont before she screwed up his plans. And who knew what else she had on Reynard? What about her granddaughter's complaint against her stepfather? His behavior in attempting to get rid of the servants had been suspicious. Fibers found on the old lady's body matched those of Reynard's camel hair coat—it was an expensive coat, perhaps too dear to dump.

"And then there's our testimony, of course," Freddie said.

"Right," I said "He broke in here and threatened to kill us all in a faked home invasion. He blamed me for the discovery of Madame's body in the cistern, and he ranted about his wife and step-daughter's deaths. He said that he couldn't allow Marie to divorce him. What he really meant was, he couldn't lose all that money. And he brought up the issue of his stepdaughter 'blabbing'?"

"Yeah, I caught that, too. The old pervert," Freddie said.

"The most Hank Sharpe can hope for is a plea agreement with the District Attorney," I said, wishing I was as certain as I sounded.

"As long as he goes to prison," Freddie said with that unsettling edge of menace in her tone. "I don't ever want to see that bastard's face again. I'd be too tempted to give him another jolt, if you know what I mean."

"Reynard had a history of heart trouble. It wasn't your fault," I said.

Freddie gave me a knowing look with those mysterious amber eyes of hers. "I bet you're really wondering if I pushed him over the edge, if you know what I mean. As am I."

She's been hanging around with those CIA types too much, I thought. Our purification ritual might be just in time.

~

Since the purification ritual calls for an abundance of smudging, incense, and candles, we decided to hold it in Heather's conservatory where we could waft around bundles of smoldering sage to our heart's content without smoking up the house.

Heather, of course, insisted that she would contribute the perfect candles for the occasion. She brought them down from her so-called meditation room in the widow's walk that crowned the Morgan mansion, built by a ship captain of the 19th century. It was Heather's wholly private place that could only be entered by means of a ladder and a trap door. (She'd been known to use that sanctuary to burn the occasional black candle. From time to time, I'd foiled that dark impulse as best I could.) It was the only place in the house that had a water view, a magnificent panorama of the entire harbor. And the candles Heather brought down from the widow's walk seemed to reflect the changing colors of the Atlantic in a subtle way. Tiny shells were embedded in the wax and a few nuggets of citrine quartz .

"Wow, those are wicked awesome," Freddie said.

"They are perfect," I agreed. "Citrine is the purifying stone. But Heather knew that."

Heather looked pleased. "I have faith in the traditional correspondences, don't you?"

"*Tradition...tradition...*" Fiona sang out as she made her usual breezy entrance like a West Wind zephyr. She wore her coat sweater of many colors and a rainbow-striped skirt; Phillipa, in her customary black—leather jacket and narrow trousers—trailed behind her.

"Tradition is the light in wise woman's lantern, its shadow links the past with the future." Fiona swirled around, skirts flying. "Let's get smudging!"

"Deidre isn't here yet," I said.

"It's not like our magical time manager to be late," Phillipa said.

But Deidre ran in just on the dot of eight, looking pale and distressed.

"Is everything all right at home?" I asked.

"Oh sure," she said "It's just that I ran into an old friend on the way over here."

"She doesn't seem to have had a pleasant effect on you. A talker, was she?"

"He"

"Okay, he. Who was he—some old flame you'd rather duck?"

"No, you don't understand. I mean I *ran into him*. With the Mazda."

Deidre's slightly hysterical tone attracted the attention of the others.

"Are you saying that you ran over an old lover with your car?" Heather demanded.

"*Friend.* I said, *friend*," Deidre replied testily, slapping down on the wicker coffee table a bunch of birch wands she had made especially for this night. "Here. Birch for purification. Something all of you could probably use."

"Dee will explain everything after the ritual," Fiona said, wrapping a plump warm arm around those petite shoulders. "Let's jiggle off the negative vibes, dear."

"Yes, later," Deidre agreed. They shook their hands and feet, Fiona's silver bangles tinkling, always a comforting sound.

The rest of us joined in. Shaking off negativity seemed a proper beginning to Freddie's purification ceremony. Soon we were performing an impromptu dance through the potted plants of the conservatory, light-footed and laughing.

"Where is he now?" I whispered to Deidre as we snaked through several hibiscus trees in great ceramic pots.

"Jordan Hospital," she muttered. "Concussion, contusions, and a sprained shoulder. At least, I hope it's only sprained. They're keeping him a day or two for observation."

Heather lit the amazing candles. Phillipa smoldered the incense sticks of lavender, rosemary, pinon, and cedar. Fiona drew a handful of lovely citrine quartz pieces out of her reticule and placed them near the candles. And I smudged—the room, the circle, and especially Freddie.

My daughter-in-law stood with her arms held out at each side, her eyes closed, murmuring her own quiet prayer.

"Remember," I whispered to her as I waved the smoking sage around her from head to toe, "you do not have the power to cause physical harm to another person by thought alone, you never have had it, and you never will. It is better so."

"It is better so," she repeated.

Fiona began to chant an ancient Gaelic blessing that we'd heard before and could follow with her.

"Deep peace of the flowing air to you,
deep peace of the rolling waves to you,
deep peace of the shining stars to you,
deep peace of the quiet earth to you,
May the moon and stars
shine their healing light on you."

All our voices echoed the blessing:
"Deep peace to you,
deep peace to you,
so must it be!"

Voicing our several wishes, we waved our new wands over and around Freddie. Each had been set with an amber stone the tip that sparkled in the flickering candlelight.

"*No harm you have done, no harm comes to you*," Phillipa said.

"*Let your works shine as pure as these flames*," Heather added.

"*Your powers are always and ever consecrated to the good*," Fiona declared.

I thought of the inscrutable chain of karma. "*May time be the river in which you are washed clean of all negative events.*"

Phillipa closed the ritual with a sprinkling of salt water on Freddie and on the rest of us with such enthusiasm that we were soon all laughing.

~

Later we grilled Deidre about the old flame/friend now lying in Jordan Hospital, a victim of her Mazda.

"How did it happen?" Phillipa demanded to know. "You're always such a careful driver with that van full of kiddoes."

"Someone from your misspent youth, I hope," Heather inquired with a knowing smirk.

"It's lucky we were embarked on a purification ritual this evening," Fiona said. "May it clear away any negative vibes from your aura." She sprinkled Deidre with a bit of corn pollen from her medicine bag for good measure. "I once ran into a storefront on Court Street. Quite a jolt to the system, it was."

"Not to-mention the shopkeeper," Phillipa murmured.

"I suspect it's more so if it's a pedestrian," Fiona continued placidly. "And someone you know! Dearie me."

"Tell us about him," I suggested, eyeing the others with an unmistakable warning to *cool it.*

Deidre sighed, a faraway look in her blue eyes. "The last time I saw Conor O'Donnell was our tenth reunion, Sacred Heart in Plymouth. We'd been good friends in high school. We didn't date, because I wasn't allowed to until I was sixteen, but we hung around together a lot. What a crazy kid, scrawny with freckles, a real Irish imp! Photography nut. Then Will Ryan enrolled in Sacred Heart. Will was such a beautiful guy back then, so tall, with that flaming hair, not to mention a basketball star. All the girls were after him, but he chose me, so there it was, kismet. Poor Conor mooned around for a while. Then, of course, he started chasing after everything in skirts. Gee, I hope he's going to be okay. I mean, in his head, after that bump I gave him. But it was his fault, really. Taking a picture of the leafless trees, walking backwards into the road at twilight. Wearing some kind of gray anorak."

"Still a camera enthusiast?" Phillipa asked.

"It's his profession now. Takes photos all over the world. You've probably seen his work in *Time* or *Newsweek* or the *National Geographic*. Very big on African stuff."

"Does his wife enjoy traveling with him?" Fiona asked, her round gray eyes all innocence.

"No wife, Fiona, as I believe you've already guessed. But Conor's still a charmer, and still playing the field. Unless, of course, he got married sometime between our tenth reunion and my running into him today. Holy Mother, what a shock when I got out of the car and saw that familiar face. He came to for a moment, but I don't think he recognized me. All he said was, *my Nikon, my Nikon*. His camera was knocked clear, luckily, onto a patch of grass. I picked it up. Seemed okay."

"I expect you'll be visiting him in the hospital, then." Fiona said. "To return the camera and all. Take him one of your amulets. The red-eyed gargoyle would be a good choice."

"Holy Hecate!" exclaimed Heather. "Do you suppose he's still a faithful Catholic? In which case, the gargoyle simply won't do, Fiona."

"Why ever not? They're carved all over the European cathedrals," Fiona protested. "The word *gargoyle* means throat, actually—often used as downspouts."

"When I saw him at the reunion, he was telling everyone at the bar that the Sisters of Providence taught him to think for himself so well that he could no longer believe in anything," Deidre said with a wry smile.

"Well, that's all right then," I said. "Would you like to bring him a dream pillow? Something to induce a restful, healing sleep maybe?"

"How about just a lovely basket of fruit," Phillipa suggested. "Something exotic. Persimmons and Asian pears would be my choice."

"Do you think he'd like a visit from Honeycomb? She's a registered therapy dog, you know," Heather suggested.

"Okay, you witches," Deidre said. "Just the lot of you *back off*, please. He's only an old, old friend. But I will go to see him, of course. To apologize, return the Nikon, and that's it."

Phillipa raised a black winged eyebrow at me behind Deidre's back, and I really had to turn away to hide a smile. What we all were wondering was, is this the Cosmos's answer to Deidre's Lammas wish for a shot of joy in her life?

CHAPTER THIRTY-FIVE

For the love of money is the root of all evil…

– 1 Timothy 6:10 KJV

"No, it can't be!" I wailed to Phillipa on my cell phone. "Murder suspects are never, *ever* released on bond."

"Phil Spector, the Rock 'n Roll mogul, was released on bond, if you remember that case. A one-million-dollar bond.. Same as Reynard. I believe the precarious state of Reynard's health weighed heavily with Judge Lax. Although, I don't think anyone actually expected Reynard to come up with the collateral, the estate from his late wife still being in probate. But he did. He put up the two Chez Reynard restaurants and just squeaked by. Had to surrender his passport, of course, and submit to an electronic ankle monitor that constantly tracks his movements. He's home at his wife's mansion in Wareham now with a full-time nurse. I can't get anyone to tell me the exact state of his health—those pesky privacy laws!"

"But the evidence! He's obviously guilty. The fox in the hen house, the hens all dead."

"If you think about it coolly, Cass, the evidence is completely circumstantial, although the Grand Jury *did* bring back an indictment. I guess there was enough suspicion to bring the matter to trial. But those fibers from Reynard's coat that were found on Madame are far from conclusive, and can be explained away. Madame was family and Reynard was in constant contact with her. Sure, the prosecution can prove motive, but that by itself is not enough. Then there's your testimony, but who's going to believe the neighborhood witch? Also, when you report Reynard's boasts about offing his family and threats to do the same to you, Freddie, and the twins, it's still merely hearsay."

I was in my office, the former borning room, trying to make sense of my Christmas orders. Apparently, there were a lot of gals out there who were going to treat their significant others to my Love Potion Number Thirteen Kit, The Complete Seduction Collection. Now, of course, I was utterly put off the happy task of selling my herbal wares by this unwelcome news. I shut off the computer and glared at the dark monitor screen furiously.

This is something I should never do. When turned off, a monitor screen is mighty like a black mirror. Perfect for skrying. A sensitive individual gazing into its depths can sometimes see a revealing little movie-of-the-mind. Unfortunately, I am such a sensitive.

I was conscious of Phillipa talking on, but I wasn't really focusing on her words. I was rapt in a tiny vision appearing in the monitor.

"Ceres save us—it's just as I feared. I see Albert Reynard getting on a plane," I said in a faint voice, feeling rather nauseous "Somehow he's going to remove that ankle thingie."

"Where's he going without a passport, Cass?" Phillipa asked reasonably.

"You don't think he can obtain a false passport? Don't you ever watch spy movies?"

"Yes, but I try to separate fact from fiction. Your prophecy of doom and gloom is duly noted, though," Phillipa chortled. "But if you ask me, not even Houdini could have managed to escape from Reynard's confinement. Not to mention he's a very sick man."

"Yeah? Maybe. But you'd better ask Stone if he's confident that Reynard is really secure in his present situation."

Phillipa groaned. "Stone has nothing to do with Reynard. Nor did he ever. Don Wolfe was involved in the arrest but now it's all up to the prosecutor, the judge, and the County Marshals. I mean, sure, I'll tell him what you said, but his hands will be tied. *Che sera, sera*. Did you ever think you might be wrong this time?"

"I pray I am. Okay, *talk later*!"

I hung up and immediately called Heather with the worrisome news.

"Bummer!" she exclaimed with her usual vigor. "That guy should never take a free breath again. Want me to burn some candles? Not black, but darkish? What about a serious binding spell? Wait—what time of moon is this? Binding spells work better at the dark of the moon."

"No, Heather, no candles, no spells without Fiona's imprimatur. Because I don't want that negativity to rebound onto you and yours. But I'm just wondering if you can wheedle anything more about Reynard and de Rochemont out of Bartie Bangs. Knowledge is power."

Heather laughed merrily. "And *power is knowledge*—according to Fiona. Just leave it to me," she said.

I hung over local news reports of the de Rochemont murder for days. They were mostly rehash and speculation.

News people kept close watch on *Chateau Marie*, but were warned by the police to keep their distance. Reynard was rarely seen. His defense attorney, Hank Sharpe, fended off questions with a brusque wave of her hand as she drove in to see her client almost daily. Medical supply trucks came and went. Francis Reynard visited his brother frequently. The property was gated but not secured, which is how Lovitt and Farrow had penetrated the house so easily in the first place.

An ambulance accompanied by a marshal from the Plymouth County Sheriff's Department took Reynard to his cardiologist for scheduled appointments. The cardiologist and laboratory personnel refused to discuss their patient. Police cars patrolled the area regularly.

Hank Sharpe filed a motion to delay the trial until her client was well enough to participate, *if ever*. She cited exhaustive medical evidence portraying Reynard as very ill, possibly dying.

On the one hand, I hoped it was true that Reynard was too incapacitated to be a threat to anyone. On the other hand, I would truly like to see him brought up on the charge of murdering Madame de Rochemont. My Libran sense of justice cried out for him to be tried and convicted, even though that might mean Freddie and I would have to testify.

A few days later, Heather reported to me with great glee that she'd invited Bartie Bangs to an intimate luncheon to discuss a new codicil to her will—just herself, her devoted attorney, and the nine resident canines—plus Ashling, who did the cooking and serving on light-footed bare toes.

Heather had plied Bartie with Vive Cliquot and had been rewarded with a few gossipy tid-bits. Madame's untimely death had both shocked and released Bartie from strictest client privilege. He'd felt duty-bound to report certain matters to the detectives assigned to the case, and now he regaled Heather.

Madame de Rochemont, he whispered, had been complaining to the firm for some time that her son-in-law might be diverting some of the income—or even the capital—from her daughter's trust funds into his own pocket. Marie had been troubled but uncommunicative, the old lady said, but her mother's intuition had always been very keen—and she smelled financial chicanery. When Reynard had made a trip to the French countryside, *he claimed,* to refresh his recipe repertoire, she suspected him of skipping over to Switzerland to open a secret bank account.

At the time, Bartie had wondered if this was Madame's old age paranoia talking, but after the bizarre discovery of her body in the cistern, he'd felt obliged to share her qualms with the murder team and let forensic accountants have a go at Marie Reynard's financial records to determine if Reynard had indeed found a way to siphon off a substantial amount of cash.

Heather was reminded of her second husband ("Roberto the Hyena") who had appointed himself her financial advisor for a similar purpose, and of her third ("Chet the Owl") a CPA, who, under the guise of straightening out the mess left by Roberto, had found a less obvious way to reroute some of her trust income to an island with three palm trees and a financial institution of reliable anonymity .

Heather's attorney had remembered those years well, for it was Bartie Banks who'd salvaged Heather's fortune in the nick of time. Heather herself had burned a few potent candles as well. She declined, however, to prosecute either of her ex-husbands. When last heard of, Roberto was in Mexico preying on rich widows and drowning in Tequila. Recently Chet had gone down in flames for his association with a massive Ponzi scheme.

"As Fiona is fond of saying," Heather summed up her rant, *"Time wounds all heels."*

"She also says *Evil is the root of all money.*" I reminded her, and we both laughed.

Curious to learn if Deidre's old flame had recovered from his run-in with her Mazda, and more, if he was still buzzing around, I decided to stop in to see her on my way home from mailing stacks of herbal orders at the post office. Scruffy and Raffles wouldn't have the opportunity to bully Deidre's poodles, because I'd left my dogs at home, complaining of gross neglect. Joe had promised to take a break from his current project—outlining the house and the garage with warm golden Christmas lights—to give them a good long walk on the beach.

The lights were an outstanding decorative touch but not my style. I tend to keep a low profile at Yule so as not to encourage Patty Peacedale, the neighboring minister's wife, to rush over with Presbyterian recruitment pamphlets "Okay, honey, but no crèche on the lawn, okay?" I'd said. "You can put a red bow around the totem pole, if you wish."

The packages having been consigned to the tender mercies of the US Post, I drove to Deidre's garrison colonial house, parking behind a banged-up grayish, dusty Range Rover already ensconced in her driveway. It occurred to me that I probably should have called first. *Oh, well. Who can expect a private moment with an old lover in a house full of children?*

I found Deidre in the kitchen making coffee. She was fussing over a new coffeepot, a double-walled French press. Since Deidre's usual brew was an insipid instant stuff, I suspected a discriminating influence.

"Conor's here?" I glanced around but we were alone.

"I have to wait three minutes," Deidre said, glancing at the watch on her wrist, a girly gold number of the sort presented at graduation. This was unusual, too, since Deidre never wore a watch but operated on some infallible inner clock. "Then I plunge this thingie down, and supposedly it's done. What a lot of bother, and it will probably be strong enough to grow chest hair. But I can add hot water to yours, if you like. Oh, Conor. Yes. He's in the backyard shooting the children."

"Shooting?" I inquired weakly.

"Yes. Did you ever see Conor's spread in *Time* magazine of children playing outside Albert Schweitzer's hospital in Gabon?"

"Gabon?"

"Used to be called the French Congo. He does have a magical way with children, I'll give him that."

"So you've been seeing him then—after the, eh, accident?"

"Yes. I did feel obligated to invite him over for a home-cooked meal after running into him. Although, he admits it was his fault entirely, stepping into the road like that at twilight in a gray hoodie." She poured me a mug of the fresh coffee. It smelled divine. I tasted it gingerly.

"Oh, this is great," I enthused.

"Want a dash of hot water in that?"

I put my hand over the mug. "No, dear, it's perfect as is." I was thinking about that home-cooked meal. Oh, well. Deidre did have a few fool-proof dishes. Her macaroni and cheese was excellent, and her meatloaf dependable..

Deidre set my mind to rest. "Mother Ryan made this incredible Irish stew. I do believe she has been quite captivated by Conor. She calls him *the dear little leprechaun*. And here he is back again today, presenting me with this contraption. Why can't he just drink tea or whiskey like all the other leprechauns?"

I looked out the kitchen window to Deidre's backyard, which sported enough swings, slides, and climbing bars to equip a municipal playground. Jennie was holding Baby Anne, and the lot of them were cavorting around gleefully. Conor was crouched down exhorting them to new merriments while he clicked away.

Deidre leaned out the back door and yelled, "Hey, Conor! Come on in for coffee and meet my friend Cass."

The kitchen was soon crowded with little Ryans, but mercifully, they were briskly sent to the living room to watch a DVD that Jenny would play for them. It was to be *Bedknobs and Broomsticks* with Angela Lansbury.

Deidre introduced us. "Conor, this is my friend Cass who I told you about. She's one of the ladies in our little craft circle. Cass, this is my old friend Conor O'Donnell, who's surprised us all be becoming a world-famous photographer."

Our little craft circle? What did the poor man think, that we were stitching potholders for the church fair? I glanced at Deidre. There was that glint of mischief in her blue eyes, actually a good thing to see after all she'd been through.

Conor was a small man, only a few inches taller than Deidre, with a freckled face, a narrow chin, an unruly crop of coppery hair, and unusual eyes—one blue and one green. His grin was pure sunshine that warmed me instantly. When he gave me his hand, my impressions were swift and sure. *He must be a Saggitarius,* I thought. Not one to settle down to hearth and home. A charmer, a story-teller, a carefree soul but with an innate kindness. There were however, some dark and hidden sides to Conor that I couldn't read with just one handshake. But most importantly, he was clearly enchanted with Deidre, and had been forever.

"Grand to meet you, Cass! Dee warns me that you have a bit of the Second Sight, and you're a dear friend who's supported her through all her troubles."

"Hello, Conor. You seem to have suffered no ill effects from that little accident. Deidre's been bragging to us about your career in photography. We're all very impressed."

"She means herself and the other ladies of the circle," Deidre explained as she poured a mug of coffee for Conor and a teacup for herself, to which she added a dollop of hot water from the kettle. She opened a tin of shortbread. I recognized the tartan pattern as one of Fiona's.

"Fiona stopped over earlier. Beat you to it," Deidre said.

"I just happened to be passing," I said. Then I asked Conor about his current projects, and he told me that he'd been commissioned by W.W. Norton to explore the mystique of Plymouth.

"And it's to be called Conor O'Donnell's Plymouth," Deidre said proudly. "Since he grew up here on the South Shore and all. His family were all commercial fishermen."

"Really! What a wonderful project! So, how long do you expect to spend in Plymouth, Conor?" Not a subtle question, I admitted to myself.

"Well, I'll want all the seasons represented, so I expect I'll be around for a year or more, between other assignments. I guess I'll rent a studio of some sort. Get my stuff out of storage and spread out a bit, you know." Conor flashed me another of his endearing grins. "What a treat for a wanderer like me!"

He glanced at Deidre, who had taken an embroidery out of her workbasket. She kept her eyes on it but I could detect a small smile as she held up the cushion cover. *A sunbeam to warm you, A moonbeam to charm you, A sheltering angel so nothing can harm you.*

Already with the Irish blessings, I thought. *Promising!*

As I was leaving, I took Deidre aside and told her that Reynard had got out of jail on a million-dollar bond, and I was not happy about it. I'd "seen" him making a run for it. "Possibly to Europe. Madame de Rochemont suspected him of having a secret bank account in Switzerland."

"Sounds like a man with a plan. I can't imagine how he'll manage to escape police surveillance and his ankle monitor, though, especially in his condition. But if he should make a run for it, you know what I think you should do?" she said.

"Got some magic up your sleeve, Dee?"

"Something more practical. Get in touch with the de Rochemont family in France," she said. "Maybe they have contacts, if you know what I mean."

That notion stayed with me all the way home. I began to wonder what kind of people the de Rochemonts were? Besides being very rich vintners. When I got home, I Googled the de Rochemont family. The apparent patriarch of the family was Claude de Rochemont, Madame's older brother, who was still active in the business although in his late eighties. Along with the many awards conferred on the superb de Rochemont wines through the years, Claude de Rochemont had received the Légion d'honneur for his participation in an elite group of railroad saboteurs known as the Fer Reséau during World War II. I made a note of the de Rochemont history and tucked it away, in case.

YULE, THE WINTER SOLSTICE, DECEMBER 21, FESTIVAL OF LIGHT AND LOVE

CHAPTER THIRTY-SIX

...it was the season of Light, it was the season of Darkness, it was the spring of hope, it was the winter of despair...

– Charles Dickens

I wouldn't want to claim that my visions are invariably accurate, but they've been a glimpse of the truth often enough so that I pay attention to them, and so do those who know me best. Time, of course, is the factor that always trips us clairvoyants. *When will it happen?* is not a question I can answer with any assurance.

In the case of Reynard, for instance, it was barely three weeks after my vision of him boarding an airplane that he did indeed escape his home confinement. Even though I'd predicted it, I was surprised and so were the rest of the circle—I mean, where were the watchdogs of law enforcement? The strong suspicion was that he had help from his brother Francis, but nothing could be proved, so we heard from Phillipa's husband, Stone.

His schedule had been simple and structured: Reynard's day nurse went off shift at five, and the night nurse came in at seven. In the interim, Albert Reynard's dinner was served in an upstairs sitting room adjacent to the master bedroom by Mrs. Spacey, a housekeeper newly hired by Francis. On the night of Albert's flight, however, the housekeeper had been sent to Chez Reynard in Chatham to pick up some culinary specialties of the season to tempt his appetite.

Mrs. Spacey had been delayed by the Chez Reynard chef while he fussed over packing gourmet fare for his boss's Christmas holiday. So, by the time the housekeeper returned and lugged the hampers into the kitchen, Albert Reynard was long gone. His ankle monitor had been cut off, which went unnoticed for more than an hour by the guy at the service center computer.

Meanwhile Reynard had been whisked away by an accomplice to places unknown. Although airport personnel were alerted, the fox had slipped under the radar, possibly to a chartered plane at some little regional airport. In spite of the terrible weather—a mix of sleet, snow, and wind gusts—there were no reports of private planes gone missing. So wherever Reynard went, he made it. But not as far as Europe, not in some anonymous small plane in terrible winter weather. I wondered if Reynard was now holed up somewhere in the States, but when Fiona, our finder, attempted to follow his route by dowsing a world map, the pendulum kept zigzagging over the northern Atlantic.

"He may have flown to Canada and then taken passage on a merchant ship. Still at sea, I'll wager," Fiona said.

"I can't understand it," Phillipa said. "Reynard had a really good shot at being acquitted. Hank Sharpe would have questioned every piece of evidence, scaring up enough shadows of doubt to rival the OJ trial. Why would he skip and become a fugitive forever?"

"Perhaps he wasn't prepared to take his chances with a jury," Heather suggested. "If he has enough money in some

Swiss bank, he might be able to live quite well abroad. Think of Roman Polanski. Or if not so openly, in some obscure little country with no extradition policy. It has been known."

We'd gathered at Heather's to mull over this latest development. Heather passed around snifters of Courvoisier Cognac while we lounged around her Victorian red parlor in various attitudes of discouragement.

"We could bring him back, I suppose," I ruminated. "We've done that before."

"Yeah, sure," Deidre said. "And how many times has that Bringing Back ritual screwed up and resulted in more mayhem?"

"Possibly because the moon was *void-of-course* at the time," Fiona mused. "When magic turns out differently than expected, oft times it's because the spell has fallen between aspects. One of us ought always to be on moon watch—quarters, signs, planetary movements—that sort of thing."

"'*Not I, said the little red hen*,'" Deidre quoted. "It's trouble enough being on ghost watch."

"Reynard's heart is his Achilles heel," Heather said, sipping thoughtfully.

"Mixed metaphor," Phillipa said sourly. "And I don't think we want to actually kill him, do we?"

I remembered the night Freddie had confronted the crazed Reynard. Surely we none of us had that power, or wanted it. "*Harm none...*" I recited the basic Wiccan creed.

"*...and do as ye will*," Phillipa completed the law.

"Or perhaps there was something a wee bit wrong with our Bringing Back spellwork," Fiona said thoughtfully. "I wonder if that cinnamon oil was as potent as it should have been. Perhaps it was diluted with soybean oil. Soy negates everything. Or maybe the heartsease wasn't harvested at the right time of the lunar cycle."

"Listen up!" Deidre commanded, taking another tiny stitch in the Irish blessing pillow cover, "As I have already suggested to Cass, since this Reynard joker is probably making his way to Europe and his secret Swiss bank account…"

"A rumor I personally wheedled out of Bartie Banks," Heather interrupted.

"…I believe that the thing to do," Deidre continued, "is to inform the de Rochemont family that the murderer of three de Rochemont ladies is in their backyard—in case they may want to seek him out and *have a word*, as the Brits say."

We thought about that quietly, sipping the excellent Cognac.

"Sounds like a plan," Heather said. "But is it *your* plan, Dee?"

Deidre blushed and smiled a bit sheepishly. "Caught! I admit it's these damned *things* I see now. Therese again. She kept saying, 'Tell Uncle, tell Uncle,' until I finally had to promise I would 'tell Uncle' just to get her out of the living room window. I was so afraid that someone else would see her and flip out—like my mother-in-law, for instance. Or…or…"

"Or Conor," I suggested.

"Why don't you borrow Conor's camera and take a picture of your ghost girl?" Phillipa suggested.

"Cool it, friends," Deidre said. "Like he'd lend out his precious camera. He probably sleeps with it."

I think all of us decided not to touch that line with any smart remarks. It would have been too easy, and we really hoped Conor would be that "shot of joy" Deidre had been wishing for at Lammas.

Fiona rummaged in her reticule and drew out a pamphlet. "I have this brochure about the de Rochemont wine dynasty—with Bordeaux addresses and phone numbers."

"Naturally," Phillipa said, raising one winged eyebrow. "What I like most about Dee's plan is that it doesn't involve breaking the law. At least, not by us."

"Okay," I agreed. "But I just want to go on record that *my* cinnamon oil is top grade stuff, absolutely not diluted with any cheap soy, and *my* heartsease was properly harvested on the eve of the new moon. There's nothing wrong with the ingredients—it must have been our method that went awry when we did the Bringing Back thing."

"It's like making puff pastry," Phillipa said. "Method is everything. Not a recipe for amateurs, my dears."

Fiona laughed her deep infectious chuckle that set us all laughing with her. "Well, truth to tell, when you send a spell out into the Cosmos, you have to be prepared for a few surprises. There's no such animal as a sure thing in magic or horse races."

~

It's not that we forgot about Albert Reynard, or Hugh Collins either, but we did put aside our justice pursuits while we celebrated Yule in a private circle at Phillipa's home. Her baronial fireplace with the immense copper hood seemed made for the ceremony of lighting the decorated Yule log, the traditional ash, with a shred of last year's wood. Deidre had outdone herself in festooning the log with green ribbons and holly, pine cones and sea shells, crystals and beads. She called it *Blessings of Earth and Sea*.

Phillipa was hostess and high priestess of our Yule celebration. With Stone absenting himself to the upstairs study, it must be admitted, we breathed the air of serenity that surrounds a circle of women when the coast is clear for magic. We savored our goddess laughter, so deep and rich and purely female. And we were glowing with an inner blaze of energy, wondering what elementals and spirits we might summon, the Ghosts of Yuletimes Past perhaps.

Phillipa cast our circle with her athame, a no-nonsense 19th century dagger, invoking the Brigid, goddess of the hearth and mistress of the arts of fire, and her mother Dagda, whose cauldron is a symbol of nature's continuing abundance. As we called the four quarters, our only illumination came from the bayberry candles and the crackling hearth fire. I had brought bunches of sage and tossed the dried sprigs on the blaze to keep us safe and protected, and we burned incense of frankincense and myrrh.

Afterwards, with the Moroccan rugs rolled up in the corner, we danced on the broad gray stone floor to build our energy. *We are air, we are fire, we are water, we are earth.* When the force of the Goddesses could no longer be contained in flesh and spirit, we let go, releasing our needs and desires to the Divine Spirit of the Cosmos.

But, just as Phillipa was about to open the circle so that we could have a merry time with "cakes and ale," we began to notice a shimmering apparition forming in the shadows of the candlelit room.

Looking like a perfect familiar, Zelda's gleaming black body had been sprawled on her yellow silk cushion, basking in the heat of flames leaping in the massive fireplace.

But now the sleek cat sprang up, her fur standing on end, then streaked upstairs with a plaintive howl.

"My Omar is a sensitive, too," Fiona murmured. "Early warning system, rather like having a canary in a mine."

The spectral phenomena escalated into a chorus of sighs, a sense of invisible presence, a fleeting glimpse of moving shadows, a cool breeze out of nowhere. Many of the candles guttered, and some went out. I felt Deidre beside me shudder and moan.

"Therese, Therese de Rochemont," she murmured. "See there in the doorway, Cass?"

Mercifully, the weird stuff began to fade a few moments later. Phillipa relit the candles with a fireplace match, and Deidre breathed a sigh of relief.

"Wow—wasn't that intense! What do you suppose Dee's ghost wanted this time?" Heather asked.

"Oh, please don't call Therese *my* ghost," Deidre whispered. "Actually, she didn't speak this time. But it's as if I feel her thoughts in my mind. I don't think she's going to leave me—leave *us*—alone until we contact the de Rochemonts family in France."

"I'll do it, then." Phillipa was our surprise volunteer. "And maybe I can talk Stone into asking Don Wolfe to check with Interpol as well."

"Good!" Deidre exclaimed. "Now maybe I can *get a life*, as they say."

Heather winked at me. "I have just the thing for that," she said to Deidre. She reached into her faux alligator bag and took out a tissue wrapped candle. "I was thinking of you today, and I made this especially." As Heather unwrapped the candle, a strong scent of roses filled the air. The candle was flower-shaped and rosy-pink with little gold and silver hearts imbedded in the wax.

"It's lovely, Heather," Deidre said, taking the gift cautiously. "Now what in Hades are you up to? This isn't some meddling little spell, is it?"

"I'm shocked, shocked I tell you, that you would think such a thing!" Heather said. "I'm only trying to help, dear. Light this up for atmosphere when you and Conor are having a nice quiet cup of Irish tea and going through the old Sacred Heart yearbooks."

"Sure, and do you want me to wear the old school uniform, as well?" Deidre said with a broad Irish accent and a lewd wink. "Have I ever heard of such shameless matchmaking in me life?"

"You should know," Phillipa said dryly. "Remember how you conjured up Stone the night that Fiona shot out Heather's bow window!"

"Ah, those unforgettable Christmas moments," Fiona said with a nostalgic sigh. "How I so miss dear Rob Ritchie's pistol! And Rob, too, of course."

CHAPTER THIRTY-SEVEN

Revenge is a dish best served cold.

– Sicilian proverb

As members of a wealthy wine dynasty, the de Rochemonts guarded their privacy assiduously, and there was no easy way to contact them directly. By the new year, however, Phillipa had managed to communicate with the firm that handled their legal affairs. Having insisted that she had information of a sensitive and personal nature to impart to Claude de Rochemont, eventually Phillipa was connected to Jacques Terrier, the firm's bilingual avocat.

The next morning, she reported her unsatisfactory conversation to the circle gathered in my kitchen for coffee and strategy.

As she'd explained to Terrier, she wanted Claude de Rochemont to know that Albert Reynard, recently charged with the murder of Claude's sister Madame Therese de Rochmont of Beau Rouge, had escaped from home confinement and fled the country.

M. Terrier replied that Interpol had already so informed the family.

"Did they tell M. de Rochemont that Reynard has been siphoning off his wife Marie's funds into a Swiss bank account, that he may have headed to Switzerland to collect his money and live comfortably in Europe?" Phillipa asked.

M. Terrier was silent.

"Reynard suffers from heart disease. He might seek refuge at a private health clinic or hospital," she added. "Such an excellent place to hide."

M. Terrier gave a slight cough. "Was there anything else, Mademoiselle?"

Phillipa was beginning to feel rather desperate in trying to communicate with this noncommittal attorney. "Reynard's wife and step-daughter..." she began.

"We understand that the criminals who killed Madame de Rochemont's daughter and granddaughter have been tried, convicted, and imprisoned," the avocat interrupted in his perfect English.

"Maybe," said Phillipa. "Perhaps Claude de Rochemont will want to look into the possibility that Albert Reynard also had a hand in those crimes, too."

"Is there any evidence that is so?" Terrier asked mildly.

"No. But he was on the scene before the police. His wife Marie's fortune was considerable, and since her daughter also died in the incident, Reynard would have inherited everything. Unfortunately for him, Madame de Rochemont was not satisfied with the investigation and was making quite a fuss about it. So he silenced her and stuffed her body in an ancient cistern where he thought it would never be discovered. But it was. So now he has to forego the inheritance and run to Europe to escape the law."

"You seem to be remarkably well informed about the de Rochemont family's affairs," the avocat said. "Exactly what is your interest in this matter, Ms. Stern?"

"Madame and I were practically neighbors," Phillipa lied. "Make of this information what you will, but do pass it along to the head of the family. Good-bye, Monsieur Terrier."

Phillipa had half-expected and feared to hear from Claude de Rochemont himself, she told us, but so far there had been no call-back from the family or their avocat. "Big sigh of relief," she said. "I mean, could I have told him that all my evidence of Reynard's guilt came from my Psychic Friends Network?"

"You've done all you can, Phil. All that any of us can. It's time that we put Reynard to rest," Fiona said. "And I, for one, am just as well pleased that we never tried to haul him home with our Bringing Back spell. I only hope we've put young Therese to rest as well."

"If there's one thing I've learned about ghosts," Deidre said, "it's that they hang around to see justice done."

"You must tell Therese that she needs to spiritualize and move along to a higher plane," Fiona said, reaching into the green reticule from which she was never parted. "The desire for revenge keeps a soul in earthly chains. I have a pamphlet on that subject which will interest you, Dee." The pamphlet she handed Deidre was titled *The Seven Spiritual Laws for Successful Exorcism.*

"Holy Mother," Deidre said. "All I want is to be free of these weirdo specters—is that asking much?"

"Calm yourself, Dee. Fiona's right. We've done our part to unlock the poor girl and set her free," Heather said. "She wanted the matter of her stepfather delegated to dear Great-uncle Claude, who no doubt will ferret out that bastard Reynard from whatever exclusive hiding-hole he's found. Phil's managed that admirably, and it's time for Therese to *shuffle off this mortal coil,* or whatever."

"So now, for mercy's sake, *let go and let Goddess*!" Fiona decreed.

"So must it be," I agreed with fervor. I never wanted to see that demented murderer again. And somehow I had faith that Deidre's way was the proper karmic choice.

And so it proved to be. Albert Reynard never returned to the United States to haunt us, so to speak.

In February, Hugh Collins was arraigned on charges of running an illegal dog-fighting operation. He pleaded guilty and was sentenced to six months in the Plymouth House of Correction, but on appeal, that sentence was later reduced to three years parole, four months of community service, and a substantial fine.

Heather was not a happy camper.

I knew that narrow-eyed, tight-lipped, grim-faced look would soon find her in the Widow's Walk room burning black candles. Peace-making Libran that I am, I attempted to deflect the possible karmic damage.

"Have you seen Collins recently? He's a marked man, Heather," I said, by way of pacifying her irate mood. "Looks like the picture of Dorian Grey. The one in the attic. And I hear there are more surgeries down the road before his face is anywhere back to normal."

We were in the Morgan mansion's conservatory, fending off restless, winter-bound canines. Heather had thoughtfully filled an insulated safari canteen with hot rum toddies, and we were sipping the heartening brew from silver camp cups to ward off the late winter freeze.

"You hear? Hear what? From whom, exactly?"

"Patty Peacedale shanghaied me into a stint at the Angels' Table. You know, the soup kitchen in Plymouth funded by the Lydia Craig foundation that Reverend Peacedale administers. *For his sins,* one might say, if you remember all the *sturm und drang* over the Craig will. Not to mention the poisonings. Anyway, while I was there doctoring up their insipid recipe for American Chop Suey with real tomatoes, garlic and oregano, I bumped into Wanda Finch."

"You know, Cass, your conversational detours are beginning to remind me of Fiona. Wanda Finch wandered in for a free lunch?"

"No, the Finch family had donated a big bunch of winter veggies to Angels', and Wanda was in the kitchen stirring up a vast vat of Portuguese Kale and Potato Soup. With sausage from Pryde's Pig Farm. So maybe that romance is back on. I've always thought Iggy Pryde and the redoubtable Wanda were made for each other."

"Right. *So what!* I mean, *so what* did the rifle-toting Finch have to say about Collins, exactly."

"Didn't your cousin Brooke used to have a *thing* for Collins? And isn't she a realtor! So you must already know that Collins has put Fresh Meadow Farm on the market. Anyway, I don't think we need to pursue Collins any further. He's probably going to take a well-deserved loss when he gives up his stables. And those pit bulls of his that you rescued—I mean, American Staffordshire Terriers—have probably messed up his classic handsomeness for life. Although he may get off with an interesting dangerous look like George Macready in *Gilda*."

"*What terriers?* I don't have any terriers at the shelter, my dear."

"Got 'em out of town on the underground doggie railroad, did you?"

"You bet your tuckus I did. Collins was calling for a court order to destroy those poor sweet babies."

"And Brooke didn't tell you that Collins plans to leave town as soon as he finishes his community service?"

"No, because, as it happens, Brooke is in McLean Psychiatric Hospital for dependency therapy," Heather said. "Booze, sex, and *who knows what else*. It's the Morgan blood, you know. Curse of the Opium Trade. Prone to a freewheeling kind of overindulgence. Thank the Goddess I've been spared from that sort of thing."

"Sure," I said.

"So I haven't heard from Brooke or anyone that the old Churchill place was on the market again. Collins is selling out, is he? Where's he going, do you know?"

"Wanda says West Virginia."

"How can he move out of state? He's on parole!"

"Yeah, he can. According to Wanda, his attorney, Ray Laratta —same slick criminal lawyer who defended Lovitt and Farrow —has got permission from Massachusetts and from West Virginia to transfer him to that parole board, as long as he has a job and lives with a family member. She says he's going to live with his cousin, Bain Collins, and work at Bain's horse farm, Thunder Gulch.

"*That bastard*! You realize, don't you, that he's just going to start up his dog-fighting operation all over again in some congenial redneck neighborhood."

"After all he's been through? The man looks as if he's been run over by a reaper. And besides, if he gets caught, he goes to jail for three years."

"Those nip-'n-tuck guys will fix him up okay, and he'll be back in the game. *No way* I'm going to allow that sadistic abuser to walk away from this, Cass."

"Well, he won't exactly be *walking away* while he's doing community service for four months," I said.

"Where and what?" Heather wanted to know.

"Don't have the faintest," I lied. But Heather, with her network of Morgan cousins, some of them in the Town Hall, would soon find out that Collins had been assigned to the clean-up crew in Miles Standish State Forest. At this time of year, that would probably mean snow-plowing and keeping the roads clear of fallen trees, and in the spring, pruning deadwood, spreading mulch around plantings, and edging borders.

I imagined Heather working some arcane spell to get an ancient, enormously tall pine to topple onto Hugh Collins and crush him to a pulp. This was as worrisome as Freddie zapping the weak-hearted Reynard.

"You really must trust Divine Justice to deal with Collins," I said. "Magic power corrupts, my dear."

But as February and March went by without news of any bizarre accident in Myles Standish putting *Paid* to the account of Hugh Collins' crimes against canines, I began to think that Heather had listened to reason and not gone over to the Dark Side after all.

Only her Book of Shadows knows.

OSTARA, THE VERNAL EQUINOX, FESTIVAL OF REBIRTH AND RENEWAL

CHAPTER THIRTY-EIGHT

And Spring arose on the garden fair
Like the Spirit of Love felt everywhere…

– Percy Bysshe Shelley

Ostara came, reverently observed in our private ritual. We wove and wore apple blossom crowns and danced to celebrate the exuberant return of spring after winter's torpor. We even did a cautious fertility rite, specifying intellectual creation—*not, for Goddess's sake, more babies,* although warned by Fiona that the Divine Spirit of the Cosmos interprets as She wills.

Later, we celebrated Easter with all our extended families at Heather's. Being New Englanders, we had, of course, made two sets of plans, one for miserably windy, sleety weather and one for a decent, merely chilly April day. Heather gave spring a hand with pots of tulips and daffodils among the padded redwood chairs on the fieldstone patio. Her three crooked apple trees obliged with fragrant white blossoms, and the Goddess of Spring smiled on us as well. A mild sunny afternoon proved to be perfect for the Circle's take on Easter: Egyptian Multi-colored Egg Hunts, Ojibwa Great Rabbit Baskets (packed by Fiona) and macho outdoor grilling, Dick

Devlin's specialty. He had to be satisfied, though, with free-range, organic chickens and some vegetarian sausages that Phillipa tasted gingerly with an affronted expression. She had brought a lamb roast, redolent of garlic and herbs—assuring Heather that all New Zealand lamb was free-range and had gamboled in the grasslands until D-Day.

"An ancient Easter symbol of innocence and sacrifice," she defended her carnivorous tastes.

Ashling had baked Irish soda breads, departing with tradition to sweeten them with honey and golden raisins. They were deeply cut with the sign of the cross, which Ashling said was in honor of the trinity and Conor claimed was to let the faeries escape. She'd also brought trays of hot cross buns, and for dessert, cream puff bunnies. I couldn't help glancing down at her feet, bare again, and barely connected to the ground. With Ashling, one continually had the impression of watching one of those magical airy ballet dances. Or, when she was really detached, some kind of newly winged angel.

Maury, the redoubtable dog trainer and true vegetarian, came bearing a vegetable lasagna the size of a small car, filled with ricotta, eggplant, spinach, mushrooms, noodles, and a fragrant tomato sauce. He buzzed around Ashling like a bee in search of nectar. And his presence seemed to settle her down a little. "With both feet on terra firma," as the expression goes. I wondered if Heather would soon be seeking another housekeeper—she did seem fated to lose them just as they became invaluable. *Oh well, we can always do another calling and see what the Divine Spirit has up Her sleeve this time.*

Speaking of what the Divine Spirit could conjure, the celebration was well-documented by Conor, who sprinted around taking countless photos of the festivities. He was wearing the *de rigueur* khaki vest, multiple pockets filled with photography gadgets, and jeans nearly as well-traveled as Joe's salt-faded ones. Conor's hair glinted copper in the sun, his strange eyes were full of mischief and fun, and his grin contagious.

The children adored him, and no wonder. Not only the four little Ryans, but also Fiona's Laura Belle and my dear grandkids toddling about with Freddie. It seemed that Conor had an endless fund of stories and rhymes about elves, faeries, and leprechauns to keep the young ones entertained while he caught their delightful antics on film.

"You have a marvelous memory for poetry," Phillipa said. She'd been listening with a bemused smile, as enchanted as the children.

"Probably a drop of Druid blood in my genealogy," Conor said. "The Druids committed their history and magic lore to memory rather than writing it down. Safer that way—but, alas, all their secrets died with them."

"A mnemonic aid to remembering. Or perhaps an early green effort to spare the trees," Phillipa said with a sly smile.

"You're a poet yourself, Miss Phil," Conor said. "I came across a volume of your poems in a Notting Hill bookstore. *Traveling Light.* The title reminded me of me, so I couldn't resist. Your poems are full of music and myth, just my thing. Unfortunately, I find it impossible to keep books for long, but maybe now that I have my own place. My Plymouth pied-à-terre." Then he sprinted away with his camera at the ready, leaving Phillipa not unpleased.

"A discerning mind, that Conor," she said. "It will be fascinating to see what he does with his book on the mystique of Plymouth. There's a depth and darkness to this town beneath the bubbles of tourism," she said. "I don't suppose today's shoot is for the book."

"These pictures are to be a gift for me, an Easter album," Deidre said, her eyes downcast on her work, sewing gauzy, glittery dresses for her summer collection of faery dolls.

Phillipa glanced at me, raising an expressive black eyebrow, then quickly turning away. Not one of us hinted to Deidre by a careless word or a suggestive look, what we all knew. This nostalgic fling with Conor was heating up and suffusing Deidre with an inner glow, the subtle but unmistakable aura of good sex. *Love and a cough cannot be hid.*

"If that Irish sprite breaks Dee's heart, Goddess help him," Heather muttered to me as I helped to lug out a tub of ice to cool white wines for us and sodas for the youngsters. "I mean, how long before he'll be off to far-flung adventures in uncharted lands where a gal with four kids could never follow? I just won't have it! Why is she fooling around with this bozo anyway, this wandering Pied Piper?"

"Because he's the Cosmos answer to the Circle's prayer. Oh, don't say we witches never fiddled around with Deidre's love-life. We all had *thoughts* about it, if you know what I mean. And then this guy arrived *out of the blue!* Literally, stepped into the road in front of her car in the blue twilight. With a little push from Fortuna Primigenia, surely. I say we've got to give him a chance to be Dee's gift from the Divine Spirit."

"Yeah, I suppose. After all, you seem to have found happiness with a sailor of the seven seas," Heather admitted.

"Well, there's not much chance of Joe and me getting bored with one another," I said. "But there are lonely times and worries. The important thing, though, is to find the right person, the soul mate."

"One of them," Heather temporized. "There's more than one soul mate on the beach, you know."

"Another garbled metaphor," said Phillipa, who had come up quietly behind us in search of more wine. "But I couldn't agree more."

"Let's make that *one soul mate at a time*, then," I suggested.

~

Conor took off soon after Easter for a photo shoot in Australia featuring Platypuses, Echidnas, Tasmanian Devils, and other rare animals; it had been commissioned by the *National Geographic*. Deidre insisted on his wearing one of her carved black teak pendants to protect against dark forces while in the wilds of the "Land Before Time."

It must have worked, because he returned only a couple of weeks later with gifts, toys, and mesmerizing tales of adventure. He appeared to be immune to jet lag, Deidre told us, and was as jaunty and merry as ever. A small smile bringing out her dimples made her look about sixteen. I noted that the worried little line that had appeared between her brows last year seemed to have faded. *Satisfying Sex: It's Better than Botox*.

"I admit I was afraid Conor might have flown the coop," Heather said to me privately later while we were catching a few morning rays on her patio. "But here he is in fine fettle, just in time for Beltane, too. I wonder if crafty Dee annointed that amulet with a little come-hither voodoo oil."

"It has been known," I said, sipping coffee from a Limoge mug. I'd turned down the offer of a Sambuca sweetener. "And besides, Conor has that Plymouth book to finish, which, as he explained, needs views of the old town in all four seasons, so that's a year at least. A year should be plenty of time for Dee to weave her magic web. After all, he's been besotted with Dee ever since Sacred Heart."

"*In the spring, a young man's fancy...*" Heather quoted Tennyson.

"*...lightly turns to thoughts of love,*" I agreed. "But what about that swarm of children buzzing about?"

"Dogs are so much less trouble," Heather said, eyeing with approval her frolicking pack in the fenced park she called her *dog yard.* "Of course, one needs a real sense of commitment in either case."

"And Conor wears responsibilities so very lightly," I said. "Saggitarius."

"*Straight to the mark.* Maybe that's good," Heather said. "Let's keep a good thought."

"Always," I said.

CHAPTER THIRTY-NINE

...if the assassination
Could trammel up the consequence, and catch
With his surcease success, that but this blow
Might be the be-all and the end-all...

– William Shakespeare

The day after Conor's return, Phillipa called me with some not-so-unexpected news. She'd had it from Stone who'd had it from Don Wolfe who'd got a memo from Interpol. The body of Albert Reynard had washed up on the shores of the Seine at dawn a week ago. "Garroted!" she exclaimed. She seemed to be struggling unsuccessfully to keep the glee out of her voice.

"*Ce qui une surprise*!" I said.

"But wait, there's more," she said. "That particular style of garrote—its knot or whatever—was recognized by some old gendarme as being a favorite with certain members of the Resistance in World War II. It was part of a kit with a blade and a slugging tool."

"A coincidence," I suggested.

"So-called coincidences are greatly misunderstood. They're all part of the Cosmos' ever-changing connections. You would have thought, though, with that weak heart, he'd have collapsed under the strain of escaping justice and died of ostensibly natural causes," Phillipa mused.

"In my opinion, he has met with poetic justice."

"I'll drink to that," Phillipa said. I thought I could hear ice cubes clinking in a glass at her end of the phone, a sound I was familiar with from the pre-dinner calls of my daughter Becky.

"At least it wasn't some spell of ours that was responsible," I breathed a sigh of relief.

"Easy for you to say. You're not the one who lit a fuse under Claude de Rochemont."

"Actually, it was Dee's doing. And she's going to be perfectly delighted if this means she's seen the last of the spectral Therese."

"Let's go over there right now! I'll pick you up in twenty minutes," Phillipa said.

"Okay, but let's call first. In case she and Conor…"

"With all those kiddos wandering about?"

"You never know what a smart girl can arrange," I said.

So I did call, and the coast was clear. Conor was off shooting the Grist Mill and flowering trees in Brewster Gardens.

Deidre made us a pot of coffee in her new double-walled French press. Usually she would have brought out a package of arrowroot cookies better suited to toddlers, but instead she arranged a plate of Anzac Biscuits with macadamia nuts and chocolate-glazed Lamington Bars, quite dazzling Phillipa.

"Conor brought them back from his trip," she said. "Did you ever wonder if I've got a thing for red hair? Will, and now Conor?"

"Will's was much darker. Conor's is coppery," I said. "And physically, they couldn't be more different."

"You can say that again," Deidre said thoughtfully. Phillipa and I gazed off into space so that we wouldn't catch each other's eye and smirk.

"Well, just look at you two witches," she said, coming back from her obvious reverie. "I guess you've *divined*, then, that Conor and I...you know."

"We didn't need to be psychic to see that the two of you are having a flaming romance," Phillipa said. "And why not?"

"Well, I feel a little guilty, you know...it's so different with Conor, so sort of glorious."

Phillipa and I remained quite silent, hoping for more details, but that's all we got.

"So, what's the story?" Deidre changed the subject while putting on another kettle of water for the press. "You promised me 'thrilling news.'"

"Perhaps I shouldn't have said thrilling. After all, the man is dead," I said.

"You mean, a murderer has been executed," Phillipa said, and went on to relate the discovery of Reynard's body and our suppositions to Deidre.

"Oh, good. Now maybe Therese can rest in peace," Deidre said. "And so can I. I've been terrified that Conor or the children would see her lurking outside the French doors in the living room."

"Have they?" I asked.

"No. Apparently she's not visible to anyone else. Except Baby Anne maybe. One time when Therese was hanging around watching us play Monopoly, Annie pointed and burbled on about 'the light. Fortunately, no one paid any attention to her."

"Well, let's hope Therese is off to the enchantments of Summerland now," I said.

"So must it be," Phillipa and Deidre chorused.

CHAPTER FORTY

Each friend represents a world in us,
a world possibly not born until they arrive.

– Anïas Nin

"Tell my fortune," I asked Phillipa. "I'm in a strange restless mood today, like someone is walking on my grave."

"Banish that thought," she replied automatically.

As always when a reading was in the offing, Phillipa took a few deep meditative breaths and consulted her own inner energies. Psychic work can be quite draining if a person isn't in top form. Then she nodded affirmatively and took out her well-worn Ryder deck from the red satin bag that protected it. A purple sodalite stone to enhance psychic awareness fell out as well.

Phillipa shuffled and asked me to cut the cards (with my left hand, toward my heart), then arranged the cards as they came off the deck in her favorite Celtic cross layout. She studied them with a disapproving expression, the dark wings of her hair falling forward, her brows pressed together.

She closed her eyes and laid her olive-skinned hand over her heart dramatically. "Good Goddess!" she exclaimed. "Is there no end?"

"All right, Phil. *Cut that out* and tell me exactly what you're seeing," I said sharply.

I was seeing a burning tower, a knave sneaking off with swords, a heart pierced by three swords, a woman in a boat being poled across water…okay, not the most peaceful of spreads. Except for those gals garlanded with flowers—the four of wands. But Phillipa would see more than the face illustrations—somehow she saw *through* the cards to a reality beyond them.

With her eyes still closed, Phillipa intoned somberly, "Something or *someone* will be stolen, a heart will be broken, turmoil and disruption will follow, you will journey across water to rescue what has been lost—or maybe all of us will—but in the end, we will find something to celebrate."

"So," I said, "*same old, same old…*"

"Perhaps…" Phillipa said thoughtfully, tapping the woman being ferried. "But I feel in my bones that a trip will be involved this time."

"Let's not get fanciful now. A trip across water could be, like, simply driving over the Cape Cod canal. Although Fiona did give me what she called a "traveler's grimoire" on my birthday. Crimson suede, almost too beautiful to mess up with words. She'd written a few chants and rhymes for a safe journey on the first three pages. In dragon's blood ink."

"Yes, I remember," Phillipa said. "Doesn't that seem like a long time ago!"

"So much has happened since last fall. I think I could really use a rest right now. When's this thievery-heartbreak deal going to happen, Phil?"

"Hey, Cass. You know very well that time is always the variable. *Sometime in the future*, that's all I know."

"Yeah, all time is one time, and not only in the psychic realm. I think that's why science is unable to prove that effect always follows cause. In the world of particle physics, at any rate. Sometimes effect may come first," I said.

"Our bodies are chronological though," Phil said. "So anything else is academic—as they say when they mean *worthless in the real world*"

"Fiona said I should use the book to record my own magical notes and reflections during my trip. If you're right about this, how did she know? That woman is truly awesome."

"Maybe I don't want to be invited along. Our last trip together was very nearly a disaster," Phil said.

"If you weren't such an irrepressible flirt, things might have gone better." It's the moral duty of friends to remind each other of foibles they might wish to forget..

"Oh, hush up. I was merely civil to a shipboard acquaintance."

"Wouldn't it be nice if our husbands could go with us this time—wherever in Hades we're going," I said.

"Maybe," Phillipa said without enthusiasm." Quickly she pushed the layout together in a heap and stashed them away in their satin sanctuary. "Oh, they're just cards anyway. Let's not get our thongs in a twist."

"Surely you jest," I said, secure in my Fruit of the Loom 100% cotton briefs with stylish waistband that "caresses without binding."

"If there's one good thing about being our age," Phillipa said with a grin, "it's never having to be trussed up the backside like a roasting chicken."

"Amen, sister, amen," I said.

Phillipa made us cups of frothy, cinnamon-scented cappuccino in her upscale does-it-all coffee system and brought them into her living room on a tray. Zelda was sprawled in a ray of strong sunlight coming through the floor-to-ceiling windows. There was a triangle-shaped planter built into the floor where the windows met at a right angle. Succulents flourished there in winter and a golden hibiscus bloomed that quite took my breath away. I sat comfortable against silk cushions on the sofa, gazing at the blossoms in wonder and sipping my restorative brew. The sunlight bounced off a Moroccan brass table right into my eyes.

As happens to me sometimes, I gazed too long in wonder at the sun-gilded flower and soon felt myself slipping away into a vision trance. As I watched, there was a sudden fierce storm with thunder and lightning piercing through the sky. I could see the silhouette of a man struggling to bring a frightened horse from paddock to barn. Suddenly a bolt of electricity came down from the heavens like a sword and threw the man to the ground where he lay motionless and sizzling. The horse ran off into the fields.

Then I was conscious of Phillipa shaking my shoulder. "Cass, Cass, what on earth is wrong with you. Oh, Good Goddess, I don't even have any smelling salts."

"I'm all right, Phil," I croaked. "Just give me a minute."

I felt certainly I had glimpsed an accident at Thunder Gulch where Hugh Collins was working out his parole. But when? Had it happened, or was it going to happen?

"Okay, girlfriend. What did you see?" Phillipa asked, picking up the cup that now lay on the stone floor in several pieces.

"Oh, dear. I am sorry."

"I'll get you another cup. But I want answers!

"It was nothing really, Phil. Just a thunder storm somewhere. I'm sure it had nothing to do with us."

"Okay, keep your secrets there, Cass. Time will reveal all."

"Yes, I'm sure that's true. And I wouldn't want to jar anything askew with loose pronouncements"

And I wouldn't want anything to get back to Heather that might make her feel guilty for her ill wishes. If that was Hugh Collins being struck down by Thor's Hammer we'd hear about it one of these days. No need to rush justice in the Goddess' good time.

BELTANE, MAY EVE, FESTIVAL OF FERTILITY, LOVE, AND JOY

CHAPTER FORTY-ONE

Wine comes in at the mouth
And love comes in at the eye;
That's all we shall know for truth
Before we grow old and die.
I lift the glass to my mouth.
I look at you, and I sigh.

– W. B. Yeats

On Beltane, May Eve, after I'd returned from our Sabbat at Phillipa's, which involved a lot of merry leaping over fires, Joe and I went for a moonlight walk in Jenkins Park. We didn't invite our canine companions this time, much to their annoyance.

We'd taken the precaution of slathering ourselves with my herbal bug-off. In his well-traveled old khaki backpack, Joe carried a blanket, "in case we feel like stopping for a rest" and a bottle of very excellent sauterne, gold magic. There were places in the park where the pine trees had made a comfortable carpet of brown needles with no pesky undergrowth or scratchy bushes, and I knew where they were.

Soon we found the very one to our liking. Joe spread the blanket with a gallant gesture, and we made ourselves comfortable, leaning against a grandfather pine. The scent of its resin was pungent, and the strident music of crickets was loud in the absence of any other sound but the *swoosh* of wind in the treetops. Looking up, we saw the full moon which by now had risen high above the forest. It might have been my imagination, but She seemed to be smiling approval.

Joe opened the wine and poured it into two pressed glass tumblers he'd brought from the kitchen. I would have chosen plastic, but thin Victorian glass was much more romantic. The sauterne was delicately fruity and sweet. I could feel Joe's warm thigh pressed against mine, and his arm protectively circled my shoulder. It was a moment for a deep sigh of contentment. We drank, and we sighed.

"Isn't there something we're supposed to do tonight for the sake of fertile crops?" Joe asked, contriving a tone of innocent inquiry.

"As you know full well from my many lessons in earth lore and nature spirituality," I replied. "Sometimes it's called the Great Rite, the sacred marriage. It simulates earth's creation and the beginning of all things on the earth. Presumably, earth rewards the celebrants with abundant crops and flocks. When you get right down to it, many primitive rituals were connected to fertility."

"Let's," Joe said. "Let's get right down to it." He leaned over me and kissed my throat in that place he knew to be wildly sensitive. The scent of his body filled my senses. "And if I remember my lessons correctly, there's no time like Beltane for a rollicking fertility rite."

"Hmmmm," I said. *And why not?* Making love outdoors is one of the earthly pleasures, providing one avoids the poison ivy patch and the mosquito raid.

He pushed his hand under my shirt and those little stars of excitement shot through my veins. "And anyone can perform the Great Rite, even Greek Orthodox guys?"

"Sure. No dogma, no pressure. We were handfasted by Fiona, a very spiritual union. And legalized by the Reverend Peacedale, to the great relief of my children."

"And not just spiritual," he said. "I'm glad you wore a skirt tonight."

"Oh well, I guess this must be what we had in mind all along," I said, shifting down so that I lay flat on the blanket.

He studied my face, what he could see of it in the shadow of the pines. "Pretty lady. Even in the dark, your eyes are green," he said.

"Actually, the moon is bright as day. I hope there's no one else out and about."

"No one else is as crazy as we are. Especially at our age," he reassured me, pushing up my skirt with a practiced hand.

"The Druids had a thing," I whispered. "If, at the moment of orgasm, we send our wish into the Cosmos, there's some very powerful magic."

That's one excellent thing about married sex. Chances are you can manage a simultaneous orgasm. There was actually more of a problem with a simultaneous wish, and one didn't want to stop the momentum with a discussion of options.

"Never mind," I said, and abandoned myself to the moment and the melting sweetness of surrender.

"No, I like it," Joe said. "Whatever you want, I want that, too."

And the Druid magic worked out quite well, I thought. With the remarkable sensual import of the woods at night, we were soon there and everywhere together.

Later, as we were finishing the sauterne, Joe said, "And what did we wish for, sweetheart?"

"More of the same," I said. But in my deepest being, I knew that I was also thinking of going away on some fabulous romantic adventure with Joe, instead of his going away without me, for once.

Thoughts are things.

CHAPTER FORTY-TWO

Build on, and make thy castles high and fair,
Rising and reaching upward to the skies;
Listen to voices in the upper air,
Nor lose thy simple faith in mysteries.

– Longfellow

A week after Beltane, Joe was off on another Greenpeace operation, this time to help mount a protest in support of two Japanese whistleblowers who'd exposed the embezzlement of whale meat from the Southern Ocean Hunt. Now the whistleblowers were on trial instead of the embezzlers. This gig really wasn't part of Joe's job description, but Greenpeace officials had noted how coolly he'd handled the near-arrest of crew members from the *Esperanza* with the help of Harou Sato, the physics professor who doubled as a Greenpeace chef on his sabbaticals. So Sato and Joe were off to Japan.

Meanwhile, Adam was spending two weeks in London hiring personnel for the new Iconomics branch—not a bad assignment at all. Probably more fun than hanging around in a Japanese courtroom. But I hoped The Company had not given my son any "parcels" to deliver while he was there. That sort of side-line makes a mother nervous.

Freddie and I being work widows in the merry month of May, she offered to drive down to Plymouth and take me to lunch at any eatery of my choice. When it comes to daughters-in-law, I really lucked out.

"How about if we invite Ashling, too," I suggested. "I know there's stuff you and I won't be able to discuss with Ashling along, but I was just thinking, since you are both somewhat psychokinetic, you might be able to give her a few tips on control." (*Somewhat psychokinetic*—what an understatement!)

"Yeah, like I'm so perfectly controlled now myself."

"Well, you haven't suckered the slots in a while. Have you?"

"No, Cass, I've been a model of restraint. And besides, I'm way too busy troubleshooting hackers for Iconomics and being the mother of twins to play at the casinos, alas."

We had to pry Ashling away from Heather, who wanted to know exactly what we were up to and why. "You wouldn't want to join us," I assured my animal activist friend. "It's Winston's New England Nuovo, which you have so often picketed for serving Provimi veal."

"Heartless bastards! I'd like to see them stuffed into crates. Okay then, *bon appetit.*"

Ashling, too, was hesitant to be whisked away from her Morgan sanctuary—and from Maury—but we swept her along into Freddie's Porsche for her own good. I glanced down and was pleased to note that she was wearing pearl gray ballet slippers under her Pre-Raphaelite diaphanous dress.

As the waiter escorted us to a very nice table overlooking the gardens at Winston's, I linked arms with her just to be on the safe side. It was like holding onto an armful of helium balloons.

Winston's, even though upscale and pricey, was bustling with business; I wondered if the place had profited from the demise of the two Chez Reynard restaurants, which had been seized in lieu of the million-dollar bond.

We ordered Prosecco cocktails, assuring Ashling that the lovely stuff was only at one remove from ginger ale. After a few cautious sips, Ashling said, "As long as we're having this chance to talk, there's something I've been wanting to ask you, Cass. I mean, you've been so helpful about my little troubles in the past."

"'Little problems' like the abusive ghost of Archie?"

"Well, I wouldn't want to use the word *abusive*. *Distressed wanderer of the spirit world*, perhaps," Ashling insisted.

Freddie's eyes rolled upward. I shot her a warning glance.

"Tell me about it," I suggested in my best therapist voice.

"Well, I guess you know from Serena that I have this small problem of *detaching* from time to time. I don't really mean to *uplift*, but somehow it happens. And Maury thinks... Maury suggested...that you would be just the person...to... you know."

Well, well. No segue into teaching mode would be needed, after all.

"Ashling dear, those episodes of levitation are part of a psychic ability called psychokinesis. All perfectly natural for some few rare souls. *Mind over matter*, it's often been called. And it just happens that Freddie has the very same ability."

Ashling turned to Freddie with a pleased look, as if she'd just learned that they were long-lost sisters. "You levitate, too! Oh, how wonderful. I mean, I have felt really alone with this affliction, and here I find that you..."

"Actually, Ashling, I don't exactly *take off*, if you know what I'm saying. My psychokinesis takes a different form, like, I move *things*. Or bend them. Which is still mind over matter."

At Ashling's puzzled frown, Freddie said, "Wait… I'll show you." She stared at the spoon in Ashling's place setting. And stared and stared. Slowly the spoon began to inch almost imperceptibly toward her across the yellow linen tablecloth. When it had slid about halfway and got stuck on the centerpiece of daffodils, Freddie picked up the traveling spoon, hummed a little to herself, and stroked it with her fingers. We watched with some fascination. After a few minutes, the bowl of the spoon bent over as if it were made of butter. Freddie smiled and fanned herself with the menu. "Whew! Hot work, that!" She pushed the spoon over to Ashling, who looked at it with dismay as if it were a toad on the table.

I was glad for once of slow service. But just then the waiter finally appeared at my elbow, and after we'd all ordered, Freddie said, "Oh by the way, would you mind bringing this young lady another spoon? Hers seems to be bent or something."

The waiter looked at Ashling's spoon with some surprise. He picked it up, then dropped it back on the table. "It's burning," he said.

"Use a napkin," Freddie suggested.

The skewed spoon was replaced by a new one, and Freddie put her hands in her lap to avoid any further mishap.

"This is all very well and good," she said to Ashling, "until it happens when you don't intend to demonstrate your quirky talents, like for instance, when you've been invited to meet your fiance's parents. I don't mean to brag, but I can addle almost any computer, static a radio, or stop a watch.

Occasionally my 'talent' draws unpleasant attention my way, if you know what I'm saying. So I have to exercise some control, as taught to me by my sainted mother-in-law, here—the genius."

Ashling looked at me hopefully. "Oh, would it be possible for me to control this...*thing*? That would be such a blessing. I used to drive Archie into fits when I couldn't control my feet. One time he tied me to...well, never mind. What do I have to do, Cass?"

Our orders arrived, with fronds of fennel and canoe-shaped potato chips stacked like tepees over the sizzling salmon entrees. As soon as the waiter left, I launched into my spiel about breath control and the four magic words that I use to center myself.

"*Greatness*," I said. "That's the word I use to summon the freshness of air, the vigor of winds, the East. *Brightness,* to bring forth the force of fire, the primal energy of the South. *Wellness*, to call the healing properties of water, the power of the West. And finally, *Oneness*, for the grounding of earth, the strength of the North. Concentrate on slow, steady, measured breathing and say the four words to yourself, visualizing those four elements and directions. Soon you will find that you're in control of the runaway psychic phenomena that seem to have been mastering you."

"You make it sound so easy," Ashling sighed.

"No, it's like that old joke, *How do you get to Carnegie Hall? Practice, practice, practice.* Control takes time, effort, and persistence. Even magic doesn't happen by magic."

"I've never asked you, Cass," Freddie said, "but I wonder which psychic effect did you have to get a handle on yourself? It must have been a doozy."

"It was—and it is. I'm not as controlled as I would like to be. Unless I'm very, very careful, I tend to float like Ashling, although not physically. I seem to glide through the veils of time."

Freddie and Ashling looked completely mystified.

"Weird, eh? I guess it's hard to explain. So I'll just say that, for me, it's a struggle to stay in the here and now. Not to slip constantly into a trance state and see too much."

"And what's that called?" Ashling asked.

"That's called *being a Cassandra*," I said. "Clairvoyance. My nemesis and my craft."

"Hey, mother-in-law, let's lighten up there," Freddie said. "There are some very good things about being whatever it is we are—we know how to make change happen when change is needed. We know how to protect ourselves and others from *the slings and arrows of outrageous fortune.* And we know how to love and be loved." She drew a quick pentagram in the air above us. "May the Divine Spirit bless us with Her infinite energies."

"So must it be," I said. And we three smiled at each other, the smiles of Wise Women that leave so much unsaid but are perfectly understood.

The Circle

Cassandra Shipton, an herbalist and reluctant clairvoyant. The bane of evil-doers who cross her path.
Phillipa Stern (nee Gold), a cookbook author and poet. Reads the tarot with unnerving accuracy.
Heather Devlin (nee Morgan), an heiress and animal rescuer. Creates magical candles with occasionally weird results. Benefactor of Animal Lovers Pet Sanctuary in Plymouth.
Deidre Ryan, recent widow, prolific doll and amulet maker, energetic young mother of four.
Fiona MacDonald Ritchie, a librarian and wise woman who can find almost anything by dowsing with her crystal pendulum. Envied mistress of The Glamour.

The Circle's Family, Extended Family, and Pets

Cass's husband **Joe Ulysses**, a Greenpeace engineer and Greek hunk.
Phillipa's husband **Stone Stern**, Plymouth County detective, handy to have in the family.
Heather's husband **Dick Devlin**, a holistic veterinarian and a real teddy bear.

Cass's grown children
Rebecca "Becky" Lowell, the sensible older child, a family lawyer, divorced.
Adam Hauser, a computer genius, vice president at Iconomics, Inc.,
married to
Winifred "Freddie" McGarrity an irrepressible gal with light-fingered psychokinetic abilities and they are the new parents of twins, **Jack and Joan Hauser**.

Cathy Hauser, who lives with her partner **Irene Adler**, both actresses, mostly unemployed.

Fiona is sometimes the guardian of her grandniece **Laura Belle MacDonald,** a.k.a. **Tinker-Belle**.

Deidre's family

Jenny, Willy Jr., Bobby, and **Baby Anne**

Mary Margaret Ryan, a.k.a. **M & Ms**, mother-in-law and devoted gamer.

The Circle's Animal Companions

Cass's family includes two irrepressible canines who often make their opinions known, **Scruffy,** part French Briard and part mutt, and **Raffles,** his offspring from an unsanctioned union.

Fiona's supercilious cat is **Omar Khayyám,** a Persian aristocrat.

Phillipa's **Zelda**, a plump black cat, was once a waif rescued from a dumpster by Fiona.

Heather's family of rescued canines is constantly changing, and far too numerous to mention, except for **Honeycomb,** a golden retriever and so-called Therapy Dog who is Raffles' mother.

Phil's Sautéed Butternut with Black Olives

May be served hot or at room temperature.

Olive oil
1 large butternut or 1 ½ medium peeled and cut into chunks (easier if you buy already-peeled squash)
1 clove garlic, minced
Pinches of dried Italian herbs—oregano, basil, thyme
Salt and pepper to taste
1 (14-ounce) canned tomatoes, drained and chopped, reserving juice
¾ cup pitted kalamata olives (if you like them) or canned drained black olives
Fresh flat-leaf parsley, chopped.

Heat the oil in a 12-inch skillet with a cover. Sauté the butternut until some of the pieces are lightly browned. Add garlic, herbs, salt and pepper, and sauté for 2 minutes longer.

Add tomatoes. Cook with cover ajar, stirring often. If the squash seems to be too dry, add a ½ cup of the reserved juice. When the squash is almost cooked through, stir in the olives and continue to cook until the largest pieces are fork-tender but not mushy. Total cooking time 30 minutes to ¾ hour. Squash cooks much more slowly by this method than if you boiled it.

Just before serving, sprinkle with fresh parsley.

Makes 6 servings or more

Cass's Salmon Dijon

3-pound salmon fillet
Olive oil
1 bunch scallions, chopped
Dijon mustard
2 cups fresh bread crumbs
White pepper and paprika

Preheat the oven to 400 degrees F.

Rinse and pat dry the fish. Pour a little oil into a baking pan that will fit the fish. Scatter the scallions over the oil. Turn the fillet over in the oil, ending with the darker side on the bottom. Spread a thin skim of mustard over the fish. Sprinkle with the crumbs. Drizzle with more olive oil. Season with white pepper and paprika.

Bake for 20 minutes on the top shelf, or until the fish flakes apart at the center.

Makes 6 or more servings.

Phillipa's Apple Coffeecake

Topping:
¾ cup brown sugar
3 tablespoons butter
3 tablespoons flour
1 tablespoon cinnamon

Coffeecake:
2 ¼ cups flour
1 ½ cups granulated sugar
1 ½ teaspoons baking soda
¾ teaspoon baking powder
½ teaspoon salt
¾ cup soft butter
2/3 cup milk
2 eggs
3 cups finely chopped, peeled apples (size of small dice)

Heat the oven to 350 degrees. Spray a 9 x 13-inch pan with cooking spray.

In a food processor, blend the 1st four ingredients to use as a topping; set aside.

Sift the flour, granulated sugar, baking soda, baking powder, and salt into the bowl of an electric mixer. Add the butter, milk, and eggs, and beat until well blended. Add the apples, and beat about 1 minute more.

Spoon the batter into the prepared pan, and smooth the top. Sprinkle the topping on evenly. Bake the coffeecake in the middle shelf of the oven for 40 to 50 minutes or until a cake tester inserted in the center comes out clean.

Cool in pan on wire rack. Serve warm or at room temperature.

Makes about 12 servings.